THE LOVE

Paul Miller
A gifted jazz pianist and Dessie's best friend. His music was the world to him, even when it became a world of junkies and crime.

Tony Matos
Her Svengali, her partron. Rich, mysterious, it seemed he wanted nothing in return. But this ruthless Cuban crime czar wanted everything, even her life.

Bram Howard
Wealthy, handsome, arrogant. He swore he loved Dessie, but then he did something that spoke of cruelty. . . .

Grayson
Dessie's first child. The baby she neglected because her career came first. Would it be too late to win his love?

BLUES IN THE NIGHT

Elizabeth Jordan

FAWCETT GOLD MEDAL • NEW YORK

A Fawcett Gold Medal Book
Published by Ballantine Books
Copyright © 1987 by Elizabeth Jordan

All rights reserved under International and Pan-American Copyright Convenitons. Published in the United States by Ballantine Books, a division of Random House, Inc., New York, and simultaneously in Canada by Random House of Canada Limited, Toronto.

Library of Congress Catalog Card Number: 87-91542

ISBN 0-449-13289-7

All the characters in this book are fictitious, and any resemblance to persons living or dead is purely coincidental.

Manufactured in the United States of America

First Edition: December 1987

for Clinton

1

I AM LIGHT. I AM ONE WITH THE LIGHT, SHINING WHITE, A pillar crowned with gold. Sequins glitter, wrapping me in a million tiny stars. My dazzled eyes see no faces, only the blinding glare of the spotlight, bright as the blazing sun. But I am not alone. Ten thousand voices speak to me as one voice: Dessie! Dessie! Dessie! Their love flows over and around me, caressing me and overwhelming me with its warmth and weight.

Three minutes pass with no let-up in the applause. I turn to the man on the podium. What shall I do? He smiles. Give them what they want. More music. An encore. He lifts his baton.

But something is wrong. The applause has become jeering laughter. Love has turned to loathing. The conductor leaves his podium and stands over me, his baton raised. The baton has grown, sprouted into a mighty staff. And he! He is no longer the sleek, handsome, continental gentleman who had declared his love for me moments before the curtain rose, in a scene that had left us both breathless and weak from passion. Now his face is swollen and distorted, a hideous grotesque.

The jeering grows louder. The monster is going to strike me! He raises his arms, high, higher still. I scream as the baton comes crashing down, barely missing my skull.

The blow from the pointer shattered my pencil and scattered my books. Miss Maddson pushed her gargoyle face close to mine. Her breath smelled like burning rubber.

"I suppose that's one way to get your attention, Dolores. I have been calling your name for the past five minutes. Would you care to tell us what you were thinking about? It wasn't William the Conqueror, I'll wager that much."

I saw the smug, grinning faces of my classmates. I would die before I would share a single moment of my precious fantasy with any one of them. Particularly Jean-Ellen Thomas, sitting in the front of the room, right in front of Miss Maddson's desk. I saw her lean across the aisle and whisper something to one of her chums. The two of them looked at me and giggled.

I hated everything about Jean-Ellen and her set: the saddle shoes and Shetland sweaters in pastel shades that they wore; the way they huddled giggling in the girls' bathroom between classes, trading lipsticks and bitchy appraisals of the pitiful specimens of manhood milling through the halls; the way they fell silent whenever I approached, only to erupt into a grating chorus of giggles after I passed.

"Did you read the chapter I assigned last night?" Miss Maddson barked.

I slunk lower in my chair. "No, ma'am."

"I thought not. Very well, you will return to this room at three-fifteen and you will copy the entire chapter, from the textbook, into your notebook. I will check it before you leave to make sure you haven't missed a single word. Is that clear?"

"But Miss Maddson, the choral society—"

"I will add another page for every minute you are late." Hearing a snigger behind me, Miss Maddson whirled, her pointer raised. Flesh drooped from her upper arms like bags of suet. "If anyone wants to join Dolores in her activity this afternoon, he or she is welcome."

As she stumped back to the front of the room on her short legs, Faro Hill murmured, "That wasn't the kind of activity I had in mind with Dessie."

Miss Madison resumed her lecture on the Norman Conquest. I had never hated her more.

I tried vainly to recapture the vision of myself that I had been fashioning and embroidering for weeks: tall and slender, with golden hair, and a radiant smile. But that Dessie Heavener had vanished. The theater was silent, the musicians' chairs were empty, and I stood alone in my worn cotton skirt and stretched-out sweater, with no one to listen to my song.

Picking up the remains of my pencil I wrote in my notebook, "Evil Smelling Old Bitch." Just venting my rage that little bit made me feel better. I drew a picture of Miss Maddson: sagging bottom and breasts, tightly crimped hair, jowled face, wire-rimmed spectacles. I added horns, a tail with an arrow point on it, and a pitchfork in one of her lumpish hands. I labeled the portrait "Devil Bitch Emily." After that I felt a lot better.

". . . thank you for enlightening us, Jean-Ellen," Miss Maddson quacked. "Yes, the Norman Conquest changed the face of Great Britain and hence the world."

"I wish somebody'd change her face." Billy Teasley's breath, reeking of chewing tobacco and Sen-Sen breath mints, fanned the back of my neck. "Hey, Dess, let me see that."

"Shut up, Billy."

"No, come on, gimme." His long arm snaked around me and his huge hand wrested the notebook from my grasp. With hands the size of shovels and long prehensile fingers, Baboon Billy could palm a basketball. I heard him snort with pleasure. "Hey, it's old Turkey Gizzard herself. Looka here, Willo." Ignoring my whispered protests, Billy passed the book to Alvin Henry Willoughby, also known as Boiler because of the mass of large yellow pustules that blossomed on his face and neck.

"Whoo-whee," he chortled, "will you look at that? Devil Bitch! That's what she is, all right."

"Boiler." I jabbed him with the tip of my pencil. "Give me that."

But Boiler was already sharing the joke with Faro Hill. Faro got a good laugh out of the cartoon.

"Devil Bitch!" he wheezed as he handed it back to Boiler. "Miz Maddson sure is that."

By this time, heads were starting to turn in our direction. Miss Maddson interrupted her account of the Norman Conquest and swooped down, hawklike, on Boiler, whose dim brain managed to grasp the potential explosiveness of the drawing he held in his hand.

"I didn't do it," he whined. "Billy give it to me."

Quicker than a snake's wink, Billy pinned the blame on me. "Dessie drew it, ma'am. She's been showin' it around to ever'-body."

As Miss Maddson gazed at my drawing, her face swelled and turned crimson, like a birthday balloon. "You!" she said in a choked whisper. "You—dare! This . . . this is disgusting!" Miss Maddson's arm lashed out. She grabbed a fistful of hair and dragged me to my feet. "We shall see what Mr. Motley has to say about this. Bring your belongings. I doubt that you will be returning to this classroom for a long time to come."

Miss Maddson marched me down the aisle, right toward Jean-

Ellen, who smirked. I couldn't help myself. As we passed her, I reached out and slapped her smug little face. She started to scream as though she had been murdered.

"Ow! Ow! Did you see that? Did you see what that dreadful girl just did to me?"

Miss Maddson shifted her grasp from my hair to my upper arm. Her fingers bit into my flesh. "I do believe you've lost your mind, Dolores Heavener. There's a place for people like you: the County Home for Mental Incurables!"

I tried to squirm away from her. "I don't have to be crazy to know that you're an evil old woman and I hate you!"

This brought fresh gasps of horror from Miss Maddson and the whole class. Miss Maddson dragged me out the door and down the long length of the hall toward the principal's office.

We swept past the reception desk, ignoring Billie Wainwright's protestations that she must announce us, and burst in upon Mr. Alvah Motley, surprising him with his stockinged feet up on the desk and the Munford *Bugle* draped over his face. When Miss Maddson barked his name, he righted himself and threw off the newspaper.

"Mr. Motley, this disgusting creature has no business attending school with the children of high-minded citizens. She is indecent, uncivilized, and anti-social as well. As you know, she is barely passing history. In fact, she failed her last test miserably. And yet she has the nerve to sit in the back of the classroom chewing gum and making . . . ," she sputtered and fizzed a little, "making these obscene drawings!"

I thought I detected an amused twitch at the corner of Mr. Motley's mouth as he inspected the evidence, but when he looked up again his expression was grave. "I am very sorry you had to be subjected to such a hideous insult, Miss Maddson," he said in a slow, heavy voice that he must have used in the pulpit when he filled in for the Methodist preacher. "I promise you, Miss Heavener's punishment will be appropriately harsh."

"She passed that filth all around the room." Glaring at me, Miss Maddson spat out her words like an angry cat. "Not content with that, she actually slapped Jean-Ellen Thomas right across the face as I was taking her out of class, and then she told me that she hated me! I do believe the child's gone crazy. She has no business sitting in class with the sons and daughters of decent people."

"I deeply regret this upset, Miss Maddson." Mr. Motley

heaved a deep sigh. "Now, why don't you get back to your class? You still have twenty minutes—"

"I will not." Miss Maddson folded her arms over her sagging breasts, pressing them down into the high-riding bulge of her belly. "We are going to settle this matter right now. Summon her father at once. I want to make my complaint directly to him. This girl of his is running wild. I understand that his wife is incapacitated," she dragged out the word so that we would be sure to appreciate her irony, "but in a case like that, then a father's just got to do a little more, doesn't he? Well, are you going to call him in here or do I have to do it myself?"

Alvah Motley may not have liked being ordered around by one of his teachers, but he knew when he had to submit. He lumbered to the door.

"Miss Wainwright, would you please find out where Arthur Heavener is teaching this period and ask him to come in here for a few minutes?"

Turning my back to them, I sang a furious song inside my head, a blues song I composed on the spur of the moment:

>Nobody loves me, nobody understands.
>Nobody loves me, nobody understands.
>Everybody's shouting and moaning
>And waving their flabby hands.
>
>This whole world is pressing me down.
>Stamping and squashing me right into the ground.
>I'm going to pack my bags soon
>And take myself far away from this old town.
>
>Oh, yeah.

Dessie Heavener's silent lament.

As I was composing a second verse—to the accompaniment of Miss Maddson's quacking, "trash, Dessie Heavener is trash, pure and simple"—my father entered the room. In any part of the country outside of the Confederacy folks would have called him Lincolnesque. He was tall and gaunt, with large features and the sad eyes of an aging hound dog. Although his movements were somewhat loose and shambling, he had a way of commanding attention when he stood in front of a classroom or a choir. Unlike Lincoln, however, my father rarely cracked a smile, and he never, never told a joke. His demeanor made it clear to everyone that he carried an enormous weight on his shoulders, although in his case the weight was not that of a nation divided but rather a pair of rebellious women—a wife and a daughter who simply would not, could not, do what was right. With each passing year he grew a little more stooped, a little more grim, a little more lined and anxious.

When he saw me, his mouth drooped even lower at the corners and he winced, visibly.

Mr. Motley started to explain the situation, but Miss Maddson cut him off. She waved the offending drawing under my father's nose as she shrilly described my hostile behavior and uncooperative attitude. Then she took him roundly to task for failing to discipline me properly. My father listened silently, occasionally jerking his head in a brief nod that looked more like a painful spasm than a gesture of comprehension or assent.

"That is enough," he said after two solid minutes of Miss Maddson's quacking. "I have heard enough."

To my surprise, Miss Maddson fell silent. My father's brown eyes were filled with anger and reproach. He pointed to the drawing.

"Did you do this, Dessie?" His voice was solemn and aggrieved.

I cocked my head to one side. "I sure did. Not a bad resemblance, is it?"

He reared back and slapped me so hard that I executed a complete three hundred and sixty degree spin before falling against the front of Mr. Motley's desk. My cheek stung and my eyes blurred with tears of pain and embarrassment. Whimpering, I threw my arms up to cover my face. He struck them aside and hit me again and again. I tasted blood as my teeth cut into the inside of my cheek. Blows continued to rain down on me. His voice cut through my screams:

"Damn you, you've been nothing but trouble since the day you were born. I should have beat some sense into you long ago."

Through a gray veil of tears, I saw Mr. Motley standing openmouthed, his pale blue eyes glazed with shock, as though he had just witnessed the sudden transformation of Dr. Jekyll into Mr. Hyde. Miss Maddson, on the other hand, was smiling a strange, tight little smile. Behind her glasses, her eyes glistened like bright colorless marbles.

"Stop!" I sobbed. "Please stop! Please!"

"Arthur, that's enough!" Mr. Motley, fearful of having to explain a corpse on the floor of his office, finally interceded by throwing his arms around my father's middle and dragging him away from me. "You don't want to kill the girl."

I covered my face with my hands. That's exactly what he does want, I thought.

My father was breathing heavily. "I'm sorry, Alvah. Sorrier than you know. That a daughter of mine should be responsible for filth like . . . I . . . I don't know what else to say." He ended the sentence on a sob. He sounded bone-weary and burdened almost beyond endurance. "Whatever further punishment you want to administer, I'm behind you one hundred percent."

"Well, you came down pretty hard on the girl, Arthur, so maybe we ought to end the matter right here and—"

Poor old Motley. Miss Maddson let him know right away that a simple verbal apology and a light thrashing could not compensate her for the mortal insult she had suffered.

"I am sick of her brazen face, Mr. Motley, and I don't want to see it in my class, not for a month at least. She can sit in the study hall during the third period and fail the course—she'd do that anyway."

My father added his two cents. "I think Dessie needs some time to think about her sins. If you do decide to suspend her from class, I will personally guarantee that she does not leave the house until the period of her suspension is over. In fact, I will keep her locked in her room to insure that she doesn't."

"Daddy, no!"

My father ignored me. "She will keep up with all her assignments and her studies at home, and she will pass all her exams in January, I promise you. And she will not be a disruptive influence when she returns to class in November. You have my word on that."

I glanced at the portrait of Robert E. Lee hanging behind the principal's desk. The general's sour expression gave me no comfort. I had disgraced myself and the Confederacy.

Mr. Motley sighed. "Will that satisfy you, Miss Maddson?"

"I suppose I will have to be satisfied," Miss Maddson snapped. "But let me warn you, Dolores, that your final exam will be the hardest test you have ever taken in your life. Do I make myself clear?"

I gave a listless nod. My father jostled my arm and demanded that I respond verbally. I said in a tear-choked voice, "Yes, ma'am."

"She will pass that test, Miss Maddson," my father vowed. "I will see that she keeps up her studies not only in history but in every other subject as well."

"You might have taken charge of her sooner," Miss Maddson sniffed. "Before she started running wild and causing all this trouble. You're just lucky that she hasn't gotten up to anything worse, if you know what I mean."

My father turned to me again. "I'm taking you home, right now. Somebody else can clean out your locker. Alvah, will you ask Miss Wainwright to watch my class until the end of the period? I won't be gone long, just until I get Dessie settled in and put a new lock on her bedroom door."

It seemed like everyone in town was out that morning, as if they had been summoned to witness my humiliation. I followed heavy-footed in my father's wake, past Swede's Drugstore and the bus stop, past the bank, past the *Bugle* office and Reese's Emporium. We made one stop at Bob's Feeds and Hardware so my father could buy a bolt, then we continued our journey. I kept my head lowered. I didn't want to see their looks of scorn or pity. I didn't want them to remember me as poor little Dessie, whose father beat her and whose mother didn't care about her at all.

We reached the corner of Maple Street and Creek Avenue and turned left. Our house was the third one on the right, a two-storied, white frame dwelling, distinguished from the other homes on the street by its rundown condition: sagging shutters, broken steps, unpainted clapboards. Although my father worked incessantly, teaching music and French at the high school, leading the high school chorus and the marching band, playing the organ and directing the choir at Honor Baptist Church, he barely managed to stay out of debt. He had no skills as a carpenter or handyman himself, and he couldn't afford to hire anyone else to work for him. We were poorer than almost all the other white families in town, possessing neither car nor phonograph, nor any worldly goods worth mentioning except a radio Mr. Reese had traded to my father for a lifetime of piano lessons for his daughter. Our only luxury was Clara Mae Grayson who cooked and cleaned for us six days a week. Actually, Clara Mae was a necessity, not a luxury. She had been working for us for twelve years, ever since we moved to Munford from Charleston. The house I called home would have been unbearable without her.

My father opened the front door and shoved me inside. He shouted for Clara Mae, who emerged from the kitchen wiping her hands on her apron.

When she saw my face she cried out, "Oh, Miz Dessie, what you been up to now?" I ran to her and buried my head under her collarbone. Her arms closed around me. She was nearly as tall as my father and her dark flesh was spare on her bones. Her nose was long rather than flat, and hooked at the end, a gift from her Seminole great-grandfather, she said.

"This young lady is restricted to her room until I say she can leave," my father told her. "I expect you to enforce this punishment, Clara Mae. You will take her meals up to her on a tray. She will have a chamber pot in her room and clean it out herself once a day, under your supervision. Visitors are forbidden—and that includes young Miller when he gets home."

"But, Papa, Paul and I were planning—" seeing my father's grim expression, I snapped my mouth shut. Better he didn't know what Paul and I had been planning.

From the other side of the parlor doors came the sound of snoring. I slid open one door a crack and looked in. My mother was asleep in her chair. A trickle of saliva made its way down her chin. An empty coffee cup lay in her lap. She had managed to stub out her cigarette in it before dozing off. I closed the door.

"Miz Heavener's jes' takin' a little nap," Clara Mae explained smoothly. "She worked hard this mornin' helpin' me get the house ready for the wintertime. We got all those old rugs out of storage and hung 'em out back to air. She's all tuckered out."

I didn't believe her lie for a minute, and neither did my father. Mama wasn't tired. She was drunk. Dead drunk.

My father grunted. "Come along, Dessie."

As I trailed him up the stairs, I turned and gave Clara Mae a beseeching look. She returned an encouraging smile, at the same time shaking her head.

My father pushed me inside my room and pulled the door closed. Then he got to work with a hammer and screwdriver. It took him a long time, but after awhile I heard the new bolt shoot home. I tried to appreciate the experience of being a prisoner, but I didn't feel much different than I always did in that house, in that room. I had tried to brighten the stained and streaked walls with pictures clipped from movie magazines and the newspaper. Laurence Olivier, as Heathcliff in *Wuthering Heights*, held the current place of honor over my bed, and the last face I saw before switching out my lights was his. My old raggedy doll, Sary, occupied the hard chair in front of my dressing table—a packing crate I had decorated with some blue paint and a few yards of rose-colored taffeta from one of my mother's old gowns. I pressed Sary to my breast, and as I did so, I caught a glimpse of my face in the mirror. My lip was split and my left eye was blackened and swollen half shut.

"Oh, no!" Gingerly, I touched my face. My looks were spoiled, ruined. I had never been a beauty, but now I was a monster, as hideous as Emily Maddson herself. Sobbing, I threw myself down on my bed. The salty tears stung my bruises, but I didn't care. The pain was nothing compared to the black despair that filled my heart.

After awhile I heard a gentle knock on the door. The bolt slid back. Clara Mae stood over me. "I brung you some ice for that eye. That crazy man might have gone and blinded you. Come on, chile. Turn over now."

I rolled over. "Oh, Clara Mae, I hate him. I hate them both! Why do they have to be so awful?"

"Hush now, chile. You gettin' yourself all excited ain't gonna help matters any. Hold this cloth to your face. That's right."

Clara Mae put her skinny arms around me and rocked me gently. "You don't want to forget your Lord and Savior," she said. "All the trouble I seen in my life, I never could have come through without Him."

She hummed a spiritual. I closed my eyes. I might have been three years old again, sitting in Clara Mae's lap while she sang to me. In those days, her songs were bawdy and decidedly secular, blues songs she had learned "on the river," and from great artists like Bessie Smith. Clara Mae had seen Bessie perform dozens of times, and when Bessie died in a car accident in 1932, Clara Mae cried for days. When I was six, however, Clara had gotten religion, and had condemned the songs of her past as low-down and dirty-minded. From Clara Mae I had learned to use music to forget my troubles, to make the unbearable bearable.

She started to sing softly. Her voice was high-pitched but rich, with lots of vibrato and a clear ringing tone:

The good Lord lifts me up
So I can see His shining face.
The good Lord lifts me up
So I can pray.
The good Lord lets me know
That I'm a child of His grace.
To Him I'll sing this song of praise
All of my days.

"Come on, honey," she coaxed, "you know this one. Help me with this song."

I hummed along for a few bars, just to oblige her. She begged me to sing, to try. My voice had a hard time squeezing through my closed-up throat, but I produced a creditable harmony while she carried the soprano line.

"See?" she said when we had finished. "Don't you feel better? Course you do. Now you lie down and I'll fetch you up a nice cup of coffee and some cookies I jes' made fresh this mornin'. You daddy ain't comin' home 'til late on account of the choral society is rehearsin', and I won't lock you up until then, awright? You hold that ice on your eye. It'll keep the swellin' down. If that don't work, I'll ask Brother Jupiter for a leech."

I shuddered. I wanted no part of Brother Jupiter and his witchcraft, although the tonics and potions he made up for Clara Mae had cured me of fevers, chills, and assorted childhood maladies. "I'll keep it on," I promised.

She went out, leaving the door open. I heard her sniff, "Chamber pot. I ain't botherin' with no chamber pots, I don't care what he says."

My father may have paid her wage, but I was her honey, her pet, the only thing—as she said—that kept her working in our house. Mr. Arthur Heavener could issue all the orders he wanted, but if Clara Mae Grayson didn't approve of them, she would find a way of disobeying without seeming to.

I slipped my hand under my pillow and withdrew a newspaper clipping, not a photograph this time but an announcement printed in bold, black letters. King Kinglsey and His Royal Court would be appearing at the Dixieland Dance Hall in Columbia, the state capital, one week from Saturday, ten days from today. Admission was fifty cents. The excitement would start at seven with a talent contest. The first prize was five dollars. But if a Grand Prize winner was selected, he or she would be invited to travel with the band as they completed their tour of the southeast. Participation was limited to those eighteen years of age and over. I had already mailed in my one dollar registration fee, along with a forged testimonial from my father—my music teacher—and one other falsified reference from our neighbor, Judge Hadley Miller.

I touched my face, nicely numbed by the ice. In just ten more days I wouldn't have to sing to forget my troubles. I would be singing for the sheer fun of it, and for the honor and glory it would win me.

2

ON THE MORNING OF THE DIXIELAND BALLROOM TALENT CONtest, I awakened to see a band of bright sunshine lying across my pillow. After nine days of rain, the skies had finally cleared. I took this as a promise and an omen of good things to come.

Lying in my bed, I listened to the rhythms of my neighborhood for the last time: Mrs. Stott hollering to her husband to come inside for breakfast; Junior Taylor revving up the engine on his Ford truck while his dog, Maple, barked hysterically. Old Ned the vegetable peddler moved up the street advertising his wares in a rapid rhythmic chant: "I got corn—sweet potatoes—red peppers—tomatoes—black-eyed peas and greens!" He stopped in front of our house. Our kitchen door slammed as Clara Mae went out to meet him.

The last morning of my childhood. I couldn't wait for it to end. I threw back the covers, and singing a happy song to myself, I brushed my teeth and splashed water on my face.

But at eight o'clock when Clara Mae unbarred the door, she found me huddled in the sprung-out armchair near the window, a blanket around my shoulders.

"Your daddy's gone. You can come down to breakfast now." She stepped into the room. "Why, chile, what you doin', all wrapped up like that? You got a fever?" She lay her work-roughened hand on my forehead. "No, you feel cool. What's the matter?"

"Nothing. Nothing's the matter."

"Well, ain't you comin' down to breakfast? I got batter for hot cakes all ready to go."

I shook my head. "I don't want anything, thanks. I have a bad stomachache." Shrugging, she turned away. I grasped her hand. "Clara Mae, will you do me a favor? It's a matter of life or death. I—I've got a lot of homework to catch up on today, and Paul said he would give me help with math and biology any time I needed it. Can you run over to the Judge's house and ask him to come here at two? Please?"

"Why sure, I'll do that. But you better eat somethin' if you don't want to fall down in a faint 'tween now and then. This here's my afternoon off, and I promised Flora Davis I would stop in an' see her. She's been doin' so poorly."

My father generally spent the whole day Saturday at the Baptist church. In between giving music lessons to his private pupils for twenty-five cents an hour, he practiced his own organ pieces and the hymns for the Sunday service. Always punctual in his habits, he came home promptly at noon for lunch, then returned to the church at one and stayed there until six.

After Clara Mae went downstairs, I threw off my blanket, grabbed a brown bottle from the shelf in my closet, and headed for the bathroom. I was too nervous to eat, almost too scared and nervous to think straight. So much depended on the success of every step of my plan. At least God had stopped the rain. At least He had done that much for me.

I climbed into the bathtub, pulled the stopper from the huge bottle of peroxide and dumped it over my head. I had never bleached my hair before, and I hadn't any idea how long to leave the stuff on. I figured about fifteen minutes ought to do the trick. I rinsed, shampooed, and rinsed again. Back in my room, I wound my hair up in pincurls and sat in a patch of sunlight to dry it.

To my great relief, my father did not deviate from his routine that day. At noon I heard the front door open. This was followed by a gentle clatter in the kitchen, just below my room, while Clara Mae gave him his lunch. A long silence from twelve-thirty until five of one, while he took a nap, then the front door opened and closed again. He was gone.

Clara Mae hollered up the stairs that lunch was ready. Did I want to come down or did I want her to bring it up? I wrapped a dry towel around my bleached head and hollered down that I still didn't feel right and that I wasn't hungry.

"Did you give Paul my message?"

"Yes, I seen Paul, and he say he comin' over at two, jes' like you ast him."

Suddenly the door at the end of the hall swung open and my mother appeared. Whenever the day began for her, that's when she looked her worst. Her hair hung in limp strands around her face. Her old silk wrapper looked like a withered peach skin, stained brown and spotted with cigarette burns. "What in hell is going on out here?" she demanded. "Can't you two harridans let a body sleep, for God's sake? I never heard such noise. S'enough to wake the dead." She fumbled in the pocket of her wrapper for a cigarette. My mother wore cigarettes the way some women wore lipstick: her mouth was never without one. She gave me a bleary look. "Your daddy at school?"

I sighed. "No school today, Mama. It's Saturday."

"Oh. Well, what are you doing inside on such a nice day? Ain't you got somethin' better to do than sit home?"

"I'm still a prisoner," I reminded her. "I've got eighteen more days to serve."

"Eighteen more days." She grunted. "I guess that's better than the rest of your life." Lurching around, she returned to her room and slammed the door.

I gazed after her, my relief mingling with regret. This was one of her bad days. She would spend the whole day in bed, not really asleep but too lethargic to eat or communicate with anyone who came near her. She would smoke about forty cigarettes and take that many sips from the bottle she kept in the drawer of her bedside table.

Clara Mae appeared at the foot of the stairs again. "I got to go," she shouted, not caring if her elevated volume annoyed my mother. "The beans are stewin' on the back of the stove. You can serve 'em up with some of that cornbread your daddy likes so much. Leave the washin' up 'til mornin'. I'll git to it after church."

"Thanks, Clara Mae. Good-bye, Clara Mae."

She must have heard the catch in my throat, because she looked around sharply. "You take care of yourself now." Not trusting myself to speak, I nodded my head.

Paul arrived promptly at two, letting himself in the back door and calling up the stairs. Throwing the towel over my head again, I ran to greet him.

"Come on up," I hissed. "It's all right. Mama's having one of her bad days and Clara Mae's gone."

He moved carefully up the stairs, favoring his left leg and gripping the banister. An attack of polio when he was four years old had left him with a limp and a weakness in his chest. But there was nothing wrong with Paul's mind. He had graduated from high school with highest honors and had gone on to the University of South Carolina at Spartanburg on a full scholarship. He came home every weekend to help his widowed father.

Judge Miller and his son had a warm and friendly relationship that I envied. The judge was training Paul to be a lawyer like himself. They discussed legal cases whenever they were together, and the judge liked to say that Paul could find a hole in almost any argument quicker than he could himself.

"Come on." I grabbed Paul's arm and dragged him into my room. I shut the door, then whipped off the towel. "Look!"

Paul's jaw sagged. After a minute he said, "Your hair! What'd you do to your hair?"

I laughed and tossed my newly blonded curls. "Do you like it? Don't you think it makes me look older? I do. I think I look at least nineteen, maybe twenty. You promised to help me fix it, remember? I feel as nervous as a cat on a griddle and my fingers don't know what to do next. This is what I want it to look like, remember?" I showed him a picture in *Hollywood Life* of Carole Lombard. Her blond curls were swept into a cluster on the top of her head and pinned all around, so that the sides and back were sleek and smooth. In the front, a golden wave crested then dipped down over one eye. "Do you think you can do that? I figure my hair's just long enough."

"I'll give it a try, but I can't promise anything. I've never done anybody's hair before."

"Paul, please!" I clutched his arm. "I want everything to be right tonight, to be perfect. Here." I smacked a hairbrush and comb into the palm of his hand and pointed to the box of hairpins on my dressing table. Then I seated myself in front of the mirror and clutched old ragged Sary to my bosom.

Paul rose to this new challenge with the same thought and care that he devoted to everything else. His long fingers lifted the strands of hair from my neck and wound them into coils on my crown. I watched his face as he worked over me. He was concentrating so hard that he was biting his tongue.

"It's a good thing you're not singing tonight instead of me," I joked.

"I'm just trying to keep from cussing," he said. "I never knew hair could be so ornery."

Once again I was putting myself in Paul's hands, trusting him to fix the hurt, bandage the scrape, wipe away my tears, make things all better. I had latched on to him within hours of our family's moving to Munford, when I was three and he was seven. Neither of us had any friends in town. We were both outcasts; Paul isolated by his polio and his brilliance, me by my outrageous mother and my own rebellious conduct. When Paul went away to college two years ago, I grieved for him as though he were dead. I had been in the habit of running over to his house every afternoon after school. I would burst in on him while he was doing his homework and drag him into the living room to listen to records. We knew all the big bands, and most of the musicians who played in them. And we made our own music—Paul playing the piano and me singing—trying out our talents on everything from Clara Mae's blues songs to our own versions of Tin Pan Alley and show tunes.

We had been preparing for the talent contest for two months. First we selected just the right song, then together we created an arrangement that would show me off to the best advantage. I rehearsed every move and gesture and intonation a thousand times, until Paul declared himself satisfied. He was a tough critic, probably the most educated listener in Cluny County. I never understood why he didn't want to be a professional musician. He was certainly good enough. But whenever I broached the subject, he told me curtly that he was going to be a lawyer like his father and that he didn't want to discuss it.

"I'm so nervous." I hugged Sary. "I feel like my heart's stuck right in my throat. I can't even breathe, much less sing."

"You'll be fine." Paul spoke through a mouthful of hairpins. "Nobody sings better than you, Dess."

"But there will be folks from all over there, from Atlanta, maybe, or Charleston—"

"I don't care if they've got a crooner from the moon. You'll still be better." He stepped back. "All right, what do you think?"

I compared the image I saw in the mirror with the photograph of Carole Lombard. Following my instructions, Paul made a few adjustments to his creation, then I dismissed him. "Now you'd better run along and change into your good suit. You're going to wear your blue tie, remember? The one that goes with my dress. And don't forget to take my suitcase." I dragged the suitcase out from under my bed. It had been packed for weeks, just waiting for this day. "Folks see you coming and going with your suitcase all the time and they won't think anything of it, but they might notice me and tell my father. I'll meet you at the bus stop in half an hour. Don't you dare be late."

When he was gone, I sat down in front of the mirror again and painted myself a new face. Ordinarily, my father forbade me to use makeup. Now I smoothed plenty of rouge and powder over my cheeks. I darkened my eyelashes with mascara and outlined my lips with crimson lipstick.

From the depths of my closet, I took one of my mother's ten-year-old dresses, a teal blue crepe de chine with a thin, black leather belt. I had altered and remodeled it, removing the collar and cutting the neckline low and square, padding the shoulders a little, narrowing the skirt and shortening it about a foot and a half. I had been working on the dress secretly for over a month. I had sewn a dream into every stitch.

I drew on the pair of silk stockings I had been hoarding, and slipped on the shiny black pumps I had found in Reese's Emporium four weeks earlier. The dress fastened at the side, under my left arm, with little snaps. It fit looser around the hips than the last time I had tried it on. I must have lost a few pounds since then, worried them off. A spritz of perfume from the five and dime completed my toilet. Then I added the finishing touches: long black gloves and a small black hat with a veil, also salvaged from my mother's closet and painstakingly made over in the current style. My old brown coat was shabby, but it would have to do. I would get rid of it the moment we entered the ballroom. Standing in front of the mirror, I appraised my appearance as objectively as I could. I looked at least twenty years old; maybe even as old as twenty-and-a-half.

I turned away from the mirror to see my mother watching me from the doorway. "You're all dressed up," she said. "You goin' someplace, Dessie?"

I swallowed. "Yes, ma'am. Paul and I—"

"Paul's a nice boy. Good-lookin', too, except for that limp. Like a Gypsy. Dark hair and dark eyes. Lord, I remember when I was your age. I always had boys followin' me everywhere I went. Hundreds of 'em. Wouldn't know it to look at me now, but I did. Why I let myself be talked into marryin' Arthur Heavener I'll never know."

"Mama, I've got to—"

"I wish somebody had told me, 'Look before you leap, Malvina. Look before you leap.' But he was a handsome cuss, and he played the piano like a regular Paderewski. How was I to know he'd turn out the way he has? He tells me I'm not much of a wife, and that I'm a terrible mother. Is that true, Dessie? Am I a terrible mother?''

I nearly groaned aloud. "No, Mama, of course you're not. Well, I'd better be getting along—"

"You're a sweet girl, Dessie. A good daughter." A tear coursed down her cheek, following a well-worn groove alongside her nose. My heart sank. When my mother got the weepy-rambles, she could go on for hours. "Seems like just yesterday you were a baby. Such a pretty little baby."

I glanced at the alarm clock near my bed. Quarter to four. The bus to Columbia was due in fifteen minutes. Grasping my mother's shoulders, I spun her around and sat her down in the armchair.

"Mama, I hate to run off like this, but I don't want to be late. Please, try and understand."

She seemed unaware that she had been maneuvered into a sitting position. "You were blond then, just like you are now. A real little towhead. I was so disappointed when your hair started to darken. When I was a girl, my hair was white-blond, too. Like golden silk."

I leaned over and gave her a light kiss on the cheek. " 'Bye, Mama. I'll see you—I'll see you again."

"Wait, honey." Her talons closed around my wrist. "I've got somethin' for you."

I wanted to scream. "Please, Mama, I've got—"

"Shhh!" Her whisper sent a gust of breath fouled by moonshine in my direction. "Here's ten dollars. I got it from your daddy's wallet last night. Buy yourself somethin' nice, somethin' pretty. I'd just spend it—well, you know what I'd spend it on." She laughed. "I'll probably hate myself in the mornin'! Now you tuck it away in a safe place where nobody can get to it. Put it in the top of your stocking. Go on, do it right away."

"I am, Mama." I hitched up my skirt and stuffed the folded bill into the stocking just above my right knee. "See? Thank you so much, but I really have to go now. Bye-bye."

She fell back with a heavy sigh. "You young girls are always in a hurry. I remember how it was—"

I left her to her remembrances and hurried down the stairs. I had ten minutes to get to the bus stop where Paul was waiting. I was grateful for the ten dollars, but I would hate my mother forever if she had made me miss the bus.

I ran up to Paul just as the clock on the Methodist church steeple was striking four. "It hasn't come, has it?" I gasped.

Paul didn't answer me. He stood with his arms at his sides and his mouth slightly agape.

"What is it? What's the matter?"

"It's you, Dessie," he said slowly. "You look so beautiful, I hardly recognized you. You're a beautiful woman. I can't get used to it."

I laughed. "You'd better get used to it, because from now on, you're never going to see me any other way. And when I've earned myself some money, I'm going to buy myself the prettiest dresses you've ever seen. Maybe even a fur coat. Won't I look pretty, parading in my mink?" I swanked along the sidewalk in front of Swede's Drugstore, where the bus would stop. Paul and I were the only passengers waiting to be picked up. "Maybe I'll get me one of those little dogs the movie stars have. A poodle. We'll go walking along the boulevard—he'll have a diamond collar, and I'll have matching diamond bracelets on my wrists. Can't you see them?" I posed for him, one hand flicked out at my hip, the other at my shoulder.

Behind me I heard the roar of an engine and the squeal of brakes. I turned, expecting to see the bus to Columbia. Instead I found myself looking into the front seat of a shining new red DeSoto convertible. The driver smiled up at me.

"Hey, there, pretty lady, I ain't seen you around town before. What's your name?"

I knew who he was. Blair Howard was a celebrity in our town. As star quarterback of the Mighty Munford Rams, he had led the team to the state championships three years in a row. Every girl in Munford swooned when he trotted onto the field, his helmet tucked under his arm and a lock of dark blond hair falling over his forehead. Just one bolt from his blue eyes was supposed to make females swoon and opposing quarterbacks tremble.

He was also the youngest son of the Howards of Woodlands, the wealthiest family in the county. Their lumber business was one of the biggest in the state. Not only did they mill thousands of board-feet of lumber every year, they also ran a big pulp and paper operation. They turned some of the paper into Howard's Crescent Toilet Paper, "The Favorite of Millions," and the pulp into the Munford *Bugle* and two other newspapers. The Howards were pillars of Honor Baptist Church, and along with the Thomases—Jean-Ellen's family—constituted Munford society.

Blair was grinning at me. "Cat got your tongue, beautiful? Parlay-voo fransay?"

"No, I speak English. I'm Dessie Heavener."

"You're not! Old Art Heavener's kid from the church choir? You're pullin' my leg. Ain't that right, son?" he winked at Paul. "She's havin' fun with me, ain't she?"

"No." Paul scanned the horizon anxiously for the bus, then checked his wristwatch, a graduation gift from his father.

"Dessie Heavener!" Blair marveled. "I wouldn't have known you, and that's the truth. What you doin' standin' out here, Dessie? Waitin' for the bus?" When I nodded, he leaned over and threw open the door on the passenger side. "Well, hop in. I'll take you anyplace you want to go."

I glanced at Paul, who had fixed his gaze on the end of the street where the bus was supposed to appear. "My friend and I are going to Columbia," I said. "That's a long way from here. I'm going to be in the talent contest at the Dixieland Ballroom."

"No kidding? The Dixieland, eh? Hell, I've been to that place more times than I've been to church lately. I'd be glad to run you up, and your friend, too. You look familiar, pal. Do I know you from someplace?"

Paul dragged his gaze around reluctantly. "We were in the same class in high school. I'm Paul Miller."

"Oh, Miller. Sure, I remember you. Debating society, president of the student council—you've got a gimp leg, ain't you?"

The remark was thoughtless, and Paul stiffened and turned red. "My infirmity has never stopped me from doing anything I wanted to do."

"Hell, I guess not." When Blair laughed, which he did frequently, the corners of his blue eyes wrinkled up and his mouth split into a wide grin. "Now me, I had a gimp brain. I never could have played football at all if some smart, pretty girls hadn't helped me with my tests and reports and all that stuff. You go to USC, don't you? I was going to Tulane down in New Orleans until two months ago. A Mississippi fullback ran me down durin' practice, broke my throwin' arm in two places. They just took the cast off. She still don't work too good." I saw a shadow of despair in his eyes. Then he shrugged. "I never could see no sense in wasting time in school if you can't play football. Well,

21

come on, folks, since I'm going your way, you might as well ride comfortable as not.''

The clock on the Methodist steeple gave two sullen bongs: four-thirty already. "Paul, let's.'' I tugged at his sleeve. "Please. We don't want to be late, and I have to be there by seven or I won't qualify.''

Paul jacked his spine straighter by a few notches. "I don't think we need to impose on Blair—"

"It's no imposition, honest,'' Blair said.

"Paul, please!'' I wailed. I could feel by the tightness under the sleeve of Paul's jacket that he wasn't going to budge. Furious, I dropped his arm and snatched up my suitcase. "Well, you can be stubborn if you want to, but I'm going to Columbia with Mr. Howard.''

Just then, the bus rolled into view. Blair saw me hesitate. "Don't pay attention to that rickety thing, darlin'. I can get you there twice as quick, and you won't have to pay.'' No passengers had dismounted. Paul was moving toward the door of the bus. I heard the driver urging him to step lively because they were behind schedule. I gave Blair an apologetic smile. "I guess I'd better go with him. He's got to play the piano for me tonight, and I don't want to put him in a bad mood.''

"Hey, wait!'' Blair called after me as I hurried to catch up with Paul. "Can I see you sometime?''

I turned and waved to him, then on impulse I blew him a kiss. "Sure, if you come and hear Kingsley's band on tour. After tonight I'll be singing with them.''

"I will never forgive you for this, Paul Miller. Never, never, never!''

We stood at the side of the bus and waited for the driver to complete his inspection of the undercarriage. Because the heavy rains of the past week had weakened the bridge on the main road, he had taken a detour along a typically rutted country lane. The bus had lurched into a large puddle and stopped dead.

The driver sat back on his heels and shook his head. "Looks like a broken axle.''

"Well, what are you going to do about it?'' I demanded. The other passengers looked more alert as they waited for his answer. They included a group of well-dressed Negroes on their way to a Bible convention in Columbia, and a large middle-aged white woman who slept soundly, her head pillowed on her three chins.

"Nothin' I can do," the driver said with a shrug, " 'less you got yourself a blow torch in that suitcase."

I rounded on Paul. "This was your idea. You and your stupid pride. Why couldn't you have accepted a ride from Blair Howard? It wouldn't have killed you. What if he did insult you? So what? Now we're stuck out here in the middle of nowhere and there isn't even a house close by where we could telephone from."

"Who would we telephone?" Paul asked in a reasonable tone.

"I don't know." Feeling my heels sinking into the rain-softened clay of the roadbed, I stepped onto the grassy berm. "There isn't anybody, not a single soul that I can think of except Blair Howard, and by now he's probably found himself another girl to pass the time of day with."

Paul sniffed. "I'd say that was a pretty fair assumption."

"I'm walking back to the main road," I said. "We don't stand a chance of getting a ride out here."

"It's at least two miles," Paul objected. "You'll ruin your shoes. And besides, I can't walk that far. Relax, Dessie, someone will come along soon. We'd better wait."

Paul sat on my suitcase while I paced anxiously and kept searching the horizon for some sign of rescue. Finally a pickup truck came along bearing a farmer in soiled overalls, his faded wife and four big-eyed, shoeless children. Yes, he was going to Columbia, sure, and he wouldn't mind taking us if we didn't mind riding in the back with half a dozen hay bales, one live sheep, and three of the four kids. He didn't think he could accommodate the Nigras, as he called them, and the fat lady was once again sleeping soundly inside the bus.

I scrambled up, gave Paul a hand to haul him aboard, and thumped on the roof of the cab to signal that we were ready to go.

No vehicle on earth could have been slower than that old truck. The farmer treated that thing like it was made of paper and string, never pushing the speed above twenty and always guiding it carefully over ruts and bumps. I closed my eyes and screamed silently inside my head. Nervousness and fear combined with anger and apprehension to produce a volatile and incendiary brew. I couldn't bring myself to look at Paul, much less speak to him. I blamed him, and I blamed myself for not having the guts to seize upon Blair Howard's offer.

At fifteen minutes to eight, the rattletrap truck and its exhausted passengers halted at the intersection dominated by the red-roofed dance hall. The parking lot was full. Even from a distance of a hundred yards, I could hear the thump of drums and the wail of a trumpet. I leaped down without even thanking the driver and raced across the road. Paul followed more slowly, limping, and lugging my suitcase.

I paid for two admissions and asked where I was supposed to register for the contest. The manager of the hall, a balding, sour-faced man who looked more like an undertaker than a purveyor of entertainment, shook his head.

"You're too late, missy. Registration was all over half an hour ago."

"But I mailed in my application! I paid my money!"

"Sorry, girlie. You might as well go on in since you're here. You're just in time to see the show."

3

THE MUSIC SWELLED TO A CRESCENDO AND REACHED A CRASHing finale. Tucking his trumpet under his left arm, King Kingsley turned to acknowledge the enthusiastic applause, then he waved to the other musicians on the bandstand, sharing the applause with them.

"He looks even better than his pictures," I said to Paul. We had pushed our way down to the front of the ballroom. I kept willing King to look at me, but he smiled over our heads. His hair was reddish brown and so curly that a thick layer of pomade couldn't suppress the impudent corkscrew that coiled down over his forehead.

King stepped up to the microphone. "Thank you, ladies and gents, one and all." His mellow baritone came as no surprise to me. Although I had never heard him speak on the radio, I had listened to his recording of the band's theme song, "Deep Purple," a thousand times. I knew every bar by heart, especially the last few measures when the music faded to a whisper and he said, "Good night, lovers everywhere, and sweet dreams." His words always brought tears to my eyes.

"We come now to the fun part of the evening, the big talent show. We've got a lot of folks backstage who are itching to show off their stuff, so we'll get started right away. Each contestant will get two minutes to impress you, but if he or she can do it in less, that's great. We score points for brevity." When he grinned, his eyes twinkled and little dimples danced at the corners of his mouth. "Now remember, you folks out there are the real judges. You and you alone will choose the winner by your applause. The bigger the noise, the bigger the vote, okay?"

A lump rose to my throat. Had I really come this far only to be cheated of my chance at fame and fortune? The stage, just inches from my face, seemed hopelessly out of reach; the musicians, dressed like King in purple blazers with golden crowns emblazoned on their breast pockets, resembled Olympian gods: serene, confident of their powers, a little bored. A large cutout of the band's logo—two intersecting K's surmounted by a crown—hung from the royal purple curtain in the rear. The colors on the music stands were reversed, purple letters on a glittery gold background. It was all so beautiful I wanted to cry.

King referred to a card he had taken from the side pocket of his purple blazer. "Our first contestant is Jepprey Snide on trombone. Jepp?"

A short man with very long arms slouched onstage from the wings. I could see his successors waiting to follow him, a nervous-looking gaggle of young men in boxy jackets, bow ties, and slicked-back hair, and a couple of housewives and some college girls with tumbles of curls and frilly dresses. I hated them all.

"What's that?" King inclined an ear. "Oh, Jeffrey Snead! Wow, somebody's handwriting is even worse than mine. Okay, Jeff, let'er wail!" Leading the applause, King stepped back to give the ape-armed man some room.

Jeffrey Snead managed about twelve torturous bars of "St. Louis Blues" before King broke in, clapping his hands and exhorting the members of the audience to give the lad a nice round of applause. The rest of the crowd obeyed. Paul looked downcast and I fumed inwardly.

A trumpet player was next. His climactic wail ended on an ear-shattering shriek. He slunk off into the wings, dragging his humiliation behind him like a sack of rocks.

A trio of coeds crooned "Stardust" in passable, if uninteresting, harmony. I listened hard to the lead singer, the one who carried the melody. Her voice was shaking with nervousness. At the end, all three looked relieved that their ordeal was over. I was curious: If performing was such torture for people, why did they do it?

The parade of amateurs continued: instrumentalists, vocal trios, vocal duos, soloists. Not one of them excited me, not one of them made my hackles rise. I had heard better music coming out of the Munford High School Choral Society under my father's direction.

The final contestant stepped up to the microphone, a tall, gorgeous brunette with long legs and round hips, a slinky walk, and a smile that showed off her perfect white teeth. Even the members of the band perked up, and one or two of them whistled. King's dimples deepened. His voice dropped a couple of tones.

"What's your name, sweetie?" He didn't bother consulting his card.

"Marcie Neeley." The brazen tramp spoke right into the microphone.

She had brought her own pianist along, too. He was terrible, and she was worse, and we had ample opportunity to judge because King let her number drag on for at least three minutes. She sang "They Can't Take That Away from Me," a fine Gershwin tune that didn't deserve to be mooed a whole tone flat.

But King must have detected something special in her delivery, for he made a big show of coaxing out louder and louder applause from the audience before proclaiming her the undisputed winner.

I grabbed Paul's hand. "Come on."

Paul and I bucked the crowd and ran around to the steps at the left side of the stage. I gave Paul a push in the direction of the piano and ran up to the microphone.

" 'Don't you walk out that door, you rascal, you!' " I shouted at King, who had moved a few steps away with Marcie. He pulled himself up short, then turned and scowled at me. "I said, 'Don't you walk out that door, you low-down rascal, you. When you step across that threshold, you and I are through.' " It didn't take Paul more than a bar or two to catch on. He sat down at the piano and played a blues riff. I went on with the song, one I had learned at Clara Mae's knee before she got religion:

> You can keep on walkin',
> But don't you turn around.
> Just keep right on walkin',
> But don't you never turn around.
> I want to see your backside, baby,
> Movin' on out of town.

From the audience came whistles and cheers. They moved closer, like a herd of cattle gathering around the trough at feeding time.

> You can go to China,
> Or you can go to France.
> Be the king of Kansas City,
> Or a pirate in Penzance.
> You can even go to Heaven, baby,
> But I ain't givin' you no second chance.

I heard an unexpected thump followed by a soft drum roll and a cymbal crash. The drummer had joined Paul. Then I heard a riff from the trombonist. My spirits soared with the music. I strutted a little and swung my hips, the way I remembered Clara Mae doing when she sang those blues ballads she had learned from Bessie Smith. Some of the people clustered in front of the stage tapped their feet and snapped their fingers. And they were smiling. Smiling at me.

> I'll be so happy, honey,
> So glad to see you gone.
> I'll be so happy, honey,
> So glad to see you gone.
> You've left my poor heart shakin',
> But I know I'll carry on.

Paul and the other men finished up with a joyous and noisy tremolo. I heard a strange noise, and looking around I saw that everybody in that hall—even King Kingsley—was applauding me. Me. For the first time in my life, I had sung to an audience of total strangers, and they liked me. I wanted to laugh out loud: I had been so engrossed in the music that I had forgotten to be nervous.

When the noise of the applause abated, King Kingsley said, "That wasn't bad, sweetheart, but we don't get much call for blues numbers these days. You know any standards?"

He wanted me to do another song! I nodded to Paul, who led me into the number we had originally planned for the audition: Jerome Kern's "Can't Help Lovin' That Man." The drummer picked up our beat, which was strong and energetic. I really opened up on the high notes at the end, still keeping them pure and not harsh, but sending my voice into every corner and pocket in that room, into every ear and every corpuscle. I knew I was good, because when I was finished I felt a strange, tingling sensation in every part of my body.

My listeners liked it, too. Their applause was like a balm, the sweetest and most soothing sensation I had ever experienced. King crossed the stage to me. He said, "You were great, honey." Then, wrapping his arms around me, he pressed the full length of his body close to mine and gave me a long and powerful kiss. I was too shocked to close my eyes. Marcie Neeley stood in my line of vision. Her arms were crossed in front of her chest and her face was white with rage.

Paul hobbled over, reaching us just about the time King released me. As I struggled to catch my breath, King said in my ear, "I think maybe we ought to talk privately, Miss—ah—what did you say your name was?"

I told him my name. He turned to the audience and said into the microphone, "Folks, I want you to meet the South's newest singing sensation, Miss Dessie Heavener. You heard her here first, and I want to predict a beautiful career for this young lady. In fact, as of this minute, she's joining our tour." He stepped back, his arm tight around my waist. "Let's you and me go backstage to my dressing room, Dessie, talk some business while the band takes a break."

"Mr. Kingsley," Paul said in a loud voice.

King waved him away as he steered me toward the wings. "This is between me and the young lady, friend. Sorry, but I don't need another piano player." He waved to a man standing just offstage. "This fellow's my road manager, Dizzy Dillon. Did you hear this kid, Diz? She was really sensational out there. A little rough around the edges, maybe, and nobody wants to hear a white girl singing colored songs, but I'm bettin' we can make some beautiful music together."

"Sure, King, sure." The manager was a small man with pale blue eyes, a button nose, and worried eyebrows that tickled his receding hairline.

"I think you need to be informed about something, Mr. Kingsley." To my astonishment, Paul grabbed King's arm and jerked him around. We were still onstage, over on the left side and far enough away from the microphones so that the people in the back of the room couldn't hear us. But Marcie Neeley and the audience down front could, and they stopped their talk and listened hard. "Do you know what statutory rape is? The age of consent in this state is sixteen, and Dessie here is only fifteen and a few months."

"Paul!" I wailed. "No! Stop!"

29

"If you so much as lay a finger on her, you'll be arrested and dragged up in front of a judge so fast that you'll wonder what happened. You'll be playing that horn of yours in the State Pen instead of places like this. Do you understand me?"

The hubbub of conversation in the ballroom had ceased. The crowd moved in closer, scenting excitement and wanting to be in on the kill. I could hear their whispers: "What is it?" "What's going on?"

King gave me a look that said he wished I had never been born. "The contestants in this thing were supposed to be eighteen. It's not my fault this little bitch lied about her age."

Paul—bookish, sedentary, serious-minded Paul who hardly ever swatted a fly—swung his fist and popped King right in the nose. "Don't you call her any of your dirty Yankee names," he shouted. "She's got more talent in one hair on her head than you have in your whole body. Come on, Dessie." He took my arm and dragged me toward the steps.

I hung back, twisting around to give King a beseeching look. "Please, Mr. Kingsley, I didn't mean any harm—"

"Get the hell out of here, both of you!" King produced a muffled roar from behind the handkerchief he was using to staunch the flow of blood from his nose. "I ought to have you arrested for this, you damned frauds. Out!" He looked around. "Where's that other little girl, the real winner?"

The ballroom manager and an assistant met us as we came offstage and hustled us through the hostile crowd toward the back of the hall. I glanced back. The brunette was appearing onstage and taking a bow as if nothing had happened. When we reached the door, the manager gave us each a hard shove. His friend had fetched our coats and my suitcase from the checkroom, and he sent those sailing after us. Paul's weak leg gave way when he reached the ground and he sprawled in the red clay of the parking lot. By the time he dragged himself to his feet, the doors were closed and the music had begun again inside.

"Why is it," he muttered as he dusted himself off, "that bullies always love to pick on cripples? Well, at least I got you away from that animal, Kingsley."

"Oh, you got me away from him, all right." Sensation was returning, and with it cold rage of a sort I had never experienced before. "You got me out of a singing job, too. Didn't you hear him? He told that whole crowd in there that I was going on tour with them! I was going to be a big band singer! And then you opened your mouth. Why? Why did you do it?"

"I had to," Paul said. "I could see what he wanted. You could have, too, if all that applause hadn't sent you right to cloud nine. And by the time you recognized the truth about him, it would have been too late. I watched him while you were singing. He wasn't one bit interested in your voice. He was looking at you like he wanted to eat you up right on the spot. Damn, I swear he even licked his chops. If you don't know what that makes him, then you're even dumber than I thought you were."

"You've been trying all day to ruin my plans, and now you've succeeded!" My voice rose to a hysterical scream. "You're jealous, aren't you, Paul? You want me to stay in that miserable town with you, like I was some sort of cripple myself. Well, you listen to me. I am never going back there, never. I've got ten dollars my mama gave me folded up in my stocking, and I'm going to get on a bus to New York and I'm going to be a singer. I'm good enough, I know that now. Didn't you hear those people in there? They loved me! I could feel their love pouring into me. I've never had love like that before, from anybody."

Paul's hard breathing showed that he was as riled up as I, but he was never one to meet screaming with screaming. "That's not true, Dess. I love you. I've always loved you, sure, but I'm in love with you, too."

I was sobbing so hard by that time that I hardly heard the last part of his speech. "I thought you did, but I was wrong. You've been like a brother to me all these years, and I thought I could trust you, but I was wrong about that, too. You betrayed me, Paul Miller. You're a damned traitor and I will never speak to you again as long as I live!"

Snatching up my suitcase and coat, I ran across the parking lot to the street and turned right, toward where I imagined the rest of the city lay. I had some vague idea that I wanted to go to the bus station, but the destination wasn't important. More than anything I wanted to outrun my pain and my rage and my sorrow. I heard Paul calling my name, pleading with me to wait, to listen to him, but I was past listening. I glanced back once. He was on his knees, brought low once again by his weak leg.

A stitch under my ribs forced me to slow down. Hearing a noise, I looked over my shoulder. A car was following me, a red DeSoto convertible. I broke into a run again. The last person in the world I wanted to see in my present state of emotional and physical disrepair was smooth and handsome Blair Howard, with his winning smile and his crinkly eyes.

The car pulled alongside. I kept walking. Blair said, "That offer of a ride is still open, Miss Dessie." I shook my head, not trusting myself to speak. Unlike Paul, he didn't deserve to be screamed at. "I heard you sing back there. I thought you were mighty fine, the best singer it has ever been my privilege to hear. And you looked mighty pretty besides, prettier than any other girl there. It made me proud to know you."

I managed to squeeze out a few choked words. "Please, please go away."

"Now why would you want me to do that? I only want to help you."

"I don't want your help! I just . . . I wish . . ." I broke down. Dropping my purse and suitcase where I stood, I lowered my face into my gloved hands and sobbed.

"Hey. Hey, now." Through the racket of my sobs, I was aware of Blair's embarrassed solicitude. "You don't need to carry on like that. It's not the end of the world."

"That's exactly what it is," I wailed. "If I could die right now, I'd be grateful."

"Shoot, you don't mean that." He left his car and stood beside me. He was tall, maybe a whole foot taller than I was. "I know a little place not far from here, nice and quiet, wouldn't be anybody you knew in there. Would you like to have a drink, maybe? Something to calm you down?"

"I don't know. I don't know what I want. Let's just get away from here."

"Sure. Come on, honey." He steered me to the car and settled me into the front seat with great care, as if I were an invalid or an old person. "You can trust ole Blair to know what's good for a broken heart. After I smashed up my arm, I went and got drunk, and I stayed that way for a month."

We rode for fifteen minutes without speaking, then Blair braked the car and switched off the engine. He ushered me into a dark little place where the air was thick with cigarette smoke and beer fumes and sweat. We chose a table in a dark corner. He left me dabbing at my eyes with a handkerchief and returned a minute later with two small glasses full of brown liquid.

"This here is bourbon," he said. "Best cure I know for what ails you."

I drank the whole glass right down, gagging a little at the taste and the burn in my gullet. I waited for my heart to stop aching. Nothing happened. I shoved the empty glass toward him.

"Can I have another one of those, please?"

Blair laughed. "I sure wouldn't have figured you for a drinkin' gal, Miss Dessie. But you can have anything you want." He disappeared and returned with some more drinks.

I sent the second shot the way of the first. It tasted smoother and it didn't burn so much. Then I felt something, a not unpleasant buzzing sensation in the back of my head. And around my heart. "Now I know what Mama's been up to all these years," I giggled. "This isn't so bad."

"See, I told you." Blair sipped the beer he had brought to chase his whiskey. "Nothin's so good or bad in this world that a little drink don't make it better. Hey, look at me." I lifted my head. "Give me that handkerchief of yours." I passed it across the table. Feeling it, he laughed. "Shoot, this ole thing feels like you just brought it in outa the rain. Just what we need." Very gently, he wiped away the streaks of mascara from my cheeks. "Now smile pretty. Come on, I know you can do it, even if you have to force yourself. A little smile for ole Blair."

I did have to force myself, but I managed to produce a weak and watery grin. He sat back, giving his head a contented shake. "If you ain't the prettiest little thing I've ever seen. And to think you've been livin' right under my nose all this time and I never knew it."

We had another round of drinks. By that time I was feeling pleasantly numb all over. The pain had receded so that even the memory of my ignominious exit from the Dixieland Ballroom didn't hurt so much.

I felt my cheeks burning, either from the whiskey or from Blair's flattering attentions. I said, "It's awfully warm in here."

Blair stood up promptly. "We'll take a little ride. I know a spot real close by where we can sit and talk."

"I'm not going home," I informed him as I stood up. I couldn't feel my legs under me, and I clutched his arm for support. "I am never going home. I am taking the bus to New York tonight. I am going to be a shing—a singer. A famous singer. I'll show them."

"Sure you will, honey."

The DeSoto's headlights knifed through the darkness, which was heavy with humidity and the ripened smells of early autumn. A half moon peeked out of the clouds that were gathering

33

just above the horizon. Out here, far from the lights of town, a few patches of stars still winked down, oblivious to my misery.

Blair stretched out his right arm and tossed away his cigarette. An ember like a tiny comet darted away into the darkness. His arm came around my shoulders again. I pressed close to him, grateful for his undemanding friendship, his kindness, the warmth of his body.

He slowed to make a turn onto a narrow unpaved road. The lights swept over a peeling sign for Fisher's Lake. It was a popular place at the height of summer, with picnic tables, changing rooms, and a small store that sold hot dogs and ice-cold soda pop. The little kids from Munford went around collecting empty bottles and redeeming them for the deposits. Every year the owners trucked in a few loads of sand to make a beach, but by the end of July the thin layer of sand was green with crabgrass.

Blair drove the car right down to the edge of the water. "Hey, we even got ourselves a piece of the moon tonight," he said. "See it, duckin' in and out behind those clouds? I'm bettin' we get ourselves some rain before this night's out. Guess I oughta put the top up, but I'll wait a bit." He stroked my cheek. "You feelin' any better, Dessie?"

"I don't know." I wished I could follow the narrow golden path laid down on the surface of the lake by the moon. I wanted to see where it went. "I'm not feeling much of anything right now."

Blair laughed. He had a nice laugh. "You put away a powerful lot of bourbon tonight, honey. You could hardly walk outa that ole gin mill. I half carried you, remember? Hey, would you mind if I took this hat of yours off? One of these feathers is pokin' my eye out. Golly, you have pretty hair. It's about the same color as a sunbeam, wouldn't you say?"

"I poured the sunshine out of a bottle this morning," I said thickly. "Least I think it was this morning."

"I don't care where it comes from. It's still pretty." He buried his nose in my curls. "So sweet-smelling. And soft."

He removed the pins and played with my curls, winding them around his fingers. It felt wonderful. His gentle touch comforted me. His fingertips kissed my hair. Wasn't there a song about that?

". . . kiss . . . ," I murmured.

"I was just about to," he said, moving my face around with his kind hands. His kissing was every bit as nice as his stroking.

As nice as King Kingsley's kiss. I closed my eyes. Kissing him was nice, not as nice as singing, but nice when you're with someone who knows how to do it right. I wondered if Paul had ever kissed a girl the way Blair was kissing me. I couldn't imagine him doing it. He would be so stiff and awkward, yet ridiculously meticulous, the way he had been when he had pinned my hair up that morning. Ridiculously meticulous. I giggled.

"What's funny?" Blair asked.

"Me. You. Paul. Everything. What are you doing?"

"Touchin' your leg. You got a pretty nice set of legs on you, Miss Dessie. In fact, you're just about perfect, from head to toe. You got a perfect neck, and perfect ears, and the prettiest, most perfect little nose I ever saw on a woman. I think that nose deserves a special little kiss all its own."

I was sinking lower and lower in the seat. I realized that my arms were locked around Blair's neck and that I was dragging him down with me. But when I tried to release him, I discovered that I couldn't. My arms were tangled and I didn't know how to unsnarl them.

"I don't want to stop holding you," I said.

"Then, don't. I don't intend to stop holding you. Oh, Dessie."

We had no more words for a long time. I wanted to hide myself in his warmth, and the more he touched me and stroked me and hugged me, the more I wanted to be touched and stroked and held. His weight on top of me felt like no weight at all, more like a blessing and a necessity, like a warm blanket on a cold night.

I grew sleepier and more languorous while Blair's energy seemed to increase. The more excited he got, the more torpid I became. I had a dream, or perhaps it was really a daydream, or the exhaust from the laboring of my overheated imagination: I am standing in the light, a pillar of ivory with a crown of gold. Love washes over me like the waves of a warm sea, love so powerful it feels like a caress. I sing to the sea, and the waves answer back with a chant of their own that is rhythmic and strong, washing me back and forth between the horizon and the shore. The tide of love swells higher and higher, until it engulfs me so completely that I must struggle for breath. Then the love pierces my heart, bringing pain but almost instant joy. The song of the waves slows, as if they, too, were getting sleepy.

* * *

A drop of cold rain splashed on my cheek. Another. I opened my eyes. The stars had all vanished, but the moon still glowed eerily down through the mist.

I heard a buzzing noise. Blair, slumped over the wheel, was dozing peacefully. I looked down at myself. My coat was open, my skirt rolled up around my waist. I still wore my garter belt and stockings, but my panties were gone. I scrabbled around on the floor until I found them. They were torn.

My dream came back to me. Rhythmic caresses? Piercing love that brought pain? Oh, no. No!

Horrified, I screamed at Blair, "What have you done to me? What have you done?" I shook the panties in front of his face. "Look at these. What did you do? Tell me!"

Shaken rudely out of his sleep, Blair yawned and scratched his head. "Aw, come on, honey, don't be like that. We had ourselves a good ole time and then we went to sleep. Happens all the time. You sure are a sweet little thing. I've never had sweeter. I didn't hurt you too bad, did I? I've heard it can hurt real painful the first time, but you didn't seem to mind." Leaning over, he tried to kiss me.

I shrank from him. "Don't touch me! Leave me alone!"

He retreated. A few more drops fell. "Guess I better put that top up after all."

I was shivering. The alcoholic fog had cleared from my brain and the chilling reality of my situation stared me in the face. "No," I whispered. "Oh, no. Oh, no." I threw open the door and jumped out of the car. For the second time that night, I ran. I crossed the parking lot and the road and plunged into the oak scrub across from the shuttered store.

"Dessie! Dessie, honey, come back here!"

The DeSoto's engine roared. The twin beams of the headlamps laid down a twin trail on the surface of the water that ended abruptly somewhere in the middle of the lake: paths without promise.

My stomach finally rebelled. I doubled over and emptied my stomach of bourbon and bile.

Blair's lights swung around and fanned the scrub. Dropping to my knees, I scrunched down and covered my blonde head with my arms. After the car had passed, I made my way back toward the road. Blackberry brambles lunged at my stockings. Slender twigs whipped my face. The rain fell harder.

The night sky was black as pitch. The moon had disappeared

and no lights shone among the trees. I prayed that I would find the road and not bury myself deeper in the woods. Just as my feet found the reassuring rutted surface, thunder rumbled and the skies opened. Guided by flashes of lightning, I stumbled back to the lake front and found shelter on the lee side of Pop Fisher's store. Strands of wet hair like seaweed slapped my face.

I had left my purse and suitcase in Blair's car. My clothes were ruined. I looked a mess. I was miles from anywhere. Still, I had Mama's ten dollars folded up in my stocking. Enough to buy another pair of stockings and a lipstick and comb, and a bus ride to somewhere, maybe even New York. Lifting my skirt, I felt all around for the folded bill, under my garters, even inside my shoes. I peeled my stockings down and patted the ground all around my feet. It was gone. Not only had I lost my virginity, but my bankroll as well. By this time I was too stunned to cry. I was in worse shape than Cinderella after the ball: flat broke, reduced to rags, and deflowered besides.

I sat in a miserable huddle by the side of the building until the storm passed. The moon reappeared, once again opening up an inviting avenue across the lake. I knew where it led and I wanted to take it, but I couldn't.

After a while, I stood up and took a first dragging step toward home. I had to go there. I had no place else.

4

"ALL RIGHT, SOPRANOS," MY FATHER SAID, "LET'S GO OVER your part one more time just to make sure you remember it, then we'll run through Dessie's solo."

Ayleen Carmody perked up. She lowered her music to waist level, which is where her choir director liked it to be held during church services. On our left, chairs shifted as the two tenors readied themselves for their turn in the spotlight. One of the two was Tremble Britten, a farmer's wife whose voice had a remarkably low range and terrific volume. Berenice Martin giggled and craned her neck so that she could see around me to where Ayleen was patting her newly-permed hair and simpering at my father as she sang.

"She's been looking at your father that way for fifteen years." Berenice thrust her face right up against my ear. "That woman will die of failed hopes."

I closed my eyes and held my breath against the odor of Berenice's dinner: greens cooked with fatback, pickled hog jowls, potatoes fried with onion. I wondered what the ladies of the choir would say if I ran screaming into the night. In the old days, I might have done it. But the humiliations I had experienced in October had accomplished what my father's harsh discipline had failed to do: they had broken my spirit.

On the morning after the talent contest, I had reached home at dawn, as pathetic and bedraggled as a stray cat. My suitcase was on the front porch, with my purse tucked down behind it. As I opened the door, I heard my father's footsteps on the stairs. He had always been an early riser. He said two things to me. The first was, "Why did you have to come back?" And the second was, "Where is the money your mother stole from me?" When I told him I had lost it, he started to whip me with his belt. Suddenly my mother burst out of the parlor, where she had obviously spent the night, and thrust herself between us.

"You touch her again and I'll kill you!" she screeched. "I swear, Arthur Heavener, I'll murder you in your bed if you touch one more hair on her head."

Numb and dazed as I was, I nevertheless felt surprised. My father thought I had run away. And he was sorry I had come back. Instead of depressing me further, this realization somehow relieved me. The hatred that existed between us was powerful, and mutual. He was as eager to be rid of me as I was to be gone.

From that time on, my father and I hardly exchanged two words. He stopped locking me in my room, and I stopped fighting him. When the period of my suspension from school was over, I returned to the classroom. I did what my teachers asked me to do. I attended choir practice and church services, and I even agreed to sing the alto solo in "The Peoples' Messiah." My father was not showing me any special consideration by asking; he simply had no other alto capable of doing justice to even a simplified version of Handel's music.

The pianist pounded out the introduction to my solo. I opened my mouth to sing and closed it again immediately. The room tilted, then darkened. When I opened my eyes, I was lying on my back amid a forest of stockinged legs and skirt hems.

They sat me up and made me put my head between my knees. Tremble Britten brought me a glass of water and mopped my forehead with her handkerchief. "Lordamercy," she boomed, "it's stuffy enough in here to make anybody drop down dead in a faint. You feelin' a little better now, Dessie?" I nodded weakly. "I'll just take you on home so that your daddy doesn't have to stop what he's doin'." She helped me on with my coat and, passing her arm around my waist, half carried me out of the church. Once outside, I broke away from her, dove for the azalea bushes near the sidewalk, and threw up my supper. Tremble shook her head. "You're gonna have to tell your daddy sooner or later, honey, or else the whole town is gonna know before he does."

"Know what?" I gasped.

"That you're in the family way, that's what. You can't fool me. I have nine already and another on the way come June."

"No!" I knelt in the grass, my arms pressed against my waist. "No, it isn't true. I'm not! I'm not!"

"With the first two, I heaved my guts out every blessed day for three months, but after that I didn't have any trouble."

I dove for the azaleas again.

Tremble escorted me home. She offered to come in and fix me a cup of warm milk, but I declined. I knew she meant to be kind, but we Heaveners had never developed the habit of admitting strangers into our house. We stood on the front porch. She said, "I'll tell your daddy after practice tonight, 'fore he hears it from someone else. Don't worry, I won't spread it around. Those old cats would just love to get their claws into you. I swear, I thought their mouths would never stop after you showed up that Sunday with your hair all bleached out and yellow. Ayleen's still talkin' about that."

I poked my head into the parlor. My mother was asleep in her armchair. The radio played a dance tune. I switched it off and went upstairs to my room.

A baby. I was going to have a baby. Tremble was obviously an expert, and even as I had shouted denials, I had known in my heart that she was right. Too numb to cry, I lay huddled in the darkness, my knees drawn up to my chin.

After choir practice, my father came into my room and stood at the foot of my bed.

"I should have known you'd do something like this," he said. "You're just like your mother. The devil entered your soul when you were born and he has been working his evil inside you ever since. If I were a truly righteous man and not a coward, I would kill the both of you." He turned away, then stopped in the doorway. "Well, that boy is not going to get away with this. I was a fool, letting you go running all over the place with him. But now he's going to pay, and that father of his, too. They'll be paying for a long time to come."

He stamped out. I heard him go downstairs, then the kitchen door slammed. I left my bed and looked out my window. My father was striding across our backyard toward the judge's house. He pounded at the judge's back door.

Paul! He thought that Paul was the father of my baby! I ran after him, down the stairs and through the darkened kitchen and into the night.

I found them in the judge's study, not only the two fathers, but Paul as well. I was surprised to see him on a weeknight, but then I remembered that he always got a long break from school around Christmas.

40

Paul and I hadn't spoken a word to each other since the night of the talent contest. The first time we had seen each other in church, Paul had smiled at me and started to walk toward me. I had turned my back on him. He hadn't been in church since.

"It's not true!" I cried. "It wasn't Paul, I swear it! It was—it was somebody else."

The judge looked stern. "You might have told your father the truth before he came storming over here making irresponsible accusations."

"Who was it?" My father gripped my shoulders. "Tell me, Dessie. Who? We'll make him pay, by God. We will take him to court and squeeze out every penny we can. Who was it?"

I stared at him. He cared more about money than he did about me. He didn't care that I had run away, but I had taken ten dollars of his money, and that had infuriated him. Now he saw a way of getting his money back with interest.

I couldn't answer his question. I hated him too much to tell him anything. Paul understood. Putting his arm around my shoulders, he led me away from my father and sat me down on the old tufted leather sofa.

"It's like a nightmare," I whispered. "Make it go away, Paul. Please make it go away."

"You have to tell us the truth, Dessie," he said. "Just tell us who did this to you and we'll take it from there. You'll be all right, honestly. Everyone understands how—how these things happen."

The judge stood over us. He was wearing an old blue bathrobe over striped pajamas. He had never approved of his son's fondness for me. There were no women in his house. All the cooking and housework were done by a taciturn black man named John. "You can go away and have the child someplace far from here," he said. "But we need to know who is responsible, so that he may contribute his fair share. You do not have to bear this burden alone."

I looked up at him. Even in his robe and slippers, Paul's father embodied the full might of the law. For the first time in weeks, I felt a flicker of hope. Maybe this baby was a blessing in disguise. I could go away, far away, maybe even as far as New York. I would have the baby and give it up for adoption. And then I could get on with my life, and my career. And there would be money, lots of money to compensate me for what I had endured.

"Blair Howard," I said. "It was Blair."

"Oh, dear God." My father's long jaw sagged down to the middle button on his vest. "Blair Howard? Dear Lord. To accuse a Howard of something like this . . ." As he considered the financial implications of what had happened, his eyes began to glisten.

Paul's arm slid down from my shoulders. He looked away, but not before I saw the pain in his eyes. The judge said, "Tell us what happened, Dessie. Did he force himself on you?"

I told them how Blair had followed me after I left the Dixieland Ballroom. I described how he had taken me to a bar and given me several drinks of whiskey, how we had driven into the country and parked beside Fisher's Lake.

"That's where it happened." I stared at my hands. "I didn't really know what was going on until after it was all over. He didn't mean to hurt me, I'm sure he didn't."

"Of course he meant it," my father growled. "The kind of beast who would prey on young girls—well, he'll pay for this. Pay through the nose!"

Beside me, Paul produced a sigh so deep and anguished it sounded like a groan.

The judge cleared his throat. "Well, Arthur, I guess you can proceed, now that we know the facts. Wait to confront the Howards until Doctor Simmons has verified Dessie's condition. Charles Howard may give you a hard time about this at first, but I daresay he'll come around. From what I've heard, this isn't the first time one of his sons has landed in a scrape like this. If you have any trouble with young Blair, just refer him to me. I will remind the young man that the law has a say in this matter, too. And now, I am going to bed. Good night."

The next morning I stayed home from school. I didn't feel like putting up with the likes of Miss Maddson and Jean-Ellen Thomas, and besides, I would have to quit soon anyway. At ten o'clock, I was sitting in the kitchen with Clara Mae. I told her everything. We had a good long cry together, then she got up and wiped her eyes and started to separate eggs and grate lemons for lemon meringue pie, my favorite.

Paul tapped on the back door and came into the kitchen without waiting for an invitation. Why not? This had been his second home for twelve years, and he always said he preferred Clara Mae's cooking to John's.

"Morning, Dessie. Clara Mae. Dessie, my dad said I could have the car today. Would you like to go for a ride?"

I gave him a bleak smile. "You know what happened last time I accepted a ride with a man."

Paul stood framed in the kitchen doorway. "I can guarantee your safety." He smiled sadly at Clara Mae, who pulled him into the room, seated him at the table, and set a cup of coffee down in front of him, already fixed the way he liked it with a little sugar and lots of milk. I watched him over the rim of my own cup. He looked haggard, the way he did when he stayed up all night studying for exams.

Clara Mae said, "You two better get out of here. This pie won't be done for a couple hours and I don't want y'all here stickin' your fingers into the meringue."

We set out five minutes later. As soon as we passed the school and the Munford city limit sign, I blew out my breath in a long sigh.

"In a few more days, I'll be gone. Finally. I hate that place."

"That's what I want to talk to you about." Paul braked close to Britten's cow pasture. He helped me through the strands of barbed wire and we mounted the slope to the ash grove, one of our favorite places in the autumn and spring. In summer, it was generally occupied by shade-seeking cows who didn't want to share. We sat on a cushion of dry leaves and leaned against a log.

After a while, Paul said, "You probably don't remember, but back there in Columbia at the Dixieland, I told you that I was in love with you. I meant it, Dessie. I could never love another woman the way I love you. I don't want you to go away. I want you to stay here and be my wife. Marry me, Dessie."

"I can't, Paul." I took his hand. "I wish I could say yes, but I can't. You know why, too. I'm going to be a singer. The kind of life you want for yourself isn't for me. Can you really see me as the wife of a small-town lawyer? I'd go crazy, and I'd embarrass you, and I'd lose you clients, and pretty soon we'd both be starving."

Paul pulled his hand away and turned so that I couldn't see his face.

"We'd fight, too, Paulie," I went on. "I know we would, and I don't want that to happen to us. I would still have my dream, and I would resent you for keeping me from it. Please understand, I love you, too. But if we were ever meant to marry, I would have known it long ago. Besides, Paulie," I tugged at his sleeve and tried to laugh, but I managed only a weak hiccup, "your father doesn't like me."

"That's not true. In fact, I think he's quite fond of you." He didn't sound convinced of that.

"He wouldn't appreciate having me as a daughter-in-law. And knowing that my—"

"Forget my father. I'm the one who wants to marry you, not him. What happened to you that night was my fault. I should have handled the situation differently. If I had explained things better to you, or spoken to Mr. Kingsley privately—"

I shook my head. "We can't change what happened. You've protected me all my life, Paulie. I couldn't expect you to behave differently, just because I had a chance to sing with King's band. You did what you thought was right. And now I'm going to do what I think is right."

Paul argued with me, but without much passion or conviction. He knew he could not persuade me to change my mind once I had decided on a course of action. Finally he said, "If you ever need me, I'll be right here. And if you ever change your mind, I'll be waiting."

The Howards were not really Southerners. They were Yankees, and carpetbaggers to boot. The present Mr. Howard's grandfather had arrived in town in 1866, hot on the heels of the Union army. Within six months, he had bought up half of Cluny County, married the daughter of a destitute aristocrat, and begun construction on Woodlands.

From a high wooded slope at the northern end of town, on the edge of the family's vast timber holdings, the mansion looked down on the town of Munford. Built of rose-colored brick, faced with white pillars two stories high, it had balconies on both the first and second floors. The grounds were as impressive as the house. In the spring and summer, garden clubs from all over the state converged on Mrs. Howard's formal rose gardens and her meticulously tended perennial beds. Now, at Christmastime, a candle flickered in each of the house's eighty-five windows, and the twin evergreens that stood just inside the wrought iron gates were trimmed with ropes of tinsel and colored glass balls.

My father and I were puffing by the time we reached the top of the cobbled driveway. Ahead of us lay a long flight of marble steps and a pair of polished mahogany doors decorated with twin holly wreaths. We paused for a moment to collect ourselves. Then we climbed the steps and my father lifted the brass, pine tree-shaped knocker and let it drop.

A Negro manservant opened the doors. He wore a black suit and red waistcoat, with a sprig of holly pinned to his lapel. He made a shallow bow and wished us Merry Christmas. My father asked to speak to Mr. Howard at once on an urgent personal matter.

"Yessa, Mr. Heavener. I'll see if Mr. Howard is available to speak with you. Won't you please come in?"

This was not my first visit to the Howard mansion. Once a year Mrs. Howard threw a big party for the members of the Baptist Church choir and the Sunday school faculty. We guests, sipping punch and lifting cookies from silver platters as big as truck tires, always talked in hushed voices, as if we were in a museum. None of us ever returned Mrs. Howard's hospitality. That wasn't why we had been invited. We were there to see and admire, and to express fulsome appreciation of our hostess's abundant and warm-hearted generosity.

After relieving us of our coats and hats, the butler tapped at a tall door to the right of the cavernous entrance hall and disappeared inside. He neglected to latch the door, which swung open a few inches. From within came the sound of masculine voices raised in argument:

". . . if you weren't my son, I'd have you arrested and thrown into jail for this."

I pricked up my ears. Had Mr. Howard heard about Blair's conduct toward me from some other source?

"Forging my signature on a check is a criminal offense!"

Not sex. Money. I awaited Blair's response.

"If I hadn't needed the money urgently, Dad, I wouldn't have done it. Why are you making such a big fuss over a measly two thousand dollars? I'll pay you back as soon as—"

"What is it, Sylvester? Who? My God, what does he want? Christmas Eve is a hell of a time to be asking for a new organ for the church. Well, send him in. Son, you and I will continue this discussion later."

Sylvester reappeared to beckon us inside the room. I experienced a momentary flutter of nervousness, and I reminded myself that I wasn't asking for anything I hadn't earned. I followed my father into Mr. Howard's library.

Although the walls were dark with walnut panelling and heavy with the weight of a thousand leather-bound books, the Christmas spirit nevertheless burned brightly here. A fire crackled merrily in the hearth. Above the elegantly sculpted pink and white marble fireplace hung a portrait of the original carpetbagger, painted when his hair and beard had turned to snow and the avaricious gleam in his eye had faded to a benign twinkle. Old Grandaddy Howard had been given an immense evergreen wreath all his own.

My father approached the massive desk in the center of the room. The two older men shook hands, then Mr. Howard gestured to a pair of wing chairs in front of the fireplace and asked us to sit down. I directed an anxious glance at the corner near the curtained windows, expecting to see Blair. But the man who gazed back at me was not Blair, although his resemblance to Blair was remarkable. He had the same chiseled profile with a high forehead, straight nose, and strong chin. But as I looked closer, I noticed that his hair was a shade lighter, and his nose was slightly crooked and thickened at the bridge. His chin boasted a thin white scar. Like Blair, he had blue eyes, but the creases at the corners were not friendly. They were watchful and wary creases, and the eyes themselves were pale and hard, like chips of granite. Blair's mouth was bent in a perpetual grin. This man's lips were pressed tightly together. I recalled that Blair had an older brother. He must be quite a bit older. Blair, at nineteen, was still a boy. This person appraising me with his cool eyes was a man.

I looked away. Despite this stranger's casual pose—leaning against the side of a leather armchair, a cigarette in one hand and a bowl-shaped glass in the other—I sensed that he was coiled tight. Mr. Howard had called him a criminal. That made him bad, and dangerous. Whatever he was, I didn't want him looking at me.

Mr. Howard rubbed his palms together. They sounded clean and dry, like paper. "Well, Arthur, this is an unexpected pleasure. Nice of you to call on Christmas Eve, but I'm sure you won't mind getting to the point. We're expecting guests for dinner in a few minutes, and Dorothy hates anything to disturb her plans. I believe you told Sylvester the matter was urgent?"

"Something has happened, Charles. Something you should know about." My father glanced at the room's other occupant.

"You remember my son Abraham," Mr. Howard said. "Bram

hasn't been around much these past few years. Don't worry, you can talk in front of him."

"Charles, I think you'd better call your other son in here. Blair. What I have to say concerns him."

"Blair?" Charles Howard looked surprised. "Why would you want to see him?"

"Because your boy has put my daughter in a family way," my father's cheeks flushed as he said the words, "and I would like to know what you intend to do about it."

Bram let out a short, sharp laugh. Coming as it did, in a moment of shocked silence, it sounded like a gunshot. We all jumped. Mr. Howard rubbed his hands on his trousers. All of a sudden, his palms weren't so dry. "I wasn't aware Blair even knew your daughter. What you're saying is mighty serious, Arthur. You'd better be sure of this before you start makin' accusations."

My father passed a piece of paper over the top of the desk. "This is a letter from Doctor Simmons confirming that Dessie is two months pregnant. If you want further proof, you can just ask her what happened. She'll tell you. Now I'm not saying she wasn't foolish and that she doesn't deserve a share of the blame for being out with him in the first place. But he took advantage of her. He—he forced himself on her. She's only fifteen and not much bigger or stronger than a kitten, while your boy—anyway, what's done is done. But somebody's going to have to pay to send the girl away and arrange for an adoption, and you know very well that I don't have any money to spare."

Mr. Howard's face had turned the color of a holly berry. He whipped around and snarled at Bram, "I see your brother is following in your footsteps. I might have known you'd corrupt him, too. You defile everything you touch!"

Bram shrugged. "It's not my fault if Blair can't control his baser impulses." He looked at my legs. One corner of his mouth curled up in what for him must have been a smile. "Can't say I blame him much for seizing an opportunity when it presented itself. The Howards of Woodlands certainly don't marry girls like her."

"Shut up, Bram. Go find Blair. I want to get to the bottom of this as soon as possible."

When Bram had gone, Mr. Howard sat down at his desk and pushed a meaty hand through his graying hair. "This is serious business, Arthur. I—I just can't believe it. Blair is such a fine boy. You remember that last game he played for Munford, that sixty yard run he made in the last minutes of the game? He was a hero. Folks carried him on their shoulders the whole length of Main Street. I've never been so proud. No, no, I just can't believe it." We sat silent for a moment, then Mr. Howard seemed to remember I was there. "Dessie." He shook his head. "Oh, Dessie, I remember you when you were just a wee mite—"

Just then, the door burst open and Mrs. Howard charged in. Her two sons followed in her wake, Bram bringing up the rear. Blair stopped near my chair. I glanced up long enough to see that he was smiling.

"What's so important that you have to see Blair right now?" Dorothy Howard demanded. "The Thomases will be here any minute, and I don't want my dinner spoiled." Then she saw us, and her expression altered dramatically. She seemed genuinely pleased to see us. "Well, Arthur! And Dessie! Merry Christmas to both of you. I'd invite you all to stay to dinner but I'm afraid we're havin' roast goose, and you know a goose only goes so far."

"This isn't a social call, Dorothy," her husband growled. "Dessie here is sayin' that Blair got her in a family way. They want some money to send her away."

The welcoming smile blinked off and the fleshy, pink-powdered face puckered into a hideous frown. "Oh, do they! I might have known something like this would happen, Arthur Heavener, the way you've been lettin' this girl of yours run wild all over town. I bet you've been congratulatin' yourselves on cookin' up a nice little scheme to bilk the Howards out of a fortune. But you are gravely mistaken, I'm afraid. My son would hardly even speak to a harum-scarum like Dessie, much less—much less do to her what you claim he did. The idea! I suggest you look elsewhere for the father of this alleged child. My Blair is innocent!" She engulfed her son in a smothering embrace. "My poor baby!"

"Well, I don't know." Blair wriggled out of her grasp. "If Dessie says I'm the one, then I guess I am." He leaned over me, his smile still intact. "Hello, Dessie. Looks like I've landed you in some trouble. I'm awful sorry. I drove around half the night lookin' for you. I left your stuff on your porch. I kept hopin'—"

"Don't you go sayin' you were sorry!" his mother boomed. "You don't know how many other boys she's gone with."

"Well, I do know she never went with any other boy before me. I was the first one."

"A virgin, by God." Behind me, Bram whooped. "You have all the luck, Blair."

"Do be quiet, Bram," his mother snapped. "This is no laughin' matter."

"Oh, for heaven's sake, Mother, just pay these people off and chalk this up as a lesson in Blair's column. This isn't the first time Dad has had to bail one of us out of a jam."

Mr. Howard slammed his palms down on the desk. "No, but it's the last time, by God! What have I done to deserve such sons? I gave you everything, everything, from the time you were babies. Maybe that's the problem. But no more. I am not going to pay any more gamblin' debts or bail money—"

Mrs. Howard sucked in her breath at her husband's indiscretion. I was surprised to hear that the Howards' lives were nearly as scandalous as the Heaveners'.

"No more!" Charles Howard bellowed. "For once, the guilty party is going to take the consequences of his actions. Bram is past savin', but Blair is still young enough to learn a lesson. I'm not payin' for somebody else to rear my grandchild. But I will pay for a weddin'. Boy, you are going to marry this little girl and be a responsible father to her baby. And you are going to work in one of my mills. I'll start you off in Hadleyville, where my daddy started me. In a few years you'll be a plant manager, and eventually you'll be sittin' behind the president's desk."

In the explosion of protests that followed this announcement, my voice was the loudest. "No! No! I don't want to marry him!" I screamed. "I don't want to marry anyone. I just want to go away and forget all of this. Please, just send me away. I'll never, never, never ask for anything from you again."

"Dessie, be quiet!" my father roared.

Mrs. Howard inclined her bulk over the top of the desk. "You can't be serious, Charles! What's happened to your mind? We can't let a girl like this into our family. It's ridiculous! I had such hopes that my boys would both make good marriages. This is the ruination of all my plans!"

Behind me, Bram chuckled. I heard the snap and flare of a match striking. "Like I said, Blair, you have all the luck."

"You can't be serious about this, Charles!" Mrs. Howard wailed. "I . . . I forbid it."

"You're damned right I'm serious. We've spoiled these boys,

Dorothy, both of them, and now we're reaping the bitter harvest. One son a wastrel and a criminal, the other a no-account who spends his days riding around in that car I let you talk me into buying him. All right, the boy broke his arm and can't play football. That doesn't mean we have to coddle him for the rest of his life."

Blair lowered himself onto one knee and took my hand. His eyes were shining. "I want to do it," he said. "I want to marry you, Dessie."

"No, don't say that!" I pleaded with him. "You don't want to marry me, Blair. You can't! You don't even know me. Just a couple of hours isn't enough—"

"It was long enough for me." He turned to his father. "Did you hear me, Daddy? I'm willing to do right by this girl and her—and our baby."

Mrs. Howard threw herself between us and dragged Blair away from me, her arms wound in a stranglehold around his neck. "My poor baby!" she wailed. "I'll protect you, darlin'. You don't have to do anythin' you don't want to do."

"But I want to do this, Mama," Blair said. "I want to marry Dessie."

The noise and the heat in the room, combined with the smoke from Bram's cigarette, were making me feel faint. I left my chair and hurried out of the room. Behind me, the wailing and shouting went on. In the grand marble entrance hall, I sat down on an upholstered bench under a hanging tapestry that pictured a white unicorn encircled by yapping hounds. I knew how the poor creature felt. Doubling over, I rested my forehead on my knees.

Someone leaned against the white marble pillar at my side. "So this is the little girl who's going to be my sister-in-law." It was Bram Howard, still smoking his foul-smelling cigarette. "What's the matter, Dessie, don't you like fairy tale endings?"

"Go away," I moaned.

"You know I believe this was what you were after all along. The Howard millions. The whole banquet, not just the soup. That story about going away and putting the kid up for adoption was just a smokescreen. Little lady, you are one of the best con artists I've ever seen, and believe me, I've seen plenty."

"If you don't put out that stinking cigarette, I'm going to be sick."

"Ah. Sorry. I forgot about your delicate condition." He stubbed out the butt in a porcelain flowerpot.

My dizziness passed, and I sat up. With my eyes still closed, I leaned my head back against the tapestry and took several deep breaths. I felt something touch my lips. My eyes flew open. Bram Howard was kissing me. When I attempted to twist away from him, he grabbed my shoulders and pressed his mouth down harder on mine.

"Dessie?" Blair came out of the library. "Are you all—damn you, Bram!"

He leaped onto Bram's back and pulled him away from me. They tussled, Blair trying to land a punch on Bram's jaw or in his gut. Bram was savvy and as quick as a lizard. He skipped lightly away from Blair.

"Take it easy, little brother. I know all the right moves, remember? And you don't know any of 'em. Nobody ever learned how to defend himself on a football field."

"I know that I'll break your skull if I catch you botherin' my wife again," Blair shouted. "All my life, I had to settle for second best, after you got yours first. You were always big and mean and pushy, and after you started boxin' at college, you got even pushier. But not this time. Dessie is mine, do you hear? I saw her first and I claimed her, and now she belongs to me!"

"Stop it!" I jumped up. "Stop it! I don't belong to anybody but myself, Blair Howard. Nobody claimed me. You're disgusting, both of you. Why, I'd sooner be married to Boiler Willoughby or Faro Hill than to you. Either of you!"

Without even pausing to retrieve my coat, I ran out of the house and down the long driveway. Half-blinded by tears, wracked by sobs of noisy desperation, I stumbled through the streets of the town. All around me, I saw wreaths and ribbons and candles burning to commemorate the fate of another girl. Like me, she had found herself pregnant through no fault of her own, and she spent the rest of her time on earth living according to someone else's plan.

5

BROTHER JUPITER LIVED DEEP IN THE HEART OF THE PINE WOODS where the sun never shone. I had been to his shack on several occasions as a child, but always with Clara Mae. Late in the afternoon after a Christmas rain shower, I followed a narrow path that wandered between the spare tree trunks, through a thick undergrowth of junk: spare tires, rusted bicycle and car parts, buckets with no bottoms, mangled scraps of bleached-out shoe leather, broken toys, shattered bottles.

The cabin door, which stood wide open in warm weather, was closed tight. Only a thin strand of woodsmoke rising from the chimney pipe revealed that the cabin was occupied at all.

I knocked. Hearing no reply, I pushed open the door and went in. The stink of dust, sweat, and moldy vegetation made my eyes water. Tied-up bunches of dried weeds and grasses hung from the rafters. Two of the four walls were lined with shelves holding an assortment of tin cans, jars, bottles, and boxes in which were stored—I imagined—a choice selection of bug wings, snake tongues, and lizard tails. I did see a collection of skulls, ranging in size from what might have been a bird to what was certainly a bull.

Brother Jupiter's four hound dogs lay snoring in a pile on the dirt floor near the small black iron stove. One of them opened a sleepy eye and closed it again after deciding I was no threat. Brother Jupiter wasn't much livelier; he sat in an armless rocking chair, his feet tucked under the stove and a tattered plaid blanket pulled around his shoulders.

When I spoke his name, he lifted his head. One of his eyes was crooked and it stared over my shoulder.

"I was wondering . . . I need . . . I'm going to have a baby and I want to get rid of it," I finished with a breathless gasp.

He said nothing. I stepped closer to his chair. The cabin was filthy. Looking down, I noticed that my ankle socks were covered with tiny black dots: fleas. I forced myself not to slap, not to jump, not to run.

"I know you've got something to help me," I said. "I've heard stories."

"You heard wrong." His voice sounded like a metal spoon scraping the bottom of a rusted tin bucket.

"Listen, Brother Jupiter, I don't have any money right now, but if your medicine works on me I'll get some soon and then I can pay you whatever you want. You've got to understand, this baby is killing me. It's digging a grave for me here in Munford and pushing me down and shoveling five thousand pounds of dirt on top of me. I want to get away, but I can't if I'm weighed down by a baby and a husband. I've got to be free."

Brother Jupiter snorted. "Free." Then he said, "I don't give dat kind of medicine to no white gals."

"You've given me other kinds of medicine," I argued, "when I had a fever or an infection. Why can't you give me this kind?"

He shook his head.

I knelt beside his chair. I tried not to think about the fleas or the dirt. "If you don't help me, Brother Jupiter, I will kill myself. Not only that, I will leave a note saying that you really did give me the medicine and that it didn't work and so I was forced to hang myself. White people will come here and they'll burn this shack down around your ears, and you won't be giving medicines to anyone but the devil. Do you hear me? That's how desperate I am. I am not going to be anybody's mother or anybody's wife. I have my own life to live. I hate this thing that's growing inside me. I hate it! I don't care how nasty the treatment is, I'll do whatever you say and I won't tell a soul. But you'd better believe I'm serious about this. I've got a piece of rope in my room at home, and I've learned how to tie a hangman's knot, and I know just how I'm going to do it, and when. Tonight, if you don't help me."

One of the dogs moaned and scratched himself, his hock thumping the hard-packed earthen floor. The pile shifted, a writhing mass of brown and white fur. I sat back on my heels and waited for Brother Jupiter's answer.

He was silent for a long time, then he said, "Guess it don't make no difference to me if dere's one less white man in da worl'."

He told me to wait outside; he never allowed anyone to watch him work his magic. I sat on the sagging front step and scratched my bitten ankles. The rain had stopped an hour earlier, but a sudden gust of wind whistled through the boughs of the overhanging pines, sending down a drenching shower.

After a while, Brother Jupiter emerged from the cabin. The dogs piled after him and dispersed into the gloom that surrounded the house.

"Mix dis powder wid a half a cup of whiskey and a half a cup of water." He handed me a blue bottle that had once held digestive salts. It was corked with a twist of filthy rag. "Drink it all down in one swallow. Won't take long, maybe couple hours. You git some pain and plenty of blood."

I took the bottle. The outside was filthy. I didn't even want to think about the contents. "I don't care about the pain. How much is it?"

"I don't want no money. Git away from here and don't never come back. And don't you tell nobody."

"I won't, I promise." I ran away from the shack. The dogs yapped and followed me a short ways, until Brother Jupiter whistled them back.

Half a block from home, I met Paul. He was wearing only a light jacket and no hat. Raindrops glistened on his dark hair, and his shoulders were damp. "I've been looking for you, Dessie. Where've you been?"

"Out walking." I knew what was coming. I could see it in his reddened eyes and quivering jaw.

"You're going to marry Blair Howard, aren't you? Your father came over this morning to tell Dad. I can't believe you would agree to such a thing. But he says you did."

I fingered the bottle in my pocket. "Not exactly."

"Why, Dessie? How could you let them talk you into something like that? It's the Howard money, isn't it? A hard-working lawyer isn't good enough for you. You want more. It's not fair. I've loved you all my life and you admit you love me, yet you refuse to marry me. But when a stranger comes along and offers money, you can't wait to say yes. You betrayed me!"

"I did not! You listen to me, Paul Miller. I am not going to marry Blair Howard or anyone else. It was all a mistake, a misunderstanding. The baby and Blair and getting married—just pretend it never happened." I tried to push past him. "That's what I'm going to do."

"You're planning something, aren't you?" Paul's hand closed around my wrist. "You're going to run away again! I'll come with you, Dessie. We'll go to Georgia and get married just as soon as—"

"No!" I wrenched free. "Damn it, Paul, stop bothering me."

He turned pale. "I'm sorry. I was only offering you my love and my life. I didn't realize it was a bother."

I got away from him before I lost my temper. At home, my father was closeted in his study, as usual. I found my mother snoring in her favorite armchair in the parlor. Her current bottle of moonshine was stuffed down between the seat cushion and the arm. I managed to extract it without disturbing her, then I poured some of her moonshine into a teacup. Upstairs, I added some water from the bathroom tap, stirred in Brother Jupiter's evil-smelling powder, held my nose, and drank it down. Then I lay on my bed and waited for the child to be purged from my body.

Brother Jupiter's potion made me mighty sick, so sick that I was sure I couldn't possibly still have a baby inside me. But I did. The blood and pain he predicted never materialized. Everything else came loose, but the baby stayed put. Two days after Christmas, I resigned myself to my fate. I was going to become a mother, and I couldn't do a thing about it.

My story about the hanging rope had been a lie, a threat concocted in case Brother Jupiter refused to help me. Now I seriously considered killing myself. Mr. and Mrs. Blair Howard and their child, Junior or Sissie. What had happened to Dessie Heavener? What had happened to the ivory pillar crowned with gold, the brilliant lights, the outpouring of love from strangers? I had no future, nothing to live for. I might as well end it.

But I was too afraid. Dead people don't listen to music, and they don't sing, either. I wasn't going to slink silently off the stage of life. Before I died, I was going to make enough noise so that people everywhere would pay attention to me. But how, or when, I had no idea.

On Sunday morning Blair Howard knocked on our door. He had come to escort me to the late church service.

"Daddy wants everything to look right, so we need to be seen together a lot." Blair leaned against the door frame. "Can I come in?"

"No," I said. "My mother passed out in the front parlor last night, after she threw up. She's still in there and the place smells terrible even though I've been cleaning all morning. See what I mean? You don't want to marry me."

He laughed. "I sure don't want to marry your mama."

I agreed to let him accompany me to church. When we walked down the aisle to the Howard family pew, the congregation let out a collective gasp. My father quelled the outburst by pulling out all the organ stops and playing so loudly that folks couldn't hear themselves whisper.

Keeping up appearances, Blair and I went out two or three times a week through January, to basketball games, the movies, even to Swede's Drugstore for a soda now and then. Plans for the wedding went forward. I was fitted for a gown, taken to the hairdresser's, measured for a trousseau. I couldn't stop the machinery, so I let it carry me along.

One week before the wedding, I encountered Paul outside Reese's Emporium. He turned and limped away.

On the day of the wedding, one of the Howards' Cadillacs picked me up at the house and drove me to the church. My father wasn't quite ready. At the last minute my mother had decided that she must go and see her baby married, and she insisted that he help her get dressed. He asked the Howards' driver to return, and he promised to join me just as quickly as he could. The car dropped me at the parsonage. Mrs. Keating, the preacher's wife, escorted me into her parlor.

"Now, you wait right here until your daddy comes, and I'll send word when we're ready for you. I'd better go over and make sure that Mrs. Swede from the Methodist church knows how to get the organ going. Seems strange to have a weddin' in the church and not have your daddy playin'. Nobody can wring beautiful music out of that thing like he can."

I sat alone in her house, a stranger even to myself. Who was the girl hiding under that mountain of snowy satin and antique lace purchased with someone else's money? Where was Dessie Heavener? What kind of bride was she, with no bridesmaids or maid of honor, no ring bearer, no flower girl, no one to fuss over her and fix her veil and make sure her hem was straight? The Howards had offered to rig up an entire wedding party and pay all the expenses, but I refused and they did not insist. The only person I wanted by my side, helping me get through the day, was Paul, and he would never have consented.

At five minutes to eleven, the front door opened and Bram Howard came in. He wore a pearl-gray morning coat, striped trousers, and gray spats. He seemed perfectly comfortable in the outlandish costume, unlike my father, who had been plucking at his collar and his cuffs all morning. "They're almost ready to start," he said. "Sent me over to see if your daddy was here yet."

"No, he's not." I buried my nose in my bouquet of pink and white roses. "My mother wasn't quite—"

"You mean she's drunk. Don't look at me like that. It's not your fault your mama's a lush."

"Somebody's been telling tales about me."

"Only everybody in town. So what? They've always had plenty of nasty things to say about me, too. I never paid any attention." He sat beside me on the sofa. "Ah, Dessie, you're a funny girl. You haven't been up to the house since you and Blair got engaged. Daddy kept asking Blair why he didn't bring you to Sunday dinner. Every single time Blair told him you weren't feeling well, because of the baby. Blair never was a very inventive liar." Bram laughed softly in my ear. "I have another theory. I think you didn't come because you didn't want to see me," he whispered.

I held my bouquet in front of my chest like a shield. "If Blair knew you were talking to me like this, he wouldn't like it."

"At this moment, Blair is sitting in the preacher's office looking as sick as it's possible for a human being to look without being dead." Bram stretched his arm out along the top of the sofa and toyed with my veil. "I do believe reality is finally beginning to sink in. One hour from now, my little brother will be a family man, and he's scared stiff." Bram touched my shoulder. "Look at me, Dessie."

"No, I don't want to."

"You're afraid I'll kiss you again."

I shook my head. "I won't let you."

"You can't stop me."

He pushed my bouquet aside, lifted my veil, and pulled me gently into his arms. I felt his kiss clear down to the bottoms of my feet. That kiss. It was a drug more powerful than anything Brother Jupiter could cook up, a magic elixir that lifted me out of myself and carried me away to someplace I had never been before. I wanted it never to end.

When we finally broke it off, Bram sat back and combed his fingers through his hair. "Well, well, well." His voice was unsteady. Hearing noises outside, he whipped out a handkerchief, wiped his lips, then handed it to me. "Better fix your lipstick. The mirror's over there."

The preacher's wife rushed in, followed by my father. "Goodness, we're ten minutes late in starting already!" Mrs. Keating exclaimed. "Bram Howard, you better get right back over to that church this minute and stand up with your brother. I don't know what you're doing here anyway. You'll bring the bride bad luck. Come along, Arthur. It's time to give your daughter away. My, Dessie, don't you look pretty! I would never have believed it. And such an attractive flush on your cheeks. A real blushing bride!"

Later that night, as I lay beside Blair in a hotel room in north Georgia, I thought back on my wedding day. The only thing I could remember with any clarity was Bram's kiss, and the way I had felt afterward. As I marched up the aisle, I had known with absolute certainty that I was about to marry the wrong brother.

Beside me, Blair stirred. I knew he was awake, too. He wanted to make love to me, but I had refused to let him touch me. Puzzled and angry, he had retreated to the far side of the bed to sulk.

"Why did you do it, Blair?" I asked him. "You didn't have to go along with your daddy. You could have refused, and your mama would have stood up for you. He couldn't force you to marry me."

"I don't know, Dess." He sighed. "I think maybe I'm in love with you. I must be, because I liked you the first time I met you, and I like you better every time I see you. Now I got a question for you." Pulling himself up, he turned toward me. "How come you ain't happy bein' my wife? I ain't such a bad catch. I mean, half the girls in that town would love to be where you are right now."

I told him the truth. "I wanted to be a singer, Blair. I never wanted anything else. Then you came along and spoiled everything. Sure, I know King Kingsley threw me out of that talent contest, but there would have been other contests, other chances. Now I'll never get away from that town. We'll have one baby, and then another and another and another and I'll get older and older. I might even start to hate you for taking my dreams away from me. In the past, I used to dream about my future all the time. Now I don't have a future and I feel like my mind and my heart are empty."

Blair frowned. "I don't understand. Why can't you sing if that's what you want to do?"

"I told you—"

"No rule says you got to sit home all the time and stitch quilts for the Ladies' Aid. You want to get a job singin'? Hell, that's okay with me. Why not?"

I propped myself up on my elbow. "But not in South Carolina," I said. "Not in Munford or Columbia or Charleston. I want to go to New York, Blair. I was headed there when Paul opened his big mouth and ruined it for me. But I still want to go. Can you understand that? I have been wanting to get out of the South since I was born. I don't belong here. I never did."

Blair said slowly, "That means you don't want to stay married to me after the baby comes."

"I didn't say that. You—you could come with me. You could be my manager, Blair. Handle the people from the booking agencies and the newspapers, help me get jobs on the radio, take care of the business end of it. You see, Blair, I am going to be very famous someday. I'll be making plenty of money, and I'll need someone like you to look after it for me. We won't even have to live in New York all the time. We'll be traveling all over the country, maybe even to Europe, to places like Paris and London. Wouldn't you like that, Blair? Wouldn't you like to shake the swamp water out of your shoes and see what the rest of the world is like?"

"What about the kids?"

I winced at his use of the plural, but I let it pass. "Why, we'll hire nursemaids, of course. Anything we want, we'll be able to afford. Think about it, Blair, you wouldn't have to start work in your daddy's lumber mill, taking orders from people who can hardly read or write. You wouldn't have to depend on your daddy for money anymore, because you'd be making plenty of your own, as my manager. Think of the things we could buy: fancy cars and boats and airplanes. Horses for racing and horses for riding. Even a whole tropical island if we wanted. All you have to do is help me become famous."

He was silent for a long time. Finally he laughed aloud. "Hell, darlin', we could have ourselves a ball, couldn't we? Travelin' all around, eatin' in fancy restaurants, meetin' baseball players and movie stars. You're right, it sure beats workin' in the lumber business till I'm old. And there's somethin' even better: If there's one thing in this world that I love, it's hearin' you sing."

I placed my hand on his bare chest. "You really mean that? You would help me become a singer?"

"Sure, I mean it. I don't say stuff I don't mean. Why you cryin', honey?"

"I don't know . . . I never expected . . . oh, Blair!" I threw my arms around his neck and hugged him.

He stroked my hair. "That's more like it. I sure hate seein' you unhappy. I want to see you like you was at the Dixieland Ballroom, havin' yourself a good ole time and makin' everybody else happy besides. Now will you give ole Blair a kiss, please? He's been dyin' for a chance to kiss you."

The revival of hope and the exuberance of Blair's lovemaking pushed all thought of Bram out of my head. I felt reborn. I wasn't alone in my desire to escape anymore. I had enlisted an ally. Blair was on my side.

We honeymooned in New Orleans. Blair promised I would love the city, and I did. On our first day there, we rode the trolley cars and ate oysters and sat for a long time in Jackson Square watching the pigeons and the other tourists. As we were strolling back to our hotel, we passed a doorway. I heard music, lively and energetic and full of fun.

"Can we go in?" I asked Blair. "Please?"

"Sure, honey, anything you like."

Through a haze of cigarette smoke, I saw the musicians seated on chairs in the center of the room, seven black gentlemen playing the richest, juiciest music I had ever heard, a happy blending of banjo, drums, trombone, clarinet, two trumpets, and a piano. Entranced, I led Blair to a table right up front. An elderly waitress came over. I didn't want to drink, I just wanted to listen, but I ordered a ginger ale, Blair a bourbon and water. Then I let the warm wings of the music wrap themselves around me. For the first time in months, I felt truly happy. I felt like singing.

"Honey," Blair said after an hour, "ain't we heard enough?"

I shook my head. I could never get enough of listening to real musicians making real music. Those men were heroes to me; they were doing what I wanted to do. "You can go back to the hotel without me," I told Blair. "I want to stay a little longer."

"You're findin' out early that you can wrap me around your

little finger," he grumbled good-naturedly. "I ought to put a stop to this before it goes too far."

By three in the morning, Blair and I were the only customers left in the place. Blair was asleep, his head pillowed on his arms. While the men packed up their instruments, the waitress started switching off the lights. The pianist came over to our table. He was as round as a melon, and his skin gleamed like hand-rubbed teak.

"Club ain't gonna make no money from folks buyin' one ginger ale and then leavin' it to spoil," he remarked. "Least your young man had the good manners to drink whiskey."

I remembered the drink I had ordered early in the evening and took a quick swallow to appease him. It was flat and warm. Seeing the face I made, the man laughed.

"My name's LeRoy," he said. "This is my place. I been watchin' you. You been sittin' here drinkin' down our music the way some folks drink down beer on a hot day."

"It's wonderful," I breathed. "It's what they call Dixieland jazz, isn't it?"

He shrugged. "Jazz, blues, Dixieland—you can call it whatever you want. It's our music, the black man's music. Up north these days, they're playin' something they call swing. Shoot, it ain't no different from this, 'cept they speeded it up and laid the percussion on heavy and added a few more instruments. But this is where it all started, honey. Right here in New Orleans. Some folks'll tell you different. They'll brag to you about Kansas City and St. Louis and Chicago. But don't you listen to 'em. The music was born right here, and it went up the river on the riverboats. It's like a child that grows up and moves away from home and gets new ideas, but it was born right here in New Orleans."

The next night after dinner, I dragged Blair back to LeRoy's again. After an hour, I got up enough nerve to ask LeRoy if I could sing a blues song I had learned from my oldest friend, Clara Mae Grayson. I told him that Clara Mae's brother, Hotshot, was a famous Kansas City jazz man.

"You know Hotshot?" LeRoy's grin widened, exposing five white teeth and empty pink gums. "Hell, him and me go back over twenty years. Ain't seen Hotshot since I played in Mother Fleet's whorehouse on Beale Street in Memphis, and that was a while back. Well, I guess I could let you take a turn after most of the crowd goes home."

I sang "Fast Walkin' Blues," the song that had stopped King Kingsley in his tracks and won me the job that I lost five minutes later. I used a trick I had learned from LeRoy's clarinet player. At the end of a line or phrase, I would bend the resolving note, hitting it properly first, sliding down a half step, then returning to the note again.

Blair applauded loudly. The musicians and the few remaining customers in the club liked the song and asked me to do another. I went through my entire repertory of old blues songs. LeRoy not only knew all of those, he offered to teach me a few more. We stayed in the club until dawn, me singing and Blair listening and sipping bourbon. My voice never got tired, and I never felt sleepy. I was drunk on music and the sound of my own voice.

As we fell into bed at dawn, Blair said, "I love to hear you sing. Any other woman sings, it sounds like a dog howlin'. But not you. I could listen to you forever."

I snuggled close to him. "Blair, I don't want to go back to Munford. Why couldn't we live here? I want to learn all I can from LeRoy, and from all the other musicians in this town. We wouldn't need to stay long, just until I started making money and made a name for myself, and then we'd go north, to New York. I'd get on radio, and I'd start making records—"

"Sure, baby, that sounds like a great idea. Now stop talkin' and start lovin'."

Over the next few days, when we weren't hanging around LeRoy's club or making love, we were planning our future. Blair agreed to ask his father to find him a job in New Orleans. We would rent a little house in the Garden District, and after the baby came, I could go to work, singing in one of the clubs or hotels.

"But only three, four nights a week," he said firmly. "No more. I want you to myself the rest of the time."

We returned to Woodlands two weeks later. I was shocked to see how bad Mr. Howard looked. He had lost weight, and he was jumpy, nervous, and short-tempered. Blair wanted to discuss our plans right away, but his father refused to listen.

"You aren't goin' anywhere until that baby of yours is born, son, so you can just put any thought of movin' to New Orleans out of your mind. On Monday mornin', you're startin' work at the Hadleyville mill. That's where my daddy put me and that's where I'm puttin' you. As for Dessie, if she wants to sing, she can sing right here in Munford, in her daddy's choir at church."

We newlyweds settled into an apartment in the west wing of the house, really a suite of rooms with a bedroom, small sitting room, bathroom, and a small kitchen. Every weekday, Blair dragged himself off to the mill at five in the morning. After the first week, he was so stiff he could hardly move.

"You're too good for work like that," I murmured in his ear as I massaged his neck and shoulders. "It's for common laborers. Look at those blisters! You'll ruin your poor hands—if you don't lose one first. I asked your daddy how long it took him to work his way up in the business to the point where he was making decent money and working decent hours. He said five years. Five years, Blair. I don't think we can wait that long."

Mrs. Howard seemed to have accepted the situation, although she made it clear that she thought her precious baby could have found a more suitable wife. She filled her calendar with events that didn't include me, committee meetings and tea parties and bridge games. I didn't see much of Mr. Howard, either. He spent most of his time in an office in town. Only Bram seemed to have nothing to do during the day, but I tried to stay out of his way. He went out most evenings, stayed out late, came home at dawn, and slept until midafteroon.

I had hoped to keep my pregnancy secret a little longer, but word got out that I was visiting Doctor Simmons on a regular basis, and I made the mistake of purchasing some maternity smocks at Reese's. Wherever I went in Munford, I was the subject of much whispering and pointing while folks calculated just how far along I was and when the baby was likely to drop. Once a week, I went into town to have my hair done—Mrs. Howard insisted that her daughter-in-law make a good appearance—and to visit my mother and Clara Mae. Blair and I attended church together, and after the service my father and I exchanged frosty greetings. Otherwise, I stayed close to my new home.

One day I discovered a cache of jazz recordings in the old playroom upstairs. Sylvester carried them down to the conservatory for me, where there was a record player. The conservatory was my favorite room in the house, a glass-enclosed porch whose southern exposure insured continuous sunlight from early morning to midafternoon. Ferns, parlor palms, and aspidistra thrived there among the white wicker furniture. Flowered chintz drapes and cushions gave the illusion of being in a very private garden.

Paul had had a fairly comprehensive record collection, but nothing like this. I found band leaders like Artie Shaw and Benny Goodman, Chick Webb and Stan Kenton, and vocalists like Billie Holiday and Ella Fitzgerald. I put on the Andrews Sisters' version of "Ti-Pi-Tin" and sang along. Very soon, the rhythm reached my feet, and I started dancing.

"You get around pretty good for a girl who looks like she's on her way home from a midnight raid on the watermelon patch." I looked around to see Bram lounging in the doorway. "I see you found my records."

"I didn't know they were yours. I'll put them back."

"Hell, I don't care if you listen to them. I'd forgotten all about them. Good to hear them again, the old songs. Why don't you get on with your singing and dancing? Don't mind me, I like a good show."

I shook my head.

"Let me see, there was one I used to like—here it is." He put on Bunny Berrigan's "I Can't Get Started." "Would you care to dance, madame?"

"No. No, please, I don't want to. I've got to—"

He took my hand and swung me around, into his arms. We started to foxtrot. He was such a strong leader that I almost forgot I was an inexperienced dancer myself.

I said, "I don't think I should be doing this. The doctor told me to take it easy."

"I suppose shaking your hips to a boogie-woogie tune is taking it easy? Relax. And stop pulling away from me. I don't mind your stomach. I've accommodated myself to a lot stranger figures than yours."

I was relieved when the song ended and I could flee to a small chintz-covered armchair that left no room for Bram. He asked if I wanted to hear another record. I didn't. I said, "You've been away for such a long time, and now you're home, and everybody's wondering how long you're going to stay."

"You mean you're wondering how much longer I'm going to be around to bother you." Bram leaned over the back of my chair. He coiled a strand of hair around his finger. "Home is where I come to hide out from nasty men called creditors. These creditors claim I owe them money. I suppose I do. Unfortunately, I am still on a losing streak and I haven't got any."

"Why don't you ask your daddy for some?"

"I have, often. But my daddy is being unusually tightfisted and stubborn these days, which is why Blair is married to you and I am enjoying an extended if not very stimulating visit to my old hometown. For once, I have no regrets. I wouldn't have missed my brother's wedding for anything. And I really do envy him the honeymoon."

His hand strayed to my cheek. I caught it and pulled it away from my face. "Please stop. I don't like for you to touch me."

"That's funny, I would have thought otherwise from the way you sat so still just now, soaking it all in. You're starved for affection, Dessie. Not surprising, considering where you come from. Obviously my brother hasn't been spending enough time with you lately. I shall have to speak to him about his responsibilities as a husband."

"What would you know about those?"

He laughed. "Not much, thank God."

"Blair's told me all about you. He says you were always in trouble from the time you were small, that you were thrown out of all the best schools in the state and a couple of colleges besides, and now you're nothing but a high-class bum who lives off cards and dice and women."

"Especially women," he agreed. "Capricious though they may be, they are still more reliable than cards or dice."

I shook my head. "You're one of those people who doesn't think he's alive unless he's making trouble for someone." Twisting around, I faced him over the back of the chair. "Why don't you leave me alone? You don't really want me. You just want to stir up trouble between Blair and me. I'm asking you to stop. Please."

He looked thoughtful for a moment, then his mouth creased into a smile and he lapsed into a thick drawl. "You are absolutely right, Miz Dessie. I have been a brute and a boor, and I do sincerely apologize, ma'am. From now on, I shall strive to be an exemplary brother-in-law."

Bram was true to his word, exaggeratedly so. He made a great show of solicitude and concern for the expectant mother. Whenever he saw me, he inquired anxiously about my health. When the family adjourned to the drawing room after dinner, he always made sure I was seated in the most comfortable chair, and he fussed around, bringing me a footstool or a cushion or a shawl for my shoulders. The rest of the family enjoyed the joke, but not I. The game was cat and mouse, and we both knew I was the preordained loser. The strain of waiting for him to pounce made me crazier than ever to get out of that house.

I increased the pressure on Blair. I talked about his low stature in his father's company, his lack of importance, the scorn with which he was regarded by the other workers. He was the boss's son, a rich boy who performed only token labor and collected pay far in excess of his true worth to the company. He told me he wanted to quit, but he felt the time wasn't right. He started drinking on the job and after work. I urged him to confront his father one more time, to make the break, but he held back while he tried to build up his courage with bourbon and big talk.

Once again, I turned to music for comfort. I had the record player moved to our sitting room, where I could lock the door and play my music all day long without fear of being interrupted by Bram.

As I listened, I learned. I learned to appreciate the way Louis Armstrong phrased a line, the way Artie Shaw designed a cadenza. Thanks to LeRoy, I understood where this new music had come from. In Benny Goodman and Mildred Bailey, I could hear echoes of Bourbon Street and Beale Street. According to LeRoy, many of the old blues and jazz men from the early days were playing in the big bands now, lending their experience and love of the music to a form that wasn't really new, just growing and changing.

That April was the hottest on record in over a hundred years. Barely six months pregnant, I felt like a bean about to burst out of its pod. In cooler weather, I had enjoyed strolling around the grounds every morning after Blair left for work. Now I stayed indoors or on the shaded verandas and exerted myself as little as possible. I even stopped going to church. I suspected every woman in the choir of hoping that I would drop my baby in the middle of the sermon.

One Tuesday afternoon, Mr. Howard came home early, complaining that the heat in his office was well nigh unbearable. He joined me in the gazebo on the knoll behind the house. Sylvester brought us a frosty pitcher of lemonade and two glasses. He poured the first round, then returned to the house.

Mr. Howard took a long swallow. "I suppose Dorothy's at one of her meetings?"

"Yes, sir. The Garden Club this morning, and she had a bridge party this afternoon."

My father-in-law and I didn't mind being silent together. We gazed out at the green avenue that ran away to the trees and through the evergreen and oak forest to the horizon. Years earlier, Mrs. Howard had complained that the trees obscured her view of the mountains, so a wide strip had been cleared. Unlike most roads, this one did not dwindle to a vanishing point as it neared the horizon. Instead, the landscapers had kept widening it as they went along, to give the illusion of a single straight avenue of green from the house to the distant mountains. In the spring and summer, the family often entertained guests in the gazebo, where they could admire what the Howard men called Mother's View.

Mr. Howard's voice jolted me from my reverie. "Blair's not happy at the mill, is he?"

"Oh, he doesn't mind it that much."

"You don't need to lie for him, Dessie. I've seen how he's been actin'. He's restless, dissatisfied. And he's furious with me for startin' him out at the bottom like I did. But I had no choice. I couldn't make him a foreman or a plant manager; he doesn't know enough and the men wouldn't work for him. So I did what my daddy did to me, I put him at the lowest rung of the ladder. He could climb pretty fast if he just put his mind to it. Why, two years from now, he could be runnin' that place. Lord knows, I've tried to talk some sense into him. Maybe you could . . ."

"I'll try, sir." I didn't tell him that I was the one who had planted the seed of discontent and nurtured it and fed it until Blair was nearly as crazy to leave Munford as I was.

My father-in-law sighed deeply. "Folks are sayin' we're going to be gettin' into that war they're having over in Europe. Part of me knows that war is evil, that it swallows up young lives quicker than fire devours straw. But so help me, this war can't come too soon for me. War means business and business means money. Lots of money."

We heard a shout. Sylvester was running toward us across the lawn. I knew that something terrible had happened. The baby felt it, too, and kicked me hard.

"Mr. Charles," Sylvester panted, "Mr. Charles, sir, you's wanted on the telephone quick. They say Mr. Blair, he's been in a accident at the mill. He's hurt pretty bad."

Mr. Howard hurried back to the house, Sylvester trotting at

his heels. A chill of dread seized me, and I was suddenly grateful for the afternoon heat. I knew that a turning point had come, for all of us. Life at Woodlands would never be the same again.

6

LOGS WERE FED INTO THE HADLEYVILLE MILL ALONG A SLIP OR delivery chute onto a spiked conveyor belt known as a jack ladder. On the afternoon of the accident, the jack ladder had jammed. Instead of ordering the power to be shut down, Blair had insisted on climbing along the logs on the belt in order to locate the trouble. The logs were slick from the water spray in the slip that cleaned away dirt and grit that would dull the saws. As Blair neared the head of the jack ladder, where the logs were fed into the powerful deck saw, the conveyor motion started again with a jerk. He lost his footing and fell into the whirling saw blade, which sliced off his left leg above the knee.

No one at the mill had any explanation for Blair's recklessness. I always believed they concealed the real cause of the accident: Blair was drunk.

Although the workers had acted swiftly in applying a tourniquet and sending for an ambulance, Blair lost a lot of blood. For several days he lay in the hospital in Columbia, near death. After a week, his strong young body began to recover. Drowsy with morphine, he was sufficiently alert to recognize the members of his family, and to smile at me and squeeze my hand.

Then one night some clotted blood broke loose and traveled to his brain. The doctors called it a cerebral accident, but it was really a death blow ineffectively delivered. Blair lived.

They brought him home in early June. He was awake, or at least his eyes were open, but no one could say how much they saw. He uttered sounds, mostly grunts and growls, but no words. Most of the time he just sat in a chair in the conservatory and stared into space. He had lost control of his bowels and bladder, and he had to be diapered like an infant. He didn't seem to understand us when we spoke to him, but sometimes he would become angry and start shouting. At other times, silent tears would roll down his cheeks. No one ever knew what was bothering him, and no one could get through to him. The doctors told us he would never recover, but they said that he could live for many years, given proper care.

The tragedy took a terrible toll on Blair's parents, particularly on his father. Mr. Howard blamed himself for what had happened. But I knew that the blame really lay with me. If I hadn't come along, Blair would have been perfectly content to follow the path that his father had laid down for him. But I had exploited his love for me. I had shared my dreams with him. I had made him ambitious for me, and filled his head with ideas of rebellion and independence. By poisoning his spirit, I had made him as dissatisfied with life in his hometown as I had always been.

He went back to his old boyhood bedroom, where his mother hoped the sight of his souvenirs and trophies would jog his memory and bring him back to life. He did not require professional nursing care, but his size alone made caring for him difficult. Mr. Howard hired a husky black orderly named Sam to help out.

An elevator was installed, at great expense. Every morning after breakfast, Sam would take Blair down to the conservatory to enjoy the sunshine. I spent most of my waking hours by his side. I owed him that much. He had been a true friend to me. He had always treated me with kindness and respect, and he had made a lot of effort to understand my wants and to fulfill them. His lovemaking had been tender and gentle, never forced or hurried. I missed that most of all. Blair Howard had treated me like a lady, and as his wife, I had become just that.

Mrs. Howard sat with him every afternoon and talked nonstop in her bright social voice, regaling him with gossip about this or that neighbor or committee person. After a while, her voice would crack and she would depart in tears. The sight of her baby reduced to a state of helpless infancy was more than she could bear. Mr. Howard came, too, but he never spoke. He just sat and held his son's hand, and his tears fell silently.

Bram's feelings were the most difficult to gauge. He had been the least accepting of all of us when told that his brother would never recover. Blair's passivity enraged him. Once he gripped Blair's shoulders and shook him violently, hoping to force a response. When he failed to elicit even a syllable, he turned and walked away. For several weeks after that he stayed away from Blair entirely.

Then one day he wandered into the conservatory while I was reading some poetry aloud to Blair.

"Have you tried singing to him?" he asked.

I shook my head. "I'm too choked up to sing. It would sound terrible."

"He won't notice. Please, sing something."

I chose one of Clara Mae's favorite spirituals, "Sometimes I Feel Like a Motherless Child:"

> Sometimes I feel like I'm almost gone.
> Sometimes I feel like I'm almost gone.
> Sometimes I feel like I'm almost gone,
> A long way from home.
> A long, long way from home.

As I sang, tears started to roll down Blair's cheeks, and he jerked his head up and down. Bram got very excited, thinking that this was some kind of miracle and that his brother was recovering his senses at last, but it was just one of Blair's moods, because two seconds later he was shouting incoherently and tossing the crockery from his lunch tray right at Bram.

Still, singing had helped me, and I kept it up. Blair seemed to like the slow songs the best, the lullabies and blues and ballads. Sometimes I would put my arms around him and rock him gently while I sang, as Clara Mae used to do with me.

One morning in late June, I opened my sitting room door just in time to see Mr. Howard leaving his bedroom, which was down the hall from my suite. I was surprised. He usually left the house quite early, before I was even awake. Generally so nattily attired, he wore no suit jacket that day, and no shoes, only trousers and a white shirt that looked like he had slept in it. His hair was disheveled, and his cheeks were rough with stubble. In his right hand, he carried a gun.

I watched him go into Blair's room. After a moment, he came out again. Of course, Sam had already taken Blair down to the conservatory. Mr. Howard moved toward the staircase.

I ran down the hall to Bram's room and burst in without knocking. He was sprawled on his back on top of his bed, wearing pajama bottoms but no top. I grabbed his shoulders and shook him. He sat up at once, instantly awake.

His mouth twisted. "Well, Dessie, to what do I owe—"

"Your daddy—I think he's going to kill Blair. He's got a gun!"

Bram leaped out of bed and rushed out of the room. I followed as quickly as I could, cursing the burden that hampered my movement. I was halfway down the stairs when I heard the first shot.

When I reached the conservatory, I saw Bram grappling with his father, struggling to gain possession of the gun. A pile of plaster dust in one corner gave witness to the destination of the first bullet. I ran to Blair, seated in his usual armchair. He was unhurt. When I spoke his name, he gave me a little smile.

"Dad, please, listen to me—"

The gun went off. I screamed and threw my arms around Blair's head, covering his ears and shielding his eyes. Daddy Howard staggered backward, his hand pressed to his chest. Then he crumpled. His mouth sagged, and his eyes stared at the hole in the ceiling. Bram turned to me. He was holding the gun.

"It was an accident. I had just gotten it away from him, and it went off."

I nodded. Tears streamed down my face. "I know. I know."

Mrs. Howard stood in the doorway. "What happened? Oh, my God, Bram, what have you done? What have you done to your daddy? Charles? Charles, speak to me!"

Bram dropped the gun. "It was an accident," he repeated in a dazed voice. "An accident."

Blair giggled.

On the desk in the library, we found a letter Mr. Howard had addressed to his wife: "My dear Dorothy, Over the past ten years, I have watched the fortune I inherited dwindle to almost nothing. The fault is entirely mine. I made some bad business decisions, and I am now so deeply in debt that I will never be able to repay what I owe. I suppose I could have stopped you and the boys from squandering what little we had left, but to my great shame, I could not bring myself to tell anyone the truth. So you see, I am a coward as well as a failure. And so I have decided that I must leave you before I drag you down even farther. As a final act of kindness, I am taking Blair with me. He has suffered enough, and to care for him would only burden you unfairly in the years to come. Your hardship will be great enough without that. All my love, Charles."

Half of Cluny County attended Mr. Howard's funeral, as well as the governor and several senators and legislators from all over the state. People clustered around Mrs. Howard, and even I came in for my share of sympathy and attention. I overheard Ayleen Carmody tell Jean-Ellen Thomas's mother that bad things always come in threes. Blair's accident, Charles Howard's death—what would be next? Perhaps she was hoping my child would be born with two heads and six legs.

All the mourners avoided Bram. Everyone knew that Mr. Howard had intended to shoot Blair and then turn the gun on himself, but it was Bram who had pulled the trigger, had slain his own father. In the eyes of the community, if not the law, that made him guilty of murder.

Since the morning of the shooting, Bram had held himself aloof from the rest of us. After his father's coffin was lowered into the ground, he kissed his weeping mother, then said to me, "Looks like your luck has turned sour, Dessie, just like mine." He walked away. When we got back to Woodlands, Sylvester told us that Bram had taken two suitcases and one of the Cadillacs and departed. A couple of hours later, we got a telephone call from the ticket agent at the bus station in Columbia. He said a Mr. Howard had left him the keys of a Cadillac, and would someone please come and pick it up.

In the days that followed, the extent of Mr. Howard's financial collapse became apparent. During the Depression years, he had borrowed extensively against his real estate holdings in order to keep his mills from closing. Now his bankers were calling in their loans, but the demand for lumber, paper and pulp was still slack. Mr. Howard's life insurance was gone, and even the profits from Howard's Crescent Toilet Paper, still the favorite of millions, had been swallowed up by Mr. Howard's efforts to stave off disaster.

In late June, the house and all its furnishings were sold at auction. Jean-Ellen's father bought up most of it, along with huge tracts of Howard land.

We had to vacate the house at once. But we had no place to go. Mrs. Howard's own family was not rich. Her aging mother and a maiden aunt were being cared for by a bachelor brother in Buford, in a house that was barely large enough to accommodate the three of them much less three or four of us. Then Preacher Keating and his wife came to the rescue, offering to let Mrs. Howard and Blair stay with them in the parsonage. But they had no room for me.

And so, eight-and-a-half months pregnant, with three suitcases full of maternity clothes and not one penny to my name, I returned to my father's house on Creek Avenue. Nothing had changed there. The girl who used to sit and dream in the back bedroom sat there still; still unhappy, still desperate to escape. Only Clara Mae rejoiced that I had come back home. She fussed over me and cooked all my favorite dishes. But my father regarded this swift change in fortune as a personal insult. He had managed to get rid of me, yet here I was again, and soon there would be another mouth to feed. My mother seemed only vaguely aware that I had been away at all.

On my first night home, Paul Miller came to see me. His semester at College had ended, and he had started working in his father's law office, as he had every summer since he was fifteen.

"I heard about Blair's accident," he said. "It must have been terrible for you. I wanted to write to you, but I . . . and then Mr. Howard—" He shook his head. "I'm sorry, Dessie. I should have come to see you right away when it happened. But I . . . I guess I was still hurting a little. I'm not a very good friend to you, am I?"

"Oh, Paul," I said, "you're the only friend I've got. The only real friend I ever had. You were right: I was going to use the Howards' money to get me started on my singing career just as soon as the baby was born. I guess it wasn't meant to happen. I'll never get away now."

Paul did not talk of marriage. I was still married to Blair, until death parted us. Although my husband was mentally and physically incompetent, the laws of South Carolina in 1941 did not allow for divorce under those circumstances.

I went into labor on a Thursday evening when my father was away at choir practice. Clara Mae had already gone home, and I was alone in the house except for my mother. I found her in the kitchen. After days of fasting, she was trying to cook herself some eggs and bacon.

"Mama, I think the baby is coming."

"Honey, do you know where Clara Mae keeps the cinnamon?" Her hands fluttered in the air like birds. "I think I'd like some cinnamon toast."

I walked through the backyard to the Millers' house. The judge and his son were sitting in the dining room enjoying after-dinner cigars. I was surprised. I had never seen Paul smoke before.

I said, "The baby is coming. I think Paul better drive me to the hospital right away."

They looked flabbergasted. Then the judge started tut-tutting and wondering aloud where he had left the keys to the car. Paul turned white and then red and then white again.

I said, "I can drive myself if you don't want to come. But I don't think I should wait much longer."

The hospital was twenty miles away over terrible roads. Paul covered the distance in record time.

"I'll be right here waiting for you," he said, as a nurse plopped me into a wheelchair and steered me toward the labor room. "I'll be right here." Leaning over me, he gave me a dry kiss. I smiled and squeezed his hand.

When I woke up from the anesthesia, I could see my feet again. The mound in my middle had diminished. A nurse told me I had a baby boy. Then she said, "Somebody's waiting to see you."

Paul came into the room, his arms full of roses. He looked exhausted but happy. "I called your father. He'll be over to see you sometime today. And Mrs. Howard. I thought she'd like to know, too. Oh, and my father. Just to let him know I wouldn't be coming into the office today. How are you feeling?"

"Like I've been pounded, wrung out, twisted, and hung out to dry in a hurricane. Thanks for the flowers, Paulie."

"You . . . you have a boy. What are you going to name him?"

"Grayson Paul. I suppose he's got to be a Howard."

"Oh, yes, under the law, even though his father is mentally incompetent, he is still—"

"It's all right, Paulie, you don't have to explain it to me now. His name is Grayson Paul Howard."

After a moment, Paul said quietly, "Did you love him, Dessie? Blair, I mean?"

I sighed. "I was grateful to him for paying attention to me."

The nurse came in bearing a bundle. "Here he is, ready for his first feeding. Now, Mr. Howard, you can take a quick look and then out you go. We want to keep the new mama and her baby as relaxed as possible, don't we?" She displayed the baby to Paul. "Isn't he adorable? Looks just like you."

Paul fled, blushing.

The infant would not take my milk, and I guess I didn't want him to have it because it wouldn't come down. After three frustrating days, he was given formula in a bottle, which improved his temper only slightly.

Grayson Paul. Little Gray. He was mine, my son, born of my body in a sea of my blood. But he was a stranger to me. I felt unconnected to him. I hadn't the slightest idea what to do with him. He wailed constantly. Was he hungry? Was his diaper soiled? Was he sick? Half the time I cried myself. He didn't seem to like being held, but he hated being put down. He didn't like singing, and he didn't like silence. He didn't even like to sleep, and when we got out of the hospital, he kept the whole family awake all night long while he demonstrated his lung capacity. He was small, not much bigger than my father's foot, but he intimidated the hell out of me. I tried to love him, but I couldn't understand how mothers were supposed to feel warm and possessive and affectionate toward their babies. I didn't know how to be that way. I had no example to follow except that of my own mother. I tried my best, but half the time I ended up hating him. Poor little Gray.

When he was two weeks old, I took him over to the parsonage to meet his father and his grandmother. Blair was having a bad day, and Mrs. Howard was at her wits' end.

"I swear," she declared, "sometimes I feel like pushin' Blair right out the window."

"I know what you mean," I said. "I feel the same way." Our eyes met. My mother-in-law and I finally had something in common.

After that, I visited the parsonage frequently, mostly to give her a rest from caring for Blair. Gray's daddy didn't mind the colicky, wailing baby. He hardly seemed to hear Gray's screams.

The people of the town surprised me by their kindness. Tremble Britten and some of the other women in the choir brought over piles of used diapers and baby clothes and a few toys. Without their contributions, Gray would have had nothing. I had no money, and my father resented even paying for my food and his grandson's baby formula.

As before, the radio was my link to the musical world outside. I had no hopes of singing professionally anymore, but music was the blood in my veins, the air in my lungs. If I couldn't sing, I would die.

I told Paul all about New Orleans and LeRoy, and we worked up a few of the songs I had learned. Paul was one of those wonderfully gifted persons who could listen to a tune once on the radio and then reproduce it perfectly on the piano. But despite my urging, he refused to consider a career in music. He had his future all mapped out. He thought he could finish his degree in two years. After he was called to the bar, he would take his place in his father's firm.

"Music is my avocation," he said, "law is my vocation. I'm looking forward to having clients of my own someday, helping people with their problems, settling disputes, arranging the disposal of property. It's fun."

"It wouldn't be fun for me. I'd hate it. Stuck in this town, seeing the same faces again and again, knowing they know everything there is to know about my life—I'd go crazy. What am I talking about? I am going crazy. Sometimes I want to walk out of the house and keep walking until I drop. Hundreds of miles, maybe a thousand. Maybe I'd be so exhausted by the time I reached the end of that road that I wouldn't even remember my name. I could start my life all over again, as a stranger among strangers."

On Sunday afternoon, December 7, we were clowning around in the living room, Paul banging out "Flat Foot Floogie with a Floy Floy" on the piano while I sang and did the strut and Mother sat in her chintz-covered chair doubled up with laughter. Father was out. Suddenly Judge Miller burst through the kitchen door without knocking and came straight on through to the parlor. He so seldom entered our house that we all stopped what we were doing and stared at him.

"I just heard it on the radio," he said. "The Japanese have bombed Pearl Harbor. We're in the war at last."

Paul's hands went limp on the piano keys. The jangling dissonance punctuated his father's announcement. Then we crowded around the radio in the corner and listened for more news of what had happened.

Every boy in town rushed to Columbia to enlist in some branch of the service. Even Paul. "They won't care about my bad leg," he said confidently. "They need clerks and secretaries and office personnel, don't they? They're sure to find a place for me somewhere."

But the Army had no use for a man who was not able-bodied. Paul's 4-F classification filled him with shame.

At home, we started saving tin cans and newspapers and rags and all sorts of things we thought might be required by the war effort. Clara Mae decided we should plant a garden in the spring and put up as much food as we could.

"Clara Mae," I said, "the Japanese aren't going to come here, or the Germans either."

"I don't care. The last time the South was in a war, folks near starved to death. Not this time."

Two days before Christmas, my father and I had just sat down to supper when there was a knock at the door. The sheriff had found my mother wandering down the middle of Main Street, oblivious of honking horns and shouting drivers. She was wearing only a thin dress and bedroom slippers on her feet.

"I just wanted to show everybody that I could still walk a straight line," she declared.

We telephoned Doctor Simmons, who came right over. He told Mother flat out that if she didn't stop drinking, she would be dead within the year. She gazed at my father with loathing. "Not that anybody would care," she said. "Some folks would be glad to see me dead."

I helped her up to bed. When I came downstairs again, I found my father sitting at the dining room table, his head cradled in his hands.

"I can't do a thing with her," he said. "Never could. Why won't the Good Lord help us?"

"The Good Lord hasn't done very much to benefit the Heaveners lately," I said. "I stopped counting on Him long ago."

During the week that followed, Mother seemed a little better, a bit brighter, and more coherent. She started eating regular meals and sleeping regular hours. I began to hope that she had taken the doctor's advice to heart.

I will never forget the last day of that year. Gray had finished his bottle and I had taken him upstairs and put him in his crib for his afternoon nap. For once, he cooperated. I went back down to the kitchen, where Clara Mae was measuring out flour for an eggless, butterless cake. I had seen the recipe in the local paper and suggested she try it so we could see what life would be like with rationing.

"I suppose they be rationin' the air soon," Clara Mae grumbled as she dipped down to the bottom of the flour cannister. "They's gonna take away everythin' else."

"We'll be all right." I dumped a soiled diaper in the covered pail in the mudroom, just outside the kitchen door. "I never thought eggs tasted that good anyway."

"I don't care, you just can't make a decent cake—"

We heard screams from the parlor and ran to see what was the matter. Mother's chair was ablaze. Flames were devouring her, licking at her face and arms and hair as she tried feebly to swat them out. The stench was terrible. I started to beat at the fire with my bare hands.

"Clara Mae, get some water, quick!" I shouted.

"Here's a blanket." She thrust something into my hands. "Smother the fire, smother it!"

While I tried to cover Mama with the blanket, Clara Mae hurried back to the kitchen and returned with a pail of water. She dashed it over the chair and its occupant, and the remaining flames dissolved in a cloud of vapor and smoke. I noticed then that the drapes were starting to smolder. I yanked them down, carried them out to the front porch, and heaved them over the railing into the middle of the lawn.

Mother's face and arms were red and blistered, and her hair was almost gone. Her dress was a charred rag that had adhered to her body. I called Doctor Simmons, who promised to come over right away. He asked me to call Orlando Smeal, the undertaker, who provided ambulance service to the hospital in Columbia. When I turned away from the phone after the second call, Mother was gasping for air. Clara Mae and I got her out of the chair and laid her on her back on the floor. Not knowing what else to do, I pumped her arms up and down and shouted at her, "Breathe, Mama, please. Breathe!" She was shivering violently. I knew she was in shock, but I didn't want to touch a blanket to her raw skin.

Mother screamed with pain when the doctor and the undertaker placed her on the stretcher and removed her to Orlando's shiny black hearse. I asked Clara Mae to stay with Gray, then I climbed into the back of the hearse with Mama. Some of the neighbor women came out onto their porches to watch and to speculate about what had happened.

The long ride to Columbia was agony for Mama, who cried out at every bump and rut. The doctor administered a shot of morphine, which seemed to have no effect. If anything, her screams grew louder. I wanted to ask him if she would live, but I didn't. I was afraid the answer would be yes.

Early that evening, the sheriff brought my father to the hospital in the police car. For the next three days he and I took turns keeping watch over the woman who had been my mother and his wife. When the end came, we were both with her.

Father drew the sheet up over her face. "I'd say she's paid for her sins." He sounded more sorry than angry. His eyes were dry.

I wept for my mother, but I had really lost her long ago. I pictured the photograph that graced the piano at home, a smiling young girl with a blond bob. I hardly remembered that smiling girl before she started drinking and turned difficult and unpredictable. After that, I never knew what to expect. One day she would kiss and fondle me and tell me how much she loved me. The next day she would scream and throw things and slap anyone who came near her. My father was right, she had paid. So had we.

We brought Mama home in the same hearse that had taken her to Columbia, only this time the vehicle served its proper function. She was buried in the Baptist churchyard. I altered the black maternity dress I had worn to Mr. Howard's funeral to fit.

When we carted out the burned and blackened armchair, we found an empty bottle underneath. We never found a glass. What had happened seemed obvious: Mother had been swilling moonshine straight from the bottle while holding a lighted cigarette in her other hand. The bottle had slipped, the liquor had spilled all over her, and in trying to mop it up, she had touched the tip of the cigarette to her clothing and ignited herself.

My own hair had been singed, and my hands and arms were burned badly enough to require medical attention. Fortunately, I healed quickly, and the scars faded in time. But for months afterward, no matter where I was, I smelled the sickening odor of charred hair and flesh. It seemed to have permeated my tissues, and no amount of shampoo or soap would remove it.

One month after my mother's death, my father made an announcement: "I have asked Ayleen Carmody to be my wife," he said, "and she has consented. I hope you will treat her with the respect and the love she deserves."

Ayleen Carmody, with her crimped hair and her falsely warm smile. Ayleen Carmody, of the wobbling soprano and the honeyed voice that concealed steel. Ayleen Carmody, my stepmother!

The wedding took place two weeks later, in the study at the parsonage. Reverend Keating officiated, with Mrs. Keating and Mrs. Howard as witnesses. My father asked me to attend, and

I did, although halfway through the ceremony Gray had a screaming fit. I didn't mind; I felt a little like screaming myself. I took him into the next room to see his father.

"You won't believe what's happening right at this very minute, just a few feet away from here." I flopped onto the settee beside Blair's wheelchair and bounced Gray on my knee. "My father is marrying the biggest gossip in Munford. I am not going to have one secret left if I'm not careful."

Blair laughed on cue.

Ayleen swept through our house with the force of a hurricane, discarding keepsakes and worn-out furniture, boxes of old letters and greeting cards, samples of my childish artwork. She stripped and repapered the parlor first thing, where the fire had blackened the ceiling and walls.

I walked in one morning just as two workmen were hauling our old Oriental rug off to the town dump. Then I noticed that the pile of music I had left on the piano was gone, including the arrangements of the blues songs Paul and I had worked up from the notes I had made at LeRoy's in New Orleans.

"Where have you put my music?" I asked Ayleen, who was supervising the changes.

"Oh, that old stuff? I gave it to the Boy Scouts for their paper drive, along with about five tons of newspapers and magazines I found down in the cellar. Your mama didn't believe in throwin' things away, did she?"

I lost my temper. "How dare you go throwing things out wholesale, without even asking permission! Those were my songs, mine! I collected them on my honeymoon with Blair."

"Dessie, honey, your daddy gave me permission to do anythin' I want in this house." The sugar coating on Ayleen's drawl thickened. "If you really wanted that old stuff, you should have said somethin'."

"What do I have to do, go all around the house and point to things and say, 'I want to keep this and this and this?' You have a lot of nerve, coming in here and disrupting our lives—"

"What's going on in here?" The noise had drawn my father out of his study.

"This woman has gone all through this house destroying and discarding things that don't belong to her," I told him.

"Ayleen has a perfect right to do whatever she wants," my father said. "This is her house now. If you don't like it, you can go and live someplace else, Dessie."

"Now, Arthur, it was just a little misunderstandin'," Ayleen cooed into the hostile silence that followed that invitation.

I shook my head. "Oh, no, I understand perfectly. I'm the next to go, the next discard. Don't worry, it will be a relief to get out of here."

I stormed up to my room and pounded my pillow for an hour. But when I calmed down, I realized that I had no place to go. No money. No job. No friends willing to take me in except Paul, and now I couldn't even marry him if I wanted to. My in-laws were as destitute as I. And I had a baby, a wailing red-faced baby whose inordinate demands on my time and attention sapped my energy and eroded my desire to sing. How could I sing? Half the time, I could barely hear myself think.

The Boy Scouts had taken my music to a shed behind the high school where the town stored the paper it was collecting for the war effort. I spent the entire afternoon sifting through piles of moldy newspapers and magazines until I found my songs.

"I've got to get out of here," I told Clara Mae the next day. "I can't stand it anymore. Every minute I stay in this house feels like a hundred years. It was always bad, but it's gotten worse since that woman came."

"Oh, Miz Ailin' ain't so bad." Clara Mae chuckled. "I never did see such a woman. She would set about organizin' Heaven if she had a mind."

"She'll probably get the chance. The devil wouldn't put up with her."

Ayleen poked her needle nose into every corner of our lives. When I came home from visiting Blair two days later, I caught her searching through my dresser drawers, looking for some sachet, she said. I told her I never used sachet. She seemed unperturbed, and went on to remark that the Howards had given me some pretty nice lingerie. I began to understand the speed with which my father had been maneuvered into this marriage. He had had no choice. The woman had the hide of a rhinoceros and the nerve of a junkyard watchdog.

Even though Ayleen had been a spinster and an only child herself, she was a self-proclaimed expert on raising children, and was generous in ladling out advice to me.

"Dessie, don't you know you shouldn't put wool against the baby's skin like that?" She plucked at the sweater I had put on Gray one chilly morning. "It'll make him itch. You've got to put a little cotton undershirt on him first, and the sweater on top of that. We don't want Gray to scratch and scratch until he's raw, do we? He's such a little sweetums, mummm, mummm."

She plucked the baby from his high chair and snuffled his belly.

The strange thing was, Ayleen seemed genuinely fond of Gray, and he seemed to tolerate her better than he tolerated me. After she had given Clara Mae and me our orders for the day, she would play with him by the hour, and talk baby talk to him, and hold him in her lap while she turned the pages of a picture book. Clara Mae and I theorized that because her own insides had dried up and she knew she would never have a baby of her own, she was determined to extract maximum enjoyment from this one.

Her friends started turning up to pay calls on the new bride. Ayleen took them all around the house and showed off the work she had done, not without remarking on how disreputable the place had been when she moved in:

"I declare, I don't know how people can live like they did. I mean, Clara Mae did her best to keep the dirt down, bless her heart, but she was swimmin' against the tide as far as the clutter went. *She* didn't lift a finger for years, and she didn't train Dessie too well, either."

"I can't stand this," I said to Clara Mae after Ayleen and her ladies adjourned to the front room to play canasta. "If I spend one more day in this house with that woman, I'll go stark, staring mad."

"You got a baby to think of," Clara Mae reminded me. "You start payin' more attention to what he wants and less attention to what you want and you forget all this nonsense."

"Clara Mae, I've got to establish myself as a singer before I get gray-haired and crippled up with arthritis. And I can't do it with Gray hanging on me."

She looked horrified. "You can't mean you would leave your child behind! You crazy or somethin'?"

"Ayleen would be good to him, and my father, too, and if they didn't, I'd come right back and take him away. Meanwhile, you'd be here to watch out for him. It's the only way, Clara Mae. I've been thinking about it and thinking about it. I'll never find any kind of decent job in Munford. No one would hire me, and besides, what could I do? All I know is music and singing. But if I got a job with a band, I could start sending money home right away. And when I was able, I would send for Gray. I've got to get out now, Clara Mae, but I can't take him with me, not yet, anyway, while he's so small. That would be cruel. To both of us."

We argued. Clara Mae scolded, I pleaded, we both wept. Finally Clara Mae touched her apron to her eyes and promised she would never leave the baby as long as she could draw a breath, and she would sing to him and make sure that Ailin', as she called her, treated him right and never spanked him.

That afternoon I went over to the parsonage to visit Blair. I sat beside him and cradled his hand in my lap.

"I just wanted to say good-bye to you," I said when Mrs. Howard left the room. "You remember all those plans we made together? Well, I'm going to make them come true. I promise, Blair. I'm going to make you proud of me."

That night, when the house was dark and everything was quiet, I dragged my suitcase out from under my bed and packed up my clothes. I hadn't done it sooner because Ayleen might have become suspicious, and I didn't feel like arguing with her or my father. All I had were maternity outfits that Clara and I had made over to fit my slimmer figure. I had four pairs of nice shoes, a lovely warm coat, two decent hats, and of course, my fancy lingerie. Right at the top I packed the blues arrangements I had rescued from the trash heap. I knew the songs by heart, and I could have written down the chords any time I wanted. But they were more than songs. They were a link with my past, with Blair, with Paul, with the South.

I wrote a letter to Father and Ayleen: "I feel that I must try and make my own way as a singer. I have no desire to be a burden to anyone. I wish I could take Gray with me, but for now I do not know where or how I will be living. But I do know that you will look after him until I can send for him. I will send money as soon as I can to repay what I have borrowed. I hope you will write to me every week to tell me how my son is doing. I guess I shouldn't be sneaking off like this, but I have made up my mind that this is the best thing for all of us. Try not to be too angry with me."

I signed it, stuffed it into an envelope, and carried it to the front bedroom, where Ayleen's treble snores now joined Father's bass ones. Silently, I opened the door and tiptoed in. My father always hung his trousers over the back of the hardback chair near the window. I found his wallet and emptied it of all bills.

I did the same to Ayleen's purse, which was sitting open on her dresser.

Finally I went into the nursery and leaned over Gray's crib. He had had a bad earache that day and had cried for twelve straight hours before falling into an exhausted slumber at suppertime. He was still restless, and had kicked his blanket down to the bottom of the crib. I pulled it up over his back and tucked it in around his shoulders. He whimpered a little, and sighed, but did not awaken.

"You'll be better off without me," I whispered, "really you will. Clara Mae will look out for you, and Ayleen's not so bad. We just don't get along, that's all. A lot of people are going to tell you that I'm a bad mother, running off and leaving you like this. They're probably right. But someday you might understand. I hope so."

A tear plopped onto the blanket. I brushed it away before it could soak in. More tears fell. If only he had never been born. If only—

I fetched my suitcase from my room and carried it down the back stairs. The watery light of morning was starting to seep into the backyards and alleyways. I filled my lungs with the air of freedom, then I headed down the street, toward Swede's Drugstore. I had plenty of time to catch the six o'clock bus.

7

ONE MONTH AFTER LEAVING HOME, I HAD MADE IT TO BROADway. To a coffee shop at Forty-fifth Street and Broadway, anyway. I studied the menu and chose peanut butter over cheese, for a savings of five cents. I could save ten cents by forgoing coffee and drinking water instead. My stomach gave a mutinous growl. I decided to splurge and have the coffee and a cigarette both.

I was grateful for a chance to sit down. For thirty days, I had been pounding the pavements looking for work. New York had plenty of jobs, if I wanted to wait on tables or take off my clothes. The owner of one jazz club told me that if I wasn't willing to strip, I would never find a job in show business. These days, he said, the soldier boys all wanted to see some skin. I told him I preferred to sing with my clothes on. He shrugged. "I got plenty of dames who can do both. You gotta be versatile, honey."

I haunted talent agencies and booking agencies. Not one was willing to take me on as a client, even after I had belted out a few bars of "Chattanooga Choo-Choo" for the receptionist. I stood in line for an audition for a Broadway musical for four hours, only to be told when I got within sight of the stage that the part had been filled. This time I tried out "Fast Walkin' Blues" on the producer, hoping to catch his attention the way I had caught King Kingsley's at the talent contest. Maybe I should have done a reprise of "Chattanooga Choo-Choo." I was still singing at the top of my lungs as two burly stagehands carried me out to the street. Another day, I did the rounds of the radio stations to see if by any chance they needed a girl to sing jingles or read advertising slogans. One station manager laughed out loud when I opened my mouth to introduce myself.

"Sweetheart, you don't really believe that I'd hire anyone who talked like that? This is New York, not a cottonfield."

I was living in a furnished room on the Lower East Side, eating ketchup sandwiches and using the same teabag three times. My money, eighty-five dollars borrowed from my father and Ayleen, would soon be gone. I thought about writing and asking them for more, but I knew my father would never lend me a nickel, and besides, I had already sent a note saying I had found employment and would repay their money soon. I had promised myself that I would not panic. If I didn't find work as a singer by the time I had one dollar left in my pocket, I would start waitressing, but only in the daytime so I could continue my search for a singing job during the evening hours.

While I chewed my peanut butter sandwich slowly, savoring every sticky bite, I opened the newspaper I had picked out of a trash can earlier. Nothing new there. Art Tatum was playing at Joe and Eddie's Club on Fifty-second Street. He was one of Paul's heroes, a wizard on the keyboard. Harry James was blowing his trumpet on the roof of the Astor Hotel. Hazel Scott was playing and singing at the Café Society. The Sentimental Gentleman of Swing, Mr. Tommy Dorsey, was performing with his trombone and his orchestra between picture shows at the Paramount in Times Square.

I flexed my aching arches. I was down to my last dollar and a quarter. Almost time to throw in the towel and admit defeat. I would make the rounds of the talent agencies and clubs one more time that afternoon. Tomorrow I would enslave myself to Marty's Third Avenue Diner.

My eye fell on Pepper Wellington's column, "All Around Town." A line printed in bold face type leaped off the middle of the page: "What royal swinger is having girl trouble—again?" I read on. "The Rumor Bird Reports royal fireworks at the Nassau Point Inn last night, when a well-known trumpet-playing bandleader and his shapely chanteuse decided to call it quits in a big way."

King Kingsley. It had to be. King Kingsley was playing somewhere near here, and he had just lost his vocalist. I called the waitress over. "Where's the Nassau Point Inn?"

"Beats me, honey," she shrugged. "I'm from New Jersey. Better ask a cop."

I forgot I was starving. I threw down two quarters and ran out of the shop without finishing the last bite of my sandwich. I asked three policeman before I found one who was able to tell me that Nassau Point was located at the eastern tip of Long Island, a three hour drive from the city. He said I might be able to get there by train from Grand Central Station. I was so nervous and rattled that I started walking west on Forty-Fifth Street instead of east. I was in sight of the Hudson River before I realized my mistake, then I turned and ran in the opposite direction.

Grand Central Station looked like it could swallow all the houses in Munford in one gulp and still have room left for dessert. I circled the crowded concourse twice before locating the information booth. The lines were long, full of men in uniform. I ran to the first ticket window I saw and asked for a round-trip ticket to Nassau Point.

"That'll be two-eighty," the clerk told me.

"But I only have seventy-five cents!"

He looked bored. "Sorry, lady. Trains cost money. Next, please."

"Couldn't you lend me the money?" I leaned through the ticket window as far as I could without climbing into his lap. "Please? I have an audition with King Kingsley's band, and I know I'll get the job if I can just get out to Nassau Point. I promise I'll pay you back—double. I swear!"

"Sure you will, lady. Next, please."

"You don't understand!" I wailed. "I'm desperate!"

"Everybody has a story. Get lost, lady."

As I turned away from the window, I spotted a group of soldiers, raw, gawking recruits who still wore their uniforms self-consciously. I went over to them.

"Any of you boys from South Carolina?"

"Yes, ma'am." A freckle-faced redhead stepped forward. "I am."

I grabbed his hand and looked deep into his eyes. "Listen, soldier, I'm in trouble, and I don't have one single friend in this city to turn to. Because you and I are from the same part of the country, I am counting on you as my neighbor to do me a favor. My name is Dessie Heavener and someday I'm going to be a famous singer, and you're going to be the one who helped me get there." The soldier and his friends chipped in for my ticket. Twenty minutes later, I was on my way to Nassau Point.

The ride out to the tip of the Island seemed to take forever. A switching problem cost us an hour, and we experienced another delay further down the line when a produce truck conked out on the track. It was nine-thirty before the train pulled into the tiny Nassau Point station. I asked the conductor where I could find the Nassau Point Inn.

"About five miles, straight out that road there. You can't miss it."

No taxis were waiting at the station. I had to walk. I struck out along the dark road. This part of Long Island was desolate and remote, as far removed from the lights of Broadway as good old Munford.

I had gone about a third of the way when I heard a car overtaking me. I stood in the middle of the road and waved my arms. The car stopped just inches from my kneecaps. The driver opened his door to shout at me.

"You crazy dame! I could have run you down!"

I said, "I'm sorry, mister, but I have a singing engagement at the Nassau Point Inn, and I don't have any way to get there. Would you mind taking me? I'd be so grateful."

"Aw, heck. All right," he grumbled. "Hop in. Dumb broad, walking around in the middle of the night and in the middle of nowhere." My rescuer was a balding man in his early forties, well-groomed, and expensively dressed. The car, a pre-war Cadillac, must have gulped a fortune in gas coupons. We rounded a few more corners and saw a rambling structure silhouetted against the white surf of Long Island Sound. I couldn't see any lights on outside, although the parking lot was full.

"Why is it so dark?" I asked him.

"Partial blackout. Someone spotted German submarines in Peconic Bay the other day. I think they must have been dreaming or drunk, but folks love to scare themselves. Human nature. So you're a singer, huh? What's your name?"

"Dessie Heavener." I climbed out of the car. "You haven't heard of me before, but you will. Thanks a lot, mister."

Inside, I told a waiter that I wanted to speak to Mr. Kingsley. "It's about a job."

"He's busy right now. You'll have to wait."

I didn't want to wait. "Is there someone else I can talk to? What's his manager's name?"

"You mean Mr. Dillon? Yeah, he's in back somewhere."

Dizzy Dillon. How could I forget?

Up on the bandstand, the members of the band were playing "Carolina Moon" in an easy swing tempo. I was relieved not to see a woman on the stage, or anyone else who looked like a singer. King faced the audience as he conducted. When he wasn't playing a hot solo, he kept his trumpet tucked under his left arm while he waved his right hand up and down, two beats to the measure. Couples were dancing. Most of the men were in uniform.

I skirted the dance floor and pushed open a door near the stage. I found myself in the kitchen, momentarily dazzled by a display of shining chrome and white tile. A busboy directed me to the dressing rooms: "Go past the sinks, straight through the pantry and turn left at the garbage cans."

I entered a drafty room whose windows had been covered on the inside with blackout paper. A metal rack held suit jackets, neckties, and overcoats. The shelf above sported at least a dozen hats. The floor was littered with open music cases, a couple of suitcases, stacks of sheet music, a broken music stand or two, some split and useless bamboo reeds, and about two hundred cigarette butts. A faded curtain concealed one corner of the room. The makeup mirrors on one wall were ringed by lightbulbs, half of which were either missing or dead. A filthy sink cowered in another corner. On the mirror above the sink someone had scrawled in crimson lipstick, "So long suckers." The departing shapely chanteuse, I guessed.

I called out, "Mr. Dillon?"

A voice came from behind the curtain. "I'm back here. Who wants me?"

I followed the voice. "Can I come in?"

"Who's stopping you?"

I pushed the curtain aside. Dizzy Dillon was seated on a sagging cot. Although his hat was pushed far back on his head, it barely cleared his eyebrows.

I said, "I don't suppose you remember me?"

He shook his head. "So many girls come through these dressing rooms. I can't remember them all. If you're looking for King's autograph—"

"I sang for you in Columbia, at the Dixieland Ballroom, about two years ago. It was a talent contest. Remember? I sang 'Fast Walkin' Blues' and 'Can't Help Lovin' That Man.' Mr. Kingsley offered me a job, but he fired me before I could even get started because someone told him I was only fifteen. Well, I'm almost seventeen now, and I'm ready to go to work. I hear you need somebody."

"Well, yeah, I do, but—nah, I don't think so. I promised to listen to a girl tomorrow, used to sing with Stan Kenton. A real pro."

"Tomorrow is tomorrow. Meanwhile, I'm betting that those soldier boys out there were real disappointed tonight not to see a pretty girl singer up on that stage."

Dizzy sighed. "Yeah, well, you win some, you lose some. That's show biz."

I planted myself in front of him. "I tell you what, Mr. Dillon, I'll sing for you for free tonight, and if you don't like me, you can listen to your other girl tomorrow. What harm can it do? Let me do one chorus of something, anything. A love song. The boys out there want someone to say the words they can't say themselves. I know the band's arrangements by heart. I've listened to all their records a thousand times, and I've heard them on the radio, and I've memorized every note. I don't sing flat and I know how to keep my tempo up. Please, Mr. Dillon. Please."

Dizzy rubbed his face with his open hands. "The management's been griping about what happened last night. Threatened to cut short our contract and take us to court. Geez, that's all we need. Oh, what the hell. If you bomb as a singer, at least you look good. Okay, get into your costume. This set's almost finished. I'll tell King when he comes in."

I said, "I don't have a costume. Just what I'm wearing."

He eyed my navy blue suit and black coat. "Looks like a Salvation Army uniform. Wait a minute, I think Mavis left some of her rags behind." He rummaged under the pile of masculine clothes on the cot and pulled out something silver and shimmery. "Try this. She said it made her look like a floozy. I don't know why she minded. She was a floozy."

I held the gown up in front of me. Mavis must have been built like a broomstick, a foot taller than me, and half my girth. "This thing is at least two sizes too small for me."

"Fine. If it splits while you're on stage, at least the crowd will get its money's worth of spectacle." He left me, pulling the curtain closed behind him.

While I was trying to zip up the dress, I heard voices. "Geez, what a bunch of deadheads," one musician groaned. "I seen livelier-looking stiffs in the morgue."

"You were lousy, all of you," King came in bellowing. "Don't blame the crowd because they've got long faces. Listening to

91

you, anybody would feel like throwing up. Wilson, you wreck that solo one more time and I'm giving it to Kenny, understand? And you, Adam, what was the big hurry with 'In the Mood' tonight? You got a train to catch? Damned drummers all think you're God's gift. Watch my lead, will you? How many times I got to tell you? Watch my lead!''

"Uh, King—" Dizzy pleaded for his attention.

"What is it now, Dizzy? Don't tell me Uncle Sam tapped you on the shoulder today." King threw back the curtain. "What the hell?"

I paused in my struggle with the zipper long enough to give him a big smile. "Oh, hello, Mr. Kingsley. I . . . was just trying this on for size."

"I been trying to tell you, King, miss—ah, this little girl is looking for a job. I told her we'd give her a try, just for tonight."

From the way King smiled back at me, I could tell he didn't remember me at all from the Dixieland Ballroom talent contest. "No kidding? What's your name, honey?"

"Dolores Heavener, sir. But everybody calls me Dessie."

He didn't remember my name, either. "Dessie. Nice. I like that. I had an Aunt Tessie, but I've never known any Dessies. Here, let me give you a hand with that."

Dizzy went on. "I figured we might as well give her a chance, huh? You got a few minutes before you go back out, maybe you could go over one or two songs with her."

King did not reply. He was too busy wrestling with the zipper. He managed to work it all the way to the top, then he dipped his head and kissed the side of my neck. I shivered. No man had touched me like that since Blair's accident. I checked my appearance in the cracked mirror that hung over the cot. The gown was a tight fit, all right. When I inhaled, I could hear the seams creaking under the pressure. Long sleeves bound my upper arms, and my breasts swelled over the top of the low-cut bodice. I decided the sleeves looked ridiculous, and besides, my hands were turning blue. I ripped each sleeve off with a few hard tugs, then I turned and faced King.

"What do you think? Will this be all right?"

His gaze plunged to my cleavage and kept on going until it reached my feet, then it reversed direction and traveled upward until it locked with mine.

He gave me a slow, sleepy-eyed smile. "You're gorgeous,"

he breathed. "You're perfect. I've never seen anyone like you. All this and you can sing, too?"

"So I've been told," I croaked, and cleared my throat. "Then, you'll give me a chance?"

"Sure, I'll give you a chance. Our book is pretty hard; maybe you ought to look at the music a little. Billy," he hollered through the curtain, "bring me my arrangements, will you?"

"Yessir, Mr. Kingsley."

Billy was the band boy. Fifty-five years old, bald except for a horseshoe fringe around the back and sides of his skull, and nearly toothless, he was the one who kept track of everyone's scores, set up the music stands and took them down after the show, hung the purple backdrop and the glittering logo, produced reed and mutes, chewing gum and cigarettes from the depths of his pockets. He entered the curtained cubicle, plopped a pile of music into King's arms, and went out without even glancing at me.

King put on a pair of thick horn-rimmed glasses. That explained the vague, dreamy look in his eyes; he was nearsighted. He sat on the cot and patted the space beside him. "Here, kid, park your carcass."

I laughed. "I can't even walk in this thing, much less sit. Don't worry, I can read over your shoulder."

I studied my solos, noted the timing of my entrances, and listened to King's advice about phrasing and dynamics.

"Come on real strong here, because the saxes are playing full blast and Fast Eddie is just finishing up his solo. This entrance is tricky. None of my girls ever gets it right the first time. But if you watch me starting here," his slender finger tapped the score, "I'll be able to cue you. Tempo on this one is *vivace*, that means real lively, almost double time."

"I know," I said. "I've studied music."

"That's a big help." He flashed his sweet smile again. I experienced a sweet, sinking sensation in my middle. "You'd be amazed at how musically ignorant some singers are. Can't even read music, some of 'em. I can see you're different, in lots of ways." He stood up. "Don't worry about a thing, baby," he said. "You'll do fine." He threw back the curtain. "Onstage, everybody. Oh, this is Dessie Heavener from South Carolina. She'll be filling in for Mavis until we get someone permanent." The men greeted my appearance with wolf whistles and lewd sniggers. "Be nice, now. Dessie is a newcomer to our business."

A few groans, and somebody said, "She can't be any worse than Mavis."

"Okay, show time. And liven it up a little. Looks like the aftermath of Pearl Harbor out there." King went out.

My skirt was so constricting I could hardly walk. I stopped one of the men who had been standing near the coat rack. "Would you mind helping me, sir? I'm not getting along too good in this thing. Just bend right over and grab the bottom of the dress, and rip it up along the side seam to someplace above my knee. I sure would hate to make my debut sliding onstage on my face."

He grinned. He had reddish-brown hair and green eyes, and a sprinkling of freckles over his nose and cheeks. "This will be a pleasure, ma'am." He knelt down and ripped the stitches very slowly while the others looked on and cheered.

Dizzy told me that I would be the next to the last to go onstage, right before King. Since I couldn't sit down, I would have to stand over to one side until it was time for me to sing. Then King would signal me to step up to the microphone.

"Oh, just one thing, Mr. Dillon. I haven't had much experience singing into a microphone before. What do I do?"

Dizzy looked nonplussed. "Do? Well, you just sing. If you're going to belt real loud, you'd better back up a little if you don't want to break their eardrums. If you want to croon, then lean in closer and they'll hear every word. You'll find you don't need to project nearly as loud. You can save a lot of wear and tear on your voice that way. You'll last longer."

I didn't care about lasting long. I just wanted to get started. King pinched my bottom and gave me a shove and I was on my way. During the band's first lively number, I stood near the proscenium and smiled out at the audience. For their second number, also a jitterbug, I started tapping my foot and snapping my fingers to the beat. Then it was my turn. The band played one chorus of "Dancing in the Dark," and King beckoned me up to the mike. I went, in a sort of sideways shuffle that would keep my back hidden. I felt such a mixture of emotions that I couldn't have singled out just one. I was scared. I was happy. I was excited. I was nervous. And I fervently hoped that when I opened my mouth, something would come out besides the chatter of teeth.

My first notes quavered, but I pushed a little harder, and my tone evened out. The range was high for me, but I sang that song as if I'd sung it a thousand times. And I suppose I had, every time I had played the record or heard it on the radio. Out of the corner of my eye, I saw King smiling. I mustn't have been too bad, because the audience applauded.

"We'll give 'em 'Chattanooga Choo-Choo' next," King said under cover of the applause, "and then 'These Foolish Things.' Think you can handle 'em?"

I nodded. He reminded me not to come in too fast after the drum solo on the first number, then he cued up the band, gave them the downbeat, and the clarinets and trumpets wailed like a train whistle. The drummer set a brisk pace, laying down a beat that sounded just like the chugging of a locomotive. I grinned and swung my hips. I couldn't wait to sing again.

With each number, the applause grew warmer. After "These Foolish Things," somebody yelled, "Hey, King, where you been keepin' her?" We did some current favorites like "The White Cliffs of Dover," and a real brisk arrangement of "That Old Black Magic" which I faked, having heard it only a couple of times on the radio. King finished up the set with the Harry James hit "I've Heard That Song Before," then we took our bows and trooped offstage.

Back in the dressing room, the men crowded around me to offer congratulations. Someone handed me a flask of whiskey, which I refused, and someone else gave me a lighted cigarette, which I accepted. I inhaled deeply and started to choke.

"What kind of cigarette is that?"

"The best kind, sugar," one of the trombonists said. His name was White Willie Wilson. His features and curly reddish hair were Negroid, but his skin was as white as mine. "Relaxes you. Good for the nerves."

"But not for the throat."

The drummer offered me a real cigarette. "I think I'm in love," he said, snapping his lighter. "Will you marry me?"

I laughed. "No, thank you."

He sighed. "Too bad. The view from the bandstand was unbelievable tonight. Did you know you keep time with your, ah, bottom when you sing? Absolutely perfect, like a metronome. We were all mesmerized. You looked like you were having the time of your life out there."

"I was."

"You know, this band needs someone like you. Us Army rejects have been feeling a little demoralized lately. I'm 4-F myself. All that football in college tore up my knees pretty bad. Don't you feel sorry for me? Over the hill at twenty-two. I'm Adam Foster, by the way."

He stuck out his hand, and we shook. I said, "You're a great drummer. Your beat holds everything together and really keeps it moving. Have you been with the band long?" I didn't remember seeing him in Columbia. He was so good-looking, with his wavy auburn hair and green eyes, that I would surely have noticed.

"Just since Christmas. I was with Goodman before that, but we didn't get along. Benny's a bigger tightwad than King when it comes to money. But I don't think you'll have any trouble in that department. King is pretty generous to his women."

"I haven't even been hired yet, officially."

"The way you look? You will be."

"What about the way I sing?"

He laughed. "Around here, talent is a secondary consideration. King auditioned you before you even opened your mouth."

King came into the room just then and put his arm around me. "You were great, baby. Just keep it coming." He turned to the rest of the group. "The management has reconsidered, gents. They want us to finish out the week. Looks like we're stuck here until Monday."

I heard a few groans, some remarks about playing the sticks and the hinterlands, but no real objections. A job was a job. King leaned close and whispered in my ear. "They think you'll be good for business. You're on, sweetheart. We'll discuss the details later."

Our next set was even livelier than the first. This time, I felt more at home in front of the microphone, more sure of myself. I couldn't stop smiling while I sang, and the faces that looked up at me were smiling, too. We were friends sharing the same pleasure, enjoying the same music.

After another ten minute break, we returned to the stage for our last set of the evening. The crowd greeted us like returning heroes, and didn't let us leave for another hour and a half. When we were finally ready to wrap it up, someone called out a request for a nonsense boogie-woogie tune, "Hava Banana," not to be confused with "Yes, We Have No Bananas."

"Hava Banana" was a conversation between two brass voices.

The saxophones and trombones played something that sounded like, "Doodle-y, doodle-y, do!" and the clarinets and trumpets replied with five notes that sounded like, "Have a banana!" They repeated this about five times, then the two voices joined in a standard boogie-woogie resolution. The song's popularity baffled me. It was so simple-minded and silly and easy to play that a group of eight-year-old musicians could have fun with it. Anyway, King gave the downbeat and the saxophones did their doodle-y do's, and when it came time for the trumpets to respond, someone in the crowd shouted, "Sing us something, sweetheart." King gave me the nod, and so I stepped up to the microphone and sang, "Have a banana" whenever it was appropriate. The second time around, I started to substitute different five note phrases like "Play the pian-a" and "I'm a sopran-a," sung with the proper operatic spirit, of course, and "Go to Havana" and "The big panorama," and at the resolution I shouted out, "Look at me everybody, I'm from South Carola-na!" and the crowd cheered. Next time through I got even sillier, not even trying to rhyme my words with banana but throwing in stuff like "Corned beef on rye bread," "Two goats in a Chevy," anything that fit the meter: "The weather is fine here," and "Hitler's a swine, dear." At the end of that chorus I wailed, "If you give me one more piece of Spam, I'm going to throw it out the window!" and the place broke up. A soldier on the bus between Richmond and Washington had told me that if there was one thing that every man in the armed forces was sick of, it was Spam. So when I looked out and saw all those uniforms, I knew just what to say.

We did three more choruses, and by that time the boys and girls didn't care what I said—they loved it. A few called out suggestions, which I used. We could have gone on for another half hour, except I noticed that King's upper lip was looking a little raw, and he was rolling his eyes at me saying he wanted to quit. So we wound it up and with it my first night as a professional singer.

The men were exhausted but pleased: they hadn't had such a warm reception in years. Members of the audience surged up on the stage and started shoving pieces of paper and autograph books at me.

"Autograph!" I laughed. "You all don't even know who I am. How can you be asking for my autograph?"

Eventually King took my arm and pulled me away. "Someone here I'd like you to meet, Dessie."

I recognized the good Samaritan who had given me a lift earlier in the evening.

"You were right," he said, "a lot of people are going to be hearing from you from now on."

King introduced Pepper Wellington, whose column had brought me to Nassau Point. In addition to his duties as a man-about-town columnist for the New York *Mirror*, he reviewed popular music for *Swing* magazine. "Pepper couldn't wait to get out here and see the funeral rites," King said sourly. "I bet he was surprised when it turned out to be a christening."

"I just happened to be visiting friends in Southampton," Pepper said, "when I got wind of the situation. You can't blame me for being curious, King. I am a journalist, after all. It's my job to report on the vicissitudes of fortune experienced by musical groups, even second-rate outfits like yours."

King's smile showed his teeth. They were very white and very even, one of his best features. "If I didn't like you so much, Pepper, I'd call you by your real name."

Pepper took my hand and raised it to his lips—the first time in my life anyone had ever done that. "You are unique, my dear, the missing link between Ethel Merman and Billie Holiday, although in looks you resemble neither of those fine ladies. Where does that voice come from? In any case, we must get together for an interview. Soon. I'd love to know where you've been hiding yourself all this time. South Carolina's loss is the world's gain, eh? Well, so long, King. If you ever need a friend, I hope you find one."

Because Nassau Point was so far from New York, the musicians were staying in the inn. King said, "They're full up, but I'll bunk in with Dizzy and you can have my room. Tomorrow I'll get somebody to pick up your stuff from the city and bring it out on the train."

"Thank you, Mr. Kingsley, that's very kind of you."

"Hey, baby, you deserve the best, and I'm going to see that you get it."

The musicians adjourned to the bar for an after-show drink. I would have liked to join them, but King held me back. "You were terrific tonight," he said when we were alone in the dressing room, "but your act needs polishing. We're going to have to spend a lot of time rehearsing your numbers in the next few days."

I nodded. "Anything you say, Mr. Kingsley. I'm just so grateful to you for giving me this chance—"

"Hey, we're the ones who should be grateful." His eyes flashed and his dimples deepened. "Mark my words, little lady, you are going to breathe new life into this bunch of wilted flowers. I've been waiting for someone like you for a long, long time."

He rested his hands lightly on my shoulders and turned on the full force of his smile. That smile really was magical. It told me I was the only woman in the world who could make him happy.

"I've dreamed about this ever since you threw me out of that talent show in Charleston," I said. "My future got interrupted that night. But here I am, and this is where I'm supposed to be. What do they call that? Destiny?"

King look startled. "Son of a gun, I thought I recognized you from someplace. Sure, you were the little girl who—" he chuckled. "You're all grown up now, aren't you, Dessie?"

"I guess so," I said. "I've got a broken-down husband and an eight-month-old baby to prove it. But I never let go of that dream, that someday I'd be up on the bandstand singing with you. I've been waiting, too. Waiting for my destiny to happen. I don't want to wait anymore."

He led me over to the cot and drew me down beside him. This time, his agile musician's fingers had no trouble with the recalcitrant zipper. "Neither do I, baby," he breathed around the sides of a soul-shattering kiss. "Neither do I."

I slept until noon the following day. King awakened me with a kiss. "One of the boys got hold of this morning's paper. Looks like you made a hit with Pepper. You're lucky. He's an Ivy League prick, but he has influence with people who count. Listen, I've been trying to get a hold of my A and R man at Glow Records all morning. I want him to come out tonight and hear 'Hava Banana.' And guess what? Dizzy's on the phone right now with the producers of the Marvel Soap Hour. How'd you like to be on radio, kid?"

I found Pepper's column and read aloud: " 'Caught King Kingsley's new silver-throated songbird at the Nassau Point Inn last night and she almost blew me off my perch. Her style is sensational, and her appearance alone could cause a riot in any crowd in which red-blooded American males are present. Dessie Heavener's her name. Pepper predicts you'll be hearing plenty from her just as soon as her new boss lands himself a Gotham gig.' "

I folded the paper up and set it aside. "I spent so many years waiting for something like this to happen to me, and now it's all happening at once. Yesterday I had seventy-five cents in my pocket and no prospect of a job. Today I'm in the newspapers and people are talking to me about records and radio." I looked up at King and smiled. "Looks like I was in the right place at the right time last night."

King wrapped his arms around me and pulled me over on top of him. "I'll say you were. You still are, baby."

I squirmed. "What about Glow Records? You were going to call them—"

"They can wait. The whole world can wait."

In King's life, sex took precedence over music, over food, over everything. He loved it, he was good at it, and he needed it all the time. His performance as a bed partner carried through the promise of his smile. When we were together, nothing else mattered. The equation was simple: One man plus one woman equals an infinite number of possibilities for pleasure. In just one night, he had restored my sagging self-respect, not only as a performer, but as a woman.

I signed a contract with the King Kingsley band, three years at a hundred and fifty dollars a week. Adam Foster told me I was making a mistake, that I should ask for a six-month contract with an option to renew, at which point I could ask for a raise.

"This is more money than my daddy ever made in a month most of the time I was growing up," I told him. "Even if I send half of this home, I can live very well on the rest."

"You're worth more."

"The money's not important. I want to sing. And I want people to know my name. Anything else is just icing on the cake."

I finished out our engagement at Nassau Point in Mavis's silver gown. When we got back to New York City, King bought me two gold lamé gowns, tightly fitted around bust and bottom, with low-cut bodices, and skirts that flared at the hem.

"Gold is better than silver," he said. "Looks richer. More expensive. I don't want people like Pepper saying I'm a cheapskate."

The band's next job was in the Sky Room of the Hanover Hotel. I moved into an apartment on West Eighty-fifth Street near Central Park. King had his own apartment in Jackson Heights, which he shared with his mother. He went out there once or twice a week. The rest of the time, he lived with me. We socialized with the other band members at after-hours clubs or at Sunday jam sessions in clubs like The Famous Door or Joe and Eddie's on Fifty-second Street, which was known in the business simply as The Street. Between King's lovemaking and getting to live and breathe music every minute of the day, I thought I was in heaven.

We played to a capacity crowd on our first night at the Sky Room. Pepper had been singing my praises in his column, and King's press agent had done his job, too. The audience kept us on stage for sixteen minutes at the end of the second set doing "Hava Banana," and they made us repeat it twice more before the evening ended.

The following morning, stupid from lack of sleep, I found myself in a recording studio for the first time in my life, singing "Hava Banana" while the band members tried their best to sound alert and enthusiastic. During a fifteen-minute break, King handed me a new ballad he and his Artist and Repertory, or A and R, man had chosen for the flip side.

"It's not much," he said as he passed out sides to the musicians. "Everybody's gonna be buying the record for 'Hava Banana' anyway." The song was called "Believe Me."

That night I mailed my father a check for a hundred dollars, the eighty-five I had borrowed plus a little extra for Gray. A week later, I telephoned him for the first time. I wanted to tell him that I would be appearing on the nationally broadcast Marvel Soap Hour the following Thursday if he cared to listen.

"I'm afraid that won't be possible," he said. "As you recall, Thursday is our night for choir practice."

"Oh." I had forgotten. That part of my life seemed to belong to another century. "How's Gray? Does he miss me?"

"Gray? He seems quite content. Ayleen is very good with him, of course, and he listens to her. He hardly seems to know you're gone."

I cried for an hour after I hung up. King returned from a visit to the barber shop that had kept him away for nearly three hours. "What's the matter, baby?"

I clung to him and wept into his shoulder. "My little boy is going to grow up without knowing me. I thought I was doing the right thing for both of us when I left, but now I'm not so sure. Do you think," I looked up at him, "do you think Gray could live with us?"

King shook his head. "Uh-uh. No brats. I've got headaches enough. Look, baby, we're going on the road after the Sky Room gig ends. You don't know what that means yet. You sit in the bus for twelve, fourteen hours. You get into your costume, play for six hours, sleep in a flophouse somewhere if you're lucky, on the bus if you're not, then ride another twelve or fourteen hours to the next job and do it all over again. It's no place for a kid. Hey, you're too old to play with dolls. Besides, you've got a man to look after now. And I'm very demanding. I want your undivided attention."

As he was talking, I noticed a smear of lipstick on the side of his neck. "That's some barber you go to," I said. "Is he always so affectionate?"

"What's that?" He looked in the mirror and laughed. "Oh, this? Funniest thing, I ran into my mom in Saks. I was looking for a present for you, something special to celebrate, you know?" He produced a long, slender box from an inside pocket. It contained a gold bracelet.

"It's beautiful," I said as he fastened it around my wrist. "No one's ever given me anything this nice before."

"That's what makes me special," King said. "I appreciate quality when I see it. She wants me to bring you out to see her sometime."

"Why didn't you just invite her over? I'd love to meet her."

He shook his head. "She's jealous of my girlfriends, and besides, she snoops. How would we explain my pajama bottoms under your pillow?"

King called a rehearsal one Saturday afternoon a few weeks later to go over some new material. As I walked into the empty hotel ballroom, Adam Foster grabbed my arm.

"Come on," he said, "I want you to hear something."

"But the rehearsal—"

"We still have a few minutes. Come on!"

We ran ten blocks to the corner of Forty-seventh Street and Broadway.

"Listen," Adam said breathlessly. "Don't say a word. Just listen. Isn't it beautiful?"

A music store was playing a newly released record over an

outdoor loudspeaker. Passersby were stopping to listen and a good-sized crowd had gathered. A few women wiped tears from their eyes.

For the first time, I was able to hear my own voice as everyone else heard it, not belting out "Hava Banana," but crooning the slow, sweet ballad on the flip side.

> Believe me when I tell you
>   that the sun will follow the rain.
> Believe me when I say
>   the scarlet rose will bloom again.
> Believe me when I promise
>   that you'll never be alone.
> Believe me when I say, I'm coming home.

There were two more verses in the same vein, then the song ended with a dramatic crescendo and a swelling coda:

> Although I may be far away
> Please believe me when I say
> That it won't be very long before
> I'm coming home to you.

Adam grinned at me. "A hit record your first time out. Congratulations, Miss Heavener. You're a star."

8

I TELEPHONED MUNFORD ONE THURSDAY EVENING, AFTER I WAS sure my father and Ayleen had left for choir practice.

"Hello, Miz Heavener's residence."

At the sound of Clara Mae's voice, so familiar and so dear, a powerful wave of homesickness swept over me.

"Clara Mae? It's me, Dessie."

Clara Mae was cool at first; she had to let me know that she did not approve of the way I had run off. But she could not stay angry with me for long. She admitted that she thought about me every day, and she prayed for me, too.

"I never thought I could miss a human bein' the way I miss you, chile. It was bad enough when you was up at the Howards', but least I got to see you once in a while. When you comin' home?"

Clara Mae was real proud of my success; I had sent Paul copies of all my records so far, as well as articles clipped from newspapers and magazines, reviews of my performances, even an interview in the New York *Mirror* Sunday supplement in which Pepper Wellington called me the hottest young singing star in the business, as pretty as I was talented. Paul had dragged Clara Mae over to his house to hear my records. He had to read my notices to her, because she could read and write her own name but not much more.

I asked to speak to Gray. Clara Mae fetched him and held the phone up to his face.

"Say hello to your mama, chile. That's your mama callin' from someplace far away."

"Hello, Gray. Do you know who this is?" My voice caught in my throat.

Gray gabbled something into the phone. At age one, his con-

104

versation wasn't very coherent, but Clara Mae understood every word.

"He say he want a cookie. I guess I better get off this phone pretty quick and give him one, or I'm gonna hear about it. Say good night to your mama, sugar."

"Goo."

Just then I heard Ayleen's voice in the background.

"Who is that you're talkin' to, Clara Mae?"

"It's Miss Dessie, ma'am. She want to say hello to her baby."

"Dessie! Give me that phone. Hello, Dessie, honey? We do appreciate the money you've been sendin' for Gray, but honestly, don't you think a long distance telephone call is a bit extravagant these days? After all, Gray's just a baby, startin' to walk and talk some, but you can't really expect to communicate with him, can you?" Ayleen gave a small, indulgent laugh at my silliness. "I mean, you don't want to get into the habit of doin' this, honey. It'll cost you the earth, and you'll just confuse the poor little mite. He probably doesn't even remember who you are. After all, you did abandon him when he was only eight months old, and I just know he's forgotten all about you by now. So I think you had better confine yourself to writin' letters when you send your checks. That would make more sense, don't you think? Now, Gray, hush. Be a good boy, or Mama's gonna spank you. 'Bye, Dessie. I'll tell your daddy you called." She hung up.

"I bet you will," I shouted to the dead receiver in my hand. "I just bet you will!" How dare that bitch threaten to lay a hand on my son? How dare she call herself "Mama" to him? How dare she forbid me to telephone my own—

"Dessie, two minutes!" someone called. I scooped the rest of my change into my purse and hurried back to the dressing room. I just had time to check my hair and touch up my lipstick.

By the time we finished performing that night, I had cooled down a little. Gray would be no better off living with me. King hated kids, and he had been right about life on the road. It was exhilarating and exciting, but grueling, nerve-racking, and exhausting, not something one would wish on a one-year-old baby. But I deeply resented Ayleen's proprietary attitude toward my baby. Mama. She had called herself "Mama" when speaking to my son. I was sure Gray called her that, too. Mama.

I tried telephoning again two weeks later, on a Thursday. Ayleen answered the phone. I hung up without saying a word. They must have changed their schedule to thwart me, or else Ayleen had dropped out of the choir altogether so that she could maintain a nightly vigil by the telephone. I wrote to Paul, asking him to keep an eye on Gray for me and to send a report. King's booking agency forwarded his reply to me in Boston, where the band had a one-week engagement at the Claridge Hotel.

"Seems I have been banned from the Heavener house as an undesirable," Paul wrote. "Your stepmother picked a fight with me the last time I was there and all but threw me out. Still, I've asked Clara Mae to drop by now and then to fill me in on what's going on. She says Gray is doing fine, growing like a weed, talking more every day. Ayleen is strict with him, but surely no more strict than my dad was with me. Meanwhile, I'm spending another summer clerking—can't wait till I'm a full-fledged, legitimate lawyer. Maybe then I'll get paid what I'm worth."

In early July, we started on a tour of army bases in the South. I sent Paul our itinerary along with a note: "Can't believe I'll be this close to Munford and not have a minute to run over and see you and Clara Mae and Gray."

The bus that took us from one gig to another was my home, and the band was my family. And despite the cramped quarters, we got along without killing each other.

King's band had four saxophone players: Rheinhold "Rhiney" Schwartz, who suffered a lot of antagonism from the other men because of his German background; Byron Fraser, who followed the horses and whose instrument case was always stuffed with tip sheets and racing forms; Buddy Best, who played hot alto sax and clarinet; and Fast Eddie Smith, who was known for his practical jokes. Eddie had almost gotten fired when he poured honey into the bell of King's trumpet. King played hot trumpet, of course, with Kelly Coates and Jo Jo Jonas on valve trumpet and cornet supporting him. White Willie Wilson, who had given me my first puff on a reefer, played the smoothest trombone I had ever heard, but Kenny Albertson, who was thirty years younger, gave him some stiff competition. Ivor Szewicki was our pianist, a self-described nervous wreck. He attributed his bad nerves to the fact that he was the only musician in the bunch who never knew what kind of instrument he would be playing— or if he would have a piano at all. Wee Geordie Douglas on guitar and Peanut Tasker on bass filled out the rhythm section, while Adam Foster's drums laid down the beat that kept us all in line.

King got carsick, so he always rode in the front of the bus

right behind the driver, his window wide open no matter what the temperature was outside. When I found the draft too chilling, I retreated to the rear of the bus, where the haze of reefer smoke was so thick that I could get high without even touching one to my lips. But I learned to like that, too. I helped myself to sips of whiskey from the pocket flasks that were passed back and forth. A few of the men, and King himself, snorted cocaine regularly in order to keep awake and alert. I tried it once, stayed up all night talking and singing and laughing, and was so exhausted by the following evening that I could hardly perform.

The members of the King Kingsley family shared toothpaste, handkerchiefs, soap, and cigarettes, as well as small cash loans and aspirins, drugs and liquor. Sometimes I dispensed Dessie's Miracle Hangover Cure, a light massage of the afflicted person's temples and neck. I had a lot of fun learning to shoot craps and play poker, although I never became expert at either. We complained together, ate together, exchanged jokes and jibes, dressed and undressed in the same cramped dressing rooms. We talked music and baseball and show business, but very little about the war. Even though we performed at army bases all over the country, Europe and the Pacific were like two geographic poles, and we were somewhere in between, untouched by what was happening on either side.

The men understood that I was King's woman. No one ever made a pass at me, not even Adam Foster, who was sweet on me. Like the others, he maintained a discreet distance and preserved a casual, friendly manner when King was around.

After evening performances, we were always too keyed up to sleep. If we happened to be playing in a town where bars and clubs were open late, we would adjourn for what usually turned into an after-hours jam session. Only then was I able to sing the songs of my past, the blues songs I had learned from Clara Mae and LeRoy. Whenever I sang them, I thought of Blair, who had been with me when I learned them, and Paul, who had learned them from me. More often, though, I got an image of Blair's brother, Bram, dancing with me in the conservatory at Woodlands, listening intently while I tried to lure Blair out of his tragic private world with a song. I wondered what had happened to Bram. He had vanished after his father's funeral, and no one in Munford, not even his mother, knew what had become of him.

The audiences at the Army bases were always appreciative.

They treated me like visiting royalty, and rewarded me with the loudest cheers and lustiest applause I had ever experienced. After each show men gathered around to demand autographs. Dizzy had come prepared with plenty of eight-by-ten glossy photographs of me, looking not unlike a glistening golden banana in a skintight gown. I basked in all the attention. I lived for it.

To my everlasting surprise and amazement, I was a celebrity. Whenever we pulled into a new town, journalists interviewed me, photographers snapped my picture, managers for local radio stations invited me to stop by and sing a song. In cities like Decatur, Atlanta, Jacksonville, Charleston, and Mobile, ordinary people stopped me in the street to ask for autographs, or simply to tell me how much "Believe Me" meant to them. I started receiving letters from soldiers who had heard the song in their service clubs or on the radio. They all said that the words made them want to win the war and come home.

In mid-July—I had sent Gray a huge stuffed teddy bear for his first birthday—we were performing at Fort Jackson, South Carolina. As I was coming offstage, I saw a familiar figure waiting in the wings. Paul Miller. He was nattily attired in a white linen suit and Panama hat. Screaming with excitement, I hurled myself at him and threw my arms around his neck.

"Oh, I've missed you, Paulie, I've missed you. You look so—so grown up!"

Paul laughed. "You look beautiful, Dessie. Just beautiful." We stood at arm's length, still touching, and beamed at each other. "Well, Dess, you always said you were going to be a star, and here you are. I'm proud of you, real proud."

"Admit it," I teased, "you never really believed I could do it."

"No," he shook his head, "I always knew you'd make it. It was just a question of when. I brought you a little something." He extracted a sheaf of music from the side pocket of his suit jacket. "I wrote a song for you. I have no melodic invention to speak of, so I stole the tune from Chopin. The lyrics were harder. I've been working on them for months."

I glanced at the first few measures:

> Paradise,
> I have seen it once or twice,
> In the evening when the setting sun
> Shines gold upon your face.
> Paradise—

The lyrics gave me chills, even in the eighty-five degree heat backstage. "I want to hear what this sounds like." I took Paul back to a dressing room where I had seen an old upright piano. I introduced him to my fellow band members as my oldest friend in the world. Paul pounded out the Chopin while I sang the words he had written for me. The range suited my voice perfectly, but then, Paul knew my vocal capabilities better than I knew them myself. He had simplified the melody, modifying it, and reducing it to the standard thirty-two bar form that most popular songs followed. It was powerful and moving and tough as blazes to sing. When we finished, the other musicians applauded.

"This is the most beautiful song I've ever heard." I blinked away tears of love and pride. "Now all we have to do is sell King on it."

"It stinks." King swaggered over to the piano and slid his arm around my waist. "It's lousy. Nobody wants to dance to Chopin."

Paul stood up from the piano stool. "I'm sorry you don't like the song, Mr. Kingsley. Looks like I'll have to peddle it someplace else."

"You will not!" I inserted myself between them. "This is my song, and nobody else is going to sing it but me."

"You're not going to sing it with this band," King informed me, "not so long as I'm the bandleader here. I don't need to solicit material from amateurs and unknowns." King looked at Paul with loathing. "I've got the best writers in the business working on numbers for me."

"Is that so?" Paul had lost a lot of his adolescent shyness. He wasn't a law student for nothing, and he knew how to argue. "You haven't had a hit since 'Believe Me,' " he reminded King, "and that was because Dessie here did the vocal. With anyone else, that song would have gone the way of the rest of your records—into oblivion. As I recall, you haven't had a big seller since 'Deep Purple.' Before Dessie came along, everybody was saying you were washed up."

"Listen, kid," King took a threatening step toward Paul.

"King, please! Paul is an old friend of mine. Why can't you try to get along?"

"Tell this punk cripple to stay away from me," King snarled, then he turned on me. "You know the rules; no visitors backstage. We've got a show to finish. By the way, Dessie, you sang that last chorus of 'Dancing in the Dark' a half-tone flat. You're going to have to cut out the late nights and the heavy drinking if you want to be a real singer. Anyone listening to you tonight would think you were a talent contest loser."

He walked away. Paul balled up his fists and started to follow him, but I held him back. "Don't pay any attention to him," I said. "He's just jealous because you're an old friend."

Paul shook his head. "I'd rather see you dying of despair and boredom in Munford than working for an animal like him. Why King Kingsley, Dessie? Out of the hundreds of bands in this country, why did you have to pick his?"

"Oh, Paul, King gave me a job when I desperately needed one. Without him, I'd be sliding sandwiches into those little compartments at the Automat. I've got everything I want now, Paulie. I'm deliriously happy, really I am. King's been wonderful to me. When we're alone together—"

"I don't think I want to hear about that." He smoothed his hair and slapped his hat on his head. "Well, so long, Dess. I don't want to get you fired."

"Oh, don't pay any attention to King. He just gets excited. I love your song, Paul. I'm not only going to sing it, I'm going to record it."

"Don't bother. It's not worth anything."

A few days after that, we returned to New York. The American Federation of Musicians had been trying to persuade record companies to compensate its members for their work every time a record was played on the radio or on a jukebox. The record companies were balking, and the union president, James Caesar Petrillo, was predicting a strike. If it actually happened, then union members would be forbidden to walk through the doors of any recording studio that had not signed a contract with the Federation. As a result, bands were rushing into the studios to record before the strike deadline.

One day after our return from the road, we went to the Glow studio to cut some sides. We did eight songs in three hours, the hardest I had ever worked in my life. I wanted to record "Paradise" on the flip side of our version of "I'll Be with You in Apple Blossom Time," but King was still opposed to it.

I had discussed "Paradise" with the other members of the band and Dizzy. Everyone agreed that the song deserved to be heard. During a ten-minute break, while King was in the booth with the recording engineer and our Artist and Repertory man, I handed out sides to the men. Ivor Szewicki played the familiar opening bars on the piano and slid into an arpeggio while Kelly Coates and Jo Jo Jonas raised their muted trumpets and the saxophones blended in with a sweet crescendo. I conducted from my score while I sang. We had reached the bridge when King burst into the room.

"What in hell do you think you're doing?" he shouted. "Whose band is this, anyway?"

I had been expecting this, and I was determined to remain calm. "You told us to take ten. If we want to jam with Paul's song on our own time, we have a perfect right."

"Nobody has any rights around here but me," King bellowed. He was furious. "Anyone who doesn't agree can take a walk. That goes for you, too, Dessie. Especially you. Right now. Plenty of other girls out there would just love to be in your shoes right now."

I threw down my music. "If they're stupid enough to put up with the bad fit, they're welcome to my shoes. You're a goddamned son-of-a-bitch, King. I take it I'm fired?"

"You're damned right you're fired. And you can take this damned song with you." He picked up my score and ripped it to shreds, then hurled the pieces after me.

I steamed and seethed for the first three blocks, then I ducked into a Schrafft's, ordered a cup of coffee, and wept noisily into a whole stack of napkins. I blamed myself for not handling the situation better. And I was furious with King. What difference did it make who wrote a song, if the song was good? Couldn't he even listen to it? Why couldn't he indulge me just this once? Every night in bed, he told me how wonderful I was, how special, how lucky he was to have me. He loved me and I loved him. Why did he have to act like such a jerk?

Back in my apartment, I ran water for a bath. I had just settled into a tub of nice hot suds when the bathroom door burst open and King came in.

"What in hell do you think you're doing? You're supposed to be cutting records today. We only have two more hours before I have to start paying overtime."

I sponged my arm. "You fired me, remember?"

"I don't remember anything. Come on, get your clothes on; we have to record that damned Chopin."

"Paul's song?" I dropped the sponge. "You mean it? You're really going to record Paul's song?"

King lifted his padded shoulders. "Damned A and R man thought it was halfway decent. But we've got to get it in the can before midnight, otherwise no record."

I threw on a dress and a pair of shoes—no underwear, no stockings. King had asked his cab driver to wait. As the taxi pulled away, King leaned over and kissed the side of my neck. "You still have soap suds in your ear." I melted into his arms. By the time we arrived at our destination, our bodies were so tangled up that the driver had to shout to get our attention.

Two weeks after it was released, "Paradise" was selling even better than "Believe Me." I was delighted, not just for myself and for the band, but for Paul. His name appeared on the record label as lyricist, right under the name of the band.

Critics and observers like Pepper Wellington declared that King's band had never sounded better. But we could have told them that. Everywhere we went, we played to sellout crowds. King was riding a new crest of popularity, and he was enjoying it to the full.

We worked without stopping all that fall and into the winter, playing Nassau Point, supper clubs in Astoria, Long Island and Atlantic City, New Jersey, as well as the famous Glen Island Casino in New Rochelle. In March, we followed the Harry James band into the Astor Roof of the Astor Hotel. Our records were selling well; "Paradise" had topped the charts for three solid months.

In early April, King's mother fell ill. I had never met her—King said it was pointless to introduce us since she had never liked any of his girlfriends—but now he began spending three or four days at a time with her, reading to her, writing letters for her, or just sitting by her sickbed.

A month went by with no change in her condition. Then one evening in late May, King turned up at the Astor with a lipstick smear on his earlobe.

I said, "There goes your mother, being overly affectionate again. I see she's changed the color of her lipstick. This shade is more coral, don't you think? It's nice she bothers, as sick as she is. Maybe I should call her and tell her how much I like it."

King laughed and told me he had run into an old classmate of his in the hotel elevator. "She's blind as a bat, worse than me without my glasses. Poor thing tried to kiss me good-bye and missed my lips by a mile."

I wanted to believe him, and when he slid into bed beside me that night and held me in his arms, I did believe him. Filled with the warmth of his passion, I would have believed anything. But in the light of day, my worries mounted and my suspicions sprouted like weeds.

In June, we finished off another successful week at the Astor Hotel. I asked King to join the rest of us at a new after-hours joint on The Street. He said, "No, honey, I promised my mom I'd spend the night at her place. She's feeling a little better, but she's scared of every little thing. Here's a couple of bucks for a taxi. I'll call you tomorrow." A quick kiss, and then he was gone.

He took the elevator to the hotel lobby. I hurried after him, reaching the entrance just in time to see him climbing into a taxi. The doorman hailed one for me, and I ordered my driver to keep King's cab in sight.

We traveled across town to the Waldorf. King paid off his cabdriver and went inside. I did the same. King wasn't expecting anyone to follow him. He never once looked behind him. A woman rose out of one of the armchairs in the lobby and greeted him with a long, unmotherly kiss. King slid his right hand down her back and cupped it under her left buttock. I knew that trick; he had done it to me a thousand times when he was ready for some loving. She got the message. Arms entwined around each other, smiling into each other's eyes, they headed toward the elevators.

I hailed a bellboy. "Who's that woman who kissed Mr. Kingsley?"

"Her?" He grinned, and whispered into my ear the name of Hollywood's biggest new star, a willowy natural blonde with awesome curves and the long, slender legs of a racehorse. "She's stayin' in the penthouse suite. Good-lookin', but no class. She's a lousy tipper."

I gave him five dollars and thanked him for the information. I waited in the lobby for ten minutes, then I took the elevator up to the penthouse suite and pounded on the movie star's door. I kept pounding until I heard footsteps on the other side.

"Whoever it is, go away!" a female voice said.

I lowered my own voice to a baritone. "Room service, ma'am. Somebody here ordered champagne."

She opened the door, and I charged through the sitting room toward the open door to the bedroom. "Where is he? Where is that lousy two-timer? King!"

"Wait a minute, you can't go in there—"

King was sprawled naked in all his glory on the oversize bed, a bumper of bourbon in one hand and a cigarette in the other. He was a fast worker. Only ten minutes, and he had already finished round one of what promised to be a long night. He sat up quickly, sloshing bourbon over his thighs and his business equipment.

"Shit! How did you get here?"

"I thought I'd pay a call on your sick mother. After all this time, I wanted to meet her." I grabbed a heavy, marble-based lamp from the dressing table and hurled it at him. He ducked, and it hit the tufted headboard of the bed and bounced off. "You skunk! How dare you make a fool of me like this! How dare you sneak around and tell lies! I could kill you for this!"

"Come on, kid," he dodged an ashtray, "you know how it is with guys like me. One dame is never enough. We've had our fling. Let's call it a day and part as friends."

I wondered how many times he had delivered that particular speech. "I hate you, King Kingsley!" I sobbed. "I hate you!"

"Dessie," he lifted his hands in a gesture of appeasement, "I swear, I never meant to hurt you. But a man can't control these things. There's no use your getting mad. I'm getting married next week and moving to Hollywood. I'm going to be in pictures."

"Married!" I laughed hysterically. "No woman would be fool enough to marry you."

"You would have," he said, "if you weren't married already."

He was right. I had loved him, and I had let myself hope and dream, and I had closed my eyes to his true character. I was a fool. I dropped the shoe I had poised to throw at him. All the fight drained out of me.

"I'm sorry," I said to the woman cowering on the other side of the door. "Con . . . con. . ." I couldn't get the word out. Congratulations.

Back in my apartment, I opened a window and hurled King's possessions into the night: pajamas, music scores, clothes, shoes, toiletries. That act of petty revenge did not salve my hurt. I had not experienced such intense rage since the night Paul

Miller had destroyed my hopes at the Dixieland Ballroom talent contest. Crying wasn't good enough for what I was suffering. Screaming and wailing didn't help, either; it only brought angry knocks on my ceiling and walls from irate neighbors. I swallowed King's supply of bourbon and promptly lost it again. I considered jumping out the window after his pajamas, but decided against it. It would be too messy. I wanted to be a beautiful corpse.

At five in the morning, I finally telephoned Paul. Thank God I got him and not the judge.

"Paul? Paulie?" I struggled to push coherent words past the sobbing and the shuddering. "It's me. Oh, God, I feel so awful. He . . . walked out on me. He's going to marry someone else! Paul, I don't know what to do!"

Paul knew exactly what kind of soothing noises to make. "Dessie, listen to me. He was no good. Honest, he wasn't worthy of you, and he's not worth what you're doing to yourself. You don't need him anymore. Do you hear me? You're a big star now. You can make it on your own from here on out. You got what you wanted from King, and he got what he wanted from you. I'm glad it's over. You will be, too, when you think about it."

He knew how to bandage my hurt, soothe my pain, blot away my tears. I could almost feel his arms around me, warm and reassuring. I grew calm, even sleepy.

"I think I'm better now," I said groggily. "I'd better go. This call is costing me a fortune."

"I miss you, Dess. I . . . I'd love to see you."

"I want to see you, too. Maybe soon. Good night."

The following morning, Dizzy Dillon came calling. "I guess you've heard. King left town this morning. Dropped the boys flat, with two weeks pay still owing."

"That bastard! What . . . what are we . . . what are you—"

"We've still got what's left of a damned good band, Dessie, and we've got you. You're a star vocalist. We don't have to lay down and die because that son-of-a-bitch dumped us. I've talked it over with the boys, and I've been on the phone. I've already got our next booking, in the biggest theater in the world."

"Radio City Music Hall?" I gasped.

"No," Dizzy smiled. "The European theater of war. The USO is looking for a band to tour the front. Now, I'll understand if you don't want to go, Dessie. It may be dangerous over there.

I don't really know. But it's the only booking I can get. If you say no, we'll have to dissolve the band, and the boys will have to look for work someplace else. The USO wants you. They think you'll be good for morale. They won't take us without you."

Tears streamed down my cheeks. "I can't face them, Dizzy. I feel like such a fool. The boys know what a fool I was. I loved him, Dizzy. I really loved him. But he never loved me, did he? They know that. They know all he wanted was—well, you know. They're laughing at me right now. Laughing themselves sick."

Dizzy stood over me and put his hand on my shoulder. "No, they're not, kid. There isn't a man in that band who wouldn't like to punch King in the mug for the way he treated you. We saw it coming, but we couldn't say nothing. We'd seen it before, lots of times. But the dames never listen. They never believe the truth until it jumps up and hits 'em in the face, like it did you. If it's any comfort, kid, you have a lot of company. The list of King's rejects would stretch from here to Jersey City. You just got to smile and tell the bastard to go shove it. Now, what about this Europe gig?"

"I don't know, Dizzy. I can't think right now."

"Tell you what. Let me give the USO a tentative yes. It'll take them some time to organize the trip, maybe as long as a month. If you decide you can't go through with it, you just let me know and we'll cancel. But if you can give me a definite yes, I can start working up some programs with the rest of the band. 'The Dizzy Dillon Band with Dessie Heavener.' How do you like the sound of that?"

"It sounds fine, Diz. I promise, I'll think it over and I'll let you know as soon as I come to some kind of decision. Meanwhile, I'm going to go home. There are some people down there I haven't seen in a long, long time."

Paul met my train in Columbia. I fell weeping into his arms. "Oh, Paul, I feel like such a dope!"

"It feels so good to hold you again," he murmured. "I'm glad you're home, Dessie. This is where you belong."

I drew away from him. "No, this is just a rest stop between broken hearts. I don't know how long I'll be staying, but it won't be forever. I made up my mind about that a long time ago."

He drove me back to Munford. When he pulled up in front of the old house on Creek Avenue, I didn't get out of the car. I just sat there with my mouth wide open. The neighborhood disgrace now fairly sparkled with fresh, white paint. The loose boards on the front steps and the porch floor had been repaired, the sagging shutters had been reattached and painted a rich, dark green, and the new porch swing even had cushions on the seat. The lawn and flowerbeds, formerly so weed-choked and overgrown, were trim and neat. A sleek blue Chevrolet sedan was parked out front. It had long running boards, a broad visor over the windshield, and plenty of chrome.

"Whatever happened to wartime austerity?" I said.

"War?" Paul climbed out and limped around to open my door. "Ayleen's never heard of it. Well, I'd better get back to the office. The way these people work me on vacations, you'd think they didn't have anybody clerking for them the rest of the time. I'll be glad when I finish up that law degree." He gave me a brotherly kiss on the cheek and patted my shoulder. "Come over any night after five-thirty. I can't wait to play for you again."

Ayleen answered my knock and ushered me into the front parlor. She was holding Gray by the hand. In my absence, he had grown into a miniature person. Nearly two years old now, he had a full head of curly blond hair, sharp blue eyes—Howard eyes—and a way of thrusting his lower jaw forward into a truculent pout. He took one look at me and cowered behind Ayleen's skirts.

She laughed. "See, he doesn't even know you. He doesn't much take to strangers."

I said firmly, "I am not a stranger, I am his mother. Nothing you say can change that simple biological fact. Gray?" I squatted down and opened the snaps on my suitcase. "Look, I brought you something." I produced a toy fire engine. It was nearly as big as a shoe box, and had ladders that moved up and down, doors that opened, miniature firemen, and even a hose that squirted water when you squeezed a small rubber bulb. "Isn't it pretty?"

I rolled it around the floor in front of him and made siren sounds in my throat. He edged closer. When he stooped over to grab the truck, I put my arms around him and hugged him tight. He screamed. Ayleen looked smug.

"See?" she said. "He hasn't the slightest notion who you are. Honestly, Dessie, honey, you can't expect a miracle after all this time. After all, he was only eight months old when you aban—"

I stood up, still holding the squalling two-year-old in my arms. "I did not abandon him. I left him with people I thought I could trust to take care of him, and I left in order to make a decent living for us both. I see you haven't failed to take advantage of my good fortune. And I don't begrudge you any of this, Ayleen. But it was my hard work that paid for that new sofa and this carpet and this wallpaper and those curtains over there, and we both know it. And like it or not, Gray is my son, and I can take him away from here quicker than a lightning bolt and you couldn't do one thing to stop me."

That scared her. "Now, Dessie, honey, you don't need to get so fired up. I was only tellin' the truth as I saw it. Come on in and have a cup of coffee and some pie. Clara Mae's been cookin' up a storm ever since we heard you were comin' home."

Home. Ayleen had replaced the old rugs with new moss green carpeting that ran smoothly into every crack and corner and surged up the stairs like some rampantly spreading fungus. Every last stick of my mother's furniture was gone; even the old grand piano had been replaced by a trim spinet with a walnut case.

Back in the kitchen, Clara Mae's antiquated coal-and-propane cookstove had gone the way of the piano. A modern electric range stood in its place, beside the shining new refrigerator that replaced the icebox. The kitchen itself looked like an illustration in a Marvel Soap ad, with yellow flowered wallpaper, new linoleum, and freshly painted woodwork.

I knew that my contributions to the household had wrought all these changes. I wasn't sorry. I wanted Gray to grow up in comfortable surroundings, and I was glad he wouldn't have to experience the same poverty and dusty clutter and dark neglect I had known when I was his age. Still, I felt I was visiting a stranger's house instead of the place I had known as home since I was three years old.

Clara Mae fixed all my favorites for supper that night, greens served in bowls with corn sticks and plenty of pot liquor, candied sweet potatoes, baked ham, and lemon meringue pie. She announced proudly that she wouldn't tolerate no rationin' in that house while I was there. She was happy as a clam in her new kitchen, and she ruled it like a queen. Ayleen seldom set foot in there anymore. She was generally too busy entertaining her lady friends in the front room.

After dinner, I announced that I had been offered a chance to go overseas with the band. My father sniffed and said he didn't

118

know what this country was coming to when hardworking taxpayers were shelling out good money to send low-class entertainers abroad. Ayleen simpered and said, "Well, if that's what you really want to do, Dessie, honey, you should certainly go ahead."

I said, "I won't be paid very much while I'm on this tour, although I'll be getting some wonderful publicity. You may have to slow down on your decorating a little until I get back, Ayleen."

Ayleen put her back up at that, but she kept her mouth shut.

Clara Mae was less tolerant. When we were alone in the kitchen, she exploded. "You mean to say you would even think about goin' over there where they's fightin', just to sing songs for them soldiers? I declare, girl, you just as crazy as you ever was. It's bad enough you runnin' off to New York and all them northern cities, but now you want to go to places I can't even say the names of and get yo'self killed."

"I haven't really made up my mind yet, Clara Mae—"

But she kept on. "And you think old Clara Mae's gonna wait here wond'rin' if you's alive or if you's dead. Well, I don't like this, Miz Dessie. I don't like it at all. Your place is with your chile," she shook her dish towel at me, "instead of travelin' around like you had no son at all. Ain't you thought about him? I ain't never seen nobody do their motherin' like you."

"Now, you listen to me, Clara Mae," I said evenly. "I intend to make a home for Gray just as soon as I can, but that takes money and I can't get money if I don't work. Besides, the publicity will be good for my career, and I'll feel like I'm doing something worthwhile."

I passed my hand over my eyes. I still had a lot of memories of King to erase.

"I also have some responsibility to the members of the band. If I don't agree to this tour, the USO will find some other band and we'll all be out of a job." To my surprise and embarrassment, I started to cry.

Paul must have mentioned my ruptured relationship with King to Clara Mae. Or maybe she just knew. She knelt down and put her arms around me. "No man's worth tearin' yo'self up about, chile," she said. "He was no good from the start, only you was too blinded by love to see it. Ain't no cause for shame."

"I did love him, Clara Mae," I sobbed. "I really loved him. Blair was sweet to me, and I was real broken up when he was hurt, but I didn't feel this way. I've never felt like this before. Like something in me has died."

"I know," Clara Mae sighed. "I know what that's like."

I wiped my eyes with a corner of her dish towel. "Poor Blair," I sighed. 'He didn't deserve a wife like me. I'll take Gray over to the parsonage tomorrow and pay him a visit."

Clara Mae pulled back. "Ain't nobody told you? Miz Howard and Mr. Blair, they livin' up at the big house again. Mr. Bram, he come back last spring with his pockets full of money and tried to buy that place away from Mr. Thomas."

My heart quickened. "Bram did? You mean he owns Woodlands again?"

Clara Mae nodded. "It took him a while, but he got it back. Mr. Thomas, he said he would never sell. He said a young scamp like Mr. Bram would live in Woodlands over his dead body. I got all this news from Sylvester—he's still workin' up there. Anyway, Sylvester said that Mr. Bram just nodded his head real slow-like and went away without sayin' one more word. Then a little while later, that daughter of theirs, that Jean-Ellen, she disappeared for a whole month, and when she came back, she was Mrs. Bram Howard. Seems he was courtin' her on the sly, and they eloped together. Well, Mr. Thomas, he was fit to be tied, but he couldn't do much about it. That girl has a mind of her own."

So Bram had worked his not-so-subtle magic on prim, prissy Jean-Ellen Thomas just to get Woodlands back, and she had fallen for it. At least I wasn't the only gullible female in the world. I almost felt sorry for her, and at the same time I envied her. I knew what it was like to be swept off your feet by a handsome man with a smooth line and knowing hands.

"Miz Howard, she's just as pleased as punch to be back home. Mr. Thomas was so disgusted that he moved out and sold the place to his son-in-law. Those Thomases never had no class anyway. Ever'body knows Mr. Thomas's daddy farmed cotton and sent his boy to school without shoes on his feet."

"That means Bram is up at Woodlands now?"

Clara Mae chuckled. "No, ma'am, he ain't. One month after the weddin', he joined up with the army and went over to Europe to fight."

Jean-Ellen's romance had been short-lived. I supposed I could count myself lucky that I had had longer than that before King's love withered. Nearly a year.

That same afternoon, I sent Dizzy a telegram:

> USO TOUR OK. SIGN ME ON.

After two days, I was itching to get out of Munford, but I forced myself to stay for a week. I needed to spend a little more time with Gray. Ayleen instructed him to call me Mama, but he wouldn't do it. Ayleen was his mama now, wasn't she? If I was Mama, what should he call her? As a result, neither of us got the title.

Ayleen and my father both declared that Gray was a handful, badly behaved, and impossible to discipline. When he didn't get what he wanted, he threw tantrums; screaming, kicking, wailing tantrums. Those displays of temper communicated something to me: My son was not happy in that house. I wished I could find a way to commiserate with him, to tell him that I had felt that way for nearly ten of his lifetimes.

Poor Gray. If he soiled his pants or dirtied his clothes playing, Ayleen scolded him. If he was noisy and rambunctious and ran screaming through the house, she hollered at him. If he spilled his milk or made a mess anywhere, she slapped his hands and told him to be more careful. Heaven help him if he broke one of her precious knickknacks. Clara Mae was kind to Gray, of course, as she had been to me, but her love was scheduled, part-time, not available evenings or Saturday afternoons. My father treated Gray just as he had treated me, with resentful neglect.

During that week, I took over Ayleen's maternal duties. My relationship with Gray was awkward at first, charged with suspicion and hostility on both sides. I was not an imaginative playmate, and his screaming tantrums upset me so badly that I couldn't eat Clara Mae's cooking. Nevertheless, I stuck with it. I was not going to let Ayleen tell her friends that after having been away for more than a year, I wouldn't spend time with my child. Every evening, I bathed Gray and dressed him in a clean sleeper suit, and held him in my lap while I sang blues songs and spirituals to him. Sometimes I took him next door and let Paul play for him while I sang. After Gray fell asleep in my arms, I brought him back home and put him in his crib and tucked him in. One night as I was laying him down, he put his arms around my neck and kissed my cheek. Tenderness surged through me. I kissed him back.

By the end of my visit, Gray was tolerating me pretty well.

On the morning of my departure, he threw a wild tantrum and called out to me as I was leaving, "Mama! Mama! No!"

I hated myself for abandoning him yet again, but I had no choice. I was still struggling to make my voice heard and my face known. I was still reaching for something that a conventional home life couldn't give me. I still wanted to be a singer more than I wanted to be a mother.

"I'm sorry, Gray," I murmured as I attempted to give him one last hug. "I'm sorry, honey. I'll be home just as soon as I can."

He didn't hear me. He was crying too loudly.

Paul drove me to the station. I sobbed the whole way. "I feel like my heart is being ripped in half. I didn't realize how much I loved my baby. But I do love him. I do! Oh, why don't I come to my senses and give up all this foolishness and stay home and be a decent mother to him?"

"Maybe you don't want to, Dess."

"You're right, I don't. But that's no excuse. Mothering's more important than singing, isn't it? At least to the child it is. My mother neglected me something awful, and I hated her for it, but here I am, doing the same thing to Gray. This is going to sound crazy, but sometimes, when I'm on stage singing for people, I forget I even have a son."

"Gray will be all right," Paul said. "Kids are tougher than we think."

I mopped my eyes and drew a long, shuddering breath. "Why didn't you tell me about Bram Howard coming back?"

He shrugged. "Guess I forgot."

Something clicked. Paul was still jealous, still resentful that I had married a Howard.

"Did you go up to see Blair?" he asked.

"No. I didn't want to run into Jean-Ellen. I might have been tempted to slap her smug little face." We both laughed. "I bumped into Mrs. Howard in town the other day. She says Blair's about the same, still has his good days and his bad days."

Mrs. Howard had no idea where Bram was stationed. The few letters she had received from him had been heavily censored.

At the station, Paul and I embraced and promised to write to each other more often. Then I picked up my suitcase and joined the soldiers who were traveling north.

9

THE JEEP LURCHED INTO A CRATER IN THE ROAD. I OPENED MY eyes. I had fallen asleep with my head on Adam Foster's shoulder. I must have been resting in that position for several hours, dead weight, but he had never made the slightest move to disturb me.

"This sure doesn't look like South Carolina," I yawned.

"Oklahoma, either."

We were passing through the bleakest countryside I had ever seen. The hillsides were scorched, the trees seared and stripped bare of leaves, the roads, cottages, and fields scarred and mutilated by the fighting.

For weeks, our USO band had been following General Mark Clark's Fifth Army up from Naples as they pushed the Italian front north toward Rome, scrapping and fighting over each acre of ground they wrested from the Germans. We slept in deserted huts, empty churches, or canvas pup tents—even under our own trucks. Some of our men were able to sleep through the shelling bombardments that the Germans unleashed at night. I wasn't so lucky. I spent many nights sitting bolt upright, waiting for dawn to break through the darkness and for the racket to stop. After we got under way in the morning, I was finally able to relax. The other band members complained of back-wrenching bumps, ruts, and jolts, but I slept peacefully in the jeep and arrived at our destination feeling rested and ready to perform.

The Dizzy Dillon Band had arrived in England in November, 1943. After a couple of tense weeks in London during the buzz-bomb attacks, the USO dispatched us to air bases and army camps all over England. We had been eager to get closer to the action, to entertain the men at the front, but the Army kept us in England for three months. Finally, in mid-February, we found ourselves on a transport plane to southern Italy—eight musicians plus Dizzy and me: Adam Foster on drums; Byron Fraser on tenor and alto sax; Buddy Best on hot alto sax and clarinet; Jo Jo Jonas on valve trumpet and cornet; Kelly Coates now playing hot trumpet; Wee Geordie Douglas on guitar. White Willie Wilson, our trombonist, was the old man of the group, and Peanut Tasker, our bass player, was the youngest.

We dressed as the soldiers did, in fatigues, heavy boots, and helmets. Like them, we ate K-rations. Our theater was whereever we happened to set up our instruments in front of a bunch of young, war-weary faces. We performed on tailgates, tabletops, barn doors, and packing crates. Once I even sang perched precariously on the massive treads of a tank. We took any elevated surface we could find and turned it into a stage.

By the end of May 1944, we were seasoned entertainers on the war circuit. As soon as we halted and unpacked our gear, I changed into one of the two gold-sequined gowns I had brought for the trip—they were as tough as tin cans and about as wrinkleproof. Frequent applications of peroxide kept my hair a dazzling white-gold, and I always applied plenty of the reddest lipstick I could find before facing my audience. I received standing ovations before I even opened my mouth.

We performed all the old standards, plus King Kingsley's greatest hits and anything else our listeners asked for. Frequently Byron Fraser and Adam Foster sparked jam sessions with frustrated musicians from the audience. They blew harmonicas, pounded on truck fenders, or just clapped their hands. We sang hymns, blues, and folk ballads that reminded all of us—soldiers and civilians—of home. When I sang "The Midnight Special" one afternoon, five rusty southern voices joined in with mine.

> Yonder come Miss Rosie,
> How'n the world did you know?
> I could tell her by her apron,
> And the dress she wo'.
> Umbrella on her shoulder,
> Piece of paper in her hand.
> Gonna ask the Captain,
> Turn loose her man.
>
> Let the midnight special
> Shine its light on me.

Let the midnight special
Shine its devil of a light on me.

I grumbled about the hardships and inconveniences I had to endure, but I was aware that I was having an easy time compared to the men who were doing the fighting ahead of us. And the warm reception we got made it all worthwhile. None of us would have traded one hour of those shows for an entire week at Roseland.

I felt especially proud of Dizzy Dillon, who had put his performing career on the shelf years ago in order to become a manager. Now he dusted off jokes that wouldn't have made a six-year-old smile back in the States, and the soldiers loved them. Mentions of Spam always got a laugh—and a chorus of raspberries. For some mysterious reason, the word *Brooklyn* evoked laughter, too. Dizzy would ask a kid where he was from. The kid would say Wheeling, West Virginia, or some such place. Dizzy would look amazed. "Brooklyn?" he would say. "No kidding? I'm from Brooklyn, too!" and our listeners would split their sides.

During those long sleepless nights, I often thought about King Kingsley. Why had I been so infatuated with him? Did I really think I was so different from those dozens of women who had shared his bed before me, and who would come after me? My marriage to Blair and my friendship with Paul had led me to expect different treatment from men. I knew now that King was a royal cad, but my heart still pounded when I recalled the pressure of his arms around me.

"Where are we going?" I asked Adam.

"You wouldn't know if you heard it. All these little towns around here have the same name. Santa Something. Santa this and Santa that. Santa Claus and Santa Monica."

"I want a bath. I should say, I desperately need one."

"I'll say you do." He sniffed the air in my vicinity and wrinkled his nose. "All right, you can have the bucket first. Hear that, boys?"

At six o'clock that evening, we pulled into the remains of what had once been a pretty little mountain town called Villa d'Este. Half the yellow stuccoed houses with their red-tiled roofs had been smashed to dust by German and Allied artillery. The nearby olive and citrus groves had been mangled by fighting on the ground and bombing from the air. The surrounding fields and roads were churned up as well. We parked in the central plaza near a fountain that still trickled water out of lions' heads on four sides of a square pillar. By some miracle, the fountain and the squat little church at the far end of the square had been spared in the shelling.

"Pick out a spot and start setting up," Dizzy told us. "I'll find the CO and tell him we're here. Maybe we'll be able to get some sleep tonight. Damn those Frenchmen."

The Fifth Army was only half American. The rest of the troops were British, French—including companies of Algerians and Moroccans—South African, and Brazilian. The French soldiers were known for the speed with which they could capture enemy-held territory, but also for their lack of thoroughness in cleaning out nests of Germans.

The previous evening, our show had been postponed while marksmen flushed enemy snipers from the trees. Only one German was taken alive and he was executed on the spot. After the noise from the shots had died away, we started the show.

I tried not to dwell on the horrors I had seen. I hadn't come to Europe to make judgments about the war and the way it was being fought. I was there to entertain the troops. When we played in the field hospitals, the sight of rows and rows of wounded and dying men filled me with pity, but I kept on smiling and I kept on singing, even while tears rolled down my cheeks.

On the road, we passed a constant stream of refugees who had lost everything they possessed. Lots of children with no fathers, no mothers. They were like my own son, Gray. Orphans. But at least Gray had a roof over his head and plenty to eat.

Our band had acquired a mascot, a cute black-eyed little con-artist named Carlo. Self-appointed guardian of our musical instruments and suitcases, he was invaluable on those occasions when local urchins showed too much interest in what we were carrying. Carlo was eight or nine and he had been fending for himself for three years. Now he was growing fat on K-rations and candy bars. He had proposed marriage to me, too. I had accepted, provided he was willing to wait ten years.

We piled out of our two jeeps. Carlo jumped down from the comfortable seat he had annexed that morning and began to unload our supplies. Jo Jo Jonas and Byron Fraser found a shady place to sit and lit up cigarettes. Adam Foster set off to scout the area for a stage. The other guys unpacked their instruments and started to jam softly in the shade of the old church.

"Geez." As Kelly Coates glanced over the wall behind him, he let out a terrible blat on his trumpet. "This place is full of stiffs. We're playing for a bunch of stiffs."

"It wouldn't be the first time," Wee Geordie said with a grim laugh. "But they were never as stiff as this."

The little cemetery behind the church had been churned up by an exploding shell. Coffins lay scattered upon the ground, some with bleached naked bones protruding. Gravestones listed. Some ancient family vaults had been smashed to powder.

"Gee, war is hell," Buddy Best sighed. He switched his gaze to the other side of the square. "What's going on over there?"

Dizzy and Adam were standing beside a jeep, arguing with a soldier. I went over to investigate. The soldier, a second lieutenant, turned to me.

"The CO won't let you folks play here, ma'am. He says they've been having some trouble with enemy planes on their way back from raids on Anzio, and he doesn't want any large assemblies."

"No large assemblies!" Never before had anyone objected to our presence. Most commanding officers were delighted to give their men a little reprieve from the boredom and the bloodshed.

"Are you Miss Heavener, ma'am?" the lieutenant tipped me a salute as I nodded. "The major extends warmest regards. He has always been a fan of yours, and he would appreciate the opportunity to meet with you. The major also suggests that he might be able to work out a schedule for short performances in the field hospital and at other scattered locations."

"We'd better talk to him," Dizzy said. "We don't want to risk putting on any shows if it means getting blown to bits."

"I'll go." I took off my helmet and fluffed out my hair. "If this major is such a big fan of mine, he probably wants my autograph. Why don't you find a place in the shade, Dizzy, and take a rest?"

"You're sure you don't mind going alone?"

I laughed. "The major wants to talk business, Dizzy. He's not going to ravish me. Okay, Lieutenant, where to?"

Shadows were lengthening as we approached Command Headquarters, a rambling villa that had once been a serene and gracious residence. Like the other buildings in the valley, it had taken a beating during the recent battles. Windows on the side toward us were blank and staring, empty of glass. Blankets thrown over their sills gave them a look of running sores, blind eyes weeping dark tears. The stuccoed exterior was the color of a dirty sunset, orange faded to pink, scored with cracks and pocked with bullet holes.

As the lieutenant and I entered the open courtyard and skirted around a dried up fountain, we were assailed by a chorus of voices: children laughing and crying, women screaming in Italian at the tops of their lungs.

"Refugees," the lieutenant explained. "Both of those projecting wings are full of women and kids. They didn't have anyplace else to go, and since we're only using the central part of the house, the major let them move in. They don't cause us any trouble."

The main door to the villa had been torn off its hinges. It formed a bridge across a muddy sinkhole at the bottom of the steps. We passed through the portal and crossed a vast, vaulted hallway, where our footsteps echoed hollowly on the stained marble floors. The lieutenant tapped at a door that was taller than my father's whole house in Munford and we went in.

The only furnishings that remained in the drawing room were an inlaid table—whose missing leg had been replaced by a packing crate—and a couple of tattered armchairs with high backs. Faded patches on the stained damask-covered walls suggested that several large paintings and tapestries had once hung there. I wondered whether they had been looted by the Germans or by the liberators, or if the owners of the house had stripped it bare and hidden everything away in the caves in the hills while they awaited an end to this disruption in their lives.

The major was studying a report when we came in. He worked by light from a kerosene lantern at his elbow. After he had initialed every page and screwed the top back on his fountain pen, he looked up and smiled.

"Hello, Dessie. Welcome to Villa d'Este."

"Bram!"

Bram nodded to my companion. "Thanks, Lieutenant. That'll be all."

"Yessir." The lieutenant snapped a salute and departed.

Bram invited me to sit. I did so, conscious of my soiled fatigues and heavy shoes. He offered me a cigarette, took one himself, and lit both with his stainless steel Zippo.

"How shall we begin this conversation? Long time, no see?

That's true, it has been a long time. You're looking well? That is an understatement, but still appropriate. How about, Are you enjoying the war?"

I finally found my voice. "What . . . what are you doing here?"

He laughed. "That's one I missed. But surely that's obvious, too? I am exactly what you see, an officer of the U.S. Army doing his duty, which consists more of writing reports than fighting these days. I know what you're doing here. I did everything I could, short of murder and blackmail—no, I even did a little of that—to get my unit scheduled for your tour. They wanted to send you over to Q division, thirty miles away from here."

"But the lieutenant says you won't let us perform."

"Unfortunately, this valley comes right under the bellies of the German bombers at night. They know we're here, and they know we have a lot of wounded men in our hospital, which is conspicuously marked by a red cross on the roof, but that seems to make us that much more inviting as a target. Still, I've made up an itinerary for tomorrow—if you don't mind taking your act to foxholes and dugouts. My men are pretty widely scattered."

"No, I don't mind. We've done it before. I usually take Wee Geordie Douglas with me—he plays the guitar—and we do a pared-down version of the full show."

"You sound like a hardened veteran."

"I suppose I am. The people at home didn't tell me you were in Italy."

"They probably don't know. So, you've been home. Did you see Blair?"

I shook my head. "I wanted to, but not with Jean-Ellen standing guard at the gates. So, you're a married man now."

He grinned. "Shocking what some men will do for a few acres of trees and a rundown shack. I gather you don't approve of my new wife?"

"It's not my business to approve or disapprove of what you do." Not seeing an ashtray, I followed my host's example and crushed out the butt of my cigarette with my shoe. The floor was littered with spent cigarette butts.

"You're angry with me."

"No. Oh, no. I guess I'm just tired." I was angry with myself for getting tongue-tied in front of him. I had met officers before, plenty of them. I had dined with Generals Eisenhower and Clark in London, and had sung for them afterward. But neither of those two gentlemen had the power that Bram had to intimidate me. The memory of the kisses he had stolen from me flamed up from the ashes of my past. I did care about his marriage, and I couldn't hide it.

"You're even more beautiful than I remember, Dessie."

I couldn't stop a blush from rising to my cheeks, so I laughed to distract his attention from it. "You should see me in gold lamé, with high-heeled shoes and long black gloves and half a ton of genuine rhinestone jewelry. I believe in giving an audience its money's worth."

"I'll bet you do. I'll bet you're sensational. Blair would have been proud of you."

I lowered my head. "I like to think so."

I became aware of a humming noise outside the villa. It grew louder and louder until it was right over our heads. I looked up at the ceiling, as if my gaze could penetrate the layers of stucco, stone, and wood. Then I heard something I had heard only once before, in London, seconds before an entire city block disappeared from the map: a piercing whistle followed by a moment of dead silence. Bram and I hit the floor simultaneously.

Outside, a brilliant flash illuminated the weed-choked courtyard. The earth trembled. I waited for the mighty explosion that would send us all to kingdom come, but it never happened.

Bram lifted me to my feet. "Delayed action fuse," he said. "It could blow any second. Get out of this house and run as fast and as far as you can. Move!"

I raced out into the hall. Bram paused just long enough to grab the lantern from his desk, then he followed me. Screaming women and children poured through the front door from the courtyard. Bram ordered them to clear out at once. He explained in pretty fair Italian that a bomb had fallen nearby, and although it had failed to detonate on impact, it could go off at any time. *"Pericoloso!"* he shouted and waved his arms. "Danger! Clear out, *presto*! *Molto presto*!"

He pushed me after the others, but he did not follow us. Turning, I saw him cross to the space below the grand staircase and jerk open a door. *"Bambini!"* he shouted. *"Bambini!"* Failing to hear a response, he ducked through the doorway and vanished.

Bambini. Why would children be billeted in the basement of his headquarters? Perhaps they were sick, or injured. An image of my own baby, my little Gray, flashed across my eyes.

Without another thought, I ran back into the villa and followed Bram through the door. I found myself heading down a flight of steep stone stairs. Bram had vanished, but I could still see the dim glow from his lantern. The corridor at the bottom of the stairs twisted sharply to the right. As I rounded the turn, I ran smack into a German officer who was just emerging from a cell, his hands held high at shoulder level. Behind him, Bram held a pistol in one hand. The lantern hung from a hook just outside the open door.

"Dessie," Bram warned, "get back!"

But the German was quicker than I. Grabbing my arms, he whirled me around and threw me into Bram. We staggered together and fell backward into the cell. Bram's pistol went off within inches of my ear. Cursing, Bram scrambled to his feet and ran after the escaping prisoner. No sooner had he left the cell than an explosion rocked the house. The closeness of the pistol shot had deafened me temporarily, and I had an eerie moment when the floor beneath me tilted and rocked and I heard absolutely nothing.

Bram managed to grab the lantern before an avalanche of stone hit the door and slammed it shut, then filled the corridor outside the cell. He hurled himself at me and dragged me to the farthest corner of the room, where we cowered against the shuddering wall and listened to the sounds of the world collapsing over our heads. My nostrils were filled with the smell of gunpowder and rock dust.

I began to tremble. "Dead and buried," I thought, "before my twentieth birthday."

My hearing returned gradually. I listened hard for the crackle of flames, but I heard only stones and timbers settling in on themselves. The air was thick with stone particles as fine as dust but as gritty as sand.

"Are we still alive?" I said in a small voice.

Bram stood up, coughing and clearing his throat. "So far." He brushed himself off. "If the section of flooring above our heads holds, we should be all right."

I was covered with dust, but miraculously I was still in one piece. I shook myself like a dog coming out of a puddle. "How long do we have until our air runs out?"

Holding the lantern high, Bram made a careful inspection of the perimeter of the cell. "See that hole up there?" He raised the lantern to reveal a small rectangular opening, just under the ceiling. "Part of the ventilation system down here. All the cellar rooms have these openings instead of windows. The one at the farthest end has a shaft leading straight up through the rock. Comes out on the side of the hill someplace. It's less than a foot wide. Not big enough to squeeze through."

"Oh, my God." As the shock wore off, realization set in. "We're trapped! They'll never find us!"

"We don't know how badly the house is damaged. There's probably a mountain of rubble on top of us. When we don't turn up outside, they'll start looking for us. Meanwhile," he waved the lantern toward a mattress in the corner, "we have Colonel van Hessen's two blankets, a jar of water, and a chamber pot. If we're careful with the water, we can last several days."

"Why were you calling for children?" I asked him.

"Children?" He looked puzzled.

"*Bambini.* I heard you. You opened the door at the top of the stairs and yelled, '*Bambini*!' "

Bram sighed. "I was calling Private Pandini. Guarding the colonel was his responsibility. He was probably upstairs flirting with the girls. He likes to try out his Brooklyn-style Italian on them. I hope he got out in time."

"Colonel van Hessen—he was your prisoner?"

Bram nodded. " I had instructions to hang on to him until a couple of officers from Fifth Army Headquarters could interrogate him. We caught him on one of those mountain roads, trying to pump up a flat tire on his staff car. His driver and his aide-de-camp had already headed for the hills. I guess the colonel wasn't much of a walker."

Bram rammed his shoulder against the door of the cell. It didn't budge. After a few more attempts, he gave up and returned to his exploration of the cell. It wasn't large, only about twelve feet by ten feet. The U.S. Army had supplied its prisoner with a London *Times* dated two weeks previously, a tin cup for drinking, a tin plate smeared with an oily residue that smelled of garlic, and two rough woolen blankets with a straw-filled mattress.

"I suppose I could fashion a tool out of the plate and tunnel out of here." Bram probed a crack in the wall with his fingertips. "Considering the thickness of the foundation walls, it should take me no more than a year." He sat against the opposite wall. "This lantern is the only light we have," he said. "I suggest we turn it off to conserve fuel. No way can any light from here penetrate to the outside. And by now, it's too dark for anyone to be looking for us. They'll have to wait until morning. We might as well do the same."

I hugged myself. "There must be a way out of here. There must be!"

"This place was a monastery back in the thirteenth century," Bram said. "These rooms were designed as cells for prisoners of the Inquisition. Believe me, the only way out is the way we came in, and that's blocked."

He turned down the wick in the lantern. I settled down on the bed of straw. Dense, dark silence closed around us like the heat on a South Carolina August afternoon. I wanted to sleep, but my heart was beating double time.

Something small and furry skittered across my foot. I leaped up shrieking.

"A rat! A rat ran over me!"

"You imagined it," Bram said. "It was probably a cobweb, or maybe a cricket."

We argued about whether or not he should light the lantern. "Damn you," I said, "I'm coming over there to light it myself."

"Don't bother. When we've used up all the kerosene in the lantern and all the fluid in my lighter and burned up all the straw in your mattress, we can sit in the dark until they dig us out of here." He snapped his cigarette lighter and held the flame to the blackened wick, then he replaced the chimney.

In the corner, light gleamed on a pair of tiny red eyes.

"See! I told you it was a rat!"

"If that's a rat, then I'm a water buffalo," Bram said with a laugh. "It's just a mouse."

"I don't care what it is, I don't want it running over me feet." Somewhat cautiously, I sat on the bed again. I shivered. "God, it's freezing down here. Hey! Hey, somebody! Anybody! We're down in the cellar! Get us out of here!" The stones returned the echo of my voice. "That's not a bad effect," I mused. "Maybe I'll stage my next concert in a mausoleum—if I ever get out of here."

After a while, I started to hum, producing random notes that formed themselves into an abstract little tune. The sound of my voice comforted me, and I started to sing softly:

> Although I may be far away,
> Please believe me when I say

> That it won't be very long before
> I'm coming home to you.

I sang two verses of "Believe Me" and the refrain. Bram said, "God, that's beautiful. You're a taste of home, Dessie."

"Why did you want me to come here?" I asked. "Just to entertain your men?"

"No. Actually, I had in mind something like this—only not quite so dramatic. Some time alone, to talk over old times. I've missed you, Dessie."

I fingered a straw that poked through the ticking. "Everywhere we sang, I kept hoping I'd see you. I looked for you. I couldn't stop myself. I looked for your face when I sang in hospitals, and I looked for your name on casualty lists. I prayed I wouldn't find it. And I prayed I would. I tried to get one of my officer friends to look up your records so I would know where you were and if you were all right. But he couldn't find any Bram Howards and the Abraham Howards he found were from New England."

"My name is Charles Abraham, like my father," Bram said. "There must be a couple of hundred Charles Howards in the armed forces. Why were you looking for me, Dessie?"

"I don't know." I shrugged. "You were always so crazy. The kind of person who took risks. I was afraid that you'd take one risk too many and then—"

And then I'd lose you. I didn't say the words. I couldn't.

"Dessie?" He stood up slowly.

I shook my head. "No, Bram. Please. My heart is still so battered and bruised that I'm amazed it can still pump."

"You've been hurt."

I nodded. "I should have known better, but I didn't. I traded my love for a career as a singer. I told myself that I'd made a good bargain. I guess I fell in love with him so that I wouldn't have to face up to what I had really done. Please, I . . . I'd rather you didn't come any closer." Dropping my head onto my drawn-up knees, I sang a song I had learned from Clara Mae:

> Go 'way from my window,
> Go 'way from my door,
> Go 'way from my bedside,
> Don't you tease me no more.

Come back in the springtime,
Come back in the fall,
And bring me more money
Than we both can haul.

I don't know how long I sat there trying to squeeze the song past the lump in my throat. I heard myself repeating the same line over and over again, like a broken record: "Go 'way from my bedside, don't you tease me no more." The child Dessie had not understood the meaning that lay behind those simple words, the sadness and heartache and longing. But the woman Dessie knew. She was living that song and every other blues song and love song and sad song she had ever heard.

Bram knelt in front of me. Placing his hands alongside my face, he forced me to look at him. "Dessie," he whispered.

"I love you!" I blurted. "I've been in love with you forever, it seems. I tried not to, but I couldn't help myself. I didn't want to hurt Blair. But that didn't change the way I felt." Tears coursed down my cheeks.

Leaning forward, Bram kissed them away. "I know." He settled down beside me and enfolded me in his arms. I pressed myself against him. "We're all alone. We can't hurt anybody. Just the two of us—"

"We might die here."

"Are you scared?"

"No. I would rather die here with you right now than be anywhere else in the world. I feel . . . I feel like I've come home."

"Yes, I feel that way, too."

We were in no hurry. We had a long night ahead of us, a night that could last for the rest of our lives.

A black shadow danced over me, its movements punctuated by a sharp drumming sound. I sat up and looked around. The lantern was burning brightly, creating a false daylight in that dark hole. In the corner farthest from the door, Bram, totally naked, was jabbing at the ceiling with a spar he had torn from the door frame. A shower of fine dust and pebbles rained down on him.

Then I heard the answering thumps above us, in the same area where Bram was pounding. Satisfied, Bram laid his spar aside and wiped his face with his uniform blouse. The sounds over our heads continued.

"They know we're here," he said. "They'll break through the floor right about here. It shouldn't take them long, maybe three or four hours." He grinned at me. "Can you think of any innovative ways to pass the time?"

"None that we didn't try last night."

"Then we'll just have to perform an encore."

Just as the flickering lantern was sucking and burning the last drops of fuel, the roof caved in and a shaft of daylight pierced the haze of dust in the cell.

"Major," a voice called, "are you all right?"

"I'm fine." Bram tucked his shirt into his trousers while I laced up my boots. "Miss Heavener is with me. She's okay, too."

Two men descended through the opening, bringing down a new avalanche of dust and chips of stone. One of them hoisted me up on his shoulder. Strong arms reached down and pulled me up.

Dizzy Dillon and Adam Foster and the boys were waiting, and behind them, a whole mob of cheering soldiers and villagers. The sun was riding high in a cloudless sea of blue. I looked around. The villa had dissolved into a heap of rubble. Only one wall remained standing, and within it a single stuccoed chimney that pointed like an accusing finger to the sky.

Dizzy told me that twenty people had been killed in the raid, and another thirty-five injured, mostly women and children who had been near the courtyard when the bomb exploded. The soldiers had found van Hessen's body when they were digging for us.

"You can thank Carlo for finding you," Dizzy said. "He was poking around this morning looking for some sign of you and he heard the major's signal. How was it down there?"

I shook the dust out of my hair. "I've stayed in worse places. Well, what are you all standing around for? We have a show to do."

In the little room that had been the church's sacristy, I made up my face and changed into my work clothes: gold-sequined gown, six-inch high heels, long black gloves, and plenty of rhinestones and glitter. When Carlo saw me, he whistled and kissed his fingertips to me.

"Bellissima, signorina," he said. *"Bellississima!"*

"I love you, too, honey." I kissed the top of his head. "Tell Signor Dizzy that I'm ready. *Presto*, Okay?"

"Sì, *presto*." He scampered out. In a minute, Dizzy was knocking at the door.

"All set," he said. "I've got 'em warmed up. Go get 'em, tiger."

"Go gettum, Teegray," Carlo echoed from Dizzy's shadow.

Geordie could play anything on his guitar, even Chopin's crashing chords in "Paradise." Together, we made good music, and because we were only two, we were more mobile than the whole gang would have been.

In the hospital, I sang a special song for each wounded man. First I asked him where he was from and if he had a favorite song I might know. Then, with Geordie accompanying me, I sang it just for him. I sang a song for each of the medics, too, before Geordie and I finished off with "Believe Me." By the time we left, I had collected five proposals of marriage and ten addresses back home in case I was ever in the neighborhood and wanted to drop in for a meal.

Next, we headed out to a bivouac on the edge of town to which the patrols would report when they had finished combing the hillsides for stray Germans. I sang and Dizzy told jokes, and any time a new man arrived back at camp, we did a little more. After that we tracked down the men who were removing or detonating mines on the surrounding roads and we performed for them. Back in town, I sought out the company's chaplain and sang "Rock of Ages" for him. I did "Stagger Lee" for the cook, who had grown up in Memphis not far from Beale Street. In early evening, I found the members of Major Howard's staff, minus the Major, holed up in what had once been a tavern. The girl who was waiting on them looked fairly grim. Geordie and I did "Have Banana" and "Mairsey Doats," before launching into a couple of romantic ballads. By the time we left, the men were smiling and the grim tavern girl was flirting with them.

Geordie reminded me that we had been playing for five hours without a break. He asked if I was tired.

"Tired? No, I'm just wondering if we missed anybody." I thought about all the men for whom we had performed that day. Every one of them had thanked us, if not with words, then with a grin or a wolf whistle or with hand-numbing applause. I was right to come here, I thought. I wouldn't have missed this for the world.

I did not see Bram again. He had told me he would be swamped with work and that I wasn't to look for him. The following morning our troupe was on the road again. But for the next month, I found myself weeping every night and at odd moments during the day. The men put it down to exhaustion and nerves; we had all been under a lot of pressure, and we were stretched pretty tight. I didn't tell them that my heart had received another blow, even worse than King Kingsley's betrayal. This time, I was deeply in love with a man who loved me in return, but our love had no future, no present, and not much of a past.

The Dizzy Dillon Band arrived in Rome on June 6, two days after the Allies liberated the city. The following day, during a performance for the men of the Fifth Army's First Division, we received word that Allied armies had landed on the Normandy coast in France. I ran to the microphone and made the announcement to the audience, then I joined in with their cheers and applause. Although I knew, and we all knew, that the war was far from over, we felt the promise of peace as well as victory. At that moment, all of us were thinking of home.

We continued to entertain the troops in Italy until the winter rains came. I did not see Major Howard again, although his company had reached Rome a few days before ours. In December, the USO sent the band to Paris for a much needed rest. Then, in March, 1945, just a few months before the end of the hostilities in Europe, we flew home.

10

"Did you see that guy out there?" The cigarette girl gave me a nudge. "At table one, with those dark glasses on? He bought up my whole stock of cigarettes, and then one of his friends broke them all up and threw them in the garbage can out back. You think he's crazy or something? Well, I guess I can't complain. He gave me a fifty and wouldn't take any change. Boy, you meet all kinds in this business, don't you?"

I though she was lucky to have any customers at all. Even on a Saturday night, the Hideaway House in the Pocono Mountains of Pennsylvania wasn't exactly jumping. A few couples moved around the dance floor while at the back of the room a group of Scranton businessmen celebrated a business deal.

But crowds had been thin everywhere since the war. We had returned from Europe expecting to be greeted like conquering heroes. We were The Adam Foster Band now, Dizzy having decided that he preferred managing over performing. We had acquired a few more musicians and a new look—snappy navy blue blazers for the men over white duck trousers and another gold dress for me—but work was slow in coming. Instead of booking us into the Waldorf or the Warwick in Manhattan, our agent sent us to Indiana, and from there to upstate New York. He counseled patience; with the war over, folks had embraced domesticity and the lure of their own hearths. Bookings were hard to get everywhere, not just in New York City. We told ourselves that the tide would turn eventually and the big bands would land on top once again, but the dry spell made us all a little nervous, particularly when bandleaders like Benny Goodman and Harry James called it quits.

We played at a hundred Hideaway Houses and waited for a phone call that would spell fame and money, but all of us, separately, I think, began to realize that the call wasn't going to come. At least two of the men had started to use heroin regularly. We were losing our unified sound. Adam Foster had begun drinking heavily. He was still a fantastic drummer, but offstage he became impossibly belligerent. The change in his personality shocked all of us. A few of the men grumbled and threatened to quit the band, but none of us had any place to go.

From the bandstand I sneaked a look at the cigarette girl's big spender while the boys were warming up the audience with a less-than-lively rendition of "Tenderly." He was seated at a table near the front of the stage, a tall glass of amber liquid in front of him. A massive gold ring gleamed on the little finger of his right hand, and two chunks of gold the size of Ping-Pong balls glittered at his cuffs.

His hair was black, smoothed straight back from a narrow, square forehead. By contrast, his skin was so white that he looked like a marble effigy. Dark glasses completely concealed his eyes. As he listened to the music, he smoked a long, thin cigar. I was accustomed to singing in smoke-filled rooms, but I moaned inwardly whenever I spotted a cigar smoker sitting near the stage. Tonight, however, the wisps of smoke that drifted up to me were sweet and flowery, like incense.

He shared his table with two companions, both swarthy and so muscular that their suits were ready to pop at the seams. They did not drink or smoke, but sat glowering at the waiters and the musicians and the other guests in the club.

When I stepped up to the microphone, the man in the dark glasses sat straighter in his chair. The quality of his listening was so intense that it unnerved me, and for the first time in my life, I missed my entrance on "Believe Me." He never smiled, never nodded to the beat, never even applauded. He just looked, aiming those opaque lenses at me like twin cannons. I had the feeling that behind those dark panes, his eyes were undressing me, examining me, dismembering and dissecting me and then reassembling all the scattered parts. I tried to relax and look elsewhere, but I couldn't take my eyes off him. By the time I got off the stage, I was sweating.

My cigar smoker turned up again two nights later in Weehawken, New Jersey, with the same two friends and the same chunks of gold weighing down his wrists and little finger. I was ready for him this time. In the interests of preserving the quality of my performance—and my sanity—I didn't look his way once, but the heady fragrance from his cigar permeated my senses, and my heart began to skip beats. Who was this man, and what did he want with me?

The following week, he reserved the best table night after night at the Juke Joint in New Haven, Connecticut. He did the same at Joe's Place in Elizabeth, New Jersey, the week after that. When we opened at Joe's, I received a note: "My dear Miss Heavener, You are the most extraordinary performer in Western Civilization. Would you do me the very great honor of joining me to discuss matters of the greatest importance to you, to me, indeed, to the entire world? Ever your servant, Antonio Matos."

His style of composition was as intriguing as his looks. At last I could put a name to the face that had been haunting me for the past two weeks. Antonio Matos. A foreigner? I was tempted to reply. But I had more important matters to think about right now. I tore up the note.

I had begun to suspect that Adam Foster was deliberately trying to sabotage my solo numbers. Nothing so blatant that your average listener would notice, just a misplaced thump or a rim shot where it didn't belong. And not every night. Just once in a while, when I was least expecting it. I didn't say anything, hoping he would give up his drinking and sulking or at least focus his hostility on someone else. But my strategy didn't work.

Our fourth night at Joe's, Adam turned downright obnoxious. He pounded his bass drum during "Believe Me," dragged the tempo on "It's Been a Long, Long Time" so that I ran out of breath on the long phrases, and used his brushes so heavily during "Blue Moon" that it sounded like a squad of janitors had come in to sweep out the room during the number.

By the time we finished the first set, I was a nervous wreck. I intercepted Adam as he was heading to the dressing room, probably for a stiff bracer.

"What are you trying to do to me out there?"

He leaned back against the peeling green wall and narrowed his eyes at me. "Shit, Dessie, don't blame me 'cause you sound like a strangled turkey. We all have our nights, don't we? I'm a little under the weather myself." He swayed slightly.

I grabbed his arm. "You're trying to make me look bad. If you have a gripe, why don't you come right out and say so? You're ruining my career."

"You tight-assed, prissy little bitch." Snarling, Adam jerked away from me. "Just 'cause you're getting old and your voice is shot, you think ever'body zhout t' getcha."

I stood glaring at him for a moment, then I said, "I'm going to sit the next set out. Or maybe I'll take the rest of the night off. We'll talk sometime when you're sober."

I had just reached my dressing room when Billy, the head-waiter-bouncer, handed me another of Antonio Matos's notes. It was identical to the first one and to two others I had received on subsequent evenings at Joe's Place. This time, instead of tearing it up, I said to Billy, "Tell Mr. Matos I'll meet him outside in five minutes."

Mr. Matos was waiting on the sidewalk in front of the club. He bowed deeply, and we shook hands. "I am delighted to be able to speak to you at last." His heavily-accented English confirmed that he was a foreigner. "Allow me the honor of buying you some champagne at the Blue Grotto. It is only a short ride." In answer to an invisible summons, a long sleek Cadillac glided up beside us. The bruiser who wasn't driving got out and opened the door.

I felt suddenly shy about entering this stranger's plush and private retreat. And I was still burning up from my clash with Adam Foster. "I could use a drink, but I think I would prefer to walk, if you don't mind."

We strolled at a leisurely pace. Mr. Matos took my hand and placed it very circumspectly on his arm. At his touch, I felt a little chill of pleasure in my spine. The Cadillac cruised along behind us. I glanced over my shoulder. "Don't they know where it is? Why are they following us so closely?"

"I pay them to take an active interest in my welfare," Mr. Matos said. "They would be remiss if they let me out of their sight for even a moment."

"You mean they're bodyguards?"

"I have many enemies, and even when I am far from home, I must be ever vigilant."

He talked like a character from the romantic novels my mother used to read. "And where is home?" I asked him.

"Havana, Cuba. Have you ever been there? A most charming city. I would love to show it to you sometime."

"I can't afford to take any trips right now, unless I'm traveling with the band."

"Then, perhaps I will hire the band," he said smoothly.

"Naturally, I will pay all their expenses, and make sure they are housed in Havana's finest hotel."

"Don't bother. They don't deserve a soft job like that right now." We walked on in silence for a minute. Traces of fragrant cigar smoke clung to his cashmere overcoat.

"You had some trouble tonight," he said, "with the band leader, the drummer."

I was surprised. "I didn't think anybody in the audience would notice."

"Perhaps no one else did. But I know your music very well by now, and I could tell immediately that Mr. Foster was deliberately trying to upset you. Did you quit?"

"No, but I'm giving him an opportunity to think about his sins. Even drunk, he knows that the band wouldn't last a week without me."

"You are right. They need you more than you need them," he said. "Perhaps you should leave them and make a career for yourself as a solo performer."

I shrugged. "I've been thinking about it. But you get used to having somebody else make the decisions—bookings, schedules, travel. I'm not good at anything except singing."

We seated ourselves in a quiet corner of the Blue Grotto. One of Mr. Matos's bodyguards staked out a table near the door. I didn't see the other one, the driver. After my host ordered our drinks, I said, "I don't mean to be nosy, but is there something wrong with your eyes, Mr. Matos?"

"In the tropics, one becomes accustomed to hiding from the glare of the sun and the stares of the impertinent." He removed the glasses and put them in his jacket pocket. Dark expressive brows rippled over his deep-set eyes, which were a curious shade of green and flecked with gold. He smiled, and the pleasant shiver in my spine spread through my middle and down into my toes.

Our champagne arrived. Mr. Matos lifted his glass to me. "To your very great talent, Miss Heavener." The champagne was delicious, not too sweet and so effervescent that it made my scalp tingle. Mr. Matos spoke again. "You toured for the USO during the war. That was brave of you. You did not need to expose yourself to such danger."

"No. But plenty of other people were exposing themselves to danger. I didn't want to sit home doing nothing."

"You have extraordinary courage. I saw that tonight. You were furious with Mr. Foster, but rather than upset or disappoint your audience, you persevered and finished the program. Anyone else would simply have walked off the bandstand in the middle of a song. Tell me, how is your son?"

I was shocked to discover that he knew everything about me. He knew all about my marriage to Blair, and the accident at the mill. He told me that Bram Howard had recently established a private hospital in Munford, so that Blair could receive quality care close to home. I hadn't even known that myself.

"How did you find all that out?" I asked.

"It is not difficult to find things out, if one has an interest. I did not mean to invade your privacy—ah, I see you are finding this somewhat upsetting. But your music means a great deal to me, Miss Heavener, and I want to help you if I can."

I was aghast at the idea of this foreigner poking around, asking questions about me. But I tried to hide my annoyance. "Thanks, but I don't need any help."

"I hope you will not take offense at this sudden intimacy, Miss Heavener. I know I seem rather presumptuous, speaking so candidly upon this, our first meeting. But I have observed you closely for some time now, and I have come to know you well. Therefore it is as a friend that I speak to you now, one who has only your interests at heart, and not the interests of your business manager or your bandleader."

I sipped my champagne. "What are you talking about, Mr. Matos? What's your point?"

"Of course, my point. Very well, I will be brief, and blunt, Miss Heavener. Your career is dying."

I jerked my head up. When I heard those four words, I knew he was right. I wasn't merely in a slump, I was on my way to professional extinction.

"Surely you realize that Adam Foster's band is third-rate. The few recordings you have made with him are satisfactory but not remarkable. They do nothing to display your talents to any advantage. If you stay with him, you will be branded as a third-rate performer yourself, and you will never achieve the kind of fame you so richly deserve."

I wiped away a line of bubbles from my upper lip. "Let's face facts, Mr. Matos. The outlook for most big bands is poor these days. If they keep folding at their present rate, then a lot of girl singers are going to be looking for work, not just me. Why do you think I'm special?"

"No reason," he said, "except for your voice. And, I think, your soul. Forgive me, I am being blunt again. We are entering the age of the crooner, the solo performer, a softer, more mellow musical sound than the raucous, brassy shouting of the past decade. You are superbly talented and qualified for success as a soloist. But if you venture out on your own right now, you will fail. You must change certain things about yourself."

"Oh? What things?"

"I do not want to upset you, Miss Heavener. Perhaps I have already said too much."

"Maybe you'd better just finish what you want to say." I felt like getting up and walking out. I'd had more than enough criticism for one evening. but Mr. Matos reached out and refilled my champagne glass. I sat still. "What would I have to change?"

"Your appearance is—please forgive me for saying this—common. What I mean is, you have calculated your gowns and your hairstyles to appeal to the greatest number, which in the past has included servicemen who had only to see your blond hair and red lips and glorious figure to fall in love with you and your music. But what is happening to those men? They are home now, most have found work, many are marrying. They are becoming solid citizens, respected veterans who are members of churches and lodges and civic organizations. They are changing, but you— you have not changed. I saw a photograph of you when you started singing for Kingsley. You looked just the same then as you do now. The songs you sing are the same ones you were singing when these solid citizens were marching off to war. In a short time, they will no longer satisfy any audience. Then there is the little matter of your speech. I have no right to say anything—my own accent brands me at once as a foreigner—but if you want to appeal to a wide audience, to listeners from all parts of this country, you must adopt a neutral way of speaking, an accent that brands you as being neither from the south nor the west nor the northeast. This accent of yours comes through when you sing, you know. The way you pronounce certain words."

"All right, you want me to change my clothes, my hair, my makeup, and my accent. Anything else?"

"Yes" he said solemnly. "Your choice of songs. You must never, never, never sing 'Hava Banana' again. For a song like that to be your trademark is nothing short of disaster."

I was sitting up so straight I thought I would pop a vertebra. "You seem to have made a thorough study of my shortcomings.

Have you given any thought to what I should do to correct them?"

"Indeed I have. In fact, I have mapped out a detailed campaign. You can follow all of it, or some of it, or none of it. It is up to you. But if you decide that my words are worth heeding, then please know that I would be honored and delighted if you would consult with me at any time. I can do much to help you, if you would let me."

"That's what bothers me." I got out a pack of cigarettes and removed one. "Why would you want to help me? Why?" I struck a match. Antonio Matos caught my hand before it reached my mouth and blew out the flame.

"I beg you, do not light that cigarette. I loathe the smell of cheap tobacco smoke. The evenings I have spent in these nightclubs would have been pure torture but for your singing—and my own cigars. The tobacco in them is grown in a high mountain field that occupies only one quarter of an acre. I select the best leaves myself, and I personally supervise the harvest and curing process. They are hand-rolled, of course, by an old man who is the supreme master of his craft in Cuba and therefore the world. I estimate that each of these cigars costs me five hundred dollars. But they are worth it."

I slipped the cigarettes out of his sight and nervously returned them to my purse.

"Your question," Mr. Matos resumed the conversation, "was why do I want to help you? Before I answer, tell me what happens when you sing. I do not mean the mechanics of vocal production and style, but what goes on inside your head. What are you thinking?"

I thought about it for a while, then I said slowly, "It seems to me that every song I sing has a voice all its own. I don't mean my voice. I mean the voice of the person whose song it is. A woman, usually, and she's telling a story. Her story. The song is only part of it, but I know all the rest. You name a song and I'll tell you all about the voice, what she looks like, how she fell in love, what broke her heart."

Mr. Matos listened intently, his eyes narrowed. "So, you step into the character of the song?"

"Yes, I guess that's what happens. Pictures go through my mind—I love someone, he leaves me, I'm all alone. I feel everything she feels."

Antonio Matos leaned forward. He gazed deep into my eyes,

as if he were trying to map the convolutions of my brain. "But what about the songs you have sung hundreds of times? Don't you get tired of them?"

"Not at all. I just put them on like an old coat or a comfortable dress. When I sing the words and feel the music, I'm right inside the song—the feelings and the pictures and the thoughts are mine. I'm living it." I laughed. "I'm not saying this very well."

"On the contrary, you express yourself perfectly. Your genius is unique, Miss Heavener. I would have expected such a cogent analysis from an experienced actress, perhaps, or from someone who has had a lot of formal training, but never from a mere singer of popular songs." He extracted a cigar from a silver case the size of a checkbook. He pricked the sides of the cigar with a gold pin, snipped off one of the tightly rolled ends with a pair of golden scissors, and lit it, not with a lighter but with a wooden match taken from the same case. "I have made a study of greatness. It is one of my passions. But only greatness among the living. Dead geniuses are too difficult to examine. Like you, I am a genius, but of a different type than yourself. I was a chess prodigy, a Grand Master at the age of thirteen. I want to see if there is a natural empathy among geniuses, a subtle communication between members of this, the highest order of humanity. I felt this with you before we ever spoke. It is our destiny."

I laughed. "I've never believed too strongly in destiny. Only in hard work and luck, and I haven't had a lot of that lately." The smoke from his cigar enveloped me in its fragrance.

"Oh, but you should. Destiny exists, no? An incident, a word, a chance meeting—the course of one's whole life can be affected by something that one may dismiss as insignificant. I felt the hand of destiny the first time I saw you. Since then I have been watching your career, waiting and hoping for the moment when your gift would be widely recognized and you would achieve international recognition. But I began to see that you were making some unwise choices, and I feared that without proper guidance, you would encounter difficulties. If that happened, you might be tempted to give up, to quit singing. That, I feel, would be an enormous loss for the world. Therefore I am giving you an opportunity to change your destiny, and my own."

My instincts told me he was right, but still I wasn't sure I wanted to put myself in the hands of a handsome stranger who wore golden nuggets on his fingers and who couldn't go anywhere without a couple of gun-toting henchmen.

"Suppose I go along with your plan," I said. "What would you want in return?"

"Only the knowledge that I have preserved an important national treasure."

I snorted. "That's a new one. I thought I'd heard every line in the book!"

His gaze never left my face. "I have no need of lines, Miss Heavener. When the time comes for us to be more than friends, we will both know."

I felt myself growing hot. Lately I had been too busy even to think about sex. Besides, after Bram Howard, all the men I met had seemed ordinary. But this one was different. And he knew it. "I'll have to think about this," I said. "You've caught me by surprise."

"Of course." He handed me a business card engraved with his name and a New York City telephone number. "Call me when you have decided, any time night or day. We shall talk further."

He offered to escort me, but I wanted to walk back to the club alone. When I got there, Jo-Jo Jonas was playing a listless cornet solo on "I Can't Get Started." The other members of the band weren't much livelier. Not that it mattered. Only three couples shuffled somnolently around the floor. I left my coat in my dressing room, fluffed out my hair, and joined the group for the last number. I sang my heart out, but no one seemed to notice.

Adam admitted he had been drinking, and apologized. "I would almost rather not play music at all," he said tearfully, "than spend the rest of my life in joints like this."

"I know," I said. "I feel that way, too."

Although it was late when I got back to my apartment, I telephoned Mr. Matos. He answered with the words, "Have you decided to take my advice?"

"I'll do whatever I have to do," I said. "Just get me out of this mess that I'm in."

"You are wise." We arranged to meet in his suite at the Plaza at noon the following day to plan strategy. Before he hung up, he said, "You will have to learn to drink your morning coffee black, no cream and sugar. You must lose twenty pounds before we can begin fitting you for new gowns."

"Twenty pounds!"

"With your voice, you do not need sex to sell your songs. Your body is breathtaking. But you do not wish to become a monument in flesh like Miss Mae West. The best singers are the hungry ones, the ones who have known suffering and want."

As he waited for me to reply, I could hear him breathing at the other end of the connection. What if I told him I had changed my mind? I suspected he would thank me politely, hang up the phone, and forget all about me.

I said, "Why do I have the feeling that I've just sold my soul to the devil?"

Antonio Matos chuckled. "A devil is merely a fallen angel, Miss Heavener. But do not worry. No matter which I turn out to be, you are in divine hands."

> "Remember Dessie Heavener, the sizzling songbird who gave us 'Paradise' and 'Believe Me' with King Kingsley's band before the war? On the skids lately with the band's remnants led by former Royal Drummer Adam Foster, 'Dorable Dess disappeared last week during a gig in Elizabeth, N.J. Foster denies any friction between them: 'We toured for the USO together,' he told me. 'She was like a sister to all of us.' The Rumor Bird Reports that Miss Heavener was last seen in the company of a well-known underworld figure. Here's hoping she has not been the victim of foul play. Top police administrators deny that they have been consulted as to her whereabouts."

At least I had made the news. Pepper Wellington hadn't mentioned me in his column since the band's return from Europe two years earlier.

My whereabouts were a well-fenced, well-guarded estate on the Hudson River just north of Hyde Park. There I rode, I strode, and I starved. Coffee took the edge off my hunger, and cigarettes gave me something to do with my hands. Neither of those vices were fattening, so Mr. Matos allowed me to continue them, as long as I didn't smoke the cigarettes in his presence. By the end of my first month, I was as ornery as a snake, and about as skinny.

My schedule was more grueling than it had been at the front in Europe: wake-up call at five-forty; breakfast at six; swimming, tennis, or horseback riding from six-thirty until ten, when I had two hours of speech therapy with a professor Mr. Matos had hired from some midwestern university; lunch at noon—a sumptuous repast of lettuce leaves and carrot sticks; voice lessons from twelve-thirty until two with a senile Italian who spoke no English; then two more hours of speech therapy followed by another vigorous session of exercise and outdoor sports. I fell into bed every night at ten and slept like a stone.

During this time, of course, I wasn't earning any money. I wouldn't have been able to send my father anything for Gray if Mr. Matos had not advanced me generous loans against future earnings.

At least I was making progress. After that first month, Mr. Matos was so well-satisfied with my dedication and the results we were getting that he allowed me to visit Munford for a week. Before that, I had paid only two overnight visits to my family since my return from Europe.

I arrived in Munford loaded up with gifts for Gray and Clara Mae, and even a few for my father and Ayleen. Gray was sprouting up; every time I saw him, he was taller, straighter, fairer. He looked more like a Howard than a Heavener. He was unhappier and more sullen than the last time I had seen him. With age had come understanding that although I was his natural mother, I had a life of my own that did not include him.

"Why can't I go back to New York with you?" he asked. "Why do I always have to stay behind?"

"Honey, I am at a very tricky point in my career right now. It's not—it's just not convenient. But as soon as I'm back on my feet, then I'll buy us a house and you can come and live with me. I promise."

"Your promises aren't any good," he whined. "You're always making promises, but they never come true."

I couldn't argue with him about that. He was right. "Don't give up on me, Gray," I begged. "I'll hit big one of these days. I've got to, for both our sakes."

Back in New York, a well-known hairdresser spent one whole day recoloring and restyling my hair. He dyed the peroxided parts to match my roots, which he described as honey-blonde and absolutely gorgeous if we lightened it just a little. He left it long, chin-length, with masses of curls swept over to one side.

Late that spring we had a stroke of luck. Glory Records released some old sides I had cut with the Kingsley band several years earlier, on the eve of the musicians' strike: standards like "Smoke Gets in Your Eyes," "The Way You Look Tonight," and "Let's Face the Music and Dance." I didn't make any money from them, but they brought my name before the public again and renewed interest in the Case of the Missing Canary, as Pepper Wellington called it.

Then in August, Mr. Matos arranged an audition for me at the Blue Room in the Warwick Hotel in Manhattan. I sang ballads and some easy blues and torch songs, tunes that would appeal to the delicate sensibilities of the Blue Room's elegant clientele. The management declared themselves satisfied, even thrilled. They hired me and scheduled my opening for October, when their elegant clientele would have returned from their summer retreats.

The time had come to costume me. Mr. Matos decreed that I must never wear gold lamé or snakeskin sheathing again. "It makes you look hard and cheap, like an armadillo. We must have softness, and darkness—we must have the dark. From now on, whenever you go into the public, you must wear black."

"I will not!" Thus far, I had given him no argument about anything he wanted me to do. But I drew the line at this. "I wore black at my mother's funeral and at my father-in-law's funeral. I won't wear it again until my own funeral—if then. I look awful in black. And it's bad luck."

"Black is the color of magic and mystery," Mr. Matos intoned. "You must wear black."

"Couldn't I wear white instead?"

My benefactor removed his dark glasses. His green-gold eyes had the power to mesmerize and intimidate me. I still got the quivers when we were alone together, but he never seemed to notice.

"Dolores, white is no color at all. But black—the color of sorrow, of longing, of loss. All the things you think about when you are singing. You cannot wear a pink dress when you sing about losing a man. Your audience will not believe you. You are a teller of stories, a diseuse, a troubadour. You want your listeners to involve themselves with the words, to be overcome by the music. Not blinded by a garish gown. I understand these things, Dolores. Listen to me."

Nobody but Miss Maddson had ever called me Dolores. I was astonished to discover that my name was Spanish. The way Mr. Matos rolled the "r" and slurred over the "l" made it sound foreign and exotic. I thought I would faint. " 'Dolores,' " he told me, "means 'the sorrowful one' in Spanish."

I don't know how I had the strength to argue, but I really hated the idea of wearing black. "My mother had a dress once," I recalled hesitantly. "The moths had gotten into it, so Mama gave it to me to play dress-ups in when I was a little girl. It was blue, dark blue. Not navy or teal. More like the color of the sky at night. Sort of . . . midnight-blue."

He stared at me for a long time. I could see the little wheels turning in his head. Finally he said, "That is the perfect color for you. Midnight-blue for a singer of blue songs."

So we assembled a wardrobe of midnight-blue gowns, one made of flowing chiffon, one studded with sparkling blue-black sequins and one with trailing blue ostrich feathers. All were modestly cut. None revealed the depth of cleavage I had capitalized on before the war.

"You will be a woman of mystery, Dolores," Mr. Matos declared. "We will cause them to be consumed with curiosity about those beautiful bosoms. You must not show them too much of yourself."

Pepper Wellington paved the way for my opening. "Waiting on Tenterhooks Department: What Heavenly singing star, absent from the scene for half a year, is planning a big comeback at the Warwick's Blue Room in two weeks? The Rumor Bird Reports that she is recovering from a tragic love affair—could it be with that French racing car driver who was killed at Le Mans this summer? Chin up, Dessie, and welcome back!"

I tossed the newspaper into Mr. Matos's fireplace. "Tragic love affair! Good grief. French racing car driver!"

"Sometimes it is necessary to give some exaggerated tidbits to the press, to bait them." Mr. Matos did not look up from his onyx and ivory chessboard. His favorite pastime when he was at home was to ponder a chess problem while he sipped one hundred-year-old brandy and puffed on one of his five hundred-dollar cigars. "We need a reason for your transformation from belting band singer to crooning soloist. Mystery, Dolores. A little mystery is very good publicity. When they see you in your midnight-blue gown, they will accept what they have read as the truth." He shifted a black chess piece and sat back with a satisfied sigh. "When you sing, you will confirm what they already know, that you have suffered, that your songs come from the heart."

To accompany me, I hired a middle-aged jazz pianist named

Freddy O'Dwyer who had once played with Paul Whiteman. I wanted a bass player, too, but Mr. Matos vetoed the idea.

"A pianist becomes invisible. He is lower than your level, and after that first glance, no one will look at him. But a bass player stands up, and he has that enormous musical instrument at his side. Both would compete for the attention that should go exclusively to you. It is not possible."

I had to agree that his reasoning was sound. Fortunately, Freddy O'Dwyer could work magic on the piano, almost making me believe that I had percussion and strings backing me up as well as brass and woodwinds. He listened to my old arrangements, came up with some new ones, and took a couple of my numbers down a few keys. We rehearsed every day for a month, refining and honing our material, but also getting to know each other so well that we could read each other's minds. After a while Freddy could sense subtle shifts in my mood and anticipate any sudden changes I might want to make in tempo or dynamics.

Finally, we were ready to open. The management of the Warwick publicized the event widely, and Pepper Wellington did his part by fanning the flames of public interest in the mystery surrounding my absence. The Blue Room was packed. A crowd of South American diplomats, friends of Mr. Matos, added Latin glamour to the occasion.

I still had no idea why this strange foreigner had come into my life. Except for those times when he made quick trips to Florida or Cuba, we had spent six months in close proximity. But I had learned nothing more about him. After my first week in the Hyde Park mansion, I gave up wondering if he would come to my room at night. He had promised not to interfere with me, and he honored his word. And yet his physical remoteness baffled me. I could sense his desire for me, and I would have melted under his touch, but something in his attitude prohibited even casual intimacy. I dared not even express my thanks with a chaste kiss on the cheek.

For the opening, Antonio Matos turned up in my dressing room wearing white tie and tails and enveloped in a fragrant cloud from one of his extravagant cigars.

"Nothing but a tailcoat would do justice to this great event," he said, bowing over my hand. "I want to give you some particle of the light you have brought into my life, although you deserve more, much more." He flipped open a small velvet box to reveal a brooch, an enormous amethyst surrounded by shoals of diamonds.

His gesture rendered me speechless. I pinned the brooch to the bodice of my chiffon gown. When I lifted my head, I felt the sting of tears in my eyes. "I've never owned anything so fine . . . so extravagant. Are you sure—?"

Mr. Matos removed his dark glasses. His smile was warm. "This is a token," he said with a dismissive wave of his hand, "a piece of metal and rock. It is merely my clumsy way of expressing the pride I feel in you at this moment. You have given me your complete trust and cooperation. I realize that this was not easy for you—you are instinctively rebellious, a nonconformist. But you suppressed your personality in the interests of building a new career for yourself. You had faith in my judgment, Dolores. I can guarantee that you will be pleased with the results."

"The reviews aren't in yet," I reminded him.

"I do not need reviewers to help me recognize genius." His eyes flashed angrily. "I am drawn to genius like a magnet to iron, like a diviner's rod to water. Most critics of contemporary culture are idiots. They cannot recognize beauty at all."

As they wrote in *Variety*, I wowed 'em. Even so, just before I went on, I experienced a moment of real panic. It was stage fright, something I had rarely suffered in the past. But the moment the lights hit me, I felt like I was coming to life after a long sleep. The months of preparation seemed like a dream. Standing in front of that audience, I understood once again why I had come into the world. I was born to sing. I had never been successful at anything else: romance or marriage or motherhood or even planning my own career. But I knew how to convey feelings and emotions through song.

In the weeks that followed, I felt like I had hitched a ride on a comet. The Blue Room wanted to sign me for an entire year at a salary that was ten times what I had earned during my time with King Kingsley. Mr. Matos gave them three months only, with an option for six that we could pick up if nothing better came along. Within three days of my opening, I was being offered appearances on radio and television and a slew of products to endorse. *Life* magazine featured me on its cover and gave me a four-page spread inside: "Torch Singer Lights a Flame in Manhattan." Their photographer took shots of me singing, rehearsing with Freddy O'Dwyer, relaxing in my new apartment on West Fifty-fourth Street.

Antonio Matos carefully avoided all the publicity and the photographs, but he was never far from my side. He continued to help me select my wardrobe, oversee new bookings, and choose new songs, and he had a permanent reservation for the best table in the Blue Room. I asked him once, half jokingly, if he ever got tired of hearing me sing the same old songs over and over.

He gazed at me for a long moment, then he shook his head. "Oh, no, Dolores," he said. "Because you never sing the same song the same way two nights in a row. It is always different, a fresh intonation here, a new surge of feeling there. I could listen to you every day for the next one hundred years and still learn more about you."

11

BY THE FRIDAY AFTER THANKSGIVING, 1947, I HAD BEEN SINGing at the Blue Room for over a month. As Freddy O'Dwyer and I were finishing up the last set of the evening, I saw a familiar figure following a waiter to an empty table. Paul. Paul Miller. His limping gait was unmistakable. With a delighted cry, I ran from the small stage and embraced him in front of the Blue Room's astonished patrons. Then I took his hand and dragged him up to the stage with me.

"Ladies and gentlemen, I would like you to meet someone very special. My first friend, my first accompanist, and the lyricist and arranger of 'Paradise,' one of my first hits. This is Mr. Paul Miller, Attorney-at-Law."

I urged Paul to play for me. He demurred, but the warm, welcoming applause from the audience persuaded him. Freddy O'Dwyer vacated the piano bench and Paul took his place.

He smiled up at me. "Got any requests?"

" 'Fast Walkin' Blues,' of course. Do you still remember how to play it?"

Paul hadn't lost his touch. In fact, his playing sounded better than ever. Later, back in my dressing room, I told him so.

He gave me a sheepish smile. "I have a confession to make, Dess. I'm a professional now. That's right, a professional musician. It's all your fault, you know. After I wrote 'Paradise' for you and you made it a hit, my whole life changed. I wore out two whole records listening to that song. It was my song you were singing. Mine. And people all over the world were listening to it. After that, I'm afraid, the law lost its attraction for me. I was spending more and more time at the piano and less and less time with my clients. My partners started complaining, and eventually I realized I couldn't stay in Munford anymore. So, here I am."

I gave him another choking hug. "Oh, Paulie, you should have told me! I interviewed fifty pianists before I hired Freddy. If I'd known you were free—"

He shook his head. "I wanted to do it without you, and with any luck, I just might succeed. You are looking at one third of the Paul Miller Trio. After you finish up here tomorrow night, how'd you like to come down to the Village Green and listen to us? The owner's promised to give us an audition. We'll be playing some time after midnight."

"Oh, Paul! Why, Paulie, that's wonderful!" I threw my arms around him. "I'm so proud of you for having the guts to leave Munford. You bet I'll be there."

We were still laughing and hugging each other when Antonio Matos came into the room. His eyebrows arched ever so slightly when I introduced Paul. "Paul has formed a new jazz trio," I told Mr. Matos. "They're auditioning tomorrow night at the Village Green. We have to go."

"But you have promised to attend the Burholme's party tomorrow night, Dolores. They have most important connections in Hollywood, and they wish you to sing for them."

I tossed my honey-blond curls. "If they want to hear me sing, they can come to the Blue Room any night of the week except Sunday. I'm not a performing seal. I'm sorry, Mr. Matos, but this is very important to me. Do you know how long I've been trying to persuade Paul to be a full-time, professional musician?"

"Professional I may be," Paul said with a laugh, "but the full-time is questionable yet."

"Are you kidding? With a talent like yours, you can't fail. Let's celebrate. Why don't you come with us, Mr. Matos? Surely I can treat myself to a hamburger on an occasion like this."

"I am sorry, but I must decline the invitation. I have some things to attend to." With a stiff little bow, Mr. Matos departed.

"Who is that guy?" Paul asked.

"Oh," I touched a powder puff to the tip of my nose, "Mr. Matos is helping me manage my career. He's a genius, Paulie. Why, in just six months, he's worked miracles with me. I look better, I'm singing better, and the people who matter are finally starting to take me seriously."

"And what is he getting out of all this?" From his tone, I

could tell that Paul thought he already had the answer, and from the way I blushed, he could have been right.

I flicked the powder puff at him. "You're not going to believe this, but all he's gotten from me so far are verbal expressions of my undying gratitude. We have an understanding. He gets a thrill out of giving my career a boost, which makes him look good to his friends."

"He doesn't look like he has any friends."

I grabbed my coat and purse. "He's a foreigner. You can't expect him to behave like us. Don't look so worried, Paulie. He is a very rich, very smart guy who just happens to think that I am a superlatively wonderful performer who deserves better than I've gotten so far. Surely you don't disagree with that?"

"No, of course not." He draped my coat over my shoulders and gave me a little kiss. "Come on, I want you to meet the other guys."

We joined the other two members of the trio at a coffee house down on Fourth Street. Jingo Lewis was a Mississippi farm boy who looked like he should have been out planting corn or shooting coons with the boys. Yet Jingo had played double bass with some of the country's top dance bands through the thirties and forties, and he had a solid reputation. But he had grown tired of the big band repertoire and wanted to experiment. "Yeah, I heard you back before the war a coupla times with King Kingsley," Jingo told me. "You really made those old songs drip with honey."

Clayton Striker, the tall black man who played alto sax, was another story. Paul told me later that Clayton was from Philadelphia, the college-educated son of schoolteachers. I never would have guessed it. He was rude, antisocial, childish, and belligerent. Two striking-looking Negro girls hung on his arms. All three glared at me, Clayton through half-closed eyes. When Paul introduced us, I could tell that Clayton recognized me, but all he said was, "White people don't know nothin' about the black man's music. Blues, jazz—it all came from the black man." Then he swung around and led his girls away.

"So, what are you doing playing with a couple of white guys, then?" I called after him. He turned back. He wasn't smiling.

"Paul is a cripple. He has a black man's soul. And Jingo's jive. Shit, Mama, I needed a gig and I needed it bad. I would have played with old President Truman himself."

Jingo explained. "Clayton just got his cabaret card back after a whole year. Some folks think he's a little tough to handle and they're avoidin' him like the plague. But he's got the meanest, hottest sax in this town. We're sittin' mighty fine as long as we have him."

Later, when Paul and I were alone in my apartment drinking coffee laced with whiskey, I asked Paul about Clayton.

"He's opening up new avenues in music," Paul said with enthusiasm. "He's a real pioneer, a trail-blazer. The young musicians coming up are all trying to sound like him."

"But why is he so hard to handle? Why did he lose his cabaret card?"

In order to keep undesirable characters from performing within the limits of their fair city, the New York City Police Department issued permits to musicians in the form of cabaret cards, which attested that the bearer was clean of word and deed and therefore fit to appear in a place of public entertainment.

Paul stirred sugar into his coffee. "He had a problem with drugs in the past. But he's clean now."

"Drugs? You mean heroin?" I knew all about the ravages wrought by the opium derivative. Musicians who had once enjoyed solid reputations became professionally untouchable when they got hooked. Besides spending all their money on their habits, they tended to be erratic and unpredictable as performers. Some went to jail. Some died. Few managed to find a cure. Billie Holiday, one of my idols, had served time in prison. She had been rehabilitated once or twice, but she always went back to heroin. It had threatened her career and wrecked her health. I had seen her perform in New York a couple of times since the war, and I thought that her technique and burning intensity were as incredible as ever, but her voice was gone. I hated heroin for what it had done to her.

"Clayton used to shoot heroin," Paul admitted, "but he just spent eight months in a rehabilitation hospital in Pennsylvania, and he's off the stuff now, for good. When we were putting the group together, he rolled up his shirtsleeves and showed me the insides of his arms. No needle marks."

"I think you're out of your mind, Paul! Joining up with a convicted drug addict!"

"You don't understand, Dess. Clayton is the one who's doing me a favor." Paul argued with the eloquence of a lawyer. "Listen, I came up here from nowhere. None of the other musicians in this town had even heard my name. But I knew Clayton's work. I tracked him down and actually got up the nerve to ask if he would listen to me play. Well, he agreed, and we went over to the house of a musician friend of his who had a piano and I played a tune I'd written that I call 'Traces.' Clayton picked up his sax and joined in. It was amazing. He listened to my music and at the same time, he improvised his way round the melody, and then we both took off together, getting stronger and stronger. I can't explain what it was like. Making love, maybe. I don't know. But it was miraculous. When we were finished, he said he thought we could make music together. That's all. The other guy, Clayton's friend, told me that he hadn't heard Clayton play like that for months and months. And I know I played better than I ever had in my life. A couple of weeks later, we found Jingo, and he fit right in. It's funny. We don't have much in common, but when we play together, we're like brothers. More. I can't explain it. You'll just have to hear us."

"But Clayton isn't even a nice black man," I protested. "How can you stand to be around him?"

Paul shook his head. "His personality doesn't matter to me. I needed him and I found him. He brought me to life. I guess that sounds strange. But I'm going to do everything I can to stay close to him."

I went to the Village Green the following night. Paul started the set with a fairly standard rendition of "My Funny Valentine," a Rodgers and Hart tune from "Pal Joey" that I often sang myself. Jingo plucked the strings of his bass, and Clayton slid in a few phrases here and there, not much more than graceful obligatos. It was nice music, well-played, but unremarkable. Then the tempo changed abruptly. Suddenly, Paul's hands were all over the keys, playing dissonant chords and arpeggios and the most fantastic runs. Jingo kept up with him, never once hitting a false note. Then Clayton, who had taken a short breather, lifted his sax to his mouth and the music really soared. It went every which way, spinning around the melody, which never really disappeared, wailing and screeching and moaning and sobbing. It was the kind of thing I always wanted to do when I sang the blues but couldn't because I didn't know how, and because I didn't have the nerve to bare my soul to strangers like that.

I listened, stunned. For the first time, I understood what the term *musical instrument* meant. The instrument was simply the means by which the musician communicated his emotions to his audience. Clayton's saxophone amplified his own voice; it articulated feelings and frustrations that he could never put into words. No singer could have done what he did: lightning-fast triplets, shouts and glissandos and jumps that spanned three octaves. "My Funny Valentine" was no longer a wistful, tender love song, but a vehicle for music that was more than music, and perhaps less.

I wasn't sure I liked what they were doing. I was certainly awed by it, and deeply moved. I think I was also frightened. I had never heard Paul play so passionately, yet so unmelodically. This was a side of him I had never seen. With me he had been a very solid musician. But here, playing with Jingo and Clayton, he sounded possessed, mentally unbalanced.

But the real genius of the group was undeniably Clayton Striker. I knew him better after listening to him play just one song than I had after meeting him in person and talking about him with Paul for three hours. I didn't like him any better, but I was awed by him. When he played, he achieved a stature as a great man of music and a promulgator of new ideas that he could never have attained without that brass instrument in his hands.

The trio finished the set to wild applause. Apparently the audience at the Village Green was educated in the intricacies of this new kind of music. I could not match their response. I just sat there stunned. After a few minutes, Paul joined me at my table. He was jubilant.

"We did it!" he crowed. "The owner has just offered us a job, two weeks at four-fifty a week. Not bad for a bunch of beginners. Well, what did you think?"

"I don't know, Paul." I was almost in tears. "I can't understand why you would take a pretty song like 'My Funny Valentine' and twist it into something that sounds like a crazy fanatic making a political campaign speech."

Paul laughed. He summoned Clayton over and repeated what I had said. Clayton nodded, and his eyes glinted. "You dig it Mama. Maybe you don't like it, but you dig it."

I promised Gray I would be home for Christmas, but early in December, 1947, I made my first album as a soloist, *Blue Heavener*, with Freddy O'Dwyer and a backup group of five musicians that we hired especially for the recording session. One of the songs on the album, Duke Ellington's "Mood Indigo," became a hit, and soon I was busier than ever, doing two or three radio appearances a night, sometimes squeezing them in between shows at the Blue Room, where I was making more money than the whole population of Munford, South Carolina. Once again, my name was a household word country-wide, and I was getting plenty of publicity and exposure. I had no time to go home, but I sent Gray a set of electric trains, hoping they would make him forget that once again I had failed to keep a promise to him. But what else could I do? Antonio Matos had made me a star, just as he had promised, and I had to ride the comet as long as it stayed aloft or I would lose momentum and crash to earth.

One afternoon in March 1948, Mr. Matos telephoned me from the West Coast.

I said, "I thought you were here in New York. I just saw you last night."

"Magnus Studios has agreed to give you a screen test. They are filming a musical extravaganza with a dozen big stars, and one of the female singers has had to drop out. They need a replacement immediately. You must fly out at once. Tomorrow."

I did, over the objections of the management of the Warwick. I made the test, and Magnus hired me to fill in for the ailing singer. My sequence was filmed in just three days, and Mr. Matos and I returned to New York. Two days after our return, Mr. Matos told me he had received a call from Magnus's president and chief executive officer. He had liked my segment so much that he wanted to sign me to a three-picture contract, commencing in May with a musical gangster film called *Monday's Girl,* in which I would play the singing moll of a dancing desperado named Jimmy Monday.

I was elated. Three films meant three years of work in one place, as well as a guaranteed income. I decided that I was finally going to be a real mother. I would buy a house in Los Angeles, hire a housekeeper—Clara Mae, if she would come—and make a home for my son.

Mr. Matos and I flew to California again. I found the perfect place for Gray and myself in Encino, only twenty miles from the Magnus studios. The Spanish-style villa stood on an isolated knoll overlooking the Pacific Ocean. It had five wood-burning fireplaces, an Olympic-size swimming pool, and gardens full of fragrant flowers. While I waited for the deal to close, I would finish out my contract in New York with the Warwick Hotel, cut another album for Glory Records, and tidy up my affairs on the East Coast. Then, right before filming started on *Monday's Girl*, I would fly down to Munford and collect Gray. I wrote to my father outlining my plans, and I sent Gray a new set of luggage and a set of toy drums.

"Start counting the days until May first," I wrote to him. "We're going to Hollywood!"

April passed in a whirlwind of activity. I saw Paul infrequently, but I was happy to know that he was making a name for himself among fans of the new music known as bebop. Whenever he could, he dragged me to after-hours clubs and jam sessions where I heard the main exponents of this fierce new jazz—Dizzy Gillespie and Charlie Parker. Paul raved about them, but I didn't share his enthusiasm. Their music made me feel itchy and dissatisfied. I kept trying to find the beauty in what they were doing, but their bleats, blats, toots, and shrieks defied my understanding.

By the last weekend in April, I had finished packing up everything I wanted to take with me: clothing, shoes, boxes of records, and mementos of my career. Late Sunday night, after I had gone to bed, the doorbell rang. I pulled a bathrobe on over my nightgown and went to the door.

Clayton Striker was standing in the hallway. I kept the chain on the door and spoke to him through the crack.

"What do you want?"

"I got to see Paul, quick."

"Paul's not here."

"Where is he? I got to see him."

"I don't know where he is. I haven't seen him for a couple of days."

"Let me in, Mama. I'm sick. I'm awful sick. I got to see Paul. Call him. Tell him I need him right away."

I balked at opening the door. "If you're sick, I'll call a doctor or an ambulance. You can wait out there."

"Shit." Perspiration poured down Clayton's dark face. He clutched his stomach, doubled over, and vomited on my welcome mat. Sagging against the door frame, he looked as though he were going to drop dead at any minute.

The man was obviously in trouble. I undid the chain and pulled him inside. He stumbled past me and collapsed onto the sofa.

After I had cleaned up the mess in the hall, I went over to

him. "You can't stay here," I told him. "I'm no doctor. I don't want to be responsible if anything happens—"

"Liquor," he said. "Gimme a drink of whiskey."

I poured a double into a glass and added a couple of ice cubes. While Clayton drank that down, I dialed Paul's apartment on East Thirty-third Street. No answer. Jingo was at home, but he hadn't seen Paul since they'd played together the previous night at Kelly's Stable on Fifty-second Street. I told him to have Paul call me at once.

"I can't find Paul," I told Clayton. "Listen, I don't want you here. If you won't let me call a doctor—"

"Leave me alone. Paul will find me. He knows what I need. He said he'd help me. Jesus." A spasm of nausea turned his complexion the color of wood ashes. The spasm passed, leaving him drained of energy. His eyes were bloodshot, wide and frantic like a frightened animal's. "Give me another hit of that whiskey," he said. "That might help. Make it a big one."

Clayton broke out into a sweat that soaked through his clothing and made dark wet patches on the sofa. Then he started to shake as though he had a bad chill. I brought out a blanket and pillow from the bedroom and tried to persuade him to lie back and relax. But he refused, and sat clutching his stomach with both arms, his head bent so far forward that it rested on his knees. Each breath seemed to require enormous effort.

All the while he kept up a whispered conversation with himself: "Gonna be all right—all right—that's right—real soon—the boy is comin' real soon—going to make everything all right. Just hang on a few more minutes—just a few more, don't let it get you—don't let it—"

He interrupted the conversation and lurched to the bathroom, where he spent the next hour vomiting and heaving. I didn't known what to do. What if Clayton Striker died? What would I tell Paul? Surely I ought to call a doctor in spite of what Clayton had said.

When he finally emerged from the bathroom, looking nearly as white as me, I flew at him. "What are you trying to do to me, scare me to death? I don't like you, but I sure as hell don't want to watch you die. Especially not in my apartment. If you won't let me call a doctor, then I'll call the police, but I can't stand around here doing nothing."

He looked down at me, his eyes bleary with tears and pain. "You ain't calling nobody, Mama, unless you want to land your good friend Paul in a whole lot of trouble. We are going to wait right here for him, even if it takes all night, and Jesus, I hope it don't."

"Trouble? What kind of trouble? What have you gotten Paul into?"

"Never you mind. Oh, sweet Jesus—" He dove into the bathroom and bent his head over the toilet again.

Nauseated myself, I went into the kitchen and poured myself a stiff bourbon. It tasted so good that I drank it down and had another. Eventually my tremors of fear and rage subsided.

I didn't know what to do. Mr. Matos might have helped me, but he was in Los Angeles, overseeing the carpenters and decorators who were remodeling my house. I had told him he didn't need to take such a task upon himself, that it could wait until Gray and I moved in, but he had said in his formal, almost stilted way, "My dear Dolores, I consider it a duty and a privilege to assure that everything will be perfect for your arrival." I didn't mind. Every task he undertook on my behalf was something I didn't need to worry about myself.

Finally Clayton emerged from the bathroom again and staggered over to the sofa. He looked wrecked and wraithlike, reduced to half his normal size. I offered him a Coke or some coffee, but he shook his head.

"Music, give me some music to listen to," he moaned. He clapped his hands over his ears, and his voice rose to a scream. "I can't stand what's going on inside my head!"

I looked around frantically. I had given away my radio and record player and sold my piano. "I can't! I don't have a thing to play music on!"

"Sweet Jesus, I need it, I need it. Sing, Mama. Sing somethin', for God's sake!"

"I . . . I don't know if I can." Anger and fear had constricted the muscles in my throat so that I could barely make a sound, but I croaked out "Sweet Hour of Prayer," one of Paul's favorite hymns. Paul liked to say that songs were better than prayers. I sang the first verse. Clayton groaned. "Jesus, woman, can't you do it any better than that? Can't you do something with those notes? Do something! Make that song into something more than it is."

"You've got a damned nerve," I snapped. "You're so sick you can hardly hold your head up, but you're not too sick to tell me how to sing." I repeated the first verse of the hymn, and embellished it with a few grace notes.

"No, no," Clayton shouted, "can't you hear it? Trite, uninspired melody, that's all that is. Listen." He sang the verse himself, embroidering on the tune, carrying that simple little song to heights it had never before enjoyed. His fingers twitched on an invisible saxophone as his rasping voice strained to imitate the saxophone's bluesy sound.

I understood what he was doing. The gospel singers I had heard as a child—like the ones he must have heard while he was growing up in Philadelphia—often built castles of soaring emotion on the melodic foundations of simple hymns and spirituals. They shouted, they moaned, they made their music tremble and shimmer. Clayton had taken this practice, and with his talent and genius, lifted it to new heights.

"Let me do it," I said when he had finished. "Let me try." I sang the second verse, but this time I took the strand of the melody and with it started to weave something much larger and more ornate. Baroque, my father might have said. But I tried to make the improvisation more than mere decoration. As my confidence grew, I sang a little louder. Clayton marked time by nodding his head weakly. His fingers continued to play an invisible alto sax.

"You're getting it," he nodded spastically. "But you don't feel it. You don't feel anything! Feel it!" he begged in an impassioned shout. Sweat poured off his face. "Feel it in your gut! Sing it again."

"I won't!" I was screaming hysterically. "I can't! I don't know how!"

"You got to compose it in your head first, know right where you're going, then sing it like you mean it. Singing's just another way of saying what everybody already knows, so you got to make 'em sit up and pay attention. I mean, you can sing, 'I love you, baby,' in five little notes, but it doesn't mean the same as if you do it like this." He used about fifty notes to sing the same four words.

I shook my head. "I can't do that. I don't have that kind of imagination."

'You learn it," he said. "That's what jazz is, Mama. Take the music and make it interesting. Without jazz in your soul, you're just another saloon singer. Shit. Might as well be singing 'She was only a bird in a gilded cage' for the rich white folks to drink their champagne by. Fuck 'em. Make your own music for your own self. Can you dig it? Jesus, it's cold in here."

I fetched another blanket for him. The clock in the bedroom said it was two in the morning. I went out and tried Paul's apartment again. Still no answer.

Clayton wanted to hear something else, a blues song. I sang a couple of verses of "Fast Walkin' Blues." He growled and shook his head.

"No, no, you don't dig what that woman is feeling." He clenched his hands. Tears joined the beads of sweat rolling down his cheeks. "She wants that man to turn around and come back to her, and every time she tells him to walk, she's really saying 'Come back, you big fool.' Make me hear it. Sing it loud! Make me believe it!"

I sang it loud, and infused it with as much passion as I could muster. Better, but not good enough. He made me keep singing, verse after verse, until my throat was dry.

"I can't sing anymore," I gasped. "I don't have enough spit left to lick a stamp."

"Get me another drink of that whiskey, and get yourself one, too. Shit, where's that goddamned Paul? Call him again. It's so damn hot in here. When's he coming?"

When I got back from the kitchen, Clayton had thrown off the blankets and stripped off his jacket and shirt and undershirt. His black skin was slick with sweat. "Bring the bottle," he said when I handed him the drink. "And get me some cigarettes. I gotta have some cigarettes."

I found a pack in my purse and lit two, one for myself.

I still got no answer at Paul's apartment. Where had he gone? What was he doing? I cursed him silently for inflicting me with this monster.

After I finished my drink and a couple of cigarettes, Clayton demanded more music. I sang "The Way You Look Tonight," just as I had sung it for King Kingsley.

"Shit, Mama, that ain't nothin' but tissue paper," he said. "I want oak. I want stone. I want blood."

"You want blood? From 'The Way You Look Tonight'?" I did my best, wringing more feeling from those sweet lyrics than I had ever suspected they contained.

"Yeah," Clayton nodded. "Yeah, that's better. The other way, you sound like goddamned Deanna Durbin, you know? Just another white girl with nothin' between her legs. A goddamned china doll. Sing it again, sing it from between your legs, not from out of your mouth."

I pulled off my bathrobe and stood in front of him, a cigarette in one hand a glass of bourbon in another. "All right, you want blood?" I said. "Here it is, then. Hold your ears if it gets too loud."

I took out those lyrics and dressed them up in a costume they had never worn before. I belted and shrieked and moaned and turned that old song into an upbeat hymn to love. For the first time that night, I started to enjoy myself. Clayton forgot his pain and grinned at me.

"Now you're singing it," he rasped. "Now you're really singing it."

I was so engrossed that I didn't hear the angry buzzing of my doorbell at first. Sure that it was Paul, I jerked the door open. I found myself looking at my neighbor from across the hall, Mrs. Foyle, a lonely widow with nothing to do and too much money to do it with. She had always been friendly and eager to gossip when we met in the halls, but now I saw real fire in her eyes.

"Miss Heavener, will you please cease that drunken, incessant wailing?" Her gray hair was coiled up against her head and stuck into place with crossed bobby pins. A quilted pink housecoat covered the uncorseted bulges in her figure. "I have been trying to go to sleep for three—oh, my God!" She looked past me, and her face turned gray.

I turned around to see what had startled her. Clayton was lying on my sofa, half swathed in a blanket, his left hand gripping the neck of a bottle of bourbon. I pulled the door closed, cutting off her view of the apartment.

"Oh, my God! Oh, my God!" She backed away from me toward her own door. Then her eyes focused on my midriff. Looking down, I saw I was holding the smoldering stump of a cigarette in my right hand and a glass of bourbon in my left. All I had on was a sheer nightgown.

"Mrs. Foyle—please—" I dropped the glowing butt into the bourbon glass and casually slipped the glass out of sight behind my back. "I'm . . . I'm sorry, Mrs. Foyle. That man—he's an old friend, a musician. We're . . . we're rehearsing. We didn't mean to disturb you. We'll be quiet. You just go on back to bed now."

Mrs. Myrna Foyle whirled and ran into her own apartment, slamming the door in my face. I heard her locks clicking into place, one after the other. Oh, my God. I heard myself echoing her own shocked reaction. What if she called the police? Oh, my God.

Time passed. The police didn't come. I spent the rest of the night on my knees beside the sofa, wiping sweat from Clayton's face and torso. Every time he began to thrash and mutter, I hissed at him, "Do you want the cops? One more sound out of either of us and that woman will call them."

At six-thirty, Paul arrived. "Is he all right?" He pushed past me. "God, I'm sorry, Clayton. There was a mix-up—I didn't have enough money. I had to borrow some—"

"Give it to me, man. Come on, quick, where is it?"

Paul handed him something wrapped in a handkerchief. Clayton grabbed it and staggered to the bathroom. Paul started to follow him, but the door slammed in his face. We stood in the little hallway waiting, saying nothing. The look of pain in Paul's eyes was almost more than I could bear. I was paralyzed, almost catatonic myself. Suddenly we heard a thump inside the bathroom. The door was unlocked, but Clayton's slumping body had blocked it. Paul and I heaved and pushed until we shifted him a little and Paul could squeeze through.

"Dess, help me!" I went in. Clayton was convulsing. Paul sent me to the kitchen for a spoon to put into his mouth so that he wouldn't swallow his tongue. Then we got him into the living room again. "Get him moving, make him move." He slapped Clayton's face. "Wake up, Clayton! Can you hear me? Wake up!" Paul slung Clayton's left arm around his shoulders, passed his right arm around Clayton's waist and tried to make the half-conscious man walk. But Clayton was too big, and Paul's leg was too weak. I shifted furniture out of the way to clear a path; then I got on Clayton's other side. Together we got him moving. After a few trips back and forth, I ran to the kitchen and brewed up a pot of powerfully strong coffee. We fed this to Clayton by the teaspoonful, in between trips back and forth across the room. I moved mechanically, and under my breath I kept repeating Myrna Foyle's refrain: "Oh, my God. Oh, my God."

We chaffed Clayton's hands, we rubbed his feet, we slapped his face and applied ice cubes to the back of his neck. The three of us walked five miles through my living room. After an hour, he started coming around. In three hours, he was gasping and drooping with exhaustion, but he was his snarling, unpleasant self again, and very much alive. Paul and I got him into my room and dumped him on the bed. He was still a mighty sick man, but he was alive.

I went into the kitchen to brew some more coffee. Paul followed me. His crippled leg was so sore he had to hang on to the walls to keep from falling down. "I'm sorry, Dess. I didn't mean to involve you in this."

I whipped around from the stove. "You fool. You stupid, jackass fool! What if that woman had called the police? We'd all be in jail right now, me included! I think you've lost your mind, getting mixed up with a character like Clayton Striker. He's isn't just sick, he's evil. He's evil through and through. A devil! Nobody could play the sax like him and not be a devil. And you're in league with him."

"Dessie, try to understand. Clayton is not—"

"I know what he is, and I know that you're half in love with him. You must be, or you wouldn't be carrying on with him like this. I never would have believed it. I always thought you loved me, but it was a lie. You're one of those men who likes other men! I've seen them—"

"That's not true!" Paul was quivering from head to toe. "I'll always love you, Dessie. If things had been different, you and I would be married now. You know that! I can't explain what it is about Clayton. All I know is, when I met him, it was like meeting another part of myself."

"You've got to get rid of him, Paulie. He's dragging you down. Find yourself another sax player and tell Clayton to get lost."

"I can't do that! Without Clayton, I'm nothing, just another piano man. I need him."

I slammed the coffee pot down on the table. "Well, get your goddamned boyfriend out of my apartment. I'm sick to death of both of you."

Paul collapsed. He slumped to the kitchen floor and buried his head in his arms. "I'm so tired," he moaned. "If you knew what I'd been through—"

"I've been through it myself," I snarled. "Thanks to you and your boyfriend."

"Don't call him that. You don't understand. Oh, God, Dessie." He started to sob. I stood back, horrified. Dropping to my knees beside him, I put my arms around him and held him close. We wept together, and I kept murmuring that I was sorry, and Paul, too, kept saying the same thing. We were both stupid with exhaustion, wrung out emotionally, drained of energy.

At about four o'clock that afternoon, Clayton woke up. He took a shower, pulled on his sweat-stiffened clothes, and announced that he and Paul had to go see a man.

"That was bad shit, Paul, real bad," he said. "Almost like somebody out there wanted to kill me. We're going to get your money back."

Without glancing at me again, Paul followed him out the door.

12

FROM THE WINDOW OF THE DESCENDING AIRPLANE, MY VIEW of the pine-covered hills around Columbia was somewhat cockeyed. I was used to that; ever since I had been cast in *Monday's Girl*, I had been tipsy with excitement over my move to California and my future as a movie star. After years of struggling, I would finally reach that pinnacle of fame where my face and voice would be familiar to millions, even to people in far-off lands who couldn't pronounce my name.

As soon as Gray and I settled into our new home, I wanted to buy a car. I would let Gray choose it—the make, the model, the color, the extra features. I wondered if he liked convertibles. Maybe we should just get a two-door sedan with wide running boards and lots of chrome. After all, Gray was nearly seven years old now, old enough to know something about cars. On weekends, when I wasn't filming, we would ride out to the hills beyond Hollywood and I would let him take the wheel. All good southern boys learned to drive as soon as their feet reached the pedals, and sometimes before.

Outside the main hangar at the Columbia airport, I approached a youthful taxi driver and asked him to take me to Munford.

"Munford? Shoot, that's over forty miles away." He screwed his mouth around and sent a squirt of tobacco juice into the dust, missing the hem of my skirt by inches. "Cost you twenty dollars—in advance."

Realizing immediately that my expensive new Yankee accent wasn't going to get me far in South Carolina, I reverted to a drawl that he would understand. "Now you looka here, boy, I wouldn't pay twenty dollars to get to the moon much less to Munford, so you can just take the ten I'm offering or I'll give my business to somebody else. I know your mama taught you to act like a gentleman, so help me with this suitcase and quit acting so sassy."

He apologized, tipping his hat to me and calling me ma'am while he loaded my single suitcase into the trunk. I had sent everything else on to California. Tomorrow morning Gray and I would fly back to New York, where we would board a commercial airliner to Los Angeles.

The car rolled through acres of pine trees, past signs that read PRIVATE PROPERTY, NO HUNTING OR TRESPASSING. HOWARD LUMBER CORP. Despite their reversals, the Howards were again in control of most of the land and timber in western South Carolina. Since the war, Bram Howard had rebuilt the fortune he had helped to gamble away. Recently the New York newspapers had reported his acquisition of a string of television stations in the southeast. He was expanding his business horizons beyond pulp and paper into the world of entertainment. My world. Perhaps our paths would cross again someday.

I wondered how I would feel, meeting Bram again. It was probably a good thing I wouldn't have time to see him while I was in Munford. I couldn't afford to complicate my life right now with any reprises of the duet we had played in that cell at Villa d'Este.

In Munford, I paid off the driver, grabbed my suitcase, and ran up to the door of my father's house. It was locked. Puzzled but not alarmed, I rang the bell, then I pounded on the window. At this time of day, four in the afternoon, Clara Mae should be home. After a few minutes, Ayleen came up the walk carrying a sack of groceries.

"Where's Clara Mae?" I asked. "Don't tell me her back is acting up on her again."

Ayleen poked her key into the lock. "I guess we forgot to tell you. Clara Mae is no longer with us."

"What do you mean, no longer with you? Oh, Lord, I suppose she was in such bad pain she couldn't work. I wish she'd see a real doctor and not let Brother Jupiter—"

"We decided to let her go. She had become too unreliable and spoiled. She was always taking advantage."

"Taking advantage! Clara Mae never took advantage in her life. She worked as hard as any two women. Three. Honestly, Ayleen. Well, where's Gray? I bet he's excited about the trip."

"I don't know where he is at the moment. You'd better ask your father. He's over at the church, practicing the organ."

The front door closed in my face and the lock sprang into place again. I just stood there and stared at it. Surely I didn't deserve this from the woman who had remodeled and refurnished her home with my money. Finally I shrugged my shoulders and set off down the street toward the church.

I heard the moaning of the organ long before I rounded the corner and saw the edifice itself, Honor Baptist Church. I paused for a moment to listen. My father played the notes correctly, but he didn't have an ounce of real music in his soul. I had never realized it before. He might as well have been pounding a typewriter.

I sat in the front pew where he would see me as soon as he looked up from his book of simplified Bach chorales. When he finally did, he stiffened. That was his usual reaction to me. He had been doing it since I reached the age of puberty.

"Afternoon," I said. "You're looking pretty well."

Actually he looked old, and like he might have the flu, but I couldn't get out of the habit of lying to him.

My father's greeting consisted of a jerky nod and a single word: "Dessie." He turned back to his music but did not lift his hands over the keys.

"I'm looking for Gray. Ayleen seemed to think you would know where he is. And what's all this about letting Clara Mae go? I never heard of such nonsense. Well, she can just pack her things and come out to California with Gray and me. We don't care if she takes advantage or whatever it was Ayleen said she was doing."

My father kept his unblinking gaze fixed on the music in front of him. "Grayson is no longer living with us."

"What do you mean, no longer living with you?" My first thought was that my son had run away, or that he was lost. I experienced a sudden attack of panic, worse than stage fright. Sweat broke out on my forehead and my breathing quickened.

"We felt that we could not provide for his needs in the way he deserved. He . . . he's living up at Woodlands now."

"Woodlands!" I jumped up. "You mean, he's with them? The Howards? That's not possible! I don't understand. Why didn't you call me—or send a telegram? I'm going up there right now and get—"

I ran down the aisle toward the door. My father's voice stopped me. "Gray went there of his own free will. We offered him a choice. He chose to live with his father's family."

I whirled. "His father's family! His father's family hasn't paid a lick of attention to him since he was born. He got the Howard name from them and that's all he got." I rushed back up the aisle and mounted the steps to the organ console. Hot tears blurred my vision, and I stumbled. "What happened? Why?"

A flash of guilt passed across my father's face, and I knew. "You . . . you gave my son away! How could you do such a thing? You knew I was coming for him at the end of April; you knew I'd be here on this very day! When? When did he leave?"

"Two days ago. The Howards sent a car."

"The Howards sent a car," I echoed weakly. "No, no, this can't be right. I don't understand. Why didn't you stop them? Why didn't you let me know? They can't do that. I'm Gray's mama. His mama! What kind of person would take a child away from his own mama?" I sank to my knees beside the organ bench and gripped my father's arm. I dug my fingers deep into his flesh, trying to squeeze out a single drop of human feeling from a man who had proved to me over and over again that he had none.

My father sniffed. "You can call yourself a mother if you want to. I've seen pigs who've mothered their litters better than you did your one boy. Running off, leaving him, coming home two or three times a year—"

"I was working!" I ended my sentence on a scream, gut-wrenching, hideous, and despairing. I had never made such a sound in my life. As tears flooded down my cheeks, I suddenly knew that, whatever I had wanted in the past, now I wanted, I needed, my son with me. "I was working," I sobbed. "I had to make a life for myself before I could provide for him. You know that. You know what kind of life I would have had if I'd stayed home. Nothing. That's what I would have had. But what about you? You've done real well out of my work, haven't you? New car, new furniture, plenty of fancy clothes for your new wife—she put you up to this, didn't she? Ayleen's the one who's been whispering in your ear like Satan: 'Why do we have to take care of Dessie's child? Why? Why?' "

"Now, Dessie . . ."

Weeping and sobbing with great hacking coughs, I dragged myself to my feet. "They paid you, didn't they? Charles Abraham Richer-Than-God Howard the Fourth and that slut Jean-

Ellen Thomas. They gave you money! Didn't they?" I struck my father, hit him with my fists, rained blows on his head, his shoulders, his back. He didn't move, didn't even flinch. "How much did they give you, Judas? Did Bram Howard give you more than I did? How many pieces of silver did it take to persuade you to betray your own daughter, your only child? How much did they pay for my boy? Judas! Judas!"

I was screaming, crying, incoherent. But my father knew what I was saying, and he knew what he had done. My father had sold Gray to the Howards. In exchange for a few dollars—I couldn't even imagine the terms of their devils' agreement—he had conspired with the Howards to steal my child.

Even now, Gray was at Woodlands, a prisoner. I had to get him out of there before they seduced him with their false manners and their finery and their elegant ways; before they persuaded him that his mother was nothing but a cheap whore who sang in saloons and cafés, in between bedding down sailors and salesmen. I had to get my son back.

"Your car." I thrust out my hand, palm up. "Give me the keys. Give them to me! Damn you, I paid for it, the least you can do is let me use it!"

Silently, he handed over the keys to the new Chevrolet parked in front of the church.

I broke every law in the book driving up to Woodlands, including driving with impaired vision. I almost wished the sheriff would try and intercept me; I would gladly have run him down.

The gates to the estate were open. I roared up the drive and halted the car under the porte cochere. I leaned on the doorbell with one hand while I pounded the heavy brass knocker with the other. After a few moments, Sylvester opened the door a crack.

"Where is he?" I demanded. "Where's my baby? Bram Howard has stolen my son and I want him back. Where is he? Where is Gray?"

Sylvester's eyes were dark with sorrow. He had always been fond of me, and I could tell that he hated having been forced into this position, but I had no pity to spare for him. "He ain't here, Miz Dessie. Young Miz Howard, she took him with her in the car this morning, said she didn't know when they'd be back. I don't know where they went."

"What about Mr. Howard? Bram? Where is he?"

"I reckon he's still down at his office, it's that new building at the edge of town, on the highway to Columbia. He said he wouldn't be back home 'til late.''

I spun away from the door and jumped behind the wheel of the Chevy once again. I shaved some paint off the right side of the car tearing through the gate, but I didn't care. My father could use some of his ill-gotten wealth to have it touched up.

I reached the new Howard Building ten minutes later. Office hours were over and dusk was falling, but lights burned in the top floor windows.

The elevator needle was stuck on five. I punched the button, but nothing happened. I found the stairs and scaled all five flights in under a minute. I ran along a carpeted corridor, passing blank flesh-colored steel doors on both sides as I went. The entrance to Howard Enterprises was at the end, behind a heavy modern partition made of brass and glass.

The outer office was empty, the secretaries long gone. In one corner of the room, I spotted a dark walnut door with C. A. HOWARD tastefully lettered in gold. I threw myself at it, and finding myself in an empty anteroom, ran toward yet another door. That led to the holy of holies, Bram's office.

For one dizzy moment, I thought I was back in the drawing room at Villa d'Este. Bram was seated behind a vast desk, his attention fixed on a sheaf of papers in his hand, just as he had been then. He did not look up when I burst in. Another man was standing at the corner of the desk, someone young and slick who might have been a lawyer or a used car salesman. I launched myself across the top of the desk, my fingernails poised over Bram's face. The younger man grabbed my arms and pulled me back.

"Miss Heavener is here to see you, sir," he said.

Bram lifted his head. His eyes told me he was remembering Italy, too. On that occasion, I had been wearing khaki fatigues. Now those blue eyes took in the short fawn-colored mink jacket around my shoulders and a pink blouse with an oversize bow at my throat before traveling down the length of my gray silk suit.

"Where's my son?" I screamed. "What have you done with my son?"

"Grayson is with my wife," Bram said softly. "I thought it best to send him away until we could talk things over calmly and rationally."

"I'm not going to talk over anything with you. I want my son and I want him now. You had no right to take him, you hear me? No right! You don't care anything about him. How could you? You don't even know him. You never took an interest in him from the day he was born. Damn you, he's a Heavener, not a Howard. I don't care what the law says his name is. He'll never be a Howard!"

"I have become very fond of the boy, Dessie. You would be foolish to take him now. He doesn't know you, and your career will never mix with motherhood. You never wanted to be a mother. And your father and Ayleen didn't want Gray, either. But I do. Since Jean-Ellen and I can't have children of our own, we thought . . . Look, why don't you sit down? Ronald, would you bring us some coffee? Maybe we can talk this over in a civilized manner." The other man nodded and left the room. Bram turned to me. "I'm sure we can come to some arrangement, perhaps divide Gray's time—"

"I'm not going to agree to any kind of arrangement with you," I said. "Gray is my son, and I want him to live with me. I've spent too much time away from him already—nearly seven years—and now I'm ready to make a home for him, like I always promised. I don't care what Jean-Ellen wants or doesn't want. Do you really believe I'd let my son spend two minutes with that insufferable woman you married?"

Bram's defensive tone told me more than his words. "Now, Dessie, Jean-Ellen's been a good—"

"I know what she is, and I know she's always hated me. You couldn't have been that attracted to her, either, or you wouldn't have joined the army a month after you married her. Bram," I dropped my voice pleadingly, "why are you doing this to me? I thought you . . . I know I . . . we were so . . ."

Bram reached across the desk and took my hand. I felt the passion in his grasp and saw it in his eyes. "Dessie. Oh, God, Dessie, I know. I know. Things should have been different. But they're not. You're still married to poor Blair. And I traded my soul to Jean-Ellen for Woodlands. We never had a chance. We still don't. I don't want to hurt you, but I can't give Gray up. I need him, and he needs me. I want him with me."

"I want him, too, and I deserve to have him. He's my son! He belongs with me!"

Bram released me and passed his hand over his eyes. "Hire yourself a good lawyer, Dessie. I intend to adopt Gray, to make him my son. In my heart of hearts, I truly believe that he'll be better off with me than he would with you. I am sorry."

Bram lifted his head. "Ronald!" When the young man appeared, he said, "Ronald, Miss Heavener has decided not to stay for coffee. Would you please show her out?"

Ronald was thin and wiry and a lot stronger than he looked. He carried me kicking and screaming through the reception area and outer office, along the corridor and into the elevator. As soon as he had inserted a key in the correct slot and the doors closed, he released me. I clawed at his face. He grabbed my wrists and twisted both arms behind my back.

"I wouldn't do that if I were you, ma'am," he said in a soft, gentlemanly drawl. "I'd hate to have to dislocate your shoulders."

Down in the lobby, he propelled me toward the main doors, pushed me through, and gave me a little shove toward the steps. I stumbled, but did not fall.

"See you in court, ma'am," he said before locking the doors behind me.

Antonio Matos flew in from California the next morning, in response to a frantic and barely coherent phone call from me. Paul came down two days later to help sort out our legal options. We petitioned the court to force the Howards to return my son to me at once. Judge Miller, Paul's father, denied the petition.

"Dad says there's no indication that Gray was taken from your father's house against his will," Paul said when we received the decision. We were holding a council of war in my room at the Pine Court Motel on the edge of town. "Your father was acting as the boy's guardian in your absence. He merely shifted his responsibility to the Howards."

"But he didn't consult me," I protested. "Nobody consulted me. Damn them! My father knew I would never have let Gray go with them, never. But that bastard paid them, I know he did. Doesn't that mean anything? If we could prove that my father received money from them—"

"It wouldn't change anything. Well, it looks like there's going to be a hearing. Dad said he'd try to schedule it for three months from today."

"Three months! I'm not going to wait that long. He can have as many hearings as he wants, but I want my son back right now. Gray's place is with me, his mother. Not that puckered up snake's ass, Jean-Ellen." I appealed to Mr. Matos, sitting wreathed in cigar smoke in a corner. He looked thoughtful but did not speak.

"The judge has to give both sides time to prepare their arguments," Paul explained patiently.

"But there's nothing to argue about. Bram Howard kidnapped my son, and I want him back."

"It's not that simple, Dess. He says he wants to adopt Gray. He is the boy's natural uncle, after all, as well as Blair's legal guardian. If Bram does succeed in adopting Gray, then Gray will naturally be in a position to claim some inheritance."

"But he doesn't need any inheritance from them," I wailed. "I'm making plenty of money. And what do you mean, if Bram succeeds in adopting Gray? He can't do that! I'm his mother. Doesn't that count for anything?"

"Of course, the court is usually sympathetic to the natural mother in cases like this, in ordinary circumstances. But Bram could well raise some salient issues."

"What do you mean, salient? What the hell kind of issues are those?"

Paul glanced at Mr. Matos, who shrugged. They both seemed to know more than I did, which frustrated and infuriated me.

"What issues?" I repeated. "What could he possibly use to take my son away from me?"

Paul let out his breath. "He could question your fitness as a mother."

I blinked at him. "My fitness as a mother?"

"Yes. Morally, fiscally, he'll be digging into every aspect of your life that could possibly have any bearing on the case. And since we know what he's going to do, we can be ready for him with witnesses of our own." Paul cleared his throat. "Dessie, I think I should say right now that I'm not competent to handle this case for you. I'm just starting to make a name for myself as a musician in New York, but I'd give it all up in a minute if I thought I could help. You know how much I care about you. But you need a sharp lawyer, the best, someone who is as ruthless and aggressive as Bram Howard is going to be. I'll do everything I can to help, but I can't assume the full responsibility for the case."

Mr. Matos finally spoke up. "Do not upset yourself needlessly, Dolores. We will engage the finest lawyers in the country. They will be guiding us to a wise decision. But for now, you must leave matters in the hands of God. Your son is safe with

Mr. Howard. He is receiving very fine care. You must concentrate on yourself and your career.''

"I don't care about my career!" I shouted. "If it wasn't for my career, I would have my son with me right now."

"But then, Dolores, you would be nothing. You would be invisible," he said. "You would be in no position to fight Mr. Abraham Howard or any other person who wanted to take advantage of you. You must listen to me, Dolores. The train of justice is in motion. You can do nothing to stop this train. You must assist your lawyers, without a doubt, but what will you do the rest of your time, for the following three months? Do not forget, you are under an obligation to the men in Hollywood who are counting on you for their film. It is best for you to go to work. The work will take your mind off your troubles. It will help you pass the time until the hearing. I will personally guarantee that everything will be done to help you win your case. You have the word of Antonio Matos on it." He leaned over and placed his heavily ringed hand on mine.

"Work? How can I work, knowing that I might lose my son?" I whispered tearfully.

"You cannot know such a thing. You have great power to fight, good friends like Mr. Miller and myself. You have much money, and I will help you with unlimited funds to retain the most skilled legal counselors. Many people will testify to your upstanding character. You must let the other side know that you are calm and stable and confident of winning. Please, you must return to California with me."

Paul joined the argument, siding with Mr. Matos. In the end, I agreed to go, because I knew that matters were out of my hands now. The train of justice. Someday I would write a song about that train.

I have no memory about the making of *Monday's Girl*. I did what I was told, smiled or wept on cue, and even managed to perform the dance numbers they taught me. When the script called for me to kiss my leading man, I kissed him and I really tried to make it look convincing. I showed up on the set on time, submitted to the tortures inflicted by hairdressers and makeup men, I wore what the costume department gave me to wear, and I never questioned the director's decisions. But I refused to be photographed off the set in the company of any man with whom I could be linked romantically or otherwise. Even so, the studio press agents labeled me "a dream to work with," and told the Hollywood columnists that I was bright, professional, and thoroughly dedicated to my art. No one knew that inside my head, I was living a nightmare.

The hearing was set for September 10, 1948. I flew to South Carolina a couple of times to meet with my lawyers. My chief counsel, Andrew McKinley, was a partner in a prestigious Charleston firm and a specialist in family law. Family law: I had always thought that families were a law unto themselves. Mr. Matos had retained two other attorneys from a New York firm to act as consultants.

The three lawyers quizzed me on every aspect of my life. I told them about my marriage to Blair, and my long pre-war love affair with King Kingsley, about which I was deeply ashamed. Then I told them what I had never told another living soul, that Bram Howard and I had slept together in Villa d'Este during the war. I added that I had had no sexual relations with men at all since the war. All three men looked dubious.

"I've been too busy," I said. "I didn't have time for any of that."

"What about Antonio Matos?" Mr. McKinley asked. "You seem to have spent a lot of time with him, and he is not . . . ah, unattractive." Mr. Matos's New York lawyers exchanged glances.

"Our relationship has always been strictly professional," I told them. "Mr. Matos never gave any indication that he was interested in me that way."

Andrew McKinley looked incredulous. "Weren't you interested in him?"

I smiled. "You're right, he is a very attractive man. But it's strictly business between us, and it always has been. If you don't believe me, ask him."

"Well, Mr. Howard won't be likely to bring the Italian incident up in court," Andrew McKinley said, scribbling. "Still, it was an unfortunate encounter from our point of view. You may be sure he's told his lawyers all about it. They will most certainly go after you in the arena of morals. Now, can you think of any other incident which might have a bearing on the case, something they could use against you?"

I thought and thought, but came up with nothing. I had been proud of rebuilding my career without having to pay for my success with sexual favors.

"Ask Adam Foster. Whatever differences we may have had, I was as pure as the driven snow while I was singing with his band and he knows it. Better yet, ask Dizzy Dillon," I said. "He'll tell you I'm not a tramp."

"I shall consult both Mr. Foster and Mr. Dillon." Andrew McKinley's pen made scratching noises on his notepad. "Well, that seems to be it. You seem to have led a somewhat blemished life, morally speaking, Miss Heavener, but all things considered, we should be able to win. The other side will try to prove that you were far worse, of course, but we'll be ready for them. They'll need to produce some pretty strong proof."

It was the worst summer of my life. Every morning I awakened with a sick feeling in the pit of my stomach. Standing, sitting, or walking, my legs trembled with shivers of fear. My appetite all but vanished. The studio costumer was the first to notice it, then the cameramen. I started drinking chocolate milkshakes at every meal, but for once in my life, I didn't even want them.

The filming of *Monday's Girl* ended on schedule, just one week before the hearing. Mr. Matos and I flew to Charleston, where Andrew McKinley told us the case was in the bag.

"They can't prove anything except that you were absent from home a good bit and that you had one fairly stable long-term attachment, which is understandable considering your husband's mental and physical condition. It's not sufficient grounds for having you declared unfit. You did, after all, send generous sums of money to your father and your son, and you visited whenever you could get away. We have your canceled checks and store receipts. We've subpoenaed your letters to your father, which show that your intention was to take Grayson out to California to live with you."

I said, "I don't understand. Why can't we show that they're unfit to be parents? Jean-Ellen is the meanest-spirited serpent in all of Cluny County, and Bram Howard is nothing but a cold-hearted, money-grubbing machine."

Andrew McKinley shook his silver-gray head. "The burden of proof is on us, I'm afraid. It's just as well. Mr. Howard is a war hero with a Purple Heart and three citations for valor. This country has a lot of respect for its heroes. He has also established the Woodland Park Memorial Hospital in Munford, the most sophisticated and well-equipped rehabilitation center in the state. That hospital has brought a lot of new jobs to the area, and people are grateful. He has received recognition not only from the local politicians but also from the governor of the state and President Truman as well. No, we won't get anywhere trying to smear Bram Howard's character."

"He is a vindictive, evil man who stole my son," I said furiously. "But I guess the law doesn't recognize outright thievery of another person's child as a crime."

McKinley tidied the papers in his folder. "Not in this case, I'm afraid. Well, I'll see you both in court."

That September was the hottest on record. The courthouse fans batted the air around like wads of moist cotton. The spectators' gallery looked like a nest of swarming termites, with sheets of paper and paddles bearing the logo of the Orlando Smeal Funeral Home fluttering like so many butterfly wings.

Mr. McKinley had been mistaken about seeing Antonio Matos in court. Mr. Matos strictly avoided occasions that might attract publicity to himself, and besides, business required that he be in New York that month. However, his two New York lawyers took copious notes throughout the proceedings and wired a summation to him at the end of each day. Mr. Matos himself telephoned me every evening to lend encouragement and to allay my fears.

I had some doubts about Judge Miller's ability to deal with my case fairly, but Paul tried to set my mind at rest. His father had never disliked me, and no suggestion of bribery had ever tainted his courtroom. He was totally objective and equitable. Besides, a change of venue would not have benefitted us, because persons outside the Howards' immediate sphere of influence were far more awed by Bram's wealth and position of power in the state than Judge Miller.

Bram and Jean-Ellen arrived with their battery of lawyers, led by Tyler J. Lloyd, a Texan with high-heeled boots, rattlesnake eyes, and a reputation for grandstanding.

I craned my neck, searching the crowd for Gray, even though Mr. McKinley told me he would probably not make an appearance in court unless we requested that he testify. My father and Ayleen sat in the rear of the courtroom, near the door. Clara Mae sat right behind me. She had told us that Ayleen had fired her within two days of receiving the letter outlining my plans for Gray.

While the lawyers outlined the facts of the case, I studied my adversary. I had never seen Bram Howard when he wasn't self-assured and completely in control. Now he looked harried, tense, angry, and even guilty, I thought. He was determined to take my son from me, but he had no right to do it and he knew it. I was just as determined to stop him.

During the entire hearing, Bram never looked at me, not once. He kept his gaze fixed either on Judge Miller or on the portfolio of papers on the table in front of him. He consulted frequently with Tyler Lloyd, who seemed quite willing to defer to his illustrious client.

Mr. Lloyd put his client's reputation into the record first thing. We heard all about the Howard family's long history of service to the community and the state, about Bram's success in business and his brilliant military career, and lastly about the sad fact of his brother Blair's infirm condition.

"To this day, Blair Howard sits in a wheelchair staring out at the green trees that surround the family home," Tyler Lloyd said, his voice throbbing. "His brother Abraham's love is his only comfort and sustenance. And Abraham has provided well for this unfortunate member of his own family." Here Mr. Lloyd brought in the hospital and the extraordinary efforts Bram had made in trying to revive Blair's vanished consciousness. Then Lloyd dug up a little family history, outlining Blair's forced marriage to one Dolores Heavener of Munford. "The Howards protested this union, no doubt aware of Miss Heavener's unsavory reputation—"

"Objection!" Andrew barked.

"Excuse me, your honor," Tyler Lloyd said smoothly. "But the fact is that Blair did consent to marry Dolores, who claimed to be carrying his child. We have witnesses who will testify that he started drinking heavily after marrying Miss Heavener, and that his drinking may have contributed to the tragic accident that left him a helpless cripple."

I jumped up. "That's not true! Blair loved me, and I loved him!"

The judge advised my lawyer to control his client. After the hubbub died down, Tyler Lloyd went on: "When her infant was only eight months old, Miss Heavener decamped to New York, leaving the babe in the care of her father and stepmother. Six years passed, your honor. Six years during which she paid only a handful of visits to her home and her child. Instead of nurturing this tiny son, this product of her ill-considered union with Blair Howard, this woman joined a band of roving musicians—"

"Here it comes," Paul murmured. He had given up an important job to help me through this crisis, and while Andrew McKinley sat on my right side with Rubinstein and Finkler, my other two lawyers, Paul sat on my left, holding my hand.

Having gilded the Howard image until it gleamed like the Holy Grail, Tyler Lloyd turned his brush on me. This time it was loaded with tar. I was greedy, careless, self-centered, ambitious, and worst of all, I spent months and months in the company of men while I bared my bosom and sang lewd songs to drooling soldiers. By the time he was through, I hardly wanted to live with myself, much less take a helpless child into my keeping.

"It's all right," Paul squeezed my hand, "our turn's coming."

The parade of witnesses began. First, Mr. Alvah Motley, principal of the high school, testified that I had been expelled at the age of fifteen for uncivilized conduct. Mrs. Howard, Bram's mother, wept as she recounted my marriage to her innocent baby boy, Blair. Ayleen virtually sprinted to the stand to describe the night I had abandoned my child.

Tyler Lloyd produced what he called some lewd and disgusting photographs of me performing with King Kingsley's band. In one, I was bending forward, displaying ample cleavage, and I was licking my lips and grinning. Lewd indeed.

Then King Kingsley appeared. He not only admitted that he had enjoyed my companionship for the entire term of my employment with him, he stated flatly that I had been equally generous to the other members of the band.

"She was one of those women who could never get enough," he said with a languid shrug. "You can't blame the guys for taking advantage."

I leaped to my feet shouting, "That's a damned lie and you know it!" Paul jerked me back down and begged me to be quiet. On cross-examination, King failed to name any particular musician with whom he had actually seen me in compromising circumstances. Then Andrew McKinley managed to establish the fact that the most recent Mrs. Kingsley had divorced King because of his insane jealousy.

"One might say, Mr. Kingsley, that you are the type of man

who is in the habit of seeing a rival behind every tree or bush. I suggest that there is no truth whatsoever in your charge against Miss Heavener."

I felt vindicated, but my triumph was short-lived. Adam Foster took the stand next. I'd heard that he had continued drinking heavily after his band broke up. He certainly looked terrible, as if he were in the throes of the granddaddy of all hangovers. Adam swore under oath that I had been intimate with him during our USO tour and long afterward, all during our professional relationship.

"That's not true!" I screamed. "Bram Howard is paying you to slander me, isn't he? Isn't he!"

Judge Miller rapped his gavel and issued a stern warning. If I created any further disturbance, he would have me removed from the courtroom. Shaking with fury, I resumed my seat.

"They're crucifying me," I hissed to Andrew McKinley. "Do something!"

"Relax, Miss Heavener. If Mr. Foster has perjured himself, we'll have no trouble discrediting him. We have witnesses of our own, remember?" He stood up. "Mr. Foster, I understand that during the last months of Miss Heavener's association with your band, there was some professional friction between the two of you. In fact, the circumstances surrounding her departure were acrimonious, to say the least."

Andrew McKinley was a skilled questioner. He made Adam look like a run-down, third-rate musician who resented my popularity and at the same time rightly feared that losing me would lead to the collapse of his band.

Before Tyler Lloyd called his next witness, he addressed a casual but poisonous remark to the court: "If these men, these musicians who have been Miss Heavener's closest companions, did indeed perjure themselves here today, then they are villains of the first order and shall be dealt with each in his own turn. But even more important, we must ask ourselves these questions: What kind of woman habitually associates with such persons? What kind of woman would want her son associating with such persons?"

Over Andrew McKinley's shouts of "Objection!" Tyler Lloyd summoned Mrs. Myrna Foyle. Seeing her bustle into the courtroom, her corseted bosoms thrusting, I felt my heart sink.

She was by no means an ideal witness. Her memory was poor, her recall imperfect, and her delivery rambling and disjointed.

But what she was and what she said were damning. She had heard someone arrive at my apartment at eleven o'clock one evening. Disturbed by noise that kept getting louder and louder, she had finally crossed the hall at four-oh-five in the morning and beat on my door. When I opened it, she had seen a naked black man lying on my sofa, a bottle of bourbon in his hand. I, too, was reeking with alcohol, and wearing only a filmy negligee with nothing underneath.

Andrew McKinley leaned over and whispered, "What in hell is going on? Who is that woman?"

Mrs. Foyle continued her tale. Although the noise in my apartment abated, the black man did not leave. A couple of hours later, Mrs. Foyle, too horrified by what she had seen even to consider sleeping, heard another guest arrive at the crack of dawn. Peeking through a crack in the door, she saw a white man this time. The man sitting at the table beside me, in fact. He stayed for several more hours, during which time strange and terrible noises emanated from behind my door. Moans, sighs, loud cries, and my voice saying, "Make him drink some more," and "Oh, thank God, we did it, we did it!"

Finally, at five o'clock that afternoon, Mrs. Foyle had seen the two men leave, their arms entwined around each other.

I looked at Judge Miller. He was staring at Paul, his face pale and set. I knew then that I was lost.

Andrew McKinley begged a few minutes to consult with his client before he cross-examined Mrs. Foyle. Judge Miller called a recess and retreated to his chambers.

"Why didn't you tell me about that night?" McKinley demanded. "Mr. Miller, you should have known—"

"It was perfectly innocent." I proceeded to explain exactly what had happened.

"A drug addict, a heroin overdose . . . my God," Andrew McKinley moaned. "Do you think they're going to allow your son to live with a Negro dope fiend? We can't tell the truth about that. Look, I'll put you up on the stand. As far as you're concerned, Striker was sick with the flu or some other disease. He's terrified of doctors, refused to let you call for help. Maybe the other side doesn't know about his record. But I doubt it. Until then, I'll try to dismantle Foyle's testimony on cross-examination."

Court reconvened. "We're sunk, aren't we, Paul?" I whispered as we rose to show our respect to the judge. Paul said nothing, but I could not shake the dark dread that was seeping into my soul.

Andrew McKinley did a good job of stripping away the embroidery from Mrs. Foyle's testimony, but even the bare facts sounded bad enough.

"How did you know this man was naked?"

"I saw him."

"You saw his entire body?"

"I saw enough of it."

"How much is enough?"

"Well, from the waist up. He had something over his legs, a blanket, maybe. But I could tell—"

"We are not interested in what you surmised, Mrs. Foyle, only in what you actually saw. Now, you say that Miss Heavener was 'reeking of alcohol.' How close were you standing to her? Four feet? Five?"

Mrs. Foyle stumbled and contradicted herself as she answered Mr. McKinley's questions, but I could just imagine what pictures the judge and spectators were painting in their minds.

Before Mrs. Foyle left the stand, Tyler Lloyd showed her a photograph of Clayton Striker. She identified him positively as the man she had seen in my apartment. Then Lloyd introduced affidavits and copies of Clayton Striker's criminal record as a drug abuser. Clayton, it appeared, had been arrested for burglary twice, and he had once assaulted a police officer.

"This, your honor, is the kind of person with whom the mother of Grayson Howard has habitually been associating," Tyler Lloyd boomed. Judge Miller turned his gaze in our direction. I couldn't tell if he was looking at Paul or at me. His expression revealed nothing. At that moment, Tyler Lloyd rested his case.

Andrew McKinley put me on the stand, followed by a parade of character witnesses including Dizzy Dillon and the lieutenant-colonel who had arranged our USO tour. Then he whispered to me, "We've got to call Gray. The other side has been coaching him, but we'll have to risk it."

We had agreed not to use Gray's testimony unless Mr. McKinley felt that my case was in jeopardy. The outcome of my suit depended on Gray now, but no one knew what he would say or do.

I twisted around in my seat as Gray entered the courtroom. He was tall for a seven-year-old, at least I thought so. And he was handsome, fair-haired and blue-eyed just like his daddy.

And like his uncle. I willed him to look at me, but he kept his eyes lowered as he took his oath on the Bible, and as Andrew McKinley questioned him gently, he kept his gaze fixed on Bram and Jean-Ellen.

"Gray, you understand what's happening in this court today? We are trying to decide your future, and we'd like to hear your opinions on the subject. Your mother wants you to go to California and live with her. Your Uncle Bram wants you to stay at Woodlands with him. That's the choice that is before you now, and you must think very carefully before you answer my questions, because a lot depends on it. Is that clear?"

Gray nodded.

"Fine. Do you know what kind of work your mother does?"

"She's a singer."

"That's right. Being a singer is a difficult job, isn't it, Gray? It's not like being a schoolteacher or a nurse where you go to the same place at the same time every day, week in and week out, year after year. Your mother has had a lot of singing jobs over the years, which required her to travel all over the country and all over the world. That's why she couldn't be home with you. But she didn't neglect you, did she? She sent you letters and presents when she couldn't be home, and she paid visits, too, didn't she?"

"Yessir."

"Do you love your mother, Gray?"

"Yessir. I guess so."

"That's good. Because she loves you very much."

Andrew finished his questioning. Tyler J. Lloyd stepped up to the witness box.

"Do you like living at Woodlands, Gray? Are they nice to you there?"

Gray nodded, and he smiled a little. "Yessir. I have a lot of fun when I'm there."

"Do you like your Uncle Bram, Gray?"

Another nod. "Yes, he shows me things and plays with me. Nobody ever played with me before."

"You say you love your mother. Don't you think it would be fun to go live in California with your mother?"

Gray glanced at me then, and his eyes grew bright with tears. "What if she goes off and leaves me again?" he sobbed. "Like she did before?"

He would not be soothed. Jean-Ellen had to take him out of the courtroom.

Tyler Lloyd delivered a brief summation: "Your Honor, that little boy's sobs spoke more eloquently than I ever could. I have nothing further to add." Andrew McKinley, on the other hand, spent forty-five minutes pleading my case to the judge.

Judge Miller did not even leave the bench to consider his verdict. As soon as Andrew McKinley, sat down, he spoke:

"This court, while not unsympathetic to the strong attachment that naturally exists between a mother and the child she bears, also recognizes that the well-being of such a child depends on much more than simple maternal affection. A child requires a stable home, a cultured and mind-broadening environment, the companionship of adults on whom he can model his own behavior in later life." Judge Miller glared at Paul and me. "The defendants have shown beyond a shadow of a doubt that Miss Heavener and her friends are not morally fit to associate with respectable adults, much less with innocent children. Therefore, we award custody of Grayson Paul Howard to his uncle, Charles Abraham Howard, and to Jean-Ellen Howard."

I was on my feet, screaming, "No! No! No!"

"Further," Judge Miller went on, "in the interests of keeping the boy's environment free of the polluting influence of his natural mother, we forbid her to see him, to visit him, or to make any attempt to communicate with him in person. We are not unmindful, however, of the affection that may persist between them, and therefore we will permit the child to receive monthly letters from his natural mother, but only so long as those letters are deemed by his new guardians not to be harmful to the child's peace of mind."

"Letters!" My legs were giving way. Paul and Andrew McKinley struggled to hold me up. "He says I can write letters!"

I slipped away from them and fell into the merciful darkness of unconsciousness.

13

. . . can't seem to stop crying. Crying is the first thing I do when I wake up in the morning and the last thing I do at night. Oh, my baby. Most nights I don't sleep at all. I hold your picture close to my heart and rock and rock, like it was you in my arms. I have no life without you. This past year has been like my soul was ripped out of my body and a carload of pain put in its place. Oh, Gray, oh, Gray, if only we could be together for a few minutes. Oh, Gray . . .

THE HALF-EMPTY BOTTLE OF KENTUCKY BOURBON AT MY ELbow tipped over, spreading a pool of brown sorrow over my letter to Gray. My son. I reached over and snuffed out my cigarette in the overflowing ashtray before sopping up the spill with the sleeve of my bathrobe. I wasn't going to go up in flames like my mother. Not today, anyway. Poor Mama. Poor Gray. Poor me. Tears dripped onto my liquor-soaked sleeve.

After a few moments I peeled my letter to Gray off the desk and tossed the sodden mass in the direction of the wastebasket. They wouldn't let him read it, anyway. A good thing, too. They were right. I had no business being a mother.

I drew another letter out of the pocket of my bathrobe and reread it. Poor Gray. He really was an orphan now:

Dear Mrs. Howard:
We regret to inform you that your husband, Blair Howard, passed away late Monday afternoon, after suffering a cerebral hemorrhage. Funeral services and interment will take place on Wednesday, September 14, at 10:00 A.M.

Only members of the immediate family will attend. There is no need for you to return to Munford at this time.

A few small mementos have passed on to your son, Grayson, from his father, but, as you know, your husband had been living on his brother's charity since his calamitous accident and the unfortunate coincidence of the elder Mr. Howard's financial collapse, so your husband's estate is essentially nonexistent.

Please contact us directly if you have any questions regarding matters of inheritance or your former legal connections with the Howards.

Again, we express our sympathy to you in this time of bereavement.

> Sincerely yours,
> Arnold Fitch
> Leslie Breakwater
> Estate Attorneys
> Columbia, South Carolina

My former legal connections. Poor Blair. So, he was gone at last. This was Thursday already. My husband had been in his grave for almost a full day before I received the letter. Maybe the Howards were afraid I would show up at the funeral. Gray might have been there. If I had known, I might have tried to see him. I tipped the last few drops of bourbon into my mouth from the overturned bottle.

The doorbell rang once, and then again. I listened for Miralda's shuffle. She had become quite adept at turning away reporters and self-described well-wishers.

I wasn't expecting anyone. One year ago, after the hearing, Mr. Matos had decamped to Cuba on what he called urgent business. He telephoned frequently, but half the time I was too despondent to speak to him. I had no other friends, not even Paul. The memory of our parting scene in the empty courtroom still brought tears to my eyes. I blamed him for the loss of my child. If it hadn't been for his peculiar passion for Clayton Striker, I screamed, his father would never have been persuaded of my evil influence—and on and on. Paul stood there in silence, taking it all in. Then he turned and walked away from me. I didn't see him again.

I waited for Miralda to give her standard spiel: "Mees Heavener is seeing no one. She is seek. I am so sorry." Instead, I heard a rapid exchange in Spanish, then Mr. Matos threw open the door and strode into my living room. He was a dazzling sight in a tropical white linen suit and pink shirt, his black hair glistening like the proverbial raven's wing. As usual, dark glasses concealed his eyes. He certainly didn't need them in my house of mourning; the windows had been shuttered and the drapes drawn for an entire year. The passing of an invalid husband wouldn't have changed things at all.

Antonio Matos coughed and pressed a handkerchief to his lips. The air in the room was foul with liquor, despair, and stale cigarette smoke.

"You must stop this nonsense, Dolores," he said. "You are only hurting yourself, and you are not helping either your son or your career."

"I have no son. To hell with my career." I flicked my cigarette toward the ashtray. It fell short, and ash sifted onto the carpet. "To hell with everybody. To hell with you. What are you doing here, anyway? I told you the last time you called that I wanted to be left alone to die."

He walked over to the windows and jerked open the drapes. The cobalt glare from the blue-tiled swimming pool outside was dazzling. My eyes filled. A year ago, I had pictured Gray and me playing in it together, splashing, dunking, racing each other. Of course Gray would win. I would pretend to be old and out of shape and easily winded, and he would always beat me. He could certainly beat me now.

"Close those curtains," I pleaded. "I don't want to look."

"You will look." He opened the French doors to the patio. The scent of orange blossoms and roses wafted in on the freshening breeze from the valley. Southern California bloomed relentlessly. I hated it.

Mr. Matos stood over me. "Look at you, as white as one of those grubs that lives under the earth. Your hair looks like a rat's nest. And your face . . . you look fifty years old, a withered hag at the age of twenty-four. Come, Dolores. Come!"

Overcoming my resistance, he half-carried, half-dragged me into the sunshine. I winced at its harshness and recoiled from its warmth. Then suddenly he pushed me into the cool water of the pool. I came up sputtering and shouting.

"What the hell do you think you're doing? What gives you the right to come here and start bullying me? Damn you; where have you been for the past year? You abandoned me. You left me!

You're just like everybody else; as soon as there's no profit to be had from Dessie Heavener, you walk away."

He stood far back from the edge of the pool, out of splashing range. "Ah, I see that you are treading water. Perhaps your death wish is not so strong as you think, Dolores."

He was right. I was peddling my legs furiously and stroking with my arms. I stopped all motion and sank to the bottom of the pool. Pushing myself to the surface once again, I swam to the edge. "I'm just waiting for the right time," I gasped. "You'll see. This world stinks, and I'm not going to live in it one more day if I can help it."

Sighing, he shook his head. "Life is like this swimming pool, Dolores. You can either stay out of it altogether, which is a form of living death. Or you can throw yourself into it and drown as the water overwhelms you. Or you can rise to the surface and let the water support and carry you. I left you alone after the hearing because I could not share your grief. I sympathize, naturally. I am your most loyal friend. But how could I possibly share your feelings? I have never been a father. I do not know what it is to put my arms around the child of my own flesh. The shock of losing your son was devastating to you. You needed time to recover, no less than a year. But no more. In the meantime, I had pressing business which required my presence in Florida and Havana. Now the year has passed. You must make a choice, either to resume living or to sink into despair and death. Which do you think will benefit your son the best?"

I dragged myself out of the pool and collapsed on the blue tiles at his feet. "Why don't you just leave me alone?" I sobbed. "I was doing all right before I met you. If you hadn't come along, I would have my son with me right now. I wouldn't have been so all-fired busy with records and nightclub appearances and movies. I'd be singing for peanuts in a crummy little joint somewhere, but at least I'd have my baby."

Mr. Matos asked Miralda to bring me a dry robe. As he helped me into it, he said, "I know what you need to make you happy."

"What?"

"Another child. Our child." He helped me to my feet and led me toward the shade of the eucalyptus tree at the edge of the patio.

I sank into a rattan chair and stared at him.

"You seem surprised." He seated himself on the opposite side of the white wrought-iron table. "Do you think me such an unlikely candidate for fatherhood?"

"No, not at all! But I never . . . that is, you never seemed . . . interested in me that way," I finished lamely.

"You were married to another," he reminded me gently. "And you were concentrating on your career. I had no right to interfere with you. But now your husband is dead. Any legal obstructions to a permanent union between us have vanished."

Miralda brought out a pitcher of cold lemonade. I dumped two spoons of sugar into my glass, gave the lemonade a quick stir, and gulped down two big swallows. At least I didn't have to worry about calories these days. Sorrow had eroded my flesh, exposing tendons and bones I never knew I had.

"You don't want to marry me," I said. "Look at me. You don't want me. You can't. Nobody wants me."

"I do want you, Dolores. I want you to be my wife, the mother of my child."

His calm, sphinxlike inscrutability annoyed me. "How can you be so sure that I want a baby, anyway?"

Mr. Matos pushed his glass into a patch of sunshine on the table. Miralda had given him too much ice. "As a boy, I was a chess player. Even though I was very young, I was successful and I won all my matches. But I never relied solely on my own brilliance and clever strategy. Before I faced an opponent over the chessboard, I always learned all I could about him. I wanted to be able to predict which move he would make. I studied his personality as carefully as I studied his game. That practice has been useful to me since then, even in the world beyond the chessboard."

"I'm not your opponent, Mr. Matos." I drew my robe tighter around my middle. "I'm . . . I thought we were friends."

"Men and women are in eternal opposition to each other, Dolores," he said patiently. "That is how nature has designed us. Out of conflict and chaos and pain, new life emerges." Rising, he moved around to the back of my chair and rested his hands on my shoulders. I quivered. I had not felt the touch of another human being in over a year. Gradually the shock and strangeness subsided. I relished the weight of his hands. Strength flowed from his sureness. "I want to redress the wrong that has been done," he said. "To restore what the stupid laws in this country have taken away from you."

Tears rolled down my cheeks. "I want a baby. I do." Reaching up, I groped for his hand and pressed it to my cheek. "Please, Mr. Matos, give me a baby. Now. Today."

He stroked my cheek. "Perhaps you are not ready for that yet."

"I need someone to hold me." I twisted around in my chair and pressed my face against his middle. "You. I need you. I love you. I do."

"You had better start using my Christian name. Call me Tony. Antonio is too formal."

"Tony. Yes, Tony." I got unsteadily to my feet. My legs felt weak, but when I started to sway, Tony's arms encircled my waist and kept me from falling. He had the strength that I lacked, the knowledge, the courage. I wasn't alone anymore.

Slowly, we made our way into the house, to the cool darkness of my bedroom. Tony removed my robe, clucking softly at my wasted figure. He seated me on the edge of the bed, then undressed himself. He took off his dark glasses last. He smiled. "I like to preserve a sense of mystery on occasions like this."

I shook my head. "I think you could take off your skin and all your hair, and I still wouldn't know what you were all about."

He sat beside me. "Does my mystery disqualify me for fatherhood?"

I rested my head on his shoulder. His flesh was firm and cool and hairless. I said, "I'm not beautiful anymore. You were right. I do look like a hag. How can you possibly love me?"

"I love you more," he said, "because now you belong to me alone, to no one else. When you are on the stage, I must share you with others. But today you are simply a woman worn down by grief. The words that come out of your mouth are true, like the lyrics of a song you have written yourself. A song you have written for me."

"I need you," I said. "I love you."

He kissed me. Still embracing, we fell back among the pillows. "Need before love," he murmured. "That is how it should be."

He made love to me, and it was gentle and undemanding and infinitely soothing. For the first time in over a year, I slept soundly, all night and well into the following day. When I awakened, I rang for Miralda. Tony came into the room himself, bearing a tray.

"You have learned to love again; now you must learn to eat," he said. "Both are necessary to sustain life. Do you want to live, Dolores?"

"Yes, I do." My own words surprised me. I tried to recall the creature I had been before he came. She was growing fainter in my memory, like someone I had met and shared a journey with, but with whom I had little in common. My hands flew to my hair. "Tell Miralda to call my hairdresser," I said. "I'm not setting foot out of this room looking like this. I want to look beautiful for you again, Tony."

"You will always be beautiful in my eyes, Dolores."

I took a bite of toast. Not many hours ago, the very idea of food had repelled me. Now I found myself relishing the texture, the warmth, the flavor, the whole idea of toast and butter and strawberry jam. "Maybe we could go someplace this evening," I said. "I haven't been outside this house for a whole year."

Tony patted my hand. "My love has worked a miracle. You really are coming back to life. Of course we shall go out, anywhere you like. Would you like to fly to Paris?"

I laughed at his suggestion. Laughter, too, was an odd sensation. Like touching. And breathing. And tasting. "No, thank you. I think Bel-Air will be good enough for my debut."

After the hairdresser departed, I gave myself a long, hard look in the mirror. My face was still drawn, but my years in show business had taught me a trick or two. I got out my makeup case and started to paint out the ravages of my grief. The process of resurrecting my corpse took three hours, but by the end of it I once again resembled Dessie Heavener, popular singer and fledgling movie star. I chose a gown of white chiffon. White, the color of new life. Midnight-blue was too much like mourning.

Tony informed me that his car was waiting. As I gave my nose a final touch with a powder puff, I noticed that my hand was trembling. I was experiencing stage fright. For one whole year, I had lived as a recluse. The world had ceased to exist for me. Time had hardened around me, encasing me in a posture of grief like a fly in amber. But now I was ready to move my wings again, to begin a different sort of life without Gray, free of ties to Munford. A new husband. A baby. I wanted to be held, and I wanted someone to hold. I would be a good mother this time. A fine mother.

Over dinner, Tony told me that *Monday's Girl* had been released two months earlier. While the reviewers had not been kind to either the plot or the production, they had raved about my performance. The critic for *The New York Times* called me "the freshest young actress to appear on the screen in several years."

I shook my head in wonderment. "I feel like I've been asleep for twenty years." I had been totally unaware of the movie's release. I did recollect a period during which the phone had rung almost hourly, until I got tired of hearing it and Miralda got tired of telling people that I was not able to speak to them. In desperation, I had ripped the wires right out of the wall. Silence reigned for a few days until someone, Tony probably, had arranged for service to be restored and my number changed.

"You are waking up. You will see, as the days pass, you will begin to notice more and more." Tony had removed his dark glasses as we entered the romantic candlelit restaurant. His green-gold eyes shone with warmth. Tony. My Antonio. I could harldy believe that my marriage to Blair Howard had kept us apart for so long. But now I was free. And Tony loved me. He summoned the waiter to refill my glass. 'I should tell you that the studio intends to hold you to your contract. They want you to start another picture right away. They have promised a better vehicle for your talents. I will inform them tomorrow that they will have to wait at least two months."

"Why so long?" I took another sip of champagne. It was working its magic. The piercing pain in my heart had dulled to a tolerable ache. "I should be ready to go back to work sooner than that."

His eyes flashed mischievously. "Because," he said, "we sail tomorrow for Tahiti."

After dinner, we drove down to a marina near Malibu. Anchored in the middle of the harbor was an enormous yacht. It was nearly as big as a cruise ship. We climbed into a waiting motor launch and rode out to her. Her running lights and all her cabin lights burned brightly in welcome.

"It's magnificent," I breathed. "Who owns it?"

"You do," Tony replied. "It is my wedding gift to you. Will you come aboard, Madame Captain? Welcome to the *Blue Dolores*."

Two men in white uniforms snapped salutes as we climbed up a ladder and set foot on deck. Tony led me down a short flight of stairs—the companionway—to the main salon. I marveled over such seagoing elegance: polished teak, gold fittings, red plush upholstery, heavy mahogany tables and chairs, a silk Oriental carpet on the floor. It even had a stone fireplace in one corner, in which a couple of small mesquite logs burned merrily. Tony poured me another glass of champagne from the bottle cooling in a bucket on the bar.

"This vessel is powerful, sturdy, and eminently seaworthy," he said. "You will never feel seasick. She has stabilizers in her hull, just like oceangoing liners."

"Tally-ho!" Laughing giddily, I raised my glass to him. "Or should I say, 'Yo ho-ho and a bottle of rum?' When do we sail?"

"We raised anchor five minutes ago."

I ran to the nearest porthole and looked out. The lights of the marina twinkled at us from the receding shore.

"But I didn't bring a thing to wear," I protested. "I can't get married in this."

"I have supplied a new wardrobe, including a wedding gown," Tony said, "and an elegant trousseau for a beautiful bride."

The *Blue Dolores* handled sudden squalls and even a violent tropical storm with the unperturbable calm of her purchaser. We reached Papeete ten days later. After we dropped anchor, a French priest came aboard. He married us on the main deck, under the light of a full moon. I wore a simple dress of ivory silk with a full skirt and a boned bodice, and a crown of fragrant tropical flowers. The next day Tony and I were married again in a civil ceremony at the town hall, following French custom.

"Not one but two weddings! This union is obviously meant to last," I said gaily as we strolled arm in arm back to the dock.

"Until death parts us, Dolores." Tony tightened his grasp on my arm. His tone was serious. "Perhaps even longer than that."

Tony insisted that we keep our marriage secret for a while. "I am thinking of your safety," he said. "I have many enemies. If they knew I had a wife, and in due time, a child, they might threaten you to gain power over me. I cannot permit that. I beg you, do not breathe a word of this marriage to anyone until I give my permission."

"But who are these enemies you're always talking about?" I asked. "Can't you make peace with them, or buy them off?"

"It is no concern of yours, Dolores." He waived my questions aside. "I will take care of them in my own way and in my own time. You need have no worries about the future. But for the moment I must demand absolute silence and secrecy. I cannot allow my movements to become known to the readers of fan magazines and tabloids."

I started work on a movie called *Songbird*. The plot was similar to *Monday's Girl*, but the script was better and the production of infinitely higher quality than my first cinematic foray. While *Monday's Girl* had been a modest hit, some even said a flop, *Songbird* promised to be a box office smash—at least that's what the Magnus Studio press releases kept saying.

During lulls in the filming, I made a few television and radio appearances with my co-star in *Songbird*, an ex-Broadway hoofer named Dan Early, who literally danced rings around me in the movie's obligatory dream sequence.

Songbird gave me the theme song for which I had been waiting all my life, a number called "Midnight Blue." Clayton Striker's heroin-crazed interlude in my apartment had cost me my son, but in a single evening he had taught me more about singing than I had learned in six years on the road with the band. I took the notes of "Midnight Blue" and ripped them up one side and down the other. Fortunately, they managed to film it on the first take. That was a good thing, because when I sang the last refrain, I was too drained of emotion to repeat it:

> I never knew how much I had to lose.
> I've got those low-down,
>   lonesome,
> Everlovin' midnight blues.

The producer and director told me I was singing better than ever. In Hollywood, compliments like that were as cheap as the breath that carried them, but this time I knew they were right. I paid silent and bitter tribute to Clayton Striker. Thanks to him, I was honestly living those stories of love and loss, not merely telling them. I had known pain and I had known heartache, and sorrow was still my closest companion. Tony's love was slowly healing some of my wounds, but whenever I sang, they opened and I bled a little.

After the filming was completed, Tony and I sailed to Hawaii on the *Blue Dolores*. I wanted to escape the studio bosses, who had insisted that I begin filming another picture at once. I was still trying desperately to become pregnant, and I hoped that a week or two in the tropical sunshine would encourage the miracle to happen.

I consulted a couple of specialists, but they could find nothing wrong with me and advised me to stop trying so hard. But I desperately wanted a new baby. That became my goal and my obsession, one which I pursued as single-mindedly and passionately as I had once chased a career as a singer. Tony was sympathetic and encouraging; he wanted a child as much as I, and he shared my frustration when another month went by with no results.

Songbird surpassed the studio's expectations, earning back all of its production costs in the first two weeks following its release in the fall of 1950.

In *Showgirl*, filmed that same year, I played a turn-of-the-century Floradora girl who falls in love with the richest man in the world, only to find true happiness in the arms of the shoeshine boy who has loved her since girlhood. The plot was almost identical to that of *Songbird*, except that I uttered my lines of deathless dialogue clad in hourglass corsets and leg-of-mutton sleeves instead of rolled stockings and beaded flapper dresses:

ME: (gazing up at the stars) Rory, I want to be a star, a big star. I want it more than anything in the world.

HE: (rubbing the side of his neck, a troubled expression on this handsome face) Well, Kitty, if that's what you want, then you'll probably get it. But fame isn't the most important thing in the world. You'll find that out sooner or later.

Dan Early partnered me again. Magnus must have decided that our weaknesses complimented each other. I was a good singer but an unexceptional dancer; Dan's baritone was almost girlishly light, but his dancing was magical. Press agents and columnists started promoting us as the new Rogers and Astaire. Theater owners billed us as "Dessie and Dan," which I told Tony sounded like a horse act.

I began writing to Gray again, newsy nonhysterical letters about my work, the people I met, the places I visited. Months went by, but I never received an answer. Certain that Bram and Jean-Ellen were hiding my letters from him, I wrote to Clara Mae in care of the minister of her church and asked her to find out what she could from Sylvester. Sylvester replied at once. His letter said that as far as he could tell, Gray was getting along just fine. The boy was growing tall and strong, eating enough to fill up two normal boys, and he was learning to play tennis and ride horses and dance the waltz. Gray sure hated his dancing lessons. Sylvester wasn't sure what had happened to my letters; leastwise, he had never seen any, and he always took in the mail at Woodlands himself.

In the summer of 1951, just a few weeks before I was supposed to begin filming another Dessie and Dan epic—in this one, we were poor sod-busters growing up on the Nebraska prairie and my dreams of fame would carry me to San Francisco just in time for the earthquake—I learned that I was pregnant. The baby was due in March of the following year.

I was thrilled, but my producer at Magnus Studios was aghast when he heard the news.

"You'll ruin the picture!" he wailed. "By October, when we're supposed to film the big dance hall scenes, you'll be as big as a house. What's worse, you're not even married. Do you realize what a scandal like this can do to the studio? A baby out of wedlock!"

I remained calm. News of my marriage to Antonio Matos had not leaked to the press, and my husband insisted that we keep it secret for a few months longer, until he could guarantee that his wife and child would be in no danger from his enemies at home.

"If it's all right for a movie star to adopt a baby when she isn't married," I asked the producer, "why can't she have one of her own? I don't see what all the fuss is about."

"Look, Dessie"—his voice had all the weight of Magnus Studios behind it—"I like you. I think you have incredible talent. But I do not like shenanigans. When you first came to Magnus, you were hired to fill in for Glendie Burke because of what the newspapers called a sudden illness. The police didn't call it that, but their investigation, which included you and your manager, Antonio Matos, produced nothing."

"I don't understand. What are you talking about?"

"Someone slipped Glendie Burke an acid cocktail that burned out her throat and ruined her entire digestive system. She'll be in a nursing home for the rest of her life. That's shenanigans, and I won't have my people involved with them. This pregnancy is the last straw. We may have to scratch this picture. When news of this gets out, you're going to be too hot to handle."

I ran home to tell Tony, who had just returned from a quick trip to Cuba. "They told me a terrible story about someone poisoning that actress I replaced in my first picture. They acted like they thought we had something to do with it! And they're threatening to cut me loose unless I marry someone right away. Can't we tell them the truth now?"

"No. Absolutely not." Tony looked up from the Havana newspaper he had brought back with him.

"But my career is going to be ruined! I'm scared, Tony." I sat beside him on the sofa and put my arms around him. "I don't understand you, Tony. You've worked just as hard for all this as I have. Don't you care?" My eye fell on the Spanish language newspaper he was reading. I saw a photograph of a man wearing dark glasses and a tuxedo, standing beside a roulette wheel. Before I could see more, Tony leaned forward and pitched the newspaper into the fireplace.

"After our child is born, you will not want to make any more films," he said. "Your maternal instincts are much too powerful. You will not wish to take the time away from our baby. I love you, Dolores, and I would like to take you back to Cuba with me right away. But the time is not yet right. Unfortunately I may have to leave you soon, without much notice."

"Tony, is something wrong? Why can't you stay?"

"Politics, Dolores. Nothing for you to worry about. You must stay in this country and make a home for our baby. Your movies have made you famous all over the world. After the baby is born, you will be able to sing wherever, whenever you wish. But mostly you will wish to stay at home and be a mother."

Miralda brought in a pot of fresh coffee. Tony poured some into a demitasse cup and sipped it slowly. He had taught Miralda how to make coffee the Cuban way, as thick and as black as tar and strong enough to eat the chrome off a Cadillac.

He was right. When Gray was born, I had been sixteen years old. I hadn't wanted to be a mother. Now I did. I wanted it more than anything.

Magnus rushed *Song of the Earth* into production. The sound stages were declared off-limits to visitors and reporters and anyone not directly concerned with the movie. The producer let it be known that I was under great strain and that I required maximum privacy. In reality, he wanted to prevent news of my pregnancy from reaching the public. The studio bosses had decided to let me work out this, the final film in my contract, and then turn me loose. I could marry or burn, as I chose, so long as the picture was a hit.

Tony received an increasing number of mysterious telephone calls from Miami and Havana. One morning he announced that he had to return to Cuba at once.

"When will you be back?"

"When the present crisis is solved, or when I am exiled." He smiled and kissed me tenderly. "If you are ever in any difficulty, you can write to me, or call me at this number." He handed me a card. "It is the Presidential Palace. They will know where to find me."

"The Presidential Palace! You're not the president of Cuba, are you?" I laughed, but Tony looked serious.

"I am the friend and close adviser of the most powerful man in the country. I told you long ago that I could recognize remarkable ability when I saw it. Even as a boy, Fulgencio Batista had an aura of destiny about him."

I was a full-fledged, bona fide movie star. My smiling face adorned magazine covers, billboards, and theater marquees. I endorsed shampoos, beauty soaps, and skin creams. In public places, strangers crowded around to ask for autographs. Magnus sent out thousands of glossy photographs of me every week: Dessie Heavener, blond and dazzling, her lips scarlet, her smile alluring. "Blue" Heavener. " 'Dorable Dess." Was I crazy, I wondered, to give it all up? But I had made my choice. I wanted another baby more than I wanted stardom, whatever that meant. When the baby came, I would tell the rest of the world to go to hell. I was tired of Hollywood. I decided to go back to New York, where I could settle down amid familiar surroundings and old friends and make a real home for my son or daughter. I would give my child everything I had wanted for Gray. And someday, my two children would meet. That was my dearest wish.

The filming of the sod-buster epic ended in mid-December. By then I was so far along in my pregnancy that the wardrobe people had me wearing shawls over my prairie gingham dresses. After informing Tony of my plans by letter, I sold my house to a promising young actress from Detroit. As I handed over the keys, I wished her luck and more happiness than I had enjoyed in the place. Then I caught the next plane for New York.

I knocked on Paul's door at two o'clock in the afternoon on Christmas Eve. After a long time, he opened it. He looked like he had slept in his clothes, and his eyes were bloodshot and bleary.

"Hi," I drawled. "I'm a hick kid from South Carolina and I've come to New York because I want to break into show business."

"My God. Dessie! Come on in."

I shed the new sable coat Tony had given me, an early Christmas present, and tossed it over the back of a sagging armchair. Two new diamond bracelets rattled on my wrist. Paul's gaze swept over my swollen figure. "Oh, no, not again."

I rested my hands on my belly. "Yes, again. Or maybe I should say at long last. I won't be making any movies for a while. In my case, the price of motherhood seems to be professional extinction in Hollywood."

"Because you're not married." He reached out and grasped my hand. "Do you think we could . . . ?"

I shook my head. "No, Paul. I do love you, but I can't marry you."

He turned away. "Why did you come? Not because you needed me. You've never needed me. Who's the father? That dancing fool . . . what's-his-name? . . . Early?"

"I can't explain now. Please don't be angry with me. We've spent too much time apart as it is. I wanted a happy reunion, not a fight." I batted my eyelids and said in my best movie-actress tones, " 'Oh, Rory, I've been such an idiot. I hope you can forgive me.' "

Paul's scowl relaxed into a grin. " 'Kitty,' " he replied in a voice dripping with earnestness, " 'when you smile at me like that, I'd go right over the moon for you.' "

We laughed together. Paul said, "I've seen all your movies at least twice and I have all your records. You sound terrific. That year you took off seems to have done you good."

"Sometimes I hurt so bad inside that I can hardly stand it," I said. "I don't know how I managed to sing at all. Maybe I have two pairs of lungs, one for singing and one for breathing."

He looked stricken. "It was my fault. I wish I could make it up to you."

"You don't need to. I'm making it up to myself, with this baby. Will you be godfather again?"

"I would be honored, ma'am." He took my hand. "I'm glad you're back, Dess. I've missed you."

Never one to be satisfied with a handshake when I could get a hug, I threw my arms around his neck. "Merry Christmas, Paulie. It's good to be home again."

14

I MANAGED TO REMAIN ANONYMOUS IN NEW YORK FOR TWO weeks, until a photographer saw me coming out of Bergdorf Goodman's and snapped my picture. The next morning, one million people looked at page one, saw my blossoming figure, and drew the obvious conclusions.

I had expected a few words of criticism when the public found out about my pregnancy, but the scandal that broke over my head amazed me.

"Having lost one child in a highly publicized courtroom battle with millionaire television, radio, and lumber magnate C. Abraham Howard," Pepper Wellington wrote, "Miss Heavener is now looking forward to the birth of another baby. The father's identity is still a secret. Screen heartthrob Dan Early has denied that he and 'Dorable Dess ever went farther than on-screen passion, but Dan's wife is rumored to be seeking a divorce."

Magnus Studios denounced me to the movie-going public. They deplored my lack of morals and promised I would be banned from motion pictures for all time to come. They also forwarded bushels of hate mail to me. "Dessie 'Heavener' ought to change her name to 'Hell,'" a man from Iowa declared, "because that's sure enough where she's going." Record and radio producers shunned me. An automobile manufacturer who had been trying to persuade me to record its advertising jingle suddenly retracted its offer. Other companies whose products I had endorsed found new spokespersons—all brunettes. One small town in Alabama burned my records and prints of two of my movies in the middle of the high school football field.

"Lie low for a while," Dizzy Dillon advised when I visited him in Queens. "After the kid is born, you can start singing in clubs. You won't have any trouble getting work, and in a couple of years, the public will discover you all over again and you'll be a bigger star than ever."

"Being a star means living your life in an aquarium." I kicked off my shoes and warmed my feet in front of his little gas fire. "Back in California I couldn't go to a public rest room without some lady shoving her autograph book under the door. At one movie premiere, the fans ripped so much fur out of my mink that it looked like it was molting. Strange men were always trying to kiss me. Everywhere I went, people took pictures of me. They took pictures of the outside of my house and my car when I wasn't even in it. I'm not sure I want to go back to all that." I almost told Dizzy about my marriage, but my promise to Tony held me back. I could divulge my secret to no one, not even to my closest friends. "I still want to sing, Diz. But I also want this baby and I'm not sorry about anything that's happened to me because of it."

After the constant pressure of Hollywood, I thought I would be relieved to stop singing for a while, but I began to miss it more and more. Before my unmasking in front of Bergdorf Goodman's, when I was still anonymous, I had stripped a record store of all their new recordings of Billie Holiday, Coleman Hawkins, and Duke Ellington, the people whose music I felt closest to.

I also bought every album Clayton Striker had ever made: *Strike Out*, *Striking Gold*, *The Clock Strikes One*. I wanted to understand the language he spoke with his alto sax. As I listened to my own recent recordings, I was pleased with how much I had learned from him already. My line had smoothed out, my phrasing was more natural, my dynamics—loud and soft—were more marked, more dramatic. I was breathing like a sax player. And I was taking chances, turning ordinary songs into blues songs by flatting the third and seventh notes of the scale, the "blue notes."

I rented an apartment just a few blocks away from Paul's. He was a frequent visitor and enthusiastic guinea pig for my experiments in the kitchen. I had developed a craving for home cooking, for certain dishes that Clara Mae used to make. The only way I could get decent fried chicken and boiled greens with ham hocks in the middle of Manhattan was to learn how to cook them myself. Jingo joined us from time to time, but never Clayton. I told Paul that I would not allow the man to enter my house. As much as I admired Clayton Striker's music, I thought he was a despicable human being. According to Paul, Clayton had been clean for an entire year, heroin-free. I wasn't impressed. I was sure that like so many other musicians I had known, Clayton was still smoking marijuana and popping amphetamines, keeping his system poisoned with some kind of drug until his craving for heroin became irresistible and he submitted to its terrible power again.

The Paul Miller Trio had been performing at Rolly Rollinson's Hi-Note Club down on Fourth Street for the last three months. They were drawing good crowds and had attracted excellent notices. They had also cut a number of albums, one of which was so experimental, so radical, that the critics were still arguing about what it meant.

I started going to the club often, three or four times a week. I loved being back on my old schedule, staying up until two or three in the morning, then moving on to an after-hours club to drink coffee and listen to more jazz before falling into bed at dawn and sleeping until noon.

Between sets at the Hi-Note one night, Clayton came over to my table. We had not spoken a word to each other since my return. "How 'bout singing something?" he said.

I drew as far away from him as the limited space between tables would allow. "You've got to be kidding." My voice trembled. "Do you really think I would share the same stage with you after what you did to me? It's hard enough just sharing the same nightclub with you."

"And just what did I do to you?"

"You . . . your antics in my apartment that night cost me my son," I said through clenched teeth. "If that woman hadn't seen you lying there half—"

"Shit. Somebody else would have seen you doing something that their nasty minds would call sinful." Clayton slid into the chair opposite mine and lit a cigarette. "You didn't have a chance, Mama. You were up against one of them rich and powerful white men, and you lost that fight before it even got started. I guess you know now how some of us black folk feel on a real bad day. Hey, no use you being mad at me anymore. Besides, you got something to say to me, you sing it. Paul and Jingo will be right there to protect you." He laughed heartily, treating me to a dazzling display of his white teeth.

My better judgment told me to keep my distance, but the artist in me wanted to see how our voices would blend. Besides, I was dying to sing again. I agreed to join them for what Clayton promised would be a tame rendition of "Just in Time."

The crowd knew me more from my movies than from my days as a big band singer. When I stepped up on the tiny stage, I heard snorts of derision and comments about " 'Dorable Dess" and loud speculation about who had knocked me up.

Paul gave me the thumbs-up. I grinned back. Jingo played two measures of introduction. The trio played the number through once, fairly conventionally, then I stepped up to the microphone and sang a chorus like a slow ballad, but flatting some notes and interpolating others and weaving a new song out of old threads of melody. Clayton followed me; in fact, he anticipated me and supported me and let me know that anywhere I wanted to go was all right with him. As I gained confidence, I started to experiment a little more, wailing and crooning and even whispering when I felt like it. Always, the mellow voice of his sax was with me, making the song a duet rather than a solo.

The second time through, we picked up the tempo. Facing each other across the top of the microphone, Clayton and I carried on a spirited dialogue. We discovered that we had a lot to say to each other, musically at least.

I must have looked a sight: a very pregnant woman swinging her hips and popping her fingers and shaking her head and wailing for all she was worth, but at the end of the number the crowd cheered and demanded an encore. Exhilarated but exhausted by my first public venture into improvisation, I declined.

Later, Clayton said to me, "You are one cool chick, Mama. You really can dig it." Paul was ecstatic. The two people he cared most about in the world, although not exactly friends, had finally performed together, communicated musically, on his stage, with his group. I felt proud of myself. I had held my own with a man many people considered a musical giant. I was more than a pleasing voice left over from the Big Band era. I was a serious musician.

After that, I performed one or two numbers with the trio every night. Pepper Wellington and a couple of other critics of contemporary music turned up to review my new act.

"You called me a jazz singer," I said to Pepper after his column appeared. "I'm not even sure what that means."

"A jazz musician is anybody who can't play the notes as they're written," he told me. "You qualify. I knew you were a jazz musician the first time I heard you sing 'Hava Banana.' You dismantled that song and put it back together. Jazz is now. Jazz is tomorrow. The one thing jazz is not is yesterday."

I thought about that for a moment. "No wonder I can't stand Beethoven."

Pepper laughed. "That's one swinging little baby you're going to have, Dessie."

I was heavy with child—thirty pounds heavier than my normal weight—and my time to deliver was drawing near. At the end of February, I curtailed my performances at the Hi-Note. A few days later, I was sitting out front listening to Clayton's interpretations of current events when I realized that his music was more irritable and fractious than usual, nastier, more aggressive. I asked Paul if Clayton was back on drugs.

Paul answered too quickly. "Of course not. I'd know it if he was."

But I saw the despair in my friend's eyes, and I knew that Clayton had started shooting heroin again.

The first week in March, a blizzard struck New York. Temperatures dropped into the teens and mountains of dirty snow blocked sidewalks and doorways. Three days by myself in my apartment were enough to give me a good case of cabin fever, and as soon as I could get out, I threw on my sable coat from Tony, warmed up my Cadillac, and headed down to the Hi-Note. The streets were barely passable, but I managed to drive the whole way without mishap and to find a parking spot around the corner from the club.

Rolly Rollinson, the club's owner, greeted me with a kiss. "Cold enough for you out there? Come on in where the music is hot. Everybody else in town is here. We've been plenty busy since the storm." We sat at my usual table and sipped our drinks, Scotch for him and a weak bourbon for me. He looked over my shoulder and scowled. Two men had come in right on my heels and staked out a table near the back of the room.

"Jesus. I wish those bastards would back off."

"Why?" I twisted around to look at them. "Who are they?"

"Narcotics cops. Feds. They've been trailing Clayton and some of his pals around town for a couple of weeks now, trying to find out where they're getting their stuff. I just went back and told Clayton he'd better not be shooting up between sets. I don't want to get closed down because one of my musicians gets caught using dope on the premises. Please, Clayton," he whispered to himself, "play it cool tonight."

I felt sick with fear. Trouble hung around Clayton Striker like a bad smell.

In the opening bars of "I Concentrate on You," Clayton grabbed the lead with his sax and improvised a wild, screeching solo that lasted almost an hour. It didn't make a bit of sense to me; in fact, I thought it sounded downright awful. I could see that even some of the sophisticated regulars in the audience were having difficulty following him. Something besides passion was flowing through Clayton's veins that night. I cast covert glances at the two men near the door. They didn't touch their drinks, they hardly looked at the stage, and they yawned frequently, obviously not used to late hours. If they were jazz aficionados, then I was a naval orange. Rolly was right. Trouble.

The set ended, and the musicians headed to the tiny dressing room that adjoined the stage. I stood up. "I'm going to go back and talk to them," I said to Rolly. "I don't want Paul involved in this." He nodded, grateful to anyone who might be able to avert trouble in his club.

Jingo was the last one off the stage. I followed him through the door of the dressing room. Clayton was standing up in the corner, a needle already in his arm. Jingo said disgustedly, "Jesus, man, can't you even lock the door?" Turning angrily, he brushed past me and returned to the main room and the bar.

"Two federal narcotics cops are sitting right outside," I said breathlessly. "Didn't you see them? For God's sake, get rid of that stuff, Clayton. Please! Paul, talk to him!"

"Shut up, Mama," Clayton said through his teeth. "This is none of your business."

The two men burst into the room. One of them flashed a badge. "Federal agents. All right, all of you, take it easy. You, Striker, up against the wall."

Clayton drew his lips back from his teeth, those gleaming white teeth, but he went on squeezing the contents of the syringe into his veins. "This is my medicine, man, my insulin. Dig? You guys are not welcome back here while I'm medicating myself, so just get out, hear?"

"We hear, but we're not listening," the shorter of the two men said. "Take that needle out of your arm, sonny boy, and get those hands in the air. We're going to make a search."

I stepped over to Paul and grabbed his arm. He was quivering, like I was. Clayton removed the needle from his vein, rolled down his sleeve, and sighed deeply. Then he bent over, dropped the syringe into his saxophone case, and came up holding a pistol.

"You guys have been on my tail for a long time now," he said. "I'm getting tired of seeing your ugly white faces following me wherever I go."

"Put that gun down, boy." Shorty reached under his baggy, gray serge jacket and whipped out a pistol of his own. His friend did the same. "Drop it!"

It was a lopsided standoff, the two of them holding guns on Clayton while he held one on them. The baby inside me did a somersault. I hoped I wasn't starting labor. According to my calculations, we still had two more weeks to wait.

Then Paul broke away from me and hurled himself between the adversaries. I screamed and hugged my belly. A gun went off. As Clayton reeled backward, clutching his neck, his pistol slipped out of his hand. Paul dove for it and came up firing, like an actor in a Wild-West movie.

Shorty threw up his arms, executed a tidy pirouette, then dropped to his knees before collapsing in a heap. The other man barely had time to look surprised before his face disappeared in a smear of red.

As suddenly as it began, the noise stopped. The room was silent, horribly silent. The baby kicked me, hard.

"Paul," Clayton wheezed. He was bleeding from a wound under his collarbone, high up and to the left. "Paul. Paul. Get me out of here, man, or they'll crucify me."

The gun fell out of Paul's hand. As he stooped to retrieve it, his right arm dripped blood.

"Paul, you're hurt!"

Footsteps pounded across the plywood stage on the other side of the door. I shot the bolt and looked around. The only other door in the room led to a typical backstage bathroom, one of those where your knees banged the wall when you sat down. The bathroom window opened onto the alley at the rear of the club.

Paul was kneeling beside Clayton, holding the big black man's upper body against his chest. He had the gun in his right hand again. "Let's go, Paulie," I pleaded. "We've got to get out of here."

"Clay," he whispered through lips drained of color. "I can't leave . . ."

"Paul, come on! You've got to help me get out of here!" I

shouted. "I don't want to have my baby in jail! You've got to help me! Please! For my baby." I grabbed his left arm and jerked him to his feet.

"Clay," Paul repeated. "I can . . ."

"Shit." Clayton Striker closed his eyes, as though he couldn't bear the sight of either one of us. "Take the white mama and get the hell out of here. I don't want no white muthafuckas helpin' me."

I dragged Paul over the bodies of the two federal narcotics agents and into the bathroom. Paul climbed out the window first and waited outside to catch me. I climbed up on the toilet, stuck my left leg out, and sat down on the sill, twisted my swollen body around, found a fingerhold, then fell out into Paul's arms. Fortunately the windowsill was only about four feet off the ground. Somewhere a police siren wailed, the crescendo of sound signaling a fast approach.

"This way!" I caught my breath and hustled Paul out of the alley. I had parked my midnight-blue Cadillac in the middle of the next block. I shoved Paul into the backseat and hurled myself behind the wheel, no easy proposition considering my swollen dimensions and the bulk of my sable. I switched on the ignition and stepped on the gas. The wheels spun around on the ice. The car went nowhere. I threw the car into reverse, smashed the grill of the Plymouth parked behind me, and jerked the steering wheel hard to the left. The minute I felt the front wheels climb out of their icy rut, I took off with a roar of my V-8 engine. I took a diversionary route back to my apartment and parked around the corner from the front entrance, where a doorman was on duty twenty-four hours a day.

"We can't stay here," Paul said. "The police will know where to look."

"We're not staying long," I said. "Just a couple of minutes while I run upstairs and grab a few things. We'll need money. You stay here, I'll be right back."

"Don't get involved, Dessie," Paul pleaded. "Maybe I should let them find me. The shooting was unpremeditated. I won't get a death sentence."

"Oh, no, you'll just get two hundred years in Sing-Sing alongside Clayton Striker. God knows what he'll tell them. The police will crucify him, all right, but they'll nail you right up there alongside him. And they'll lock me up, too, for good measure. We've got to get away from here."

215

I was in luck. The doorman had stepped out for a smoke or a pee and the lobby was empty. I took the elevator up to my apartment, where I loaded up a jewel box and all my spare cash. I also grabbed the overnight case I had packed to take to the hospital when the baby was born and a couple of midnight-blue evening gowns from my closet. Don't ask me why I thought I needed them.

I left the building through the emergency door at the side. Paul did not acknowledge my return. His lips were blue, and his eyes were closed. I think he had passed out. As I pulled away from the apartment building and turned the corner, a police car roared up my street, its red lights flashing. I forced myself to drive sedately. The cops may have known that Dessie Heavener was involved with a shooting, but with any luck, they didn't know she owned a midnight-blue Caddy.

It was after midnight and traffic was light on the snowy streets. I considered driving to Queens and hiding out with Dizzy, but I rejected the idea. I didn't want to drag him into this, too.

Instead, I headed for the Lincoln Tunnel and the whole wide country west of New York City. The man at the toll booth recognized me and greeted me by name. A bad sign. I hadn't realized I was quite so conspicuous. I glanced over my right shoulder to the body slumped in the back seat. Paul was pretty well concealed by my sable coat, which I had shed in order to give my arms greater mobility. I drove straight west, into the hills of northern New Jersey.

I needed to call Tony in Havana as soon as possible. I carried the number of the presidential palace in Havana with me night and day so that I could notify him right away when the baby was about to be born. This was a different kind of emergency, but Tony would know what to do. He might even fly his plane up to meet Paul and me in some remote spot and take us to safety.

At four in the morning, I checked us into a motel somewhere in Pennsylvania. I gave the bleary-eyed man at the desk a big smile and a twenty dollar bill as I signed a false name to his register. Then Paul and I went to our room for some rest.

"Sit on the bed," I ordered him. "And take off your jacket. I've got to look at that wound."

"No, don't touch it, I'll be all right." He kept the palm of his hand pressed over the blood-encrusted hole in his jacket.

"What's gotten into you, Paulie? At least let me clean it up.

There's no telling what kind of germs you've got festering in there."

I jerked his hand away. He was too weak to put up much resistance. Then I helped him off with his jacket and started to unbutton his shirt.

"Leave it, Dess, please . . ."

I pushed his interfering hand aside. "You've got to take this thing off. This is the only shirt you've got, and I need to clean it up. Come on."

I pulled the sleeve off his good arm. That's when I saw the red scabs and ugly white scars on the inside of his elbow.

"What—oh, God, Paul. Oh, God, Paul, what . . . ?" An image of Clayton Striker with the syringe stuck into his vein exploded into my vision. "No, No, Paul, no!" I drew away from him. He sat slumped on the edge of the bed, his chin on his chest. "No, Paul," I wept, "I can't believe it. Not you. Not you, too, Paulie! Goddamn that black bastard! I always knew he was trouble. Paul! In the name of heaven, why would you do this to yourself? Why?"

Angry thumps sounded on the wall. I realized I had been shouting. I clamped my teeth down hard on my lower lip. Whatever I had to say to Paul could wait. In the meantime, I had a lot of work to do before we could rest.

I cleansed Paul's wound with soap and water and tried to disinfect it with some eau de cologne from my overnight case; then I bound his arm with strips torn from a pillowcase. Finally I switched off the overhead light. We lay side by side on the double bed, which was as lumpy as yesterday's oatmeal and as deeply troughed as a pig wallow.

I had hoped to be on the road by nine in the morning, but Paul and I were both creatures of the night, unaccustomed to early rising. With no alarm to awaken us we slept soundly until noon. When I looked at my watch, I experienced instant panic. Racing to the window, I peeked through the gritty slats of the venetian blinds, certain I would see a cordon of police cars surrounding the motel. The parking area was empty except for my splendidly conspicuous midnight-blue Cadillac.

The time had come to summon help. After loading Paul into the car, I went to the motel office to place a long-distance call to Havana. The bleary-eyed man had vanished, and a stern-faced woman had taken his place. She was not so easily moved by the sight of a twenty-dollar bill. I made it fifty, and she told me to help myself to the phone. I hesitated, my hand on the receiver. We held a staring contest, which she lost. She left the office.

The operators were obdurate, the connection terrible, but I finally got through to Tony.

"Forgive me, Dolores," he said, "I cannot come to you now. There are severe difficulties here. I must stay in Havana—President Batista needs me."

"Why should he need you now? You've gone away plenty of times in the past."

"Last night there was a military coup in the city. Fulgencio Batista has been restored to power. We have been waiting for this for a long time, planning for it. I cannot leave now."

He told me to get to an airport and buy two tickets for Mexico City. Once there, we were to check into the Hotel Del Prado on Avenue Juarez, opposite the Alameda Park. He promised to join us as soon as things in Cuba had settled down.

"Mexico City! But I can't go to Mexico," I protested, "I don't speak a word of Spanish."

"Perhaps it is time you learned."

As I left the motel office, I saw the woman giving me a hard look. She went back inside and picked up the telephone receiver.

Paul was still waiting in the car. He was awake but feverish. "Look, Dessie, I've been thinking . . ."

"Leave the thinking to me," I said. "I'm not doing so bad. I hope you like Mexican food, because that's where we're going."

As I was driving out of the motel parking lot, I nearly ran into a car that was pulling in, a clunky '43 Chevy. As we glided past the other car, I noticed the medallion painted on the side. The county sheriff. The bitch in the motel office had reported her suspicions to the local law. A siren screamed, and behind us a red light flashed. Half out of my mind with terror, I tore down that country road, but I was no great driver and I didn't have a chance. For a brief moment I thought I had lost the sheriff, but he took a shortcut across a farmer's field and headed me off before the rutted gravel road I was driving on joined the main highway.

At my side, Paul whimpered with pain and fear. His cheeks were pink, and his eyes were glazed. I suspected that the wound in his arm had become infected. He was probably running a high fever.

"Don't worry, Paul," I promised, "I'll get us out of this, I swear."

The sheriff's car screeched to a halt beside mine. He switched off his siren and the flashing red light.

Knuckles rapped on my window. Slowly, I rolled down the glass.

"Driver's license, please, ma'am," he said grimly.

My brain was whirling, and I felt dizzy. What was I going to do? I picked up my purse and reached inside for my wallet. My fingers touched something cold. Paul's gun. My hand closed around the butt and my forefinger found the trigger. I had to do it. I couldn't let this man arrest us.

"Hell, Miss Heavener, I don't need to see your driver's license." The sheriff chuckled. "I'd recognize you anywhere. You know, I just couldn't believe it when Thelma called me. I wanted to see for myself. I reckon I could cite you for reckless driving," his blue eyes twinkled at me, "but I'll just settle for a couple of autographs."

I jerked my hand away from the gun as if it were burning hot instead of deadly cold. My whole body was trembling. The sheriff didn't seem to notice as he extended a fountain pen and small notepad through the open window.

"I been listenin' to your records a long time, Miss Heavener," he said, "and your motion pictures are the finest I've ever seen. Thelma and I think you got a raw deal from those studio folks. Banned from motion pictures! Shoot. Why, half the girls in this county are plumped up before they tie the knot. Out here that's just the natural way of carrying on. This your fellow?" He leaned in a little farther and looked at Paul.

I nodded weakly. "Charlie's not feeling well," I croaked. "I think he must have eaten some bad oysters last night. He was still feeling bad this morning, so I said I'd drive."

"Yeah, well, you gotta watch them oysters." The sheriff offered to escort me to the state line. I accepted, hoping that he wouldn't find out that he had entertained a couple of fugitives until we were well out of his jurisdiction.

"I think I'm dying, Dess," Paul said as I started up the Caddy, backed around, and followed the sheriff's car to the main road.

"Well, don't die until we get out of this county," I snapped. "Look, nobody ever died of a shot in the arm, or of wanting drugs, either. You've got an infection, and it's gone into your blood with the rest of the poisons you've been putting in there. I'll get you some medicine, but not until we're out of this state."

Late that afternoon, in Berkley Springs, West Virginia, I painted a few pink dots on my face with a lipstick, found the oldest, most near-sighted doctor in town, and persuaded him that I had chicken pox and that I wanted some penicillin in order to protect my unborn baby. I declined a shot in the rear, saying that I preferred pills if he had them. He did. I paid him, and took the pills to Paul, waiting in the car. He gulped down four with a single swallow of the Coke I had purchased for him at the local Esso station.

"Where are we going?" Paul asked as we cruised slowly out of town.

"I told you: Mexico. But we're going to make a little stop first. I don't know how long I'm going to be away, and I want to see my boy before I go."

The plan had formed itself in my mind almost without my thinking about it. I realized that I hadn't been heading toward an airport at all. I had been going home, back to Munford. I had to see my son before I left the country. I didn't know how I was going to manage it without getting myself and Paul arrested, but I was damned sure going to try.

15

I DROVE ALL NIGHT. PROGRESS WAS SLOW ON THE WINDING roads through the mountains, and soon after midnight freezing rain began to fall, but we passed through Roanoke before dawn and crossed the North Carolina border as the black rainy night faded to a gray rainy day.

DESSIE NAILS NARCS:
FBI LAUNCHES NATIONWIDE HUNT FOR SINGER.

I saw the headline on the Greensboro *Courier* when we stopped for gas at a rundown roadside station north of town. After ten years as a professional entertainer I had finally made the front page: three columns on the killings and two more on my career with plenty of pictures sandwiched in between. The mental deficient pumping my gas must not have seen the photographs, and he probably couldn't have read the headline. While he concentrated on getting gas into the Caddy's tank, I managed to scan the front of the newspaper without attracting either his attention or Paul's.

When I got back into the car, I was trembling. Clayton Striker had told the police that I had shot everybody. I came into the dressing room, he said, brandishing the pistol and raving jealously because Paul Miller, my "old boyfriend" and the father of my child, had refused to marry me. I resented Clayton because his "genius" was greater than mine, and I blamed him for alienating Paul, with whom Clayton had a pure "musical and spiritual relationship." Clayton had tried to take the gun away from me, and I had shot him. When the two federal agents burst into the room, I lost control and shot them, too. Then I made my escape, taking Paul with me as a hostage.

During the night, I had persuaded myself that the police outside New York City weren't looking for me at all. Radio reception had been poor in the mountains, and the few news reports I had heard did not mention the shootings. Now I was wanted for murder and the FBI was on my tail. Clayton Striker had cooked my goose.

My hands were shaking so badly that I could barely hold on to the steering wheel, but I aimed the car toward the Greensboro city limits. Paul slumped in the seat beside me. The penicillin didn't seem to be doing him much good. His fever was still high, and his arm was inflamed clear down to his wrist and hand. His eyes looked glassy.

"You need a doctor," I said. "We'll have to make up some story about how you were cleaning your gun—"

"No."

"But, Paul—"

"I said no." The effort of speaking made him sweat. "He'd see the needle marks. I'll be all right," he insisted. "My body just needs a chance to heal itself."

"You didn't give your body much of a chance when you started shooting that junk into your veins." I peered through the layer of rain and slush on the windshield. "I will never understand why anyone as smart as you would deliberately poison yourself like that. Oh, well, monkey see, monkey do. I suppose your good pal Clayton told you his musical powers came from heroin. You poor dumb bastard. Look where his habit has landed us. He's in jail, and we're on the run from a murder rap. It's like a bad movie. I told you that son of a bitch was no good."

"Clayton Striker is the world's finest living jazz musician."

I snorted. "He won't be the world's finest living anything if he doesn't kick those drugs. That low-down lying bastard. Honestly, I would have expected somebody with your intelligence to have more sense . . ."

"Stop the car," Paul whispered.

"Why? What's the matter? Do you feel sick?"

"Just stop the car. I'm getting out." As I slowed for a traffic light, Paul fumbled with the door handle.

I threw myself across his body and jerked his hand away from the door. "You can't get out here!"

"I will not spend another minute listening to you bitch about Clayton and . . . and heroin and how I should have had more sense," Paul said tearfully. "You're not exactly . . . you're not the world's most sensible woman yourself. Or the most moral one. Take me to the police station. I'll tell them that I forced you at gunpoint to help me escape."

"Don't be stupid. I've been your friend for twenty years. They'll know it's a lie."

"They can't prove it. Clayton and I are the only witnesses to what happened. The other two are dead. We'll tell them you're innocent. We can make the police believe that. I killed two men, Dessie. Hasn't that sunk into your fluffy blond head yet? I killed them. I'm a murderer. Let me turn myself in. Please."

"No." I couldn't tell Paul that Clayton had incriminated me. That was a burden I didn't need to share with him in his present condition. The light changed, and I pulled through the intersection. "Listen, Paul, you're my oldest and dearest friend. My son is named Grayson Paul after you and Clara Mae. Do you really think I'm going to let you rot in a cell for the next fifty years? Do you? Anyway, they'd lock me up for sure, at least for a while. I'm not going to have this baby in jail. You'll see, Tony—Mr. Matos will fix everything. He'll hire lawyers and straighten out the whole mess while we're sitting on the beach in Mexico drinking tequila and eating enchiladas. I'm sorry. I shouldn't have scolded you. But promise me, Paul, you'll never shoot heroin again. I don't care what else you do—you can drink crankcase oil and smoke hemp and sleep with goats if you want, but I don't want you putting that stuff into your veins again. Please. Promise me."

"All right, I promise."

I cruised around Greensboro for a while before pulling into "Happy Harry's Used Cars." Fifteen minutes later, as the rain poured down, I loaded Paul and my baggage into a 1949 bottle-green Chevy that looked like every third car on the road. Happy Harry had given me eight hundred dollars in cash to cover the difference between the old Chevy and my new midnight blue Cadillac. He had cheated me royally, but at least I was rid of the custom-colored Caddy.

Next I had to do something to disguise myself. I drove past a store that had a few wigs in the window, but I couldn't risk going in. I would almost certainly be recognized. Finally I spotted a Salvation Army secondhand store. I pulled my hair back into a severe bun and sprinted through the rain to the door, leaving my sable behind in the car. The Salvation Army didn't have any wigs, but I found a pair of eyeglasses with blue frames and rhinestone wings. I could barely see through them and they gave me an instant headache, but I told the old woman at the counter that they almost matched my prescription.

She glanced at my swollen belly and smiled. "I hope your baby has better eyes than you do, honey."

Lukie's Drugstore provided me with a bottle of black hair rinse and a set of pink curlers, and a blue and yellow flowered plastic headscarf. I spent half an hour in the bathroom of the Texaco station across the street, coloring my hair and putting it up in rollers. I looked at myself in the mirror and winced. Nobody would ever recognize me. I hardly recognized myself. At a nearby lunch counter, I ordered two tunafish sandwiches, ate one and put the second in my purse for Paul. I picked up a couple of sodas and a bag of potato chips and then we were on the road again.

Judge Miller owned a little cabin out near the lake where he stayed during duck hunting season. By eleven o'clock that night I had Paul bedded down on a cot next to the small cast iron stove, with a blazing fire fueled from the judge's well-stocked kindling box and some small logs I had yanked out from under a rusty sheet of corrugated iron roofing behind the cabin. I lay down on a second cot on the other side of the stove. It was lumpy and smelled of stale sweat and mildew, but the judge had left a good supply of coarse woolen blankets. Paul fell asleep immediately, but I was too worked up to relax. Eventually the heat of the fire and the weight of the blankets had their effect, and I drifted off into a troubled sleep.

When I awoke the next morning the rain had stopped, although the sky still looked bleak and threatening. I brought in some more wood and got the fire going again.

"You stay put until I get back." The warning was unnecessary. The red streaks on Paul's arm looked less angry that morning, but he was hardly in any condition to go running off into the swamps. "I'm going into town long enough to see Gray, and then I'll come right back and we can be on the road again by nightfall."

"Somebody might recognize you."

"Are you kidding? With black hair and these glasses? You didn't recognize me yourself when I got into the car with you. Honestly, it's perfectly safe. Sylvester wrote me that Gray is going to the Lane Academy, that fancy private school where old Mr. Avery used to live, on the street that leads up to Woodlands.

I can see him during the noon recess. I just need a few minutes with him, that's all. I need to make sure he hasn't forgotten me completely.''

I was still a mile from town when the Chevy began to decelerate. I managed to pull it over to the side of the road before it died completely. I tried unsuccessfully to start it, twisting the key in the ignition, stamping on the gas pedal, jiggling the gearshaft. Nothing happened. I couldn't even get the horn to blow.

I pounded the wheel. "Damn, damn, damn!" Happy Harry had sold me a dud. At that moment, to add to my troubles, the skies opened and rain started to pour down again.

I spent a few minutes digesting the situation. I would have to walk to town to see Gray, then perhaps I could borrow or buy a car or truck from one of Clara Mae's boys. Much as I hated to involve them in this, I had no other options.

The rain continued to fall relentlessly, plastering down every hair on my sable coat. My high-heeled shoes were faring even worse. Still, I trudged on, amazed that nobody passed me going in either direction. I would have accepted a ride from anybody at that point, even my father.

I reached the school at eleven-thirty. I remembered the place from my childhood as the home of an elderly bachelor, Cadwalader Avery. The son of missionary parents in China, he had been an expert on the Far East and some kind of adviser to presidents and diplomats. He was a familiar sight pottering around his garden, his fine-boned head shielded from the sun by an immense cone-shaped hat woven of yellow straw. Why he had chosen to retire to Munford was a mystery to me. Perhaps he had felt at home there, as cut off from western civilization as he had been in China. After his death, a couple of Yankees, two women with university degrees, had purchased the house, a wild monstrosity from the Victorian era with towers and porches and stained glass windows throughout. Where once odd stone lanterns and grotesque bronze animals had dotted the lawns there now stood swing sets, slides, and a merry-go-round.

I cursed the rain. It would keep the children indoors during the noon recess. These days, they probably ate their lunch in a cafeteria instead of walking home, as I had done when I was in grammar school. Nevertheless, I would wait outside the gates until Gray appeared. I knew I would see him sooner or later. I had to.

I found a little shelter under the boughs of an aged oak tree just outside the wrought iron fence. Water trickled off the plastic rain bonnet and dripped down the back of my neck. The wet sable coat weighed a ton, and my feet were soaked clear up past my knees. At least the rain on my Salvation Army rhinestone-studded glasses didn't bother me. I couldn't see through the lenses, anyway.

A sleek black car passed, coming down the hill. It braked at the corner, then backed up, the transmission purring. "Dessie?"

I knew his voice. I commanded myself not to turn around, but I couldn't stop myself. I looked over my shoulder and peeked over the tops of my glasses. Bram Howard had rolled down the window on the passenger side of his sleek, black Packard. He grinned at me. I didn't dare speak for fear of giving myself away. I hoped he would just drive on.

He said, "I thought you'd turn up here."

I clamped my teeth down hard on my lower lip. Please, God, I prayed, make him go away.

The door opened. "Get in. I'd like to talk to you."

Tears, which had been hovering close to the surface all morning, finally overflowed. "I don't want to talk to you!" I sobbed. "I came here to see my son, just to see him for one minute. If you think that's such a terrible crime, then you can call the sheriff and have me arrested right now. Otherwise, go away. Just go away and leave me alone!"

"Gray won't even recognize you in that get-up." Bram didn't try to hide his amusement. "Come on. At least you'll be able to dry off a little. You're a trifle conspicuous, you know."

His offer of dry shelter did the trick. I climbed in and pulled the door shut. When I removed my glasses and my rain scarf, Bram burst out laughing again. I ignored him and rubbed my temples. "These stupid curlers are giving me a headache. Do you have a dry cigarette?"

"Certainly." Bram swallowed his laughter and passed over a pack of Camels. He held his lighter for me. "Your nasty little escapade with Paul Miller in New York has everyone buzzing. Most of the people in this town were betting that you wouldn't come within a thousand miles of Munford. But I thought you might."

"Because of Gray. Only because of Gray." Tears spilled down my cheeks. I made no move to wipe them away. What were a few more drops of water in an ocean of trouble?

"I know. Because of Gray." He sighed. "I'd like you to know

that Judge Miller's decision came as a shock to me, too. I never expected him to be so harsh. I told him afterward that I was perfectly willing to give you generous visiting rights, but Jean-Ellen preferred to stick to the letter of his decision. She, ah, doesn't like you."

"That comes as no surprise to me," I sniffed. "Jean-Ellen is the nastiest polecat that ever lifted its tail, and for that I apologize to skunks everywhere. You can tell Jean-Ellen—oh, never mind. You wouldn't tell her, anyway."

Bram gazed straight ahead over the steering wheel of the Packard. His temples were graying, but otherwise he hadn't changed much. "I never intended to cut you off from your son, Dessie."

I hooted. "You never intended!"

"In the beginning, we didn't have that much to use against you except your prolonged absences from Munford. Two key witnesses—Kingsley and that drummer—refused to say a word against you when we first approached them. But two weeks before the hearing, they suddenly changed their tune. Both of them were not only willing, but eager, to slander you and swear it was the truth. I didn't want that kind of testimony, but Tyler Lloyd and Jean-Ellen persuaded me we couldn't win Gray without it."

"I don't want to listen to—"

"Wait, Dessie, I want you to hear this. When that Foyle woman turned up out of the clear blue sky, it was like a gift. Her story was as damning as all hell, and it was just what our side needed. By then, I was pretty sure that someone with a lot of money was working against you—and it wasn't me. I used a powerful lot of charm on Myrna Foyle before she gave me a lead, but I finally traced some payments to her from a private investigator in New York. Eight months after the hearing, I discovered who had hired him." He cleared his throat. "It was your Cuban friend, Antonio Matos."

"Tony!" I blinked away rain and teardrops. "That's ridiculous. Why, he did everything he could to help me keep Gray. If you think you can make yourself look better in my eyes by slandering him—"

"No, I'm not trying to do that." Bram sounded suddenly weary. "I know how things must have appeared to you, and I admit I wasn't blameless. I should have drawn the line somewhere, but everything happened so fast. Once the train was in motion, I couldn't stop it."

Oh, yes, I remembered that train. The train of justice. And heartbreak. It had swept me under its wheels, mauled me, mangled me, and left me for dead.

"And I did want Gray." Bram gripped the steering wheel of the motionless car. "I wanted him badly. Not using witnesses who could help me win him seemed foolish."

I stared at the cigarette smoldering between my fingers. I cranked down the window half an inch and pushed the butt out. "I will never forgive myself," I said to the tear-soaked world on the other side of the glass. "I should have taken Gray with me when I left home that first time. I never should have left him with Daddy and Ayleen so long. I should have come back for him sooner. But I got too busy, and when I reached out for him, he was gone. Nothing goes right for me, ever."

"Gray wasn't happy with them, Dessie. From what I hear, Ayleen has a pretty nasty temper. Gray's the one who made the first move in our direction, not the other way around. I never approached him. I hardly gave him a thought. But one afternoon he came up to the house. He said he wanted to meet his father."

"He didn't!" I turned away from the window.

Bram nodded. "We talked. Gray and I discovered that we had some other interests in common besides Blair. Baseball, for one. He's a red-hot Yankee fan. We had a pretty lively discussion about that. I'm a Dodger man myself."

"Baseball?" I must have looked as bewildered as I felt. "I never knew he liked baseball."

Bram nodded. "He's a bit of a loner, like I was at that age. He likes the woods, but not hunting. He told me about an injured rabbit he'd found down near the creek on the south side of town. He amputated its leg, which had been crushed by a trap, and stitched up the fur and nursed the rabbit back to health. Toward the end of the visit, Gray asked me once again if he could see Blair, and I took him upstairs. I expected him to be put off by Blair's total helplessness. But the minute Blair saw Gray, his face lit up. He thought Gray was me, that we were kids again. Gray didn't try to argue with him, just went along. Then Blair . . . well, Blair messed his pants. I wanted to call the nurse, but Gray said he'd help. We got him changed and dry. I can tell you," Bram wiped his mouth with the back of his hand, "until then I had been revolted by Blair's condition. Every time I saw him, I remembered how strong and healthy and vital he had been before the accident, and it made my stomach churn. I was so damned angry. Heartsick. I wanted him to rise up out of that chair, to be himself again, to get well. But Gray saw him as he was, an overgrown, badly behaved crippled child. I think that's why Blair responded to him so readily, because he didn't feel any of the anger and resentment that came from me."

I wiped my cheeks. "Please stop. I don't want . . ."

"Just wait, I'm almost finished. After that, Gray and I started spending a lot of time together. He came over to the house every day after school. I don't think your father or Ayleen knew where he went, or cared particularly. He'd visit Blair for a little while, then the two of us would take a walk or go out to the farm to ride the horses. He's good with horses. All kinds of animals, actually. He'd been wanting a dog for years, but Ayleen wouldn't let him have one. So I bought him a spaniel puppy, General Lee, and he and the General played together every day. One day he said he wished he could lived at Woodlands, with Blair and me. I spoke to your father that same night, and he agreed to try it for a while. He promised to tell you right away. I guess he never did."

"You paid him! You gave him money!"

"Yes, I did." Bram looked pained. "By rights I should have been supporting the boy all along. As his uncle, it was my responsibility."

"I was his mother, damn you! It was my responsibility. And I did support him—I supported all of them!"

"I know you did. I hoped that you and I could come to some sort of understanding, maybe share the boy or let him visit during vacations, but Jean-Ellen persuaded me that you would never agree. She's the one who suggested that we adopt Gray legally. She can't have children of her own, you see, and she had some notion that every man wants a son, and she saw this as the perfect solution to the problems—but we don't need to go into that. Once Jean-Ellen got into the act, of course, there was no turning back. Jean-Ellen is a very determined woman."

"So am I," I said, "but I lost because your side didn't play fair."

Bram lit a Camel for himself and took two long puffs. "You ought to know something else. About how Blair died."

I expelled a long, shuddering breath and looked at Bram. Tears were welling up in his eyes, too. "The letter from those lawyers said it was a hemorrhage."

"He was murdered, Dessie. Someone at the rehab center gave

him an injection, an overdose of a powerful muscle relaxer. His heart just quit beating." Bram brushed his hand across his eyes.

I stared at him, too shocked to speak. He went on. "The police investigated, but they cooperated with the administrators of the center to keep it quiet. Not even my mother knows. Certainly not Gray. An orderly disappeared right after it happened. He was new there. Nobody knew very much about him, except that he was Cuban."

"You . . . you're accusing Tony again!"

"I'm not accusing anyone. I don't have a shred of proof. I'm just telling you to be careful. Matos is a dangerous man."

"You're talking about my husband," I said through trembling lips. "My baby's father."

Now it was Bram's turn to be shocked. "Husband! But the newspapers never mentioned . . ."

"We were keeping it a secret until the time was right." How silly that sounded now. I had been persecuted, vilified, condemned from newsstands and pulpits all over the land. When would the time be right?

Bram stubbed out his cigarette in the ashtray. "You didn't really shoot those two men, did you?"

"No. I don't expect you to believe that."

"You're wrong. I do believe you. Gray's mother couldn't take innocent lives like that."

"Gray's mother would like to see Gray before she resumes her life as a fugitive." I pulled the edges of my coat tighter around my belly. "Since you're still so almighty powerful in this town, and since you seem disposed to act kindly toward me today, perhaps you could arrange it?"

"I'd be happy to. I'll go in and ask Miss Talbot if I can borrow Gray for a few minutes."

After Bram left, I got my compact out of my purse and touched up my lipstick. I looked awful in my dyed black hair and pink curlers, but I couldn't do anything about that.

I found myself growing more and more upset about Tony Matos. Why couldn't anything go right in my life? I couldn't win a job singing with a band without getting fired five minutes after I was hired. I couldn't accept a ride from the handsomest boy in town without getting raped. I couldn't get raped without getting pregnant. I couldn't have a career without losing my son. I couldn't have another baby without losing my career. I couldn't even listen to my best friend play the piano in a nightclub without getting involved in a shootout. And the men I loved were either married to someone else or engaged in mysterious, perhaps even criminal, pursuits that seemed calculated to destroy my happiness.

I shook myself. I did not want Gray to find me wallowing in self-pity. I swore I was not going to cry in front of him, no matter what happened.

Bram opened the rear door, and Gray climbed into the backseat. Bram leaned in and put his hand on Gray's shoulder. "I think I'll take a short walk around the block. I'll be back in about ten minutes." He closed the door, leaving me alone with my son.

I twisted around in my seat. "Hello, Gray. Remember me?"

He hesitated. "Dad said I might not recognize you because you were wearing a disguise. But I can tell it's you. You're my mother."

"Yes, I am." *Dad* said. He called Bram *Dad*. "I certainly am your mother. I've missed you, Gray. Oh, I've missed you so much! Did you get my letters? I've been writing to you faithfully."

He shook his head.

"Oh? I'm sorry. I thought you were getting them." Tears welled up again. I blinked them back. "I hear you have a dog. General Lee."

"That's right." Gray's eyes showed a spark of interest. "Mrs. Lee just had six puppies. I helped her during the whelping. The vet said he couldn't have done any better himself."

"I believe him. I didn't know you were so good with animals. But then I wasn't around very much, was I?"

He shook his head again.

"I'm truly sorry, Gray," I said. "I wish things had worked out differently. I don't have time to explain it all now. Maybe when you're older, we'll see each other again and I can tell you all about it and you'll be able to understand why things happened as they did. I still don't understand it myself. Honestly, I never wanted to give you up. I don't know how to make you believe that—"

He cast a boyish glance over my enlarged belly. "You're going to have a baby," he said.

"That's right." I smiled. "I'll be whelping or foaling or whatever it is you call it in just a few more weeks. I wanted another baby because I missed you so much. Your little brother or sister will never take your place, but maybe I won't be so lonely all the time. I'll try to be a better mother this time around." Seeing him start to fidget, I switched the subject away from myself. "Are you . . . are you doing all right in school?"

He shrugged. "I guess so. It gets boring sometimes, but Dad says that doing things that you don't like to do builds character. Miss Talbot says I might be a genius."

"Really?" *Dad* again. "A genius! I wonder who you got that from? The Heaveners have certainly never been geniuses. As for Blair . . . well, I was sorry to hear about Blair. Your father was a good man."

Gray nodded. "He liked General Lee. I always took the General up to see him when Mo—when Jean-Ellen wasn't around. She doesn't like dogs in the house. After Blair died, the General didn't understand why we couldn't go and see him anymore. I miss him." Gray rubbed a circle in the fog on the inside of the window with his fingertip. Poor kid. He was clearly uncomfortable with me. Oh, well, this distasteful interview was building his character.

I reached over the back of the seat and touched his knee. "You'll be hearing stories about me in the next few days, Gray. I'd like you to know that they're not true. None of them. I happened to be in an inconvenient place when some very unpleasant things occurred."

"Gosh." I had finally caught his interest. "Some of the other kids said you killed a bunch of guys."

"Well, I didn't. Your fa—Bram will tell you that I didn't. Do you remember Paul Miller? Judge Miller's son? You're named for him, partly. Well, there was a mix-up, and Paul got involved, and I'm helping him, that's all. I'm sure we can straighten it all out in a couple of weeks."

Bram opened the door and climbed in behind the wheel. "Gray, I told Miss Talbot you'd only be out of class a few minutes," he said. 'You'd better say good-bye to your mother now."

Gray said, "Good-bye." A moment of embarrassed silence followed. He wanted to give me a title, but he didn't know what to call me. Mother? Mommy? Dessie? None would do.

I opened my arms to him. "Please, Gray, a little kiss." I held him close for a few precious moments. Damn you, Dessie, I said to myself, don't you cry. Don't you dare cry. "I love you," I murmured. "Remember that. I do love you. I think about you every day, every minute almost. Think about me once in a while, will you? Maybe our thoughts will cross."

"Like radio waves," he said. I felt no responding pressure from his arms.

"Right." I smoothed the hair back from his forehead. "Like radio waves."

He wriggled away from me. "Will you drive me out to the farm later, Dad? Winnie's expecting me."

"Sure, son. But you're going to spoil that horse if you're not careful."

Son. Dad. I wanted to scream.

"No, I'm not." Gray started to open the door.

"Just a minute, Gray." Bram twisted around. "Your mother is in bad trouble. If anyone knows she's been here in town, she could be in even worse trouble. You're not to tell anyone that you saw her today, understand? If Miss Talbot asks, you have my permission to tell a fib. Say that one of your horses was sick, and I thought you should know. Tell no one. Not even your moth—Jean-Ellen. Okay?"

"Okay." Gray gave me a cool, speculative look. Although I smiled encouragingly at him, he didn't smile back. " 'Bye," he said again. Then he ducked out into the rain.

I squeezed my eyes closed. That didn't stop the tears from flowing. Bram coughed delicately, but he had the sense not to say anything right away. Finally he pressed a dry handkerchief into my hand. "Are you all right?"

"What do you think?" I snarled. "Damn you, I should have taken this car and grabbed the kid and beat it the hell out of here when I had the chance. I should have taken him someplace where you would never find him."

"Why didn't you?"

"Because for once I really do believe that he's better off here than he would be with me." I buried my face in the white linen square and sobbed. The smell of lavender-scented laundry soap brought back a flood of memories. Woodlands in the rain. Sunday breakfast in the gazebo. Riding to church in the family car. Dancing with Bram in the conservatory, to the music of Bunny Berrigan. "You devil!" I whirled on him. "Saying you never intended to separate us! You're a damned liar. You stole my son! He's lost to me—it's like I never had a child. He doesn't know who I am, and he doesn't want to know. He's a stranger to me. A stranger!"

"I never—"

"How dare you hold back my letters? I'm allowed one lousy letter a month which would take him two minutes to read, and you have Gray every minute of every day, and you won't share that much of him with me. What's the matter, are you afraid I'll seduce him away from you by mail?"

Bram looked amazed. "I'm sorry. I didn't realize . . . Jean-Ellen must have intercepted them. I'll speak to her about this."

"Don't bother," I said. "I may never get a chance to write another letter. Oh, damn you. Damn, damn, damn." I blew my nose and tried to pull myself together, but the tears kept coming. "It's going to be just as wet inside this car as it is outside," I gulped. "I suppose I'd better get going."

"Where?"

"My car broke down on the road to town. I need to find—" I broke off to rummage in my purse for another dry handkerchief. The one Bram had given me was sodden already. My fingertips touched the cold barrel of the pistol that had already killed two men. I had come within a hair's breadth of shooting that sheriff in Pennsylvania with it. "I don't suppose you'd care to give me a lift, for old time's sake?"

"Of course. Where do you want to go?"

I told him about the cabin out at the lake where Paul was waiting for me. I kept my head down as we rode through town, although no one could see me through the streaked and fogged windows. We were silent, except when I needed to give him directions.

Bram nosed the car down the rutted lane. We rounded a bend and the cabin appeared in front of us. It was just a shack, really: some boards and beams slapped up and roofed over with corrugated iron. A wisp of smoke rose from the chimney. At least Paul hadn't let the fire go out.

"Would you care to step inside for a moment and say hello to Paul?" I said as Bram halted the car. "He would appreciate a visitor, I know."

"Why not?"

We reached the door. I let him precede me inside. Paul looked up from his cot. "What the—?" He struggled to a sitting position. "What are you doing here?"

"It's all right, Paul," I said. "Mr. Howard is a decent, God-fearing man. A war hero. A model parent. He would never rat on us. Besides, he's going to help us with the driving. Aren't you, Mr. Howard?"

Turning, Bram found himself staring into the cold eye of the pistol. He stiffened.

I said, "It is loaded, and I will use it, so don't make any sudden moves."

Paul blanched. "Dessie, are you crazy?"

"No, I don't think so. You're not fit to drive, and I've reached the point of exhaustion. I am sure Mr. Howard will be delighted to help us make our getaway. Welcome to our little band of outlaws, Bram. Believe me, I have nothing to lose by shooting you, and I wouldn't hesitate to do it. I've gone too far to let you stop me now. Come on, Paul. You and I will sit in the backseat and take turns holding the gun to Mr. Howard's head. All right, Bram, turn around, walk to the car, take your time. I know how to shoot. I had to learn for *Monday's Girl*. Did you see it? Probably one of the worst movies ever made."

"I agree with you," Bram said. "It was a real stinker."

"Walk, mister," I barked. "Paul, you bring up the rear. I don't want you coming between Mr. Howard and me. All right, troops, let's move out."

16

I TRIED TO KEEP MY GAZE FIXED ON THE BACK OF BRAM Howard's head. Whenever my eyes slid right, to the rearview mirror, I found his eyes already there, waiting for mine. I wondered how he managed to keep the car on the road, since he seemed to be watching the occupants of the backseat so much of the time.

"I was due at a meeting in Columbia at two," he said. "They'll be looking for me. When I turn up missing, Gray will tell them that he saw you this morning."

"He won't tell," I said. "You made him promise not to, remember? And Gray's a smart boy. He'll figure out that you're helping me escape. He won't say one word." I stroked the textured handgrip of the gun with my thumb. "All the cops in the country are looking for us, anyway. A few more from Cluny County won't matter. We just have to take the risk."

At my side, Paul stirred in his sleep. He must have bumped his wounded arm, because he moaned softly.

"He ought to see a doctor," Bram said.

"That's a brilliant suggestion. We'll stop in the very next town we come to and ask who's the best doctor for treating bullet wounds."

We rode in silence for another half hour before Bram spoke again. "We're going to need gas soon." We were on U.S. 78 in western Georgia, heading for the Alabama state line. "The needle's been on empty for the past ten minutes."

"Pull into the next place you come to and ask the man to fill up the tank. Don't reach for your wallet. I'll hand him the money. And don't forget that this gun is pointed right at the back of your head."

"Thanks for reminding me." His tone was bitter. "I'm having a little difficulty adjusting to your new image as a Cuban gangster's moll."

"Shut up, Bram."

We refueled without incident. I could tell that Bram was tiring, but I didn't care. I would keep him at the wheel all night and all day if I had to. A few hours later we stopped at a drive-in restaurant for sandwiches and coffee, and for me to make one of my all-too-frequent bathroom visits.

We were somewhere in Mississippi when I felt a sharp stab of pain in my middle. Indigestion, I thought. I shouldn't have eaten the pickles in that sandwich. Forty minutes later I had another attack, followed by a more severe cramp half an hour after that. Silently, I begged the baby to wait. Not now, I told it. Please, can't you hold off for two more days, until we reach Mexico? Honestly, it will make things so much easier for all of us.

But children are willful before they have attained any age outside the womb, and in choosing the time of their birth, they can be mighty stubborn and insistent. The labor pains were still far apart and not at all unbearable, but I knew they would get worse, and more frequent.

I wanted to sob with frustration. Nothing went right for me, ever. I couldn't even get out of the country without the birth of my baby holding me up.

After I had collected my wits and calmed myself down, I made an announcement. "We're going to have to alter our plans slightly. The baby's coming tonight."

Paul, who had been staring glumly out the window, gasped in horror. "But you can't do that, Dessie! Not now! My God, what are we going to go? We have to get you to a hospital right away."

In the front seat, Bram began to laugh. He choked it off and looked guiltily up at me in the mirror. "I'm sorry," he said. "I guess I'm a little tired—I know it's not funny—but just when things were beginning to get boring . . . ," he laughed again.

I was unable to share Bram's amusement. Another spasm seized me. "Don't think this means the end of the line for you, Bram," I gasped. "I am bound and determined to get to Mexico. If we have to delay our travels for a few days to accommodate this baby, then we will. Pull over so I can look at the map. And switch on the light."

I handed the gun to Paul while I spread the map out over my knees. We had just passed Winona and were heading south on U.S. 51 toward Jackson. I knew that Clara Mae had come from

Mississippi originally. I racked my brain, trying to remember the name of her hometown. It was near the river, I knew that much. When he was only fourteen, her brother Hotshot had hitched a ride on a barge up to St. Louis, and Clara Mae remembered waving to him from the levee. A simple name, a woman's name—there it was: Grace, Mississippi, halfway between Greenville and Vicksburg and about sixty miles west of where we were.

I gave Bram directions by way of Lexington, Tchula, Belzoni, and Hollandale. "And don't you think for one minute that this gun isn't going to be looking right at your head while I'm looking over your shoulder, mister," I added.

"Yes, ma'am."

We had gone halfway when my water broke. The rutted roads between Tchula and Belzoni weren't doing anything to slow down the process. Between pains, I told Bram to hurry. He ran a red light in Belzoni, and almost immediately a police car glided out of a shadowy side street with its light flashing and its siren shrieking.

"Damn, damn, damn!" I cried. "Step on the gas! Outrun him!" I hoped Bram could do a better job of evading the law than I had in Pennsylvania.

He did. He was good enough to be a Hollywood stunt driver. The Packard fairly flew along the roads, squealing around turns on two wheels. The police car dropped out of sight.

Teeth clenched, I endured another attack of pain. "You're having the time of your life, aren't you, Bram?" I panted when it subsided.

He grinned. "I'm sorry, Dessie, I just can't help myself. Are you ready for me to pull over and deliver that baby?"

"Not yet."

When we reached Grace at one in the morning, my pains were coming five minutes apart. I told Bram to drive around until he saw a house with some lights. There weren't any. Grace was small, run-down, and desperately poor. The inhabitants must have been farm workers in the surrounding cotton fields who rose with the sun and went to bed soon after dusk. Just when I thought we were going to have to start knocking on doors and waking people up to ask for Clara Mae's kinfolk, we spotted a light in the direction of the river.

It was a roadhouse, a tumbledown shack plastered with rusted signs for Coke and Valvoline and Red Indian chewing tobacco.

The crudely painted sign over the door read "Moonies." A half dozen jalopies were parked outside. Four of them had no wheels, and were hoisted up on blocks. From the inside I heard the voice of a trumpet, so mellow and sweet that it brought tears to my eyes. Please, God, I prayed, let that be Hotshot Grayson.

I pressed the muzzle of the gun against Bram's right temple while Paul went inside to inquire. A stab of pain nearly doubled me over, but I forced myself to keep my hand steady.

"I hope you're being careful with that thing," Bram said. "If you get one of those pains when your finger's on the trigger, you could hurt somebody."

I glared at him but said nothing. I needed all my strength for what lay ahead. But I was careful. God knows I didn't want to kill him, even though he deserved it for stealing my son.

"Have you considered that it might be easier just to turn yourself in?" Bram said. "Things may look bad for you right now—aiding a fugitive, leaving the scene of a crime, speeding, not to mention murder and kidnapping—but a good lawyer could straighten them out."

"A good lawyer let you steal my son," I hissed through gritted teeth. "By the time another good lawyer got through showing off his rhetorical style in front of a judge on my behalf, I'd be sitting in a jail cell myself, and I would have lost another child. I swear to you, Bram, nothing is going to come between me and this baby. Nothing and no one. Ever."

The voice of the trumpet fell silent. Feet crunched on the oyster shell gravel outside the car. I held the gun steady while the door on the passenger side of the car opened and a black face peered in at us.

"Lawdy, I don't believe it! Is you really Miss Dessie? Hotshot Grayson at your service, ma'am. Lawdy, I surely have heard a lot about you. What you doin' down here, and how come you holdin' a gun on that fella?"

"Look, Hotshot, I need help. I don't want to put you or your friends at risk. Just find me a place to hide for a few days—" I cut off, gasping, as another pain seized me. "Can you deliver a baby, Hotshot? I don't have much time."

"Oh, my, Lawdy me! Lemme talk to Moonie." He disappeared. A few seconds later, more doors opened and four black faces looked in at me. The fattest and roundest one spoke to me. "That white dude in there say he was jivin' with Clay Striker when the police busted it up and shot Clay. Man, that Clay can really blow the sax. The white boy, he tellin' the truth?"

"Yes. That's Paul Miller. He's an old friend of Clara Mae Grayson's, just like I am."

"No kiddin'? Ah'm Moonie," he said, giving me a grin as wide as his namesake. "I used to be sweet on Clara Mae, but that was a long time ago. What about this fella?" He gestured toward Bram.

"This man took my son away from me. My son, Grayson. I named him for Clara Mae."

"Yeah? And this dude took him away? That's not nice, mista, takin' a child away from his mama like that. You want us to look after him for you, Miss Dessie?"

"Yes, Mr. . . . ahhh." I doubled over with pain. "Mr. Moonie—Hotshot!"

"Now don't you worry none, Miss Dessie," Moonie said. "My wife's getting the bed upstairs ready for you right now. She's had three of her own. She knows what to do."

I handed the gun over to him and climbed out of the Packard. "You'd better hide the car. And watch this man closely. He's as slick as a snake."

Hotshot and one of the other men half carried me up a narrow and treacherously steep staircase. I found myself in an A-shaped attic room with a single dormer window that overlooked the levee and a broad turn in the Mississippi. Mrs. Moonie was waiting for me. Tall, shapely, hung with rhinestones and glitter and wearing a low-cut red dress that revealed the upper portions of generous black breasts, she looked like a handmaiden in Hades. Her vermilion lips glowed like rubies in the weak light from the kerosene lamp that stood on an upended crate near the brass bed. And she had the devil's own temper.

"You rich white gals got no business bringin' your troubles down on our heads," she snarled. "Don't know why you can't have your baby in a hospital like all them other rich folks. Oh, no. Instead, you got to come 'round here botherin' old Moonie."

"Now, Rolantha," Hotshot said, "you be nice to Miss Dessie. She done—"

Mrs. Moonie turned on him. "I heard what she done. I'm too old to be waitin' for my man to get out of prison again, Hotshot. And what about Pearlie and Cherisse? With your fancy white gal takin' up the bed, how we gonna make any money, you tell me that?"

So Mrs. Moonie was a madam, and I was going to have my baby on the stained sheets of the brass bed where her prostitutes plied their trade. Lucky me, I thought.

I learned against the wall. "I'll pay you whatever you lose on me, and then some," I said weakly. "Please, Mrs. Moonie, I don't have anywhere else to go."

Hotshot and the other man left. Under Rolantha Moonie's hostile gaze, I undressed myself and pulled the pink curlers out of my hair. I lay back on the bed, and she bent over to examine me. "We won't have to wait long for this one. I can see the top of his head startin' to bust out. You ever had a baby before?"

I gritted my teeth and nodded.

"Well, that's somethin'. Least you knows what to expect. I better tell Hotshot to play somethin' fancy and to play it loud. I got me a nosy neighbor up the road. If she hears you hollerin', she'll start to wonderin'. Ain't no other gals 'round here near their time, black or white."

She departed briefly, and returned carrying a load of clean rags and a basin of steaming water. I heard the first sweet notes of Hotshot's trumpet. He really was a superb musician, with a pure tone and a way of caressing the notes lightly, as if he were flirting with them.

Then I heard something else, a piano, out of tune but oddly appealing. Paul, trying out his wounded arm. Paul and Hotshot were jamming.

I screamed. The music got louder. "Push!" Mrs. Moonie shouted. "Come on, girl, take a deep breath and push hard. That baby needs a little help from you. I'm helpin', too. Come on!" I felt her hands press down on my belly.

My baby came into the world to the accompaniment of "Smokehouse Blues." When Mrs. Moonie told me I had a daughter and that she was fine and healthy, I burst into tears. My sobs and the infant's thin cries blended with the two instruments downstairs. We were all jamming together, improvising a jazz hymn to new life.

I named my daughter Grace Ann for her brother, Grayson, and because we were in Grace, Mississippi, and because that's what she was, my Amazing Grace, a gift to me from God. She had a full head of black hair and perfect plump limbs and a lusty squall that demonstrated fine lungs and a strong heart. I had a little trouble getting her to nurse at first, but Mrs. Moonie brought me something to drink to help the milk come down. It smelled like asafetida and tasted worse, but it did the trick. It also knocked me out as soon as my daughter had drunk her fill. Mrs. Moonie tucked us in, me lying in the depression in the center of the bed and Grace nestled against the curve of my body. We were both exhausted. I had had a hard day: hiking in the rain, meeting my son, kidnapping Bram Howard and forcing him at gunpoint to drive us westward across three states. And Grace Ann Matos was the world's youngest fugitive from justice.

The next morning, Mrs. Moonie, breathtaking as ever in her red dress, brought me a working man's breakfast of grits, ham, and eggs. I was surprised to find I was ravenous. Grace also did justice to her breakfast, and then promptly dozed off again.

When Mrs. Moonie returned an hour later to take away the dirty dishes, she was shocked to find me out of bed and walking around the room on shaking legs.

"Clara Mae told me that she went out and chopped cotton just two days after having her first son," I told her when she began to scold. "I'm just as strong as she was."

"And just as stupid," Mrs. Moonie rejoined. "Clara Mae Grayson never did have no sense, runnin' off with that witch doctor."

"Who?" Clara Mae had neglected to supply this chapter in the history of her life. "What witch doctor?"

"Called hisself Brother Jupiter. Sold some kind of hair oil and a tonic for the fever. It was the same stuff in different bottles."

"I know him," I said. "He's still selling it. Clara Mae swears by it. She took me out to his shack in the woods a couple of times when I was sick. But I didn't know he and Clara Mae . . ."

Mrs. Moonie snorted. "Clara Mae grabbed that baby of hers and followed that no 'count fool when he was run out of town. Next we heard she was livin' up north somewheres."

"South Carolina isn't the north," I said.

"It's north of here, ain't it?"

Some time after noon Paul came upstairs. He held Grace Ann for a while, but he was restless and uncommunicative, and he only stayed for a few minutes. Before he left, I asked him what Hotshot and Moonie had done with Bram. He said he didn't know. A few minutes later, I heard a plink, plink, plink. Paul was tuning the piano.

Mrs. Moonie didn't know what had happened to Bram, either, or if she did, she wouldn't tell me.

"I don't wanna know nuthin' 'bout nuthin'," she declared. "You and your no good friends gonna get us all lynched."

I said, "This is 1952, Mrs. Moonie." I wondered if I should try calling her Rolantha, but her attitude discouraged familiarity. "Nobody lynches Negroes anymore."

"That's what you think. White gals comin' down here, bringin' their troubles with 'em . . ." She was still muttering when she left the room.

My hair was filthy, and I wanted to wash the black rinse out of it, but I didn't have enough water and I didn't have the nerve to ask Mrs. Moonie to cart more up for me. Besides, we couldn't stay here, and I would need my disguise again when we left. I had to be satisfied with a good stiff brushing.

I spent a pleasant day resting and nursing my baby and watching the bend of the river through the dormer window. The roadhouse was quiet during the day, except for the hum of idle conversation and the gentle clink of glasses in the bar downstairs. Toward dusk, I saw three men approaching from the riverbank, two blacks dragging a white man between them. Bram.

A few moments later, I heard footsteps on the stairs. An unseen door slammed nearby, then someone knocked on my door. Moonie poked his head in. I was sitting up in bed wearing the frothy white nightgown and robe I had bought for the occasion of my lying in, never dreaming I would be using them in the attic room of a gin mill in a poverty-stricken corner of the Mississippi delta.

Moonie said, "That fella you brung has hisself a nasty temper, Miss Dessie. We had him locked up in Old Parsnip's blacksmith shop and he darn near got away. Pried one of the boards loose from the wall. Good thing Old Parsnip needed a little piece of iron when he did. Anyways, we can't think of no place else to put him, so he's in the little storeroom in the front, just the other side of that door." Moonie pointed to a panel under the eaves that I had assumed was some kind of closet. "Don' worry. He won't try nothin' funny. If he does, Beebee's right out there in the hall, and he's got his shotgun 'cross his knees and your pistol in his hand."

I looked past Moonie through the open door. A strapping black youth was settling himself down on an empty nail keg. He grinned at me over the barrels of both guns.

"Ain't no other way out of here unless that fella wants to jump out the window, and I don' think he'll be doin' much jumpin', the shape he's in." With that tantalizing statement, Moonie retreated and closed the door.

Oh, God, I hoped they hadn't hurt Bram. I didn't want that. From that moment on, I could not rest. I could feel Bram Howard's presence on the other side of that door. His electricity charged the air in my room. Even little Grace Ann felt it. She awoke whimpering and would not be comforted, even after I changed her diaper and rocked her in my arms for an hour.

Night crept into the room smoothly and silently, like a practiced thief. I drew the tattered muslin curtains over the lower portion of the window and lighted the kerosene lamp by my bedside. By this time, Grace was in the mood to eat.

I was sitting on the edge of my bed, the baby suckling quietly in my arms, when the little connecting door opened and Bram crawled through.

"I don't suppose you have an aspirin?" he said.

He was rumpled, filthy, and haggard, so totally unlike his normal impeccable self that I could only stare at him. Then I saw the purplish bruise on his forehead. "Bram, you've been hurt!"

"I had a rude encounter with one of Old Parsnip's blacksmith tools." Bram pulled himself stiffly to his feet, and just avoided bumping his head on the low ceiling. "I have the double granddaddy of all headaches."

I said, "I have a little bottle of aspirin in my purse. The water in that jug is still fit to drink."

"Thanks." Bram found the aspirins and swallowed a couple. "Would you like to see another example of Parsnip's handiwork? He's a real artist with iron, that guy." He hitched up his pantleg. A four-inch cuff of thick black iron had been fastened around his ankle. Moonie was right, Bram could not jump with that stiff weight around his leg. He could hardly walk, much less run.

"Oh, Bram," I said, "I'm sorry." The sight of the manacle shocked me. "I shouldn't have involved you in my troubles, but I was at my wits' end yesterday morning, and seeing you and Gray together and hearing him call you Dad and then having him treat me like I was some kind of visiting aunt from Charleston damned near destroyed me. You'll come out of this all right, with no more marks than the ones you have right now. Then you can say anything you like about me and Paul. But I hope you will leave Moonie and Hotshot and the rest of these folks out of it. They didn't really have a choice, any more than you did."

"Maybe you should have thought of that before you set course for this place." The lines in Bram's face eased as the aspirin took effect. He stood in the dormer and gazed out the window. It was the only place in the room where he could stand upright.

I said, "I suppose that means you have every intention of taking revenge against these people? Don't force me to see to it that you can't. Moonie and Beebee are just looking for an excuse to take a nice moonlight ride in a rowboat and toss you into the river, with a big load of rocks tied to that bracelet on your leg."

He turned, and I saw that he was grinning. "Where do you get ideas like that," he asked, "Hollywood?"

Little Grace finished her nursing. I hoisted her gently onto my shoulder and patted her back until she gave me a burp worthy of Sir John Falstaff. I laughed. "She's just like her mother. No table manners. She wouldn't fit in at Woodlands. No, sir. Such appalling behavior for a young lady!"

"So, you have a daughter. Congratulations."

"My raven-haired beauty," I said. "Her name is Grace Ann."

"Like Grayson?"

"Yes, and like Grace, Mississippi, where she was born."

"It's a good thing we didn't stop in Tchula or Belzoni, then."

"Chula or Belle." I nuzzled the baby's soft cheek. "They're nice names, too." I walked slowly up and down the length of the room, holding the baby close, crooning to her. I knew that hospitals kept women on their backs for at least a week after they gave birth, but I didn't believe in it. Cows and dogs and horses were all up and around within hours of having their babies. Why should humans be any different? But I tired quickly. After a few minutes I sat on the bed and rocked Grace Ann gently in my arms.

Bram watched us for a long time. "You're very beautiful," he said. "The two of you."

I looked up at him. Tears filled my eyes. "I wish . . ."

Limping from the weight of the iron cuff around his ankle, Bram approached the bed. "Could I . . . do you think I could hold her for a minute?"

I clutched the baby tightly. "If you think I'd let you put your hands on another one of my children . . ."

He looked pained. Grace Ann began to wail. "Oh, Dessie," he sighed, "you know I'll give her back to you." He sat beside me, at the foot of the bed. I showed him how to slide his arm under the length of the baby's body, and how to cup his hand under her head until he got her settled against his chest, in the crook of his arm. She stopped crying the minute he touched her and opened her eyes in astonishment. Gazing down at her face, he brushed her cheek with his fingertip. "So small," he murmured. "You're so very small. And as pretty as a flower. How do you do, Little Princess Grace Ann? I am honored to meet you." He kissed her tiny hand, and she gurgled.

Just like her mother, I thought disgustedly. Believes every sweet and flattering word that falls from a handsome man's lips.

Bram looked up. I flushed, hoping he wouldn't read my thoughts in my face. "I wonder sometimes what would have happened if my father hadn't died when he did," he said. "If I hadn't been so weak, if I had stayed and faced things, I could have found a place for all of us, Blair and Mother and you. If we had stayed together as a family until Gray was born, things might have been different."

I shook my head. "I was Blair's wife. And I would have left that town, anyway, sooner or later. I had to get out."

"You're probably right. Still, I can't help wondering."

"Bram." I grasped his arm. "Give me my son back. Send him down to Mexico. Give him back to me now."

His shoulders sagged, and he lowered his head over the baby. "I can't do that, Dessie. I love him too much."

My tears started to fall again. I wiped them away. How many would I shed before I stopped feeling the hurt of losing Grayson? A million? Two million? I remembered a phrase from high school algebra: x approaches infinity. X number of tears.

I took Grace from him, laid her in a nest of rags in the middle of the bed, and covered her with the edge of the blanket. She sucked on her fist as she dozed.

Downstairs, things were getting lively. Cars had been arriving since dusk, and the talk and the laughter had grown steadily louder. A trumpet fanfare brought momentary silence, then shouts of delight and encouragement. I heard a piano arpeggio. Paul had spent several hours tuning the old piano, now he was doing what he loved to do best. He started to play an old-time dance tune, "Barrelhouse Boogie." The audience responded with polite applause. Then Hotshot joined him, and the result was magic.

"He needs somebody else." I listened to the music coming

up through the floorboards. The noise didn't seem to bother Grace at all. I could swear I saw her keeping time with her tiny foot. "Paul never could have made it with just his own talent. He knows it, too. He draws life from whoever he's with, whether it's me or Clayton or Hotshot. It's his way of having a love affair, maybe. I don't know. I'll never understand what goes on inside people's heads." Grace was sound asleep. I gathered her up, rags and all, and placed her in the wicker basket Mrs. Moonie had given me for a cradle.

After the boogie, Paul and Hotshot got into some slow blues. Hotshot started to sing. He had a rough, gravelly voice, somewhere between a baritone and a bass, and he could put over a lyric as well as I could.

"I know that song!" I laughed as I recognized the tune. "I haven't heard it in years. It's pretty funny." Softly, I sang along with Hotshot:

> You can come in the evening,
> You can come in the night,
> You can come in the morning,
> And everything will be all right,
> But just keep it comin', baby.
> Bring it on home to me.

"I learned that song from Clara Mae before she got saved," I told Bram as the last bars of music dissolved into applause. "When my father heard me singing it, he paddled me first, then washed out my mouth with brown soap." I laughed at the memory of my father trying to thwart his daughter's destiny. "Hotshot Grayson is a brilliant musician." I stepped over to the dormer and looked out at the dark hump of the levee and the black river beyond. "Why isn't he famous? Why doesn't every person in this country know his name?"

"Maybe he gets just as big a kick singing for those folks downstairs as he would for an audience of thousands," Bram said. "Fame isn't everything."

"You're right about that," I said passionately. "I wanted to be famous ever since I was a kid. Then I got famous, and I found out what it was all about. Fame and fortune. If you don't have someone to share it with, it's like a slap in the face." I returned to the bed and sat. "Since I lost Gray, it hasn't been fun anymore."

The dual voices of trumpet and piano reached a crescendo, which was swallowed up by wild applause. Bram leaned across me and turned down the wick in the lamp. The flame flared up, then went out.

"Dessie—"

"No." I found myself trembling. "Please, no. I'm tired and sore and I feel like I could cry for a week."

"Hush. It's all right. Don't be frightened." He slid closer and put his arms around me.

"You took my baby away, and you won't give him back," I sobbed. "You say you love him, but I love him, too. I'm his mama. He's growing up without his mama, and now he doesn't need me anymore. I love him so much. I'll never stop missing him. Never."

"I know. I wish things had been different. Hush now."

He held me while I cried. My distress at being touched by him vanished. We sat together, our arms around each other, and listened to the sounds of a world far away: the music in the room below, the sounds of the river at night, the drone of a tugboat horn, the cry of a night bird. In her makeshift crib, Grace sighed and whimpered, then was quiet.

"So, this is what it's like," I sighed. "Not to be alone. Safe. I feel so safe."

Downstairs the crowd was getting rowdier. Grace awakened and demanded to be fed. I picked her up and opened my nightgown. Bram put his arms around both of us. Grace kneaded my breast with her fist as she nursed. She smelled warm and sweet, like laundry soap and hay and the fur of kittens.

The only light in the room came from the rising moon. Grace finished nursing. I changed her diaper and settled her back to sleep in her basket. Then, with my nightgown folded down around my waist, I dipped a cloth into the basin that sat on the upended crate by the bed and started to wash myself. I didn't feel shy in front of Bram. I had known him forever.

Bram said, "What are you going to do when you get to Mexico? How can you be sure that this Matos person will be there to help you?"

"He's my husband. I have to believe what he says. He's been so good to me."

"Murdering your husband, making sure you lost your son . . ."

"He didn't do those things! I can't believe it. I won't. You don't know him—you've never even met him. He's always been so gentle and considerate. He never even raises his voice."

"Why should he, if he can pay his henchmen to do his dirty work for him?"

I collapsed on the bed and buried my face in my arms. "I won't listen to any more lies about him. He's my husband. He loves me. And I love him. I do. I love him."

I remembered what the producer at Magnus had told me about Glendie Burke. Someone had given her acid to drink, to insure that she would never sing again. Who? Who would do such a terrible thing? Someone who desperately wanted her part in that movie, for herself or someone else . . . ?

"I've got to trust him." I twisted the edge of the threadbare sheet between my hands. "I've got to. There isn't anybody else."

"There's me." Bram ran his hands over my still-misshapen body. "Dessie—"

"Please go away. I've just had a baby," I said. "I can't. I don't want to . . ."

"You don't have to do anything." The heavy iron cuff on his ankle clanked against the brass footboard as he lay down beside me and pressed the full length of his body against mine. "I love you, Dessie. I won't hurt you. Remember Villa d'Este? I do."

I closed my eyes. The old feelings came rushing back: a powerful sense of having come home; of wanting to be with this man, in this place, at this moment, for the rest of my life, for eternity.

"Lord help me, I'm still in love with you," I sighed. "I don't understand it. If I knew how to stop myself, I would. But I can't. I can't."

"Maybe you don't want to." Bram kissed my throat.

"I do!"

"No more talk." His hand slid between my breasts, swollen and heavy with milk. His lips followed. "Let me taste the love you give your child," his whispered. "Let me love you."

Hotshot's trumpet screamed raucously and repeatedly before falling in a long, drawnout wail that softened to a sigh, a voice pleading for someone to pay attention to him, to want him, to love him. I knew that song. I had sung it often enough myself, in a hundred different versions.

Just before dawn the next morning, I roused Beebee, who was dozing just outside my door. "Find Old Parsnip and tell him to take that piece of iron off Mr. Howard's leg. And make sure he cleans himself up—he needs a bath and a shave. We're leaving today."

I packed up my belongings and the few rags Mrs. Moonie had given me for Grace, put the pink curlers back in my hair, and made sure my rhinestone-winged glasses were in my purse where I could find them when I needed them.

An hour later, a bleary-eyed Moonie pulled the Packard up in front of the door and we piled in, Bram behind the wheel, and Paul and Grace and me in the backseat. Since my arms were full with my baby, I made Paul hold the gun.

I pressed three one-hundred dollar bills into Moonie's hand. I had already given Mrs. Moonie the two evening gowns I had brought with me. She seemed somewhat mollified, and declared they would fit Cherisse perfectly.

"Thanks for everything," I told Moonie. "And don't worry about Mr. Howard. He won't bring down any trouble on your heads."

"I hope not." Moonie yawned and scratched his armpit. "I was kinda thinkin' it's time for me and the Missus to take a little trip ourselves, close the place up for a few weeks now we got a little extra money. Hotshot, he say he gonna be headin' over to Kansas City sometime soon. Maybe we oughta go with him."

"That might be a good idea."

Bram let in the clutch and put the car into gear. Twisting around, I watched Moonie's roadhouse vanish around the corner and the rising sun turn the river into a sheet of liquid fire. When I faced front again, I found Bram's eyes waiting for mine in the rearview mirror. His smile was warm, full of remembrance and promise. I did not smile back.

We drove all day, down through Mississippi, then across Louisiana and into Texas. Grace was a good traveler, a regular little gypsy. She slept all the way except when she roused herself sufficiently to demand food. Once her demands were satisfied, she dropped off again.

Night eased down over the flatlands of eastern Texas. Towns were few and far between, and the darkness felt thick and heavy, like tar. I took the gun from Paul and handed him the baby. Then I asked Bram to pull the car over to the side of the road.

"The ride feels awfully bumpy back here," I said. "I think the right rear tire may be going flat."

"Really? I don't feel anything up here," Bram replied. "Car's handling as well as ever."

"Well, you'd better get out and look. I'll be right behind you with the gun, so no funny business."

Bram walked around to the back of the car, squatted down, and ran his hands over the tire. "I can't tell," he called out. "It feels all right to me. Still, it's pretty dark. Hand me the flashlight. It's in the glove compartment."

I slid into the front seat. I made sure all the doors were locked, then I revved up the engine and pulled away. In the mirror, I could see Bram bathed in a cloud of exhaust and dust and the reflected red glare from the taillights. He looked like a refugee from hell.

I drove for ten miles before stopping again. This time I shook the bullets out of the gun, then I hurled it as far as I could into the darkness. It landed with a soft splat, probably in a cow pat in some rancher's field. I hoped it wouldn't hurt anyone else, ever again.

17

TOURISTS AND BUSINESSMEN IN THE LOBBY OF THE HOTEL DEL Prado hardly noticed me sweeping past the big Diego Rivera mural on my way to the reception desk. In my swirling green skirt and yellow blouse, with a gaudy printed shawl knotted around my hips, I looked like a colorful tropical bird. But the other North Americans, the gringos, dressed just as outrageously. I blended into the flock.

I had ditched my pink curlers and Salvation Army glasses before we crossed the border. Then, when we got to Mexico City, I cut my hair short and dyed it a flashy shade of auburn. I never went anywhere without donning a wide-brimmed straw hat and dark glasses. But it was the infant in my arms that provided the most essential element of camouflage; movie stars don't carry screaming babies and straw baskets full of diapers, rattles, and stuffed animals.

I stepped up to the desk and spoke to the clerk on duty. I didn't know his name, but we were old acquaintances. The Del Prado staff knew me as Lillian Hayes, a gringa lady who had stayed at the hotel for three months until her money ran out. "Do you have any news for me today, señor?"

I expected the same reply I had heard a hundred times before, "No, Señora Hayes, not yet. Why don't you leave your address? We will send a message to your hotel."

But today, after five long months of waiting, the answer was different: "Yes, Señora Hayes. Señor Matos checked in late last night. He is in the Presidential Suite. Manuel will show you where it is." He tapped the bell on the desk. A bellhop scurried over. I knew him, too. When I had checked out of the Del Prado two months earlier, my funds so low that I couldn't give him a tip, Manuel hadn't even carried my suitcase from the lobby to the sidewalk.

A bodyguard answered the door of the Presidential Suite. After a moment of shock, I realized the person was a woman. She was enormous, six feet tall and at least two hundred pounds, and she wore a man's suit, but with female bulges in the right places and a less natural bulge under her left armpit. Her jaw was hairless, and her hips were as broad as a Pontiac.

"Where's Tony?" I spoke in English.

She was expecting me. Stepping back, she opened the door wide enough for Grace and me to pass through. In the hallway, Manuel craned his neck to get a better look at the occupants of the suite. The Amazon tossed him a coin and slammed the door in his face.

"Come this way." Her English was American with flat Wisconsin vowels. "Mr. Matos is expecting you."

She led me through an elegant sitting room toward the master bedroom. A trace of Tony's fragrant cigar smoke lingered in the air, inviting me to a rendezvous with my past. I thrust aside the countless memories the smell evoked. I wanted to concentrate on the present.

Tony was sitting up in bed, a breakfast tray on his lap and newspapers in three languages spread out over the coverlet. He was speaking into the telephone. The curtains were drawn; his dark glasses lay folded on the corner of the nightstand, beside a chessboard from which most of the pieces had been removed. The game was nearly over.

He said into the phone, "King's knight to queen's bishop three." Then he hung up, shifted a piece on the board, and smiled at me. "Come and kiss me, Dolores."

I glanced at the character hovering in the doorway. "Can't we be alone? I have so much to tell you . . ."

"Of course. Matilda."

Matilda nodded and went out, closing the door softly. I deposited Grace on the cushions of a brocaded loveseat, then tossing aside my hat and glasses, I ran to the bed and embraced my husband for the first time in nearly a year.

"We've been waiting here for five months!" I wailed. "Five months, and not one word from you! Didn't you get my telegrams? I tried to phone, but the number you gave me had been disconnected and the information operators wouldn't help me. I nearly went mad. I couldn't imagine what had happened to you.

I didn't know if you were dead or sick or in jail. You promised to help me, Tony, but you didn't come and you didn't even send word to me. I couldn't afford to stay here. I had to leave before I was completely broke. I've sold almost everything I owned. You should see where we live now, the three of us crammed together in one room, with cockroaches as big as rabbits and mosquitoes as big as vultures. I thought I could trust you, but you . . . you abandoned me!"

Tony patted my shoulder and waited patiently for this torrent of reproach to end. "I wanted to come, Dolores," he said when I was quiet. "I missed you. But the American FBI agents have been watching me closely, hoping I would lead them to you. I couldn't take any chances. Just last week, they were finally called back to Washington. I ask your pardon a thousand times, a million times."

Tony glanced over my shoulder, at the squirming bundle on the loveseat. "In the meantime, I have been busy solidifying my position with the new regime. President Batista and I are old friends. Good friends. During his exile in Florida, I visited him constantly, advising him, and reporting to him on conditions back home, helping him plan the coup that would return him to power. I have made myself indispensable to him. But dictators require inordinate amounts of flattery and attention."

I marveled at how little I knew about this man. All the while he had been managing my career in show business, he had been conspiring with a former president-turned-dictator to overthrow the democratically elected government of Cuba. Why hadn't I been more curious about those sudden trips back home, those flights to Florida, those long telephone conversations in Spanish?

Grace started to whimper. I mopped my eyes with the hem of my skirt and went over to pick her up. "I came here every day to see if they had word from you. But it was so risky. You never know who you'll run into in a place like this. One morning I saw Dutch Hadley—he directed the first picture I ever made for Magnus. Honestly, we turned tail and ran that day, didn't we, Grace?"

Tony left his bed and came toward us, silk pajamas rustling. "So, you named her Grace." He stretched out his hand and stroked the baby's dark head. "You have given me a fine daughter, Dolores. That pleases me. Daughters love their fathers unreservedly, without judging them. Give her to me." He took the baby from me and held her in his arms. Grace seemed startled to see a strange man staring down at her. She screwed up her face, but decided not to cry.

"Beautiful," he crooned. "You are so beautiful, my little daughter. Why don't you come and live in Cuba with your Papí, no? I will take good care of you. Everything will be the best: schools, clothes, toys. All the things I never had when I was a child. Your friends will be the children of the rich men, the members of the Yacht Club, the masters of society. But you will outshine all of them with your beauty and your charm. Their sons will fall in love with you, and their daughters will envy you. And when you are fifteen, you will have your *quinze*, your debut into society. It will be the most lavish party the island has ever seen. Your gown will be white, like a young bride's, and trimmed with real flowers, thousands of pink rosebuds. And gifts—I will shower you with gifts. A little car. Money. Trips to New York and Paris—anywhere you wish to go. And you will love your Papí more than anyone else, yes? Little Gracia and her Papí."

Coldness settled over me like a breath of winter. To anyone else, his words would have sounded like the fanciful promises made by any father to his infant daughter. But I knew better. Tony Matos had no capacity for fancy. He was dictating the future to his child, and he would do everything he could to make sure his predictions came true.

Little Gracia and her Papí, whom she would love more than anyone else. He would buy her affection with his gifts and his attentions and his flattery. Where was I in his plans for the future? He was going to take my baby away from me. It had happened once before. Like Bram Howard, Antonio Matos was a man accustomed to getting what he wanted.

"What about the shooting?" I said, trembling. "Have you talked to any American lawyers about Paul and me? How do things look back in New York?"

Tony shook his head. "At the moment, very bad. The black man, Striker, has just been convicted and sent to jail on charges of possessing drugs. But he testified that you shot those two federal agents, not Mr. Miller. You are wanted on a charge of murder. If either you or Mr. Miller sets foot on American soil, you will be arrested. My lawyers say that public prejudice is still high. If you returned now, things would go badly for you."

"But I'm innocent," I cried. "You know that. Only I can't prove it unless I go back, and if I go back, they'll throw me into jail and leave me there to rot. And I'll lose Grace. Oh, my baby," I reached out to grasp my daughter's tiny hand, "what's going to become of us?"

"You can depend on me to take care of you now, Dolores," Tony said. "And the little one. You will be quite safe in Cuba. Batista would never permit the Americans to extradite you. And I can offer protection, the best protection money can buy. How do you like Matilda? She and her sister Maria take very good care of me."

"I'll bet they do. Where did you find them?"

"In a lesbian show at the Flamingo Club in Havana. They were wrestlers who challenged all comers—men, women, even chimpanzees. When they had no one else to wrestle, they fought with each other. What a magnificent spectacle that was! But they are no longer young, and they were having a hard time beating some of the men who came up against them. When I offered them a job, they accepted. I promised them lifelong financial security, plus the guarantee that they would never be separated from each other."

"What happened to your old bodyguards?"

Tony shrugged. "I had some doubts about their loyalty to me. I could not, in good conscience, continue to employ them."

I wondered briefly what happened to bodyguards whose loyalty Tony questioned. I took a deep breath. "Bram Howard told me that you were the one responsible for getting Mrs. Foyle to testify against me, and that you paid King Kingsley and Adam Foster to lie about me on the stand. Is that true?"

Tony's eyes never flickered. "Your happiness is my first and only concern, Dolores," he said smoothly. "It always has been, from the time we met. Mr. Howard is badly mistaken. Why would I want to jeopardize what I have worked so hard to achieve for you?"

"I don't know." I shook my head. "None of it makes sense to me. Bram also says that you hired someone to kill his brother. I didn't believe him. I couldn't. It's just too awful to think about. But everything happened so quickly, remember? You came back to California just a few days after Blair died, and a few days after that, we were married."

"I learned about your husband's death through perfectly legitimate channels," Tony said with a tight smile. "An obituary column in the newspaper. As you know, I am an enthusiastic reader of newspapers. Ah, Dolores, is it a crime to court a beautiful widow whom one has loved for many years? And you did want a child, did you not? Little Gracia. Is she not the most precious gift I have ever given you?"

"Of course she is. I love her with all my heart. I'm sorry, Tony. I guess I'm . . . I'm just a bit on edge."

"I understand." He took my hand and raised it to his lips. "Your accusations wound me to the heart, but I deserve them for neglecting you. I love you, Dolores. And I forgive you. Grace is my gift, too, you know. Your gift to me."

He paraded around the room, cradling the baby in his arms. I watched from the loveseat. "You surprise me, Tony. I wouldn't have thought you were the sort of man who liked children."

"My own child," he said. "My own dear daughter. She is the bond between us, Dolores, a permanent bond that can never be broken. I am her father; you, her mother. No matter what else happens, that can never change. I wanted that."

"You always seem to get what you want," I remarked. "You're a lucky man."

"I do not believe in luck," he replied sharply. "A man sees an opportunity, he seizes his chance, and everyone wants to call it luck. Bah. I make my own luck. I always have. A starving orphan from the *barrio* becomes the second most powerful man in Cuba. Luck? No. Genius. Intelligence. Courage. When a man has those, he has no need of luck."

As I listened to his credo, all my dreams vanished, and cold reality settled into my bones. Antonio Matos did indeed make his own luck. He had poisoned Glendie Burke to make me a movie star. He had given me his child to enslave me to him forever. He had robbed me of Gray and murdered Blair to achieve his purpose. That's what he called making his own luck.

Everything Bram had told me was true. Tony Matos did not love me. Tony Matos was evil incarnate, and he wanted to possess me. He wanted absolute power over me. And through Grace I had given him that power.

I stretched out my arms to take my baby from him. I tried to keep my voice steady. "We'd better be going. Paul will be wondering what happened to us."

Twisting away from me, Tony shielded Grace with his body. "Nonsense, your place is with me now, Dolores. We will fly back to Cuba together, tomorrow. I will send Matilda to fetch your friend."

My mouth went dry. I struggled to control the panic that was hammering viciously inside my brain. "I'd rather not send a stranger," I said. "Paul is so terrified of everything these days. I don't want to frighten him. Why don't I go back and tell him you're here, and we'll move in with you this afternoon?"

"Grace will stay here with her Papí," he said firmly. "Such a pretty child. My beauty, my—"

At that moment, Grace decided she had been patient long enough. She let out an earsplitting scream. Tony tried his best to comfort her, patting and jiggling and speaking persuasively to her, but he was no match for one of her temper tantrums. Her face got redder, her shouts louder, her kicks more violent. Even then, he would not turn her over to me, but kept insisting that he was her Papí, that he loved her, that if she were quiet he would reward her with a new toy.

Then suddenly the expression on his face changed. He wrinkled his nose and held the squalling infant away from him at arms' length.

"She is wet," he said, "and soiled. Do something."

I left him holding the baby while I pretended to search my bag. "Oh, dear, I don't have a clean diaper. I seem to have forgotten her dusting powder, too."

"I will call room service." Tony sounded desperate. "They will find something you can use."

"No, I'd better take her home." I took Grace from him and boosted her up on my shoulder. "Along with everything else, she's overdue for a feeding and a nap. I'll bring her back as soon as she's decent, and Paul, too." I slapped my hat back on my head, put on the dark glasses, and picked up my straw bag. "Good-bye, darling." On my way out of the room, I gave Tony a warm kiss. "I can't wait to be a family again. I've missed you so much. I love you."

As I passed through the sitting room, Matilda, who had been lounging on a sofa reading *Confidential* magazine, jumped to her feet. Her sister Maria emerged from another bedroom. She looked just like Matilda, as big and beefy as a truck driver, but she had bleached her hair blond. A darker mustache colored her upper lip. I hugged Grace closer.

Our hotel was near the *zócalo*, the square in the oldest part of town. By the time I lugged poor Grace up four flights of stairs to our hot little room, I was puffing and sweating and she was screaming with renewed vigor.

Paul was sitting in front of the window, an American news-

258

paper open on his lap. I don't know where he had gotten it, but I cringed when I saw the headline: HEROIN ADDICT SENTENCED; SEARCH FOR KILLERS GOES ON.

He lifted his head. His face looked like a death mask. "Clay's in prison."

"A good place for him, the bastard. I hope they keep him there until he rots." I dumped the squalling baby on my bed and dragged our suitcases out from underneath.

"He . . . he told them you shot those men! You, not me! I've got to go back, Dessie, and tell them the truth."

"No! Don't you understand, Paul? They'll take Gracie away from me."

"No, they won't. I'll tell them what happened; I'll them them I did it."

"They'll never believe you. Why should they? It's your word against Clayton's. Mine doesn't count." I threw myself to my knees in front of Paul and gripped his arms. "Listen to me, Paul, don't think about Clayton now. Tony's here! He's at the Del Prado. But he's not going to help us. He's . . . he wants Grace. He's going to steal Gracie away from me!" I bent my lead over his lap and sobbed hysterically.

"Dessie, that's silly." Paul gave my shoulder a halfhearted pat. "Why should he want to do that? Anyway, he can't."

"Oh, yes, he can. He's my husband. He's Grace's father!"

Paul was stunned. "Matos? Antonio Matos? But I thought—everybody thought—that dancer fellow, Dan Early . . . ?"

"I was married to Tony all along. Secretly. He married me right after Blair died. I was so mixed up, and after losing Gray I wanted a baby. I didn't know, never suspected . . . then Bram told me that Tony murdered Blair, and Tony paid those people to testify against me, Mrs. Foyle and King and Adam. He . . . he poisoned that singer, I know he did! He's a devil, he's crazy, he must be crazy to do such things. But I never knew that about him, I swear. I thought . . . I thought he loved me. Oh, God, I'm so scared. We've got to get out of here." I stumbled over to the dresser and started to empty the drawers.

"But where . . . ?"

"It doesn't matter where. Someplace where he can't find us. We'll change our names again. I'll dye my hair a different color—purple or blue if I have to. And you . . . we'll get you a pair of dark glasses and a cane and tell everybody that you're blind and deaf and dumb. But that man is not going to find us. I won't let him take my baby away. I won't!"

Paul closed his eyes. Twin tears coursed down his cheeks. "This is all my fault," he said. "I did this to you. You're an accused criminal, a fugitive, and now we're on the run from the one man in the world we thought could help us. We can't go home, we can't stay here, we're almost broke, and I can't work."

"Paul, we don't have time to feel sorry for ourselves." I put my arms around him and pressed my cheek against his. "We still have each other. I help you, you help me. That's the way it's always been with us. Now let's get going. I told Tony we would move into the Del Prado this afternoon. When we don't turn up, he'll start looking for us. We've got to get out of here right away."

We took a taxi to the central bus station and bought third-class tickets to Acapulco. Our luggage wasn't heavy—just a couple of thin skirts and dresses, a pile of diapers for Grace, and a new suit for Paul that we had gotten in Monterray. My sable coat was gone. I had sold it in Brownsville, Texas, to raise some extra cash. We had had to pay the border guard a two-hundred-dollar bribe to admit us without papers. I had given him some story about running away from my ex-husband, but he was only interested in the cash.

We stayed in Acapulco for three weeks. Our severe straits were affecting our diets and lodging. I ate tortillas and fried beans and drank plenty of cheap Mexican beer, which provided the calories I needed to keep producing breast milk for Grace, but Paul's weight dropped alarmingly. He disdained spicy food, and lived on pulque and tequila and cigarettes so cheap that they sometimes exploded, scattering cinders and ashes all over. I forbade him to smoke them when he was watching the baby.

One day when I was in the market shopping for fruit, a policeman approached me and asked to see my papers. I told him in my halting Spanish that I had left them in my hotel. He demanded to see them, and insisted that we return there at once. I opened my purse and offered him all the money I had, thirty-seven American dollars and a fistful of pesos. He helped himself to the dollars, leaving me with the equivalent of eight dollars in pesos. Then he strolled away. Terrified, I ran back to our room near the beach and told Paul that we had to move again.

I pawned what was left of my jewelry—a pair of gold earrings and a diamond brooch Tony had given me—so that I could pay our bills and buy bus tickets.

We ended up in Mazatlán, a tiny fishing village on Mexico's Pacific coast. The police were not interested in us; neither were the occasional tourists from southern California, but one day I recognized a stuntman who had worked on one of my pictures. He had come to Matzalán for the deep sea fishing. We moved again, inland to Durango, then down to Zacatecas and San Luis Potosí, and finally to Guadalajara. In Guadalajara, we were so desperate for money that I collared a tourist from New Jersey and told him such a convincing hard-luck story that he peeled off two twenties from his roll of dollar bills and handed them over to me.

Then he looked at me sharply and said, "You sure seem familiar. Like that actress they had a few years back, what was her name? Destiny Something?"

"That's what everyone tells me." I fled. Two hours later, our tired little trio was on its way to Tampico, on the Gulf Coast.

But Tampico felt too close to Texas and the American border. We drifted south to Tuxpan, and then to Veracruz. There Grace caught a cold that developed into pneumonia, and Paul collapsed from malnutrition and a liver infection. We were exhausted, all of us. Unless we slowed our pace, my body would begin to fall apart, too. Then who would look after Grace?

We were too worn out to run any farther, and too broke. We needed to stay in one place long enough to get medical help for Grace and Paul, and for me to find some kind of work so that I could build up our reserves. And I liked Veracruz. It was a wide open, lively town, Mexico's largest seaport and the port from which Cortez had shipped millions of pounds of gold to Spain.

I found an apothecary who gave me some penicillin for Grace and Paul for just a few pesos. Lodgings in the old part of town were reasonable, too—about fifty cents a night for the three of us in two rooms with a bath down the hall. Food, especially seafood, was abundant and cheap. On several occasions, I begged a whole fish at the dock where the fishermen were unloading their boats. I cooked it myself over an open fire on the beach. On days like that, we feasted for nothing.

Music was the lifeblood of the town. You could sit on a bench in the *zócalo*, officially named Constitution Plaza, and nibble on shrimp you had just purchased for a few cents from a street vendor while you listened to the strolling marimba bands warring for attention in front of the hotels that lined the side of the square opposite the cathedral.

One evening I noticed a woman singer strolling among the tables of the sidewalk cafés. A handsome mulatto with wide hips, a broad smile, and a flashing gold tooth, she accompanied herself on a small harp. Her pitch was simple: "Songs for sale, who wants to buy a song?" To please the tourists, her repertoire included many tunes that were popular north of the border, like "La Paloma" and "Spanish Eyes."

I said to Paul, "We could do that."

"Do what?"

"Sing for our suppers. Have you ever played the guitar?"

"I fooled around with one once, but I'm no expert."

"All right, you'll learn to play while I learn a few songs in Spanish. Grace will collect the money."

Grace, a year old, was an outgoing child who made friends easily. She had no fear of strangers, whom she entertained with a combination of English, Spanish, and baby babble. Dressed up like a native *Veracruzana* in a white dress and embroidered shawl, she would be irresistible.

Paul said, "Aren't you afraid someone will recognize us?"

"I don't care. At this point, I'm desperate for money and I'm desperate to sing. We'll deal with trouble when it comes. Right now, we've got to make some money. Come on."

We seated ourselves at a sidewalk table in front of the Hotel Colonial, ordered two beers and a glass of orange juice for Grace, and asked the mulatto street singer to join us.

"You want to buy a song?" Her gold tooth flashed.

"Many songs, señora. I will pay you to teach me all the songs you know."

Niña—that was her name—was incredulous. "Why should I do that? Besides, you don't need to pay to learn songs. You just learn them. Simple."

"Simple for you," I said. "But my Spanish is very weak and I don't want to make stupid mistakes when I sing."

When Niña realized we would be competing for business, she started to leave. "Stay just a moment longer, please, señora," I begged her. "If I do not sing, my child will go hungry. I cannot find any other kind of work because I speak such poor Spanish and I am not trained to do anything else. Music is all I know. Surely there are enough customers to go around?"

Grace won her over in the end. She sat in Niña's lap and tried to take the gold tooth out of her mouth. When I saw that Niña was weakening, I ordered another round of beers and coaxed her own story out of her. She told us that her boyfriend had run off with another woman to Mexico City, leaving her with three small sons and another on the way. She, too, had no other skills except singing.

"All right," she said, "meet me near the fountain tomorrow morning at eleven. We will start our lessons then. I suppose there are worse ways to make a living than singing."

I said warmly, "I can't think of any better ones."

Despite his moodiness and his melancholy, Paul was still a musician to his fingertips. He bought a thirdhand guitar and taught himself to play it in just a couple of weeks. Soon he was playing as well as most of the locals. I was thankful that he finally had some music in his life again. He used it like a drug. He picked up the guitar as soon as he got up in the morning, and he played off and on throughout the day, between sips from his everpresent bottle of tequila. Our landlady didn't mind the noise. Often, when she finished her chores, she came upstairs to listen, and she would sit knitting or mending on Paul's cot in our kitchen while he practiced.

I made a tiny costume for Grace, and I bought her a miniature straw hat. Half-Cuban, she was identical in coloring to the Mexican babies her own age, but her features were more delicate and fine-boned.

I sewed a costume for myself, a swirling Flamenco-style dress cut from a bedsheet which I dyed red then tediously embroidered with roses and butterflies. From the leftover scraps I made a matching vest for Paul. I dyed my hair again, raven black this time. Now I bore only the scantest resemblance to the honey blonde with the cherry-red lips who had warbled love songs on the world's movie screens. I called myself "La Rosita," the Little Rose.

One month after I hatched the plan, we made our debut in front of the Hotel Diligencias. Paul and I approached a table full of Mexican tourists and asked if they wanted to buy a song. They had been drinking and were feeling cheerful, and we struck a bargain: three songs for five pesos, about thirty cents. I was shaking with nerves, more scared than I had ever been on occasions when I faced five thousand people, but I gathered my courage and gave Paul the nod. Anyway, we were well-rehearsed—both Paul and I being sticklers for perfection—and we did a good job. Niña had agreed that my Spanish accent was dreadful, but she had coached me thoroughly, and our listeners did not seem to realize we were foreigners. When Grace trotted out in her little dress and tiny hat, the men cooed with delight and tossed us another five pesos for three more songs.

A marimba band came along and set up shop two tables away from us. Two men played guitars and two more manned the marimba. A fifth man pounded out the rhythm on an elongated Caribbean drum, while a sixth strummed a long notched gourd with a wooden stick. They all sang at the tops of their lungs, hoping to drown me and Paul out and to drive us away.

But I had learned my craft in crowded dance halls and on army bases where the competition to be heard was terrific, and I wasn't about to let six men with a dried squash overpower me. I just opened my throat and sang a little louder and with a little more bite in my tone. The audience loved the duel, and we raked in fifteen pesos, almost a dollar and a half. Enough to feed us and pay the rent for two days. We were on our way.

After that we played every day except when *El Norte* blew in from the Gulf bringing cold weather and rain. We arrived at the *zócalo* in time for the beginning trickle of lunchtime trade. We performed for a couple of hours, then retired for an extended siesta until six or seven o'clock in the evening, when tourists and locals crowded into the square. The festivities lasted until midnight or later. On Sundays, lunch hour and cocktail time overlapped, so we performed between noon and four, rested until seven, then returned for the evening shift.

Grace turned into a terrible ham. She started performing herself, doing little dances, singing her own garbled versions of her favorite songs. The *Veracruzanos* and the tourists from Mexico City loved her and filled her hat with coins.

"You're exploiting that child," Paul protested.

"I'm exploiting you, too, and you're exploiting me," I retorted. "In this world, everybody does whatever they can to survive. We're all exploiting someone. Haven't you seen how these Mexicans operate? Just look around. You've got two dozen little kids out here peddling shrimp and chewing gum and shoe shines—some of them not much older than Grace. Are their parents driving Cadillacs? No, they're not. They need the money those kids bring home to live on, and the kids know it. It makes them feel wanted, needed, important. Grace is learning some valuable lessons, which I didn't learn until I was almost grown.

If you want to succeed, you can't rely on anyone else. You've got to get out and do it yourself."

Paul shook his head. "I believe you're becoming cynical, Dessie."

"No, I'm just being realistic. In the old days, I left too many details to people like Dizzy and the King and Tony because I was too dumb or too lazy to take care of them myself. Then they got the idea that they owned me. From now on, nobody runs my life but me."

Our lives improved materially and spiritually. Paul was happier now that he was making music again, and so was I. I fell in love with the music of Mexico: the sound of the mariachis with their mellow guitars and sassy trumpets; the Caribbean flair of the marimba bands; the dance tunes and the folk tunes and the love songs. For the gringo tourists, we widened our repertoire to include some American songs that Niña helped us translate into Spanish. But we shunned Dessie Heavener's biggest hits, songs that would have unmasked me quicker than anything.

A year came and went, and then another. From time to time, I thought about the life I had left behind, the lucrative recording contracts, the big cars, the fur coats. But I didn't miss them. So long as I was singing, and so long as I had my daughter with me, I was fairly content.

Not so Paul. After the first couple of months of euphoria, he lost interest in our music and our new life. He started drinking even more than before and he ate hardly anything. Under his tan, his features were sharp and gaunt, and his mouth curved downward in an unhappy arc. He forced himself to keep going. His guitar playing settled into uninspired mediocrity, but Grace's antics and my singing more than made up for Paul's lack of luster and frequent fumbles.

We had no trouble with the authorities and no sign of recognition from any customers. The other musicians around the *zócalo* tolerated us. Niña became our special friend. Of course, Grace was everyone's favorite. The waiters in the hotel dining rooms and in the sidewalk cafés always made sure she had plenty to eat and drink while we were working. As her features filled out and she began to get chubby, she looked even more like the other children peddling their wares in the square. We became a familiar sight, La Rosita and Gracia and sad, limping Pablo. Grace, ever more eager to hog the limelight, started demanding solo numbers of her own. Her lisping renditions of "La Paloma'' and a popular Mexican torch song, "Mi Corazón," always brought down the house. One of the marimba players gave her a tiny guitar, and when she strummed it and sang "Cielito Lindo" with its chorus of "Ay, yay yay yay's," I hugged Paul and laughed until I wept.

"We're your family," I told Paul later that evening as we sat on his cot in our tiny kitchen. "Like it or not, that's the way things are now. You and me and Gracie. Stop fighting it, Paulie. Stop thinking about the past. For God's sake, let yourself be happy. You're entitled to it. Everyone is."

His sad eyes grew dark. "Clayton Striker's in jail because he was taking drugs that society called illegal, but he wasn't hurting anybody else. I shot two men. Yet here I am, a free man, playing my guitar in the public square and pretending to be the husband of one of the world's most beautiful women and the father of her child."

I put my hand on his arm. "You are Gracie's father, more than Tony Matos could ever be. And I'm your wife, in every sense of the word except the real one. But there's no reason why we couldn't have that, too." As I talked, I unbuttoned my blouse. Taking his hand, I placed it on my breast. He trembled. "You still want me, don't you?" I whispered. "I want to be wanted. I need it, Paul."

We kissed and fondled each other. The room was hot, my passion hotter. We stripped off our clothes, every scrap, eager to eliminate all barriers to intimacy. I was breathing hard in anticipation. But try as he might, Paul could not match my pitch of excitement. Maybe it was the tequila. Or terror at the prospect of fulfilling the fantasies that he had nurtured since boyhood.

"I can't!" he moaned. "I can't, I can't, I can't. Oh, God!"

"It's all right," I said soothingly, "really, it doesn't matter. Just calm down, Paulie."

I stroked his head. Suddenly he pulled away from me and leaped to his feet. He lurched into the table, upsetting it with a mighty crash.

"Don't be nice to me!" he shouted. "I hate it! I hate you. I'm a failure. I've always been a failure at everything I tried. Law, music, friendship, love—everything! You know it's true. You don't have to pretend otherwise. I'm sick of pretending. I know what I am. I know what you've done, sacrificed everything for me . . . your career . . ."

"Which had come to a grinding halt because of Grace," I tried to remind him, but he swept on, unheeding.

". . . your rights as a United States citizen. Everybody back home thinks you're a killer, and you're content to let them think so! Your name is a household word, all right, but not as a singer or a movie star. Oh, no, you're known as a murderess and a kidnapper and an accomplice to a drugged-up piano player. It's not right. I don't want your love and I don't want your pity, and I don't want your body in bed at night, and most of all, I don't want you turning me into a model citizen and a husband and father because you want me to be happy. Can't you get it through your empty blond head that I don't want to be happy?"

Grabbing his guitar by the neck, he smashed it against the wall. The sound of his anger reverberated inside the belly of the instrument, and throughout the little apartment.

"Señora! Señora!" My landlady pounded on the door.

"Señor Pablo is a little bit drunk," I called back. "We're all right. I'll try to calm him, señora. I'm so sorry."

Paul ricocheted around the small space, clearing surfaces with sweeping movements of his arms, hurling crockery, smashing our few plates and glasses, grabbing the tablecloth and dishtowels and tearing them to ribbons. Then, having nothing else to destroy, he attacked the guitar again, pulverizing what was left of it with his bare foot, reducing it to sawdust and splinters while he sobbed and cursed in English and Spanish. I approached him, calling his name softly. He whirled around, swinging his fist in a mighty roundhouse punch. I ducked and Paul lost his balance and fell heavily to his knees. All the fight went out of him. He collapsed in the middle of the floor, weeping and repeating the same phrases over and over: "I'm sorry, I'm sorry, I'm sorry . . ."

"Mamí?" Grace stood in the doorway, a small, ghostly apparition in her white nightgown. She rubbed her eyes with her fists. "Why is Papí crying?"

I hustled her back to our bedroom and stayed with her until she was asleep. When I checked on Paul again, I found him right where I had left him, snoring heavily. I put a pillow under his head and covered him with a blanket. Perhaps those compassionate gestures were the last straw for Paul; when I walked into the kitchen the next morning, he was gone.

In the month that followed, I searched for Paul in every cantina and flophouse and bordello in the city. One night someone told me they had seen him in a bar down near the docks, a notorious dive where the liquor was cheap and any kind of sex could be had for a few pesos. I rushed over. The dark room smelled of sin and despair. The bartender pointed out a drunken gringo lying facedown in a corner, his clothes drenched with piss and liquor and his pockets turned out. My heart pounding, I turned him over. It was a stranger.

I was too worried and upset to perform, but Grace and I quickly ate up our meager savings from the past two years. We had to start working again. And I had to have an accompanist. I hired Jaime López, the sixteen-year-old son of one of the marimba musicians, who was a reasonably good guitar player. We didn't starve, but Grace's straw hat didn't seem to fill up as fast as it had when Paul was playing with us. Paul's sad face and crippled leg had been worth another fifty pesos a night.

One night when the *zócalo* had nearly emptied out and I had bade farewell to young Jaime, a party of young men in front of the Hotel Colonial called me over and asked for a love song.

"I am very sorry, señors." With Paul missing, I had no one to speak English to, and my Spanish was improving. "My guitar player has gone home. No more songs tonight." Grace, clinging wearily to my skirt, had danced her feet off that night. She was ready to go home, and so was I.

"We can make music on the tabletop." A boy in a red shirt beat out a rapid rhythm with the palms of his hands. "See, who needs guitars? Now, what about our love song?"

"Oh, all right. One song, and then I take my daughter home and put her to bed. Do you want a happy love song or a sad love song?" I asked. "There are as many kinds of love songs as there are kinds of love."

"How about a Cuban love song?" another man said. He had big ears and a thick mustache. " 'Weep My Lady.' Do you know it?"

I did know it, a slow tune that reminded me of the blues Caribbean-style. The men, five of them, listened attentively while I sang. When I finished, I was surprised to see tears in their eyes.

"Thank you, señora." Finally one of them broke the silence. His accent sounded a little different from the others. Like them, he wore slacks and an open-necked shirt. His hair was long, luxuriant and wavy, and he sported the beginnings of a beard. Lean and handsome, with a pallor not often seen in this part of the world, he cut a striking figure. His ethereal beauty made the macho toughness of his companions seem crude and excessive. He looked like a poet. "Have you ever been to Cuba?" he asked.

I shook my head. "I know one Cuban, but I would rather forget him."

"Really? What is his name?"

"Matos. Antonio Matos. He has some position with the government, I think."

Their faces closed, and their eyes grew cold. "Yes, he does," one of the others said. "We have all heard of him. A very influential man, is Señor Matos."

I said, "I regret the day I met him, and I don't say that about too many people."

"Really?" The bearded young man looked curious. "Why is that?"

I shook my head. "I can't talk about it. One never knows who might be listening."

The man with the big ears laughed. "She sounds like us, looking for spies—"

"*Ché*! Be quiet, Raoul." The bearded poet, though younger than his friends, was clearly their leader. "Señora, will you have a drink with us?"

"No, thank you. I must take my daughter home."

"Ah, your daughter is very beautiful. I envy your husband."

"I have no husband," I said. "And my friend has been missing for a few weeks. If you see him, a thin limping man with a sad face and hair that is turning white, send him home to his Rosita."

I hoisted Grace up on my hip, told the young men good night, and walked away. I had almost reached the waterfront when I heard footsteps behind me. The pale young poet caught up to me.

"Perhaps you will permit me to walk you home." The exertion made him wheeze. He caught my look of concern and smiled. "It sounds worse than it is. I am asthmatic. But the condition rarely stops me from doing what I want to do." He reached for Grace, who was sound asleep. "Let me carry her. You seem tired. I do not like to think of a respectable woman alone on the streets at this hour."

I hesitated to hand my child over to a stranger. "How do you know I'm respectable?"

"*Ché!*" He grinned. "A man always knows."

"*Ché?*" The word was unfamiliar to me.

Smiling, he explained that the expletive was characteristic of the Spanish spoken in Argentina. I repeated it, liking the sound.

"You see," he said, "soon you will sound like an Argentinian yourself."

His name was Ernesto. Born in Argentina and educated to be a doctor, he had practiced as a field surgeon and diagnostician among the poor before participating in an abortive revolution against the British in Guatamala. He had fled to Mexico, where he joined forces with the Cuban exiles led by Fidel Castro. Having failed to overthrow the government of General Fulgencio Batista in an uprising on July 26, 1953, Castro's men had come to Mexico to reconnoiter and to plan their next move.

I put Grace to bed in our little room, then I sat beside Ernesto on Paul's cot in the kitchen. While we sipped coffee and ate oranges, he talked passionately about the forces at work on Tony Matos's little island. He described the corrupt and inefficient government, the passive military, the harsh and even brutal police presence. The peasants were apathetic and ignorant. Those in the more remote areas of the country were denied basic education and rudimentary medical care. American gangsters controlled Havana's profitable gambling casinos, as well as its night clubs and brothels.

"Everyone takes from the Cuban people," Ernesto ripped the peel from an orange with a violence that matched his angry tone, "and no one gives anything in return. It is the old story, repeated again and again in countries all over Central and South America. The peasants are starving, the bloated Americans run the banana plantations and the sugar mills and take the profits home with them, and bastards like Batista and your friend Señor Matos fly around in private airplanes and take their vacations in the south of France. If you cut them open, those men, do you know what you would find? Not hearts, oh, no. Lumps of filth hardened into lead. But Fidel has the power to change all that. I have never known anyone so obsessed with justice, so determined to right ancient wrongs."

"You sound like you're describing yourself."

"Me? Oh, no. I am still a student of revolution. Fidel is the master. A genius." Castro, he said, had been born into a respectable middle-class family in Oriente, Cuba's easternmost region. In law school, he had turned his powerful intellect to the problems facing his fellow Cubans. Just two years ago, he had been arrested after attempting to take over the Moncada Barracks in Havana with a band of followers. Released during a recent general amnesty, Castro had fled with his disciples to Mexico.

"The first time I met him, we talked for ten hours." Ernesto's eyes glowed at the memory of that encounter. "I felt like I was meeting my own brother, the brother of my soul. When Fidel returns to Cuba to lead the revolution, I will go with him. But for now, we must train recruits, gather arms, and prepare ourselves."

"What are you doing here, in Veracruz?" I asked.

After searching my face for a moment, he seemed to reach a decision. "We are waiting for a shipment of guns from sympathizers in Florida." He took my hand. "You see how much trust I have in you? I could have made up a lie, but I didn't."

"Why not?"

"I don't want to have secrets from you. Secrets separate people. The truth brings them together. Now, tell me how you know Matos. He was your lover?"

I shrugged. "My Svengali. My patron. My guardian. My betrayer. And finally my husband. A devil, although you might not know it at first. If I have to run to the other side of the world to get away from him, I will. He wants my child, my Grace. She is his daughter. I didn't find out what a villain he was until she was born. We—" I caught myself, and shook my head in amazement. "Why am I talking like this? I hardly know you."

"Because we have no secrets from each other. I have penetrated your last secret as well. I know who you are." He touched my cheek. "In Buenos Aires they call you Dolores from Heaven. Your movies are very popular there. I used to see all of them. The stories were ridiculous, but you were magnificent. And your singing! Your singing gave you away tonight, you know. You have a way of closing your eyes at the saddest moment of the song . . ."

"Yes, you're right. My directors always scolded me for that. But I couldn't help it. I've tried to stop."

"You did it tonight, when you sang for us in the *zócalo*. That was when I recognized you. Don't worry. I won't tell anyone, not even my friends."

"I know you won't." I gazed down at our meshed hands. "I feel like I've known you for a very long time."

271

"I feel the same."

We smiled at each other. Without saying another word, he pulled me close and kissed me. My heart began to swell and pound. Here I was, about to make love to a stranger, a man I had picked up in the *zócalo*. I was no better than a Gypsy or a prostitute. But I longed to be held, to be caressed. The longing was so powerful it had even prompted me to throw myself at Paul. Poor, tortured Paul. Where was he now?

Ernesto whispered, "Tonight, at least, we two exiles don't have to be lonely."

With a grateful sigh, I gave myself to him.

We made love one last time in the gray light of early morning. I brewed coffee while Ernesto pulled on his clothes. "That shipment is supposed to come in today. We will be leaving the city as soon as we get what we came here for."

"I won't see you anymore."

"I don't believe that." He placed his slender hands alongside my face. "I think we shall meet again. And when we do, remember: *Ché!*" He laughed. "I use the expression so much that my friends have given it to me as a nickname. And you are my friend."

"Yes. And you are mine. Good-bye. *Ché!*"

"Farewell, Dolores." We kissed once again, then he slipped away. The revolutionary and the street singer. I would not see him again, I was sure of that. We might have been a couple of characters from a Hollywood movie. Only someone had forgotten to write us a happy ending.

18

"Mamí, I want to paint a picture."

"I think you'd better eat your supper first and paint the picture afterward."

Grace squirmed on her chair. "I'm not hungry. Can I go to the club and sing with you tonight?"

"No, it's too close to Carnival. The club is crowded and you might get lost."

"How can I get lost if I'm up on the stage with you?"

"Because I have to be up there a lot longer than you would want to stay, and I would prefer that you remain with the Señora until Papí and I get home." I dipped the spoon into the tomato and rice stew on her plate. "One more bite, Gracie, and then I have to go check on Papí. Paul, are you almost ready?"

From the bedroom came the strum of a guitar. Paul was supposed to be practicing. I listened hard for an indication that he wasn't too drunk to perform. These days he was never sober.

Grace continued to plead her case while I put on my black wig and sat down on Paul's cot to check my makeup case. I wore a simple skirt and sweater, and a jacket over that. *El Norte* had been blowing for three days, threatening to put a crimp in the public's enjoyment of Mardi Gras. Between Christmas and Ash Wednesday, Veracruz was transformed from a simple, fun-loving port into a three-ring circus that overflowed into every street and square in the city. Costumes, parades, street dancing—and music, always music.

For the past year, I had been singing in the lounge of the Mocambo, a resort hotel on the beach a few miles south of town. The hotel manager, a man named Valdez, had heard me singing in the *zócalo* and had asked Paul and me to come see him. The next day, in the empty lounge of the Mocambo, we performed a few numbers for him, Mexican standards and love songs, some rhumba and cha-cha pieces that were enjoying a vogue, and a few American popular songs. Paul alternated between piano and guitar. He complained later that he was rusty on the piano, but Señor Valdez didn't notice. He hired us to perform six nights a week between the hours of eight and two, with Sundays off, at a salary that was four times what we made on our best weeks in the *zócalo*. Best of all, I had a roof over my head when I sang.

The piano became a conduit for Paul's emotions. In our first months at the Mocambo, he often went to the lounge during the day to practice, and some nights he stayed long after the last patron had departed. All the things he could not tell me, he told that piano. I couldn't listen to his private music. It was too painful, and too sad.

Our relationship had changed. A few weeks after I had given up searching for him, he had turned up in the *zócalo*, ragged, emaciated, just skin and bones. He wouldn't tell me where he had been. We never again talked about anything important or meaningful, and he wouldn't let me touch him, not even in a casual hug. I blamed myself for having destroyed our friendship, but I could not erase what had happened.

What remnants of affection Paul could still muster, he bestowed on Grace, who needed them less than any child in Mexico. Spoiled and petted by everyone she met, she had learned the lessons of her infancy well. Whenever we went into town or stopped to have a drink at one of the cafés near the *zócalo*, she would join Niña or one of the marimba bands and perform. Señor Valdez at the Mocambo was crazy about her, too. On slow nights, Monday or Tuesday, I would take her with me to the lounge and let her sing a song or two. Señor Valdez always rewarded her with sweets and kisses, which was bad enough. But it took me months to break her of the habit of grabbing a hat or a coffee cup and making the rounds of the room to hustle the customers for tips.

Our landlady arrived to babysit and contribute her efforts to spoiling my daughter. She brought a basket of needlework and a pile of mending. I kissed Grace good-bye and tapped on the bedroom door. "Time to go, Paul."

After a moment, I heard his voice. It was thick with alcohol.

"I can't make it tonight, Dess. You'll have to get somebody to fill in for me."

"I will not!" I opened the door. He was lying on the bed I shared with Grace, his arm thrown across his face, his new guitar propped against the headboard, an empty bottle of tequila on the floor. "Come on, we have a job to do."

"I'm not well. A fever—"

"Fever, my ass." I stepped out of the room and asked the Señora to take Grace downstairs for half an hour. When they were gone, I removed my wig and put a pot of coffee on the little stove, then I returned to Paul. He wept and resisted, but I pulled his clothes off and dragged him out to the sink in the kitchen, where I forced him to throw up what tequila remained in his stomach. Then I cleaned him up, poured some coffee into him, shaved his face, and dressed him again in clean clothes.

"I want to die, Dessie," he wept. "Please leave me alone. You don't understand me. You never tried to understand me. Just let me die."

By the time I got Paul presentable, we were too late to catch the bus. We found a taxi, but it cost us fifty times the price of two bus tickets.

The Mocambo stood on a rise overlooking the Gulf of Mexico. White, rambling, spacious and airy, it was Moorish-nautical in style, with wide arches filled with oversized captain's wheels, broad verandas, terraced hillsides dotted with palm trees, and red-tiled roofs. I asked one of the waiters to escort Paul to the piano, then I hurried to the small dressing room just off the lounge. Hearing the opening chords of the currently popular "Moonglow," I breathed a sigh of relief. He was rarely so drunk or filled with despair that he couldn't play.

I made up my face, brushed and patted my wig into place, then got into my costume, a tight-fitting black sheath on which my landlady and I had stitched thousands of red sequins. Black strapped sandals with high heels, long black gloves, and cheap dangling jet earrings completed my transformation into La Rosita. I was glad I had been able to afford the wig. At least I didn't have to dye my hair anymore.

The room in which we performed was small, with a bar and about twenty tables, which were filled on Friday and Saturday nights and during the Carnival season. Sweeping onstage, I hailed a few of our regular customers at the bar. Paul struck up the opening chords of "Mi Corazón" in a peppy cha-cha arrangement we had worked out several months earlier. The crowd was friendly and their applause was warm.

A producer from Mexico City had wanted to record that song. He had offered a generous advance, and it broke my heart to turn it down, but I couldn't risk becoming too popular, too well-known. Records meant record covers and personal appearances and tempting invitations to sing in better clubs, plus the chance that someone would recognize my voice. For Grace's sake, I had to cling to obscurity.

We moved on to another up-tempo tune, a nonsense song called "Los Mosquitos" about a girl who is so popular that the boys hum around her like mosquitoes. That one always went over big with the Mocambo patrons. We programmed a ballad next, something to bring their blood pressures down: "Ho Perdido Mi Amor." It had an easy beguine beat, and Paul liked to improvise a tinkling obligato in the upper registers of the keyboard while I was moaning low.

During the bridge—"My love, my love, my ungrateful love"— I noticed a bit of activity at the corner table near the bar as the waiter seated a new arrival. A man, alone, wearing a white linen suit and blue sport shirt open at the neck. As he hitched his chair closer to the table, the light from the candle caught his face: Bram Howard.

The song died in my throat. I heard the bizarre croaking sound I was making and incorporated it into theatrical sobbing as we reached the final climactic measures. That little display of genuine emotion brought the house down.

By this time, my body was streaming with sweat under my wig and the heavy sequined sheath. Two more numbers and Paul and I could take a break. Only two more, I had to get through them somehow, and then I had to get out.

What was he doing here? Had he come for Carnival? Veracruz attracted many American tourists at that time of year. He didn't recognize me, I was sure of that. These days my voice was husky and thoaty, more suited to Latin songs and Latin sentiments. And my disguise was impenetrable. Paul, too, had changed so much that Bram could not possibly recognize him. His hair was nearly white, he wore glasses, and he was so thin that he resembled a cadaver or a ghost more than a man. No, Bram wouldn't know us right away. But he might, after a few more songs, start watching us too closely.

As I was leaving the stage, I paused by the piano. "Bram Howard is here," I hissed. "Come on, we've got to leave."

Paul shook his head. "If I tried to stand up, I'd fall flat on my face. I'd better stay here."

"Paul!" If a person could wail in a whisper, I did it. "Oh, God. Well, keep playing then. If anyone asks where I've gone, tell them I got a sudden headache, a migraine."

Back in my dressing room, I whipped off my gloves and gown. I was just zipping up my skirt when the door opened and Bram stepped in.

"Hello, Dessie. Show over?"

"It is for me. I'm going home." I peeled off my false eyelashes and scrubbed off my heavy makeup with cold cream and cleansing tissues. "Sorry, I didn't mean to cheat you out of a full evening's entertainment."

"You really were most entertaining." He grinned. "I hardly recognized you."

"That's the point of all this false hair and paint."

"What are you afraid of? American law doesn't mean much down here. I'm not looking for revenge for the way you treated me back in Texas, although I had a mighty long walk back to civilization. My feet still remember that trip. I hope the car behaved itself?"

"Perfectly." I put my gown on a hanger and pulled on my jacket.

"Paul looks really bad. Life in exile doesn't agree with him. It does with you, though. You're prettier than ever. Even in that ridiculous wig."

"Look," I said, "you obviously feel that we have a score to settle. Well, I don't. Nothing I did hurt you half as much as taking Gray hurt me. So go away and leave me alone, Bram. I suppose you think you're real cute, penetrating my disguise and then confronting me like this. But my life is hard enough—"

Bram leaned against the door. "Gray is here. We sailed down together from Corpus Cristi."

My mouth dropped open and I stared at him for half a minute. "Gray . . . here? He's not . . . he's not sitting out front, is he?"

"No, I left him with the boat. We had rotten weather all the way and the sailing today was particularly rough. He's pretty tired."

I sank down on the stool in front of the dressing table and gave myself a hard look in the mirror. I was almost thirty years old. Framed by the black wig, my face looked small and sad and pinched and sallow, years younger and at the same time years older than my actual age. A waif. A crone.

The tension under which I had been living for the past four years had stretched me thin and pulled me tight. As I thought about Gray on a sailboat in Veracruz harbor, just a few miles away from the place where I paraded nightly in a homemade red dress and a cheap black fright wig, I felt myself starting to break. Dropping my head onto my arms, I wept.

Bram didn't speak. I knew if I looked up, I would find his eyes in the mirror, waiting for mine. Someone knocked on the door. Bram opened it and spoke softly in Spanish. The visitor went away.

After some minutes, he said, "Would you like to see him?"

"No! No, I can't. I—I don't want him to see me. I've gotten old—and ugly."

"I don't agree with you, and neither would he. He's nearly fifteen now, Dessie. He wants to see you."

I lifted my head. Sure enough, those cool blue eyes hooked mine. "You knew I was here. You knew right where to find me."

He nodded. "I met a man from Mexico City who told me about a singer he'd seen in Veracruz. He wanted to record her, but she refused. That didn't make much sense. A singer in a second-rate hotel turning down a chance to make a record for a first class outfit? I sent someone down to investigate. He told me La Rosita had a husband who played the piano and a four-year-old daughter who appeared on the bill with her sometimes. The child's name was Grace. I was mighty glad to hear you were alive."

"Yes, I'm alive," I said heavily. "Just barely. Paul is trying to drink himself to death. I've begged and I've hustled and I've sung songs in the streets to make a few pesos so that I could support my child. Things are better now, but once in a while, when I can't stand the loneliness anymore, I pick up a man and go back to his hotel room for a few hours. That's the kind of woman your son has for a mother. Keep him away from me. If you have any feeling for me at all, you'll keep him away."

"I'm sorry you feel like that. Gray will be disappointed."

"He'll get over it." I unscrewed the lid on my pot of rouge and started to put some color back into my cheeks. "Well, I guess the show had better go on as planned. I hope you've satisfied yourself that there isn't anything you can do to punish me that I haven't already done to myself. Tell Gray . . . tell him you made a mistake. Dessie Heavener isn't living in Veracruz. Tell him to forget her."

"I could bring him here."

I turned with my hand upraised. My fingertips were stained crimson from the rouge. "Don't do that. I beg you, Bram. I don't want him to see me like this."

Bram pulled himself away from the door. "The name of the boat is the *Golden Vanity*, and she's docked at the foot of Calle Zapata. We'll probably stay in port until the weather clears. So long, Dessie."

I tried to concentrate on my makeup, but as quickly as I applied a layer of face powder, my tears washed it away.

"Wait, Mamí, you forgot these." Grace handed me my dark glasses and the old silk scarf I always wore to keep the wind from blowing my wig off.

I thanked her and put them on. Before we left the apartment, I looked in at the body slumped in the chair near the bedroom window. "Are you all right, Paul?"

"No worse than yesterday. No better. I suppose that makes me all right."

On the Monday before Carnival, the hotels were filled to capacity. The streets were crowded with tourists and visitors from neighboring towns wearing colorful masks and costumes. The excitement would reach its highest pitch at midnight the next day, when abruptly it would end. The merrymakers would fade away and the streetsweepers would move in with their wide brooms. By dawn on Ash Wednesday, the happy chaos of laughter and music and fantasy would be a dream.

Grace and I cut across the *zócalo*. We waved to Niña and to Jaime López's new marimba band playing in front of the Hotel Colonial, but we did not stop. I let Grace carry my purse, and she tripped along beside me, looking like a miniature tourist with an oversized suitcase. The musicians hailed her and asked her to sing for them, but she shook her head and passed them by. I had told her we were going to see her big brother, and for once her curiosity was stronger than her desire to show off.

The boat was still there, tied up at the foot of Calle Zapata. The *Golden Vanity*'s sails were furled at the base of her tall wooden masts, the decks sparkled, bright with new varnish, towels dried on the side rails. On the roof of the cabin, a young man wearing white slacks and a T-shirt lay stretched out on his belly, reading a book.

"Mamí, I want to take a ride on the boat," Grace said in Spanish. The boy glanced over at the dock and saw us.

"Hello, Gray," I said.

He closed his book and sat up. "Hello."

We gazed at each other over the railing. His eyes searched my face, looking for some recognizable feature under my scarf and the black wig. He still didn't know how to address me. Dessie was too informal. Mother or Mom belonged to someone else.

I said, "I can't believe how much you've grown." He had, too. He was nearly as tall as Blair now, but without a grown man's bulk. In fact, he was so slim that I feared a gust of wind might carry him overboard. "This certainly is a beautiful boat."

"It's a ketch," he corrected me. "They call it that because it has two masts. But we have an engine, too, in case we get becalmed. She's thirty years old."

"Just like me." I became aware of Grace tugging at my skirt and chattering to me in Spanish. "This is Grace Ann. She's your half sister." I switched to Spanish. "Grace, this handsome young man is your big brother. His name is Grayson. You see, we have two graces in the family."

Bram appeared at the top of the companionway ladder. "Welcome aboard, Dessie. Gray, you lift your sister over and I'll help your mother."

I handed my little girl up to Gray. My daughter, my son: meeting, touching. My legs were trembling so violently I thought I might fall into the gap between the side of the boat and the dock. But Bram took my hand and told me where to step.

"I'm glad you came," he said. "We were going to pull up anchor tomorrow."

"You must have known I couldn't stay away."

"I hoped you wouldn't. Not just for Gray's sake. Would you like a tour of the boat?"

The main cabin was surprisingly spacious, with a compact galley, twin sofas that converted to beds, tables that folded into the walls when not in use, and plenty of cupboard space. Toward the front of the boat lay a bathroom complete with stall shower, and a smaller cabin with a single large bed, a desk, and a bookshelf.

"She sleeps six comfortably, eight in a squeeze," Bram said.

"And there are just the two of you?"

"That's right. We're both pretty good sailors, and we spell each other at the wheel. Crossing the Gulf was tricky because of the lousy weather, but Gray handled himself beautifully. But then he's good at most things he tries to do. Care for a cup of coffee?"

"I'd love one." I took off my dark glasses and pulled off my scarf and my wig, then I ran a comb through my short honey-blond curls.

Gray and Bram and I seated ourselves around a table in the galley and sipped coffee from heavy mugs. Gray stared at me. Grace sucked a lollipop and played with Bram's sextant, all the while keeping up a stream of chatter in her own peculiar blend of Spanish and English. I was glad I had brought her along. Small children have a way of distracting attention from more serious matters.

"She's going to be a beauty," Bram said. "I hear you let her get up on stage with you once in a while."

"I can't keep her off," I said. "She loves to perform. She steals the show every time."

Gray, who had been silent for several minutes, suddenly spoke up. "Did you kill those two men in New York?" he asked. "Dad says you didn't."

Bram started to reprimand Gray, but I cut him off. "He has a right to ask. No, Gray, I didn't shoot anyone. I know certain people said I did, but they were mistaken."

"That black man really shot both of them, didn't he?"

"No, Paul Miller fired the shots. His friend was in trouble and he thought he could help." I did not take my gaze from Gray's face. "I got involved for the same reason. My friend was in trouble and I thought I could help."

"You shouldn't have run away," Gray persisted. "If you really were innocent, then you had nothing to be afraid of. You should have stayed and told the police the truth."

I sighed. He was so young, so earnest. Had I ever been like that? "I didn't think anyone would believe me. I knew how it looked to the police, and I knew I couldn't give myself up. I would have gone to jail, and Grace would have been born in a prison hospital. They would have taken her away from me and put her in a foster home. By the time things got straightened out, she wouldn't have known who I was. The law took you away from me, Gray. I didn't stand a chance then, and I sure didn't stand a chance after that business in New York."

"You never wrote to me after you came down here. Never."

"No," I sighed. "I didn't. I guess I wanted you to forget about me. You should have."

He looked so hurt and confused that I regretted coming. It wasn't worth it, seeing his pain and feeling my own. "But . . . aren't you ever going to go back?"

"Maybe someday, after Grace gets bigger and doesn't need me so much. I wanted the two of us to be friends, you see, so that if we were ever separated for any reason, at least she would remember me." My eyes filled with tears. "I didn't . . . I didn't want us to be strangers, the way you and I . . . ," I turned my face away.

Bram said, "Gray, take your sister up on deck and show her the life preservers. She might enjoy playing with them."

"But, Dad—"

"Please do as I ask. We can talk about this later."

Gray spoke to his little sister in fractured Spanish. She grabbed his hand and they went up the companionway ladder together.

Bram said, "He thinks that because I have plenty of money and some degree of influence with people who count, I ought to be able to get you out of this jam. I've been putting out feelers ever since you left, but the consensus seems to be that you should stay away a little longer. The newspapers weren't kind to you, I'm afraid."

I blew my nose. "I didn't expect them to be."

"I didn't realize how much this had upset Gray. For some reason, I keep expecting him to be like me. But he has more feeling than logic. He's impulsive. Kind of stubborn. Good-hearted and compassionate. And loyal to a fault."

"He sounds like a regular Boy Scout," I sniffed.

Bram chuckled. "I always loved him, of course. But as he grew older, I began to realize that I liked him as well. You have a wonderful son, Dessie. He's a little hot-headed and emotional sometimes, but basically sound. He says he wants to be a lawyer, but I can't see him sticking with it. He'd be too bored in the corporate world."

"I want to know if—" I drew a long, shuddering breath. "Can he sing?"

Bram looked startled. "This will sound strange, but I don't know. Jean-Ellen made sure he had piano and violin lessons, of course, and he's done very well. But I've never heard him sing. In church he just stands there with his mouth closed."

"Because of me. He hates me. He'd rather die than do anything I do."

"No, he's angry and hurt and he's trying to make the pieces fit together, but he doesn't hate you."

We heard Gray's voice from the deck. "Dad, take a look at this."

We went up the ladder. A yacht was motoring slowly into harbor. It was sleek and white and nearly as long as the *Queen Mary*. It had already passed the Isola des Muertes and was heading for the *faro*, the lighthouse.

Bram whistled. "I'll bet that baby cost a fortune. What a beauty. Who has money like that these days?"

I gripped the rail. "I know one man who does." Frantic, I ran below and put on my wig, scarf, and dark glasses. "Where's Grace? We've got to get out of here." I found my daughter playing in a locker near the boat's wheel. She had unraveled a length of rope and wrapped it around herself ten times. I snatched her up, rope and all. She looked startled and began to wail in protest. "Help me with her!" I said to Bram. "I've got to get home—to warn Paul."

He stepped ashore and held out his arms to Grace. "What's the matter?"

I was distraught, nearly out of my mind with fear. I started gabbling in Spanish, "He has come. I knew he would come, but I didn't know when. He doesn't know I'm here—there is still time to get away."

"Mother!" Gray leaped onto the dock beside us.

Stunned, I looked into my boy's eyes. They were on a level with mine. He would be tall. The Heavener and Howard men were all tall. I grasped his hand. "I love you, son," I said. "I wish things had turned out differently, in all sorts of ways. But I've always had lousy luck. Good-bye, Gray." I hugged him and kissed him on the cheek. He didn't recoil. After a moment, his arms came around me in a clumsy embrace. I turned to Bram, who was watching the oncoming yacht. "Good-bye, Bram."

With Grace riding my hip and tears running down my cheeks, I hurried back to the old part of town and our apartment on Calle Zaragoza. We had a lot to do, bags to pack, tickets to buy. We would head for Mérida, in the Yucatan, I decided. I had heard good things about Mérida. But no more singing, no more music. I might as well hire a skywriting plane to scrawl "Dessie is here!" in fluffy white letters over the town.

"Dessie!" Bram came pelting after me. I didn't slacken my pace. "Gray's watching the boat. Is that Matos's yacht?"

"Yes," I gasped. "Got to tell Paul. Please, God, I hope he's not too drunk to move. I've been so stupid. Did I really think I could hide from him? He knew! All this time, he's been like a cat watching a mouse, waiting for the right time to pounce."

"He can't touch you here," Bram argued.

"Oh, no?" I halted and faced him. "He can do anything he wants. He can take Grace and I'll never see her again. And that's just for starters."

My landlady was waiting for us when we got home. The police had come, she said, asking for papers. Señor Pablo had gone with them.

I rushed upstairs. Sure enough, the little apartment was empty. "They'll be back. What are we going to do? Paul! They've taken Paul. They were just waiting for instructions from Tony. He knew—"

"Dessie, please, slow down."

"You don't know!" I shrilled. "If you think Faust is just a character in an opera and Svengali is just a Victorian bogeyman, stick around. I sold my soul to Antonio Matos years ago, and now he's come to claim it."

"Look, you're overwrought—"

"How do you think I got where I was, and so fast? My career was at a standstill. Tony found me singing in a dive in New Jersey, and one year later I was starring in my first Hollywood movie. He had his methods. The girl who was supposed to play my part lost her voice. Somebody laced her cocktail with acid. And what about Blair? That was murder, and you know it. I couldn't believe it when you told me, but I do now. I thought I could get something for nothing. Tony Matos was a guardian angel who stepped into my life and straightened out my affairs. He didn't want anything from me, not even sex. Just the success I wanted for myself. Do you think he couldn't have gotten me out of that jam with Paul and Clayton in New York? Sure he could. In a minute. But he didn't want to. He wanted to show me how much I needed him. He's had people watching me, I know he has. All this time . . ."

Between my shouts and Grace's wails, Bram must have wanted

to cover his ears. But he grabbed my shoulders and ordered me to calm down.

"I'll help you. Did you hear what I said? I love you, and I want to help you. That's why I'm here."

I broke away from him and ran to the window. "Do you believe it, there's a man standing under the street lamp! Just like in the movies. Half the world learns how to behave from Hollywood!"

"Is there a back way out of here?"

"Are you kidding? That's in the movies, too, but not here. The customers in the restaurant downstairs use the same door we do, only they don't have to walk through the kitchen. The cops can just sit tight outside and wait to grab us." I flopped down on Paul's sprung-out cot. A Carnival mask fell to the floor. I had planned to wear it tomorrow when Grace and I went to see the parades.

Bram picked it up. "Do you have a costume to go with this?"

"Same one I wore last year, a white flamenco dress trimmed with red silk roses. Grace has one just like it. And Paul has a mask."

"The police are looking for a woman with a child, not a woman alone. Suppose you put on your costume and mask and walk out of here? I'll wait for half an hour, then follow with Grace. They won't stop me, and if they do, my passport's in order. I am an American citizen, after all, and a pretty rich gringo besides. I think we can pull it off."

"What about Paul?"

"We'll get you and Grace safely stashed aboard the *Golden Vanity*, then I'll see what I can find out. A few judiciously placed bribes ought to do the trick. As soon as he's aboard, we can cast off and get away from Señor Matos."

While Bram entertained Grace in the kitchen, I got into my costume and low-heeled pumps. I left my wig behind. I hoped the police would be looking for a statuesque brunette rather than a runty blonde.

I kissed Grace good-bye. She had gotten over her tears, and she wasn't frightened. She was accustomed to seeing me in costume six nights out of every seven, and she was always happy when she had a new man on whom she could practice her charms.

I reached the bottom of the stairs just as a group of costumed Americans was leaving the restaurant. They had had a lot to drink, and when I attached myself to one of the men and told him he was the cutest l'il ole thing I'd seen since I'd left Georgia, they laughingly accepted me into their company. We progressed unsteadily down the avenue, passing within inches of the plainclothes policeman keeping vigil under the street lamp. As soon as we neared the *zócalo*, I bade them a merry farewell and hurried toward the docks.

The *Blue Dolores*, ablaze with colored lights, was riding at anchor in the middle of the harbor. A small motor launch plied back and forth, carrying party-goers out to the yacht. Laughter and music drifted across the water. Tony appeared to be making the most of Mardi Gras in Veracruz, rewarding his servants, paying off his spies and his agents. How many of my friends were in his employ? Jaime López? Señor Valdez? Niña?

A light burned in the cabin of the *Golden Vanity*. Softly, I called out Gray's name. He came up on deck.

"Can I come aboard?"

He gave me a hand, and we went below. I explained what had happened to Bram and Grace. In order to make him understand the need for such subterfuge, I told him about my relationship with Tony Matos. I didn't leave out any of the sordid details, not even the suspicious circumstances that surrounded Blair's death. I wanted my son to know the worst.

Gray listened silently, then he said, "This man Matos, does he love you?"

"No. I don't know. I thought he did. He wants to own me. I was a challenge, a problem to be solved, like chess. I'm still a challenge. That's why he's followed me here. He doesn't like loose ends. And he wants Grace."

"Oh." He sat on the edge of the starboard bunk and stared at the floor, his clasped hands dangling between his knees.

"I was a fool, Gray. I've made some bad choices in my life. But I can't rewrite history."

"You left me alone. You hardly ever came home." He lifted his face. His cheeks were scored with tears. "You never asked me if I liked living with Grandpa and Ayleen. You didn't care about me."

"I did care!" I said. "Maybe I didn't know how much until I lost you to Bram. Then I wanted to die. Having Grace was the only thing that saved me. I'm not going to make excuses now. I did the best I could. Hell, Gray, I'm no genius. I'm not as smart as you or Bram. But I did try. I'm just sorry that things are so bad between us now. I'd do anything to make them better."

For the first time, he almost smiled. "At least you got rid of that crazy wig. You looked pretty silly in it."

Bram and Grace arrived two hours later, by which time I had paced off the cabin floor about six hundred times. Grace was sound asleep, her head lolling against Bram's shoulder. He handed her over to me.

"The cops pulled us in. I played the loud-mouthed gringo tourist and threw around plenty of twenty dollar bills. With all the bluff, I neglected to tell them which hotel I was staying in. We can't stick around too much longer. They're bound to start checking the boats."

"And Paul? Did you hear anything about Paul?"

"No, and I ran out of pocket money before I could buy the information. Besides, if I'd started asking too many questions of them, they would have discovered the link between me and La Rosita. I'll get to work on it first thing in the morning. In the meantime, you and Grace make yourselves at home. You can have the forward cabin. I'll bunk out here with Gray."

I looked down at Grace's soiled dress and my own flounced skirts. "We didn't come away with too much in the way of baggage, did we?"

"We can do some shopping when we get where we're going, wherever that is?" He gave me a questioning look.

I shook my head. "I can't think any more tonight. I'm fresh out of ideas. Besides, what does it matter? He'll find us wherever we go."

Bram looked grim. "Not if I have anything to do with it. Try and get some sleep. It's out of your hands now, Dessie."

I lifted my head. His keen blue-eyed gaze captured mine. When I found my voice, I said, "Bram, I'm not worth it."

He glanced at Gray. "You're the mother of my son, aren't you? Gray would never forgive me if I left you in the lurch now. He has a pretty high opinion of me. I'd hate to disillusion him. In the past few years, I've found myself trying to live up to his expectations of me. Besides, he's going to have to get used to the fact that his father is deeply in love with his mother."

Gray flushed. "I'll go up and check the ropes."

When he was gone, Bram said, "Things getting any better between you two?"

"I don't know. I'd like to think they are."

"He'll warm up. As soon as he gets to know you better."

287

"I hope so." I rose and hoisted my sleeping child higher on my shoulder. The boat swayed slightly and I lost my balance. Bram caught me and held my arms until I felt steady. And maybe a little longer. "Good night, Mr. Howard."

"Good night, Dessie."

Grace didn't understand why we had to stay inside the cabin of the *Golden Vanity* on Mardi Gras day. I had promised floats, parades, costumes, marimba music, dancing in the *zócalo*. What were we doing indoors on such a day?"

"We're going to take a ride on this wonderful boat," I told her, "but only if you're good, and that means you can't let anyone see you. Otherwise they might not let us go."

I was about to suggest a game of hide and seek when I heard voices on the dock. Pushing aside the short curtains over the porthole, I saw two pairs of legs ending in official-looking shoes. "Police!" I said to Gray in a frantic whisper. "Where can we hide?"

"Engine compartment." He lifted a hatch in the floor which I hadn't seen until that moment. Grace and I shinned down the short ladder, then he handed me a flashlight and told me to crawl forward as far as I could. We did so, and the hatch closed over our heads. At least we weren't wearing our flamenco costumes. Gray had lent me a pair of khaki trousers and a baggy sweater. To Grace he had given a T-shirt that I belted around the middle with a ribbon to make a dress.

"Now comes the best part of the game," I said to Grace, "but it's hard, very hard. We have to stay down here for a little while and we're going to see how long we can be quiet, absolutely quiet, not even a whisper, okay? Whoever makes a noise first has to take a bath." My would-be singing star hated to bathe.

Footsteps thudded over our heads as the two policemen searched the boat. I wondered what Gray had done with our dresses. Then the hatch opened. I switched off the flashlight and clamped my hand over Grace's mouth. She squirmed a little, but she made no sound, not even a whimper.

The beams of another flashlight cut through the gloom down in the hold. "Nobody down here," a voice said in Spanish. "Let's push off."

"I think I want to go down and check—"

"Are you crazy? You heard the kid, he doesn't know anything

about the woman. Come on, will you? Bah, it's Carnival, you idiot. The streets are filled with pretty girls ripe for the taking. Look, I even have my mask in my pocket."

"If it's Carnival, then what's that kid doing on the boat? Isn't that what the gringo tourists come down here for, to see the parades and watch the women?"

"Who cares about some gringo kid? He's too young to know what women are for. Not like our boys. Let's go. I want a beer."

The hatch closed, and their footsteps retreated up the ladder to the deck. I didn't dare breathe until the hatch opened again and I heard Gray say, "It's okay, they're gone. You can come up."

"Thank God." I switched on the flashlight.

"You talked, Mamí!" Grace trilled. "Now you have to take a bath."

The day dragged on. Gray showed me how to light the small propane stove, and I cooked an omelette for our lunch. I found our flamenco costumes in a big lobster pot, with smaller pots and pans thrown on top. Gray grinned when I applauded his quick thinking. Then, in searching for a spoon, I opened a drawer and saw a pistol lying among the cutlery.

"What's that for?"

Gray had been pretending to read a book while he watched me prepare the meal. He looked up. "Pirates. Dad says it's a good idea to be able to defend the boat."

"Do you know how to use it?"

He shrugged. "I'm a pretty good target shooter. I never shot anything that moved. I don't like to hunt. Dad and I have started taking our cameras out to the woods instead."

I closed the drawer. "That's a good idea."

"I don't understand how anybody could shoot another person."

His voice was tense. He knew Paul might be coming back to the boat with Bram, and he wasn't sure how to treat a man he knew to be a murderer.

I said, "It's easy to judge people if you've never lived inside their skins and seen the world through their eyes. Sometimes, when a person loves another person too much, love becomes a kind of insanity. Paul shot those federal agents for the same reason I helped him get away, because a person he loved was in trouble. I love Paul very much. I hope you will learn to like him, too. He's a fine man. Or he was. He's not in very good shape right now. I'm not happy about what happened, and neither is he. But I can't condemn him as a bad person because of it, because I know better. He's a good man who made a bad mistake."

"If you break the law, you should be punished."

I stirred the eggs in the pan. "Paul would agree with you. When you see him, you'll know that he has been punished. He would have preferred going to jail to the life he's been leading down here."

The sounds of Carnival reached the docks, echoes of laughter and fireworks and music. Darkness draped the city, and still the fun did not diminish. Gray switched on the running lights and lighted a lantern inside the cabin. I tried to restrain my impatience and passed the time sewing a doll for Grace out of the skirt from my flamenco dress. I gave her blond hair made of bits of twine, and painted a broad smile on her face with a ballpoint pen.

"La Rosita," Grace said when I had finished. "She looks like La Rosita, Mamí."

She fell asleep, the doll clutched to her breast. I put her to bed in the forward cabin and then joined Gray in a game of gin rummy. Neither of us could concentrate, and we both missed countless opportunities to score. Finally we heard the soft thump of feet on the deck above our heads.

"Dad?"

"It's me, Gray. Paul, too. Let's cast off. I want to get out of this harbor before the tide drops any further."

Gray sprang into action to help. I went up on deck. Paul was seated on the locker in the stern, his head in his hands.

"Paul!" I flung myself down beside him. "They hurt you!"

"A few cuts and bruises," Bram said in passing. "I think his hangover hurts worse. Take him below and give him some brandy. You two are just in the way up here."

In the galley, Paul clutched a plastic tumbler in shaking hands. "It was almost a relief, being in a cell," he said. "I can't explain it . . ."

I smoothed his hair. "You don't have to. I know, Paulie. I know."

The engine started. I could hear Bram giving Gray orders and the slap of ropes being hauled in from the cleats on the dock. Then Gray leaped across the chasm to the deck and Bram threw the engine into reverse. Peeking through a crack in the porthole curtains, I saw a star glide past.

When we were under way, I went up on deck. The *Blue Dolores* dominated the harbor, colored lights ablaze, every porthole a small sun. Tonight she was a duchess tarted up for a costume party. But tonight was still Mardi Gras. Tomorrow was Ash Wednesday, the first day of Lent, the season of sorrow and atonement.

19

WE HEADED INTO HEAVY WEATHER. WAVES RAN TEN TO TWELVE feet in the Bay of Campeche, the portion of the Gulf of Mexico that lies between Veracruz and the Yucatan peninsula. I wasn't about to venture topside to see for myself, but Bram kept us advised. Neither Paul nor I had any knowledge of things nautical. We knew only that the boat was heeled over at a dangerously sharp and uncomfortable angle, so that preparing meals or going to the bathroom was an awkward and messy business. Sleep was impossible.

"Big storm coming down from Canada. Blizzard conditions in parts of Texas and Oklahoma." Bram had no difficulty interpreting the hisses and squawks that came from the radio. It was all unintelligible gobble to me.

"Hadn't we better head for shore?" I clutched a railing in the galley to keep from tumbling into the bulkhead.

"No reason to. This old ketch was built to handle weather like this. Anyway, we wouldn't make it before the storm breaks. We're almost a hundred miles north of the coast. We're better off out here where there's nothing to smash into. Gray, are you all right up there?" Bram shouted up the ladder to where Gray, covered with yellow oilskins, was wrestling with the wheel. A plume of spray answered first, splashing through the companionway into our upturned faces. Gray called back that he was fine, but that the wind seemed to be picking up. Bram turned to me. "Batten everything down, and that includes Paul and Grace. We don't need any broken bones on this trip." Grabbing a rail, he swung himself easily up the ladder.

Gray and I had rigged a hammock in the forward cabin for Grace. She was having a fine old time, laughing and hugging her new doll while she swung from the rafters. After making sure the hammock was secure and not likely to bash into anything if it swung too wildly, I wedged myself into a corner and told her a story. To my astonishment, she dozed off after a few minutes.

Paul sat huddled against the bulkhead. He had exhausted Bram's liquor supply on our first day out, and now he was being forced to dry out. He was sick and getting sicker. He had eaten no food for two days, and when he vomited, all he brought up was yellow bile. I forced him to take a few sips of water so that he wouldn't dehydrate too badly, then I bolstered him with cushions and strapped him down so that if the boat gave a sudden violent pitch he wouldn't end up on the floor. I was starting to feel pretty queasy myself. Although I wasn't sure I believed Bram's advice to come up on deck if I felt sick, I put on a slicker and struggled up the ladder.

The wind swept the hair straight back from my face and drove needles of spray into my cheeks. Waves crashed over the decks. The sails were short and taut and every rope and line strained against the pressure of the storm. It was a terrifying sight.

Bram had taken the wheel. Gray, a line tied around his waist, was trying to untangle another rope he had found in one of the lockers. I crawled to a corner of the cockpit behind the wheel, where the curve of the rail supported my back, and hung on for dear life.

Bram and Gray had been acting with such smooth confidence that I had managed to control my fear as long as I was below deck. But now I watched horrified as a wall of water rose up in front of us. The prow of the boat nosed up, the wave crashed over it, and with a wrenching thud, we dropped straight down into the trough. The process repeated itself again and again. I wondered how much longer my heart could stand the strain, much less the hull of the *Golden Vanity*.

Our boat was so small, so vulnerable, tossing around that endless expanse of gray sea. But at the same time, it was well-constructed and sound, strong enough to weather many storms. Just like people.

"Well, if we drown, that's the end of my problems," I said to myself. The idea struck me as funny, and I began to laugh aloud. Bram turned his head and gave me an odd look. I shrugged elaborately and tapped my temple with my forefinger. "Dolores La Loca," I shouted. "Don't mind me." But I couldn't stop laughing.

We got no rest that night. The storm struck head-on, and we had no choice but to ride it out. I wouldn't have believed that the waves could have gotten any higher or the wind any stronger, but they did. Down below, Grace slept fitfully and Paul screamed and cried and wished for death. I went below decks again. I tried holding him, but that only seemed to make it worse. He complained that he was suffocating, that the pressure of my arms was driving nails of pain into his flesh. And so I left him, after getting him into a life jacket and strapping him down again. Grace and I wore our life jackets, too. Just in case.

Conditions were so bad up on deck that Bram told me to stay below. He and Gray were hanging on to the wheel as they struggled together to keep us on course. Both of them were tethered to the mizzenmast. The main sail was down and lashed to the deck, and the jib was only half unfurled, just enough to give them control over the boat and keep it headed into the waves. I sat on a bunk, braced my feet against the chart table, leaned my head back, and closed my eyes. And then I started to sing. Blues songs, folk songs, spirituals, standards—anything I could think of. Even a few verses of "The Golden Vanity":

> Then up jumped the cabin boy
> and boldly out spoke he,
> And he said to the captain,
> "What would you give to me
> If I should swim alongside
> of the Spanish enemy
> And sink her in the lowland,
> Lowland low,
> And sink her in the lowland sea?"

Bram passed through on his way down to the engine compartment. "Are you scared?"

I stopped singing long enough to gaze up at him. "A little. Singing helps. So does having you here."

He leaned over, soaking me with the runoff from his oilskins, and brushed my cheek lightly with his lips. "That's for being such a good sailor," he said into my ear.

"I also sing my songs on dry land."

"I know. I like them there, too."

He finished checking the bilges and went back up top. After he left, I noticed that all the songs I was singing were love songs.

Suddenly a deafening crash split the air like lightning striking a tree. The boat gave a mighty lurch that almost tossed me off the bunk in spite of my cords. Water poured through the companionway. Over the roar of the storm, I could hear Bram and Gray shouting to each other.

"Cut her loose! Cut the ropes!"

"Dad, help!"

"Gray! Oh, my God!" I added my voice to the general cacophony, but no one heard me. I struggled to untie my bonds and to right myself, but I didn't know which way was right in that topsy-turvy place. The hull was groaning and creaking so loudly I was sure it was about to break apart.

Grace screamed shrilly. I found the floor with my hands and slithered over unfamiliar objects toward the forward cabin. I didn't want her to be trapped there if we started to sink. The lantern was still lit, swinging from the ceiling, etching the darkness with criss-cross patterns of light and shadow. I crawled over Paul. He was so still and cold that I wondered if he really had died. After a moment of searching, my fingers found a pulse in his neck. At least his heart was still beating.

Then, as suddenly as it had capsized, the boat righted itself clumsily. I found Grace's hammock, peeled her out of it, and held her against me. We sobbed and clutched each other.

Bram stuck his head in. "The foreward mast snapped clean off. We had to cut the ropes loose and let her go. The mizzen is damaged, too, but we won't know 'til morning how bad it is. Everyone all right down here?"

"Gray! What about Gray?"

"He went over, but I hauled him back in. He's soaked to the skin, but he probably was before." Bram disappeared up the ladder again.

My old luck was working. I couldn't even make an escape by sea without getting caught in the worst storm of the century.

At dawn the winds died and the clouds broke and scattered. The seas were still rough, but nothing like the towering thirty-foot walls of water of the night before. While Grace slept in her hammock and Paul lay groaning in his bunk, I went up to assess the damage. The foremast had indeed vanished, leaving an ugly jagged stump. The top had snapped off the mizzenmast, taking with it the pulleys that hoisted sail. Bram said we would have to make the rest of the trip using the engine. Fortunately, he had taken on ample fuel in Veracruz, more than enough to take us to Campeche on the western side of the Yucatan peninsula.

At eight o'clock, Paul staggered up on deck. He leaned over the rail for awhile, then sat beside me on the locker behind the cockpit, where Bram was manning the wheel.

"Where are we going?" His voice was hoarse, barely audible. His face looked ashen. Only a few years older than I, he looked twice my age, like a man in his mid-sixties. Despair had taken an even bigger toll on his health than alcohol and drugs, of that I was convinced.

I told him we were headed to Campeche, and that we would hide out in Mérida for awhile.

Moistening his lips with his tongue, he said with great deliberateness, "I want to go home."

"What?"

"You heard me. Home. Back to the States. I want to turn myself in and take my punishment. I don't think I'll have to serve too much time at Sing Sing."

I understood. He thought of himself as a dying man.

"I don't want to drag you down anymore, Dess. I've had enough. I'm going back. I'll tell them what happened that night. I'll make them believe me. Clayton will back me up. I'll make him. I'll force him to tell the truth. You'll be completely exonerated." He glanced up at Bram. "I trust Mr. Howard to make sure they don't come down too hard on you for aiding and abetting a felon. He's got a lot of clout. When the real story breaks, the publicity may even help you get your career back."

I was stunned. My career? I had been thinking of myself as a fugitive and an exile for so long that I could hardly imagine myself back in my own country, a free woman. Having a career. Walking the streets of New York. Singing in my own language. Shopping. Listening to jazz in the clubs on Fifty-second street. Were they still there? Singing. Had the country changed much in our absence? Singing. Singing.

"I can't," I said. "They'll take Grace. I'll never see her again."

Paul and Bram exchanged glances. Bram said, "I'll petition the court to make me her guardian until your legal troubles are straightened out. You never had any run-ins with the law before the night of the shooting, and there were extenuating circumstances, emotional factors that compelled you to escape. A psychiatrist could testify that your mental condition was unstable due to the fact that you were pregnant and had already lost one child in a court battle."

I jumped up, lost my balance, and nearly fell over the side before I grabbed the railing and steadied myself. "This is a plot! You two have been plotting against me, trying to take my baby away from me. I won't let you do it! I'm not going back, ever. You can tell the judge anything you like, Paul. It has nothing to do with me. I don't care if I have to keep running for the next twenty years. They're not going to take Gracie away from me!"

Furious, I hurled myself down the ladder and into our cabin, where I threw myself onto the bunk under Grace's hammock and sobbed. The rhythmic rocking of the boat brought me no comfort.

Several minutes passed, then someone sat beside me on the edge of the bunk. It was Gray. "I think you should come back. You won't lose Gracie, honest. Dad will look after her and so will I. She's my sister, isn't she? She'll be okay. Besides, they probably won't put you in jail at all. Paul says the most you could get would be a couple of years and they'd probably suspend the sentence."

"I nearly died when they took you away from me," I sobbed. "I couldn't live if it happened again. I just couldn't. And I won't let you have a mother who's a jailbird. It's bad enough, me singing in nightclubs and hiding out and running from the FBI and Tony Matos and God knows who else. But I won't let anyone make fun of you because your mama's in jail."

"I don't care about that. Honest. Besides, I can defend myself. Dad taught me how to box." He stuck out his chin a little. "I can handle anybody who steps out of line."

"Oh, you can!" I fixed him with an angry glare. "You're just like your fa—like Bram. If you can't buy your way out of a situation, you'll bully your way out. You're no son of mine, Grayson Paul Howard." I buried my head again because I couldn't stand to see the stricken look on his white, pinched face. He didn't deserve that outburst. But I didn't have a speck of love in me to give anyone just then.

"I love you, Mommy."

I made no response, so he said it again, louder: "I love you, Mommy."

"Oh, Gray." Sitting up, I gathered him into my arms. When I felt him hug me back, the tears spurted from my eyes. I wanted that moment to last forever. After a long time, he started squirming and I released him. He looked embarrassed and wiped his nose with the back of his hand.

"I don't understand you," he said, not looking at me. "But Dad says it's all right to love somebody anyway, even if you can't figure them out."

I took his hand and squeezed it hard. Just then, over our heads, Grace awakened from her morning nap. I pulled her out of the hammock, sat her in my lap and rocked her a little, singing the little song I had sung to both of them when they were babies: "Hush, little baby, don't you cry." I sang the words softly, and to my surprise I heard Gray singing along with me. His voice was changing, and it wavered back and forth between a childish alto and an uncertain baritone, but to me it sounded like a choir of angels. I smiled at him. He even remembered some of the crazy verses I had made up for him long ago:

> Hush, little baby, don't you cry,
> Mama's gonna bake you an apple pie.
> If that apple pie gets burned,
> Mama's gonna get you a butter churn.
> If that butter churn gets broke,
> Mama's gonna tell you a funny joke.

Grace loved those verses, too. We finished up on a chorus of laughter, the three of us. Paul appeared in the doorway.

I said, "You can tell your captain and co-conspirator that he'll be taking some extra passengers back to Texas or wherever he's going after he gets this tub fixed up. Whatever happens after that, you can blame yourself."

"I know, Dess." He nodded slowly. "I always do."

After putting the children to bed that night, I went up on deck. The sky was dazzling, a vast blue-black velvet canopy studded with sparkling sequins, fabric I wouldn't mind wearing myself. The engine pulled us slowly through the choppy water. The only other sound was the gentle slap of waves against the hull.

Bram stood in the cockpit, his hands resting lightly on the spokes of the wheel. He checked his instruments periodically to make sure we were staying on the course he had charted.

"Everything quiet below?"

I nodded. "The kids are both asleep and Paul's through being sick for the time being. I put him to bed. He needs a doctor."

"He needs liquor. He'll find plenty once we hit land."

"But this is his chance to quit," I protested. "He's almost halfway there now. If he could hold out a little longer until I get him to a doctor or a hospital—"

"He wants to die, Dessie. You can't stop him from killing himself if that's what he really wants to do."

I sat on the starboard locker where I could see his face. "Do you think he's making the right decision about going back?"

"I do. And so are you. The right decision for you and your children. And for me."

I gazed out over the water, ruffled by the breeze and last night's turbulence into whitecaps that glistened in the pale light of a half moon. "I won't be seeing much of you for a while, any of you."

"Don't even think about it. You've set your course, now stick to it. You've always been good at that. I'll help you all I can. So will Paul, by telling the truth."

"On top of everything else, we kidnapped you. That's going to make us look even more crazy and violent."

"Nobody knows about that. I never told anyone, and Gray never breathed a word about seeing you outside his school that day."

I stared at him. "But you were missing for days and days— and your car! What did you tell them about losing your car?"

Bram grinned. "I told them I ran into some old Army buddies in Columbia who persuaded me to join them at a high stakes poker game that night in Atlanta. I lost my shirt, got drunk, and ended up in Texas without my wallet and without the Packard. I had no idea how it all happened. I made a collect call to the office to wire me some money. Jean-Ellen was furious with me. She knew I'd been a gambler before she married me. Gambled away half the family fortune. And gambled some more to get it back."

"I'd forgotten that about you."

"Yes, ma'am, I played for big stakes in those days. Every time I lost, I passed the chit over to Dad. Why not? I thought his reserves were limitless. The Howards of Woodlands. He always bawled me out and threatened not to pay, but in the end he'd say, 'I think we can just about cover this one. But you shouldn't play for big money unless you're halfway sure you can win, son.' I never paid any attention to him until it was too late."

"You've done pretty well," I remarked, "considering that you came home broke."

Bram nodded. "I was able to persuade my father-in-law to cosign some loans for me. Then I borrowed to my limits and beyond. The future was in television, I was sure of that. I put every nickel I could scrape together into buying my first station. Some folks said I was crazy. I guess I was still gambling, only this time I was taking my father's advice: I never played for big money unless I was halfway sure I could win."

"You haven't changed much since the old days, have you?"

Bram's grin brought a blush to my cheeks. "I'm still the same rascal who stole a kiss from you on your wedding day. Remember that?" He gave the wheel a fraction of a turn to starboard. "I have every record you ever made, and then some. I have recordings of concerts and nightclub appearances you've probably forgotten, hundreds of them. And I have copies of your movies, too. I started the collection because of Gray. I knew he would be curious about you, and I thought someday he might value all that stuff. But I listened to those records more than he did. Whenever I wanted to remember that night at Villa d'Este, I'd go to my study and put on a record, and then I'd sit back and close my eyes," he breathed a deep, nostalgic sigh, then laughed softly. "I was glad I caught your act at the Mocambo the other night. You still have the old magic, Dessie."

I grunted. "I bet Jean-Ellen had fits whenever she heard my voice coming out of your room. I'm surprised she didn't take a sledgehammer to your collection."

"Jean-Ellen and I went our separate ways a long time ago. We came together to win Gray away from you, but that was the first time we ever agreed on anything. And the last. We're getting a divorce, by the way. It's not going too well. She wants Woodlands as part of her settlement. I married her to get it back, and I'm not about to give it away. But I'll keep upping the ante. She'll come around sooner or later."

"You never loved her."

"No." He sounded surprised that I could even think such a thing. "I loved you, the raggedy little Heavener kid with the bleached blond hair and the big voice. I loved you even when you were holding a gun to my head. It wasn't really necessary, you know. I was ready to help you any way I could. Hell, I would have driven you all the way to Mexico City, clear down to Buenos Aires if you'd wanted to go."

"But you never said anything!"

"How could I? You were still furious at me because of Gray. You wouldn't have believed me. But it's no good loving a woman who's a thousand miles away. I want you to come home with me, Dessie. You'll divorce Matos, I'll divorce Jean-Ellen, and we'll be together, the way we were meant to be. Hell. I'm not a poet. I'm not a singer. I don't know the right words or even the right tune. I love you, Dessie. What more can I say?"

"Not much." My heart was thumping. "You said your piece pretty well."

He smiled. "I've been rehearsing. All I needed was a chance to be alone with you."

"Goodness. I . . . I can't think . . ."

Bram drew me gently to my feet and placed his hands alongside my face. "Then don't."

His kiss tasted of salt spray and the night wind. Our tongues met and probed. The beating of my heart outraced the gentle throb of the boat's engine. I broke off, hovering somewhere between laughter and tears.

"What's the matter?"

"My crazy luck. I can't even lose my son to a man without falling in love with him."

We found a nest on a pile of canvas, the folded-up sail that had once hung from the broken mast. We kissed again, and this time our hands got busy. I wriggled out of the trousers Gray had lent me. Bram shed his clothes, all of them. The lashings of spray that came in over the side failed to cool our fever.

For a while we rubbed bodies but something kept getting in the way, and we both knew that what we wanted was for him to be inside me. Even then we tried to stretch out the excitement, but I didn't want to wait, and neither did he. We knew, too, that we would have a next time very shortly, and so we let the tidal wave of passion that was rising between us crest, break, and ebb away.

"Who's driving the boat?" I asked. A long time had passed with no words.

"It's driving itself. I locked the wheel at twenty degrees north-northwest. We'll just go around in a big circle until we're ready to stop this nonsense and get ourselves back on course."

"And when will that be?"

"Never, I hope."

The motor chugged. Overhead the stars revolved slowly, and

the *Golden Vanity* went around and around like a toy boat in a bathtub. The night was long and patient and we were in no hurry.

A pale streak divided the sky and the sea. I watched, fascinated, as bolts of red pierced the grayness at the horizon.

Bram sat on the locker behind the wheel. One sneakered foot rested on a spoke, which he nudged gently whenever the nose of the boat veered off its heading. His left hand held a mug of coffee. His right arm was wrapped around my shoulders. Both my arms were around his middle. We were fully dressed and back on course, if not completely sober.

"It seems a shame to let you rot in jail," Bram sighed. "What a waste of a good woman."

"Can't you get me out on bail?"

"No trouble at all, my dear. My credit is good everywhere. I will personally take responsibility for your actions. I won't let you out of my sight until your case comes to trial."

"How boring for you, playing nursemaid to a grown woman." I nuzzled his neck.

"No, how delightful for me."

By the time the purr of the other boat's engines drifted across the water to us, it was already looming large on the horizon.

Bram reached for his binoculars. "Privacy is getting to be the world's scarcest commodity."

We watched, only vaguely interested, while it drew steadily closer. Then suddenly Bram said, "I recognize that turret—and the radar scanner!" He studied the boat through his binoculars again. "It's Matos! He's caught up with us!" He pulled out the throttle. The *Golden Vanity* picked up speed. "There's a .38 revolver—"

"I know where it is."

I brought him the gun. He told me to take the wheel while he checked our heading. "I guess we shouldn't have spent all that time going around in circles last night. Damn! We're still two or three hours away from Campeche."

I stared at him for a moment, my face stiff with terror, then I forced myself to look at the approaching yacht again. "Can we outrun him?"

"Not a chance. I could radio a distress call, but he'll be here before help reaches us. Maybe he intends to escort us into harbor and confront us there. We'll wait and see. Meanwhile, I'm not letting him or any of his men set foot on this boat. You'd better wake Gray. I might need him."

Filled with dread, I went below. Gray was sound asleep in his bunk, his hair falling over his eyes, his head resting on his arm. I touched his cheek. He awoke instantly, and pulled on his shirt and trousers while I explained what was happening. His body was straight and strong, like Bram's.

Despite the increase in our speed, the *Blue Dolores* was drawing nearer. In order to make the *Vanity* lighter, Bram ordered Gray to toss the useless sails overboard. Then we emptied the galley and lockers of pots, pans, books, utensils—anything that might weigh us down. I glanced back at the *Blue Dolores*. The distance between us seemed to have widened a trifle. Perhaps we really could evade them until we reached the harbor at Campeche.

The *Blue Dolores* dropped back. "We've done it!" Gray whooped. "We're losing her!"

"I wouldn't celebrate prematurely." Bram sounded grim.

He was right. After letting herself fall behind for a few minutes, the other boat picked up speed and closed the gap.

"Jesus," Bram muttered, "that bastard must have the biggest diesel engines made." Our throttle was already open as far as it could go.

Our wake was littered with plates, cups, blankets, coils of rope, pillows, none of which deterred the *Blue Dolores* in the slightest. The roar of her engines grew louder; her white hull looked like a looming iceberg. I remembered the *Titanic*, and I trembled.

Down in the forward cabin, Paul was sleeping so soundly that I decided not to wake him, but I got Grace up and carried her up on deck. Her head bobbed against my shoulder. I wanted to assure myself that she was safe, whatever happened. I wanted my arms around her.

Bram and Gray and Grace and I huddled in the cockpit like a group of refugees, our eyes fixed on the rapidly approaching yacht.

"What do you think he'll do?" I asked Bram.

"You know him better than I do. What do you think?"

"I don't know. He's capable of anything."

The yacht pulled abreast on our starboard side, less than twenty-five yards away. Men were moving around on her decks, but I didn't see Tony.

Then abruptly she changed course and swerved into our path. Bram jerked the wheel hard to port, but the *Vanity*, whose engine was designed primarily to pull the weighty wooden craft in and out of marina slips, was slow to respond. The prow of the *Blue Dolores* caught the starboard side of our craft amidships, crushing the timbers of the hull before sliding away with a sickening scraping and ripping sound. The impact threw us all to the deck. The *Golden Vanity* lurched violently to port, recovered itself, then heeled over to the starboard, the side on which she had been wounded.

"She's taking on water. I've got to get Paul!" Bram hurled himself down the ladder. Under our feet, the deck was listing at a forty-five degree angle. Grace clung to my neck and I clutched the port railing, but I knew I couldn't hang on indefinitely. The *Vanity* groaned, a piteous, almost human sound. The pitch of her decks grew sharper.

Gray said, "There's an inflatable dinghy in the starboard locker—if I can get to it." He wrestled awkwardly with the catch while he clung to the wheel to keep himself from sliding into the Gulf.

Meanwhile, the *Blue Dolores* had lowered a small craft of her own, a twelve-foot shell with an outboard motor. A man standing in the prow raised his arm and fired a pistol over my head. I was so startled that I lost my grip and fell backward. Our arms wrapped tightly around each other, Grace and I rolled across the deck like a couple of marbles on a playground slide. We kicked Gray in passing. My shoulder struck the starboard railing, which was already submerged. We went over, then under, then bobbed to the surface again, gasping and shivering. The motorboat swung around and strong arms hauled us aboard. Before we could even shake the water out of our eyes, the boat had turned again and was heading back to the yacht.

A combination of prodding and cursing and pushing and pulling got us up the ladder to the main deck. Tony was waiting for us, casually attired in a pale yellow sweater and white slacks. Dark glasses masked his eyes.

"Welcome, my dear. And little Gracia. Ah, she is beautiful, Dolores. But of course, with two such handsome parents—"

I leaned over the rail just in time to see the stern of the *Golden Vanity* drop below the waves as the forward section of the hull reared up toward the heavens. I saw Gray treading water a few feet away, but no sign of either Bram or Paul.

"Gray!" I shouted. "Over here! Swim!"

He started to swim toward the *Blue Dolores*. One of Tony's thugs fired his pistol. It sent up a geyser of water just three feet in front of Gray's face. He stopped stroking. "Mommy! Mommy!"

I threw my leg over the rail, ready to jump in and save him. One of the deckhands dragged me back and clamped a rough hand over my mouth. As we grappled together, I managed to bite down on one of his fingers, but I might as well have been gnawing an old shoe.

Someone said in Spanish, "Shark." A thrusting dorsal knifed through the water.

"Tony!" I screamed. "My son! You've got to save my son! Tony, oh, God—don't do this! Gray! Gray! Tony, help him—"

"Let's go." Tony rapped out an order. With a roar of her powerful engines, the *Blue Dolores* pulled rapidly away from the sinking ketch.

I could not pull my gaze from the speck that was Gray. I was still watching and screaming as the prow of the *Golden Vanity* slipped beneath the water and disappeared.

20

ALONG THE WALL THAT EDGES BOTH OLD AND NEW HAVANA lies the Malecón, a wide boulevard that separates the elegant nightclubs, sleek hotels, towering office buildings and the old colonial villas and palaces from the whole wide expanse of the Gulf of Mexico. I loathed all that water, and I developed a neurotic fascination with it. I watched it for hours, from the windows and terraces of Tony's villa, from the path along the Malecón where I walked every morning. I spent endless days staring out at the waves, the boats, the birds, hating all of them.

"Today's the day." I said aloud. "I swear, when we go to the beach today, I'll do it." I made this promise to myself every morning. I would walk out into the surf and drown in those same cruel waves that had taken my only son. And my best friend. And my love. Oh, Bram.

But I never kept that promise. I couldn't. I couldn't leave Grace. I couldn't abandon her to Tony Matos. Her new Papí. Every day, I forced myself to go on living.

At high tide, the sea hurled itself at the city of Havana, crashing against the sea wall and sending towering columns of spume into the air. At those times drivers on the Malecón used their windshield wipers and their headlights. And their horns. Always their horns.

Havana was the noisiest city I had ever experienced. Back in the days when the automobile was still a new-fangled invention and a menace to pedestrians and animals, the law had required drivers to sound their horns as they approached intersections. The advent of stop signs, traffic lights and policemen had not broken the Cubans of this habit. They still blasted away like a bunch of frustrated rejects from an oompah band.

I turned my back to the sea. To my left lay the pastel-colored dwellings and shaded streets of Old Havana. The capital building glimmered in the hazy sunshine like an oversized wedding cake. Havana. I could not imagine Tony Matos living anywhere else. Havana, whose superficial beauty concealed veins of ugliness and corruption. Havana. Where children pimped for their sisters and died of the diseases that accompanied starvation; and where visiting Americans gambled away thousands of dollars at the city's luxurious municipal casinos and even the lowliest policemen grew fat and rich during their years of service. Long ago in Mexico, a young man had told me terrible stories of midnight arrests and torture at the hands of President Batista's police. Ernesto. *Ché*. I would never forget him—or his tales of horror. A woman tortured. The police executioner driving twenty-four nails into her skull. Thrown into her grave with her living child in her arms. Her husband forced to watch. For the glory of the Cuban police. These were the friends, the companions of Antonio Matos.

To the west lay a cluster of new resort hotels, including the high-rise Havana Hilton. In the four years since Batista's latest grab for power, the city had expanded as a mecca for tourists and gamblers from the States.

The black Lincoln following me blocked traffic, provoking an impassioned chorus of beeps. Tony had given me the car and its accompanying thugs for my convenience and protection, so he said. I had not used it once, but it trailed me on my daily walks like a faithful monster. I walked for miles, for hours. I wanted to tire myself out, to drop into a sleep so deep and dreamless that I would not hear my son's voice calling for help, or see the slim prow of the *Golden Vanity* sliding beneath the water, taking with it the bodies of Bram and Paul.

I turned onto the Prado and headed for the center of town. The car kept pace with me, but I ignored it as I would ignore my own shadow. I wandered around a little park for a while and found a seat on a marble bench beneath a laurel tree. Across the way, a man was reading the morning paper while an urchin shined his shoes. To his left a pair of young lovers held hands and giggled. The world was a cold, unfeeling place. I grieved alone.

After a few minutes, a woman came and sat down beside me. Her perfume was overpowering, even sickening, and a single sidelong glance revealed the costume of a whore: bleached hair with black roots, thick makeup inexpertly applied, short tight skirt worn over fishnet stockings, absurdly high heels.

She lit a cigarette and addressed herself to the plume of smoke she exhaled. "You are Señora Matos, yes? I have a message for you. Do not turn your head. I will leave my handkerchief on the bench."

"Wait, who sent you?" I asked. But she was gone.

I was puzzled, but I maintained a wooden expression in case one of Tony's goons was watching. After the woman had gone, I put my hand down on top of the handkerchief and felt a crisp piece of paper inside. Using my purse as a shield, I unwrapped the message: "Gran Hotel Colón, Av. Obisbo No. 431, Rm. 114." It was unsigned.

The prostitute had known my name. How? No one other than Tony Matos and his coterie of villains knew I was here. Who wanted me to go to the Gran Hotel Colón on Avenida Obisbo? I was almost too depressed to be curious, but what did I have to lose? It was still early and I wasn't ready to return to Tony's villa yet. Grace was occupied with her new nurse Maria and the playmates Tony had found for her, Juana and Pedro, a pair so well-dressed and well-scrubbed and well-spoken that they might have been little robots. Later we would all take a picnic lunch to Varadero, where Cuba's finest beaches were located, a two-hour drive to the east.

I stopped at a café for a cup of coffee, which was offered in three sizes, for three, four, and five cents. I asked the waiter for directions to the toilet. A door near the bathroom led me to an alley behind a row of nightclubs. The back door to one of those places was open, and a Chinese boy was slopping water on the floors inside.

"Can you let me out the front?" I asked him in Spanish. "I am meeting my boyfriend, and my husband is following me."

He shrugged, demonstrating his supreme lack of interest in my love life, but he cooperated. Instantly I recognized the morning smell of nightclubs the world over: stale beer, stale sweat, stale cigarette smoke, and stale dreams. For a moment, I wished I could stay. I wanted to sit in the dressing room, sip a Coke, and work on a crossword puzzle until it was time to get ready for the show. Then I would put on a new face and a sparkling gown and stand in the spotlight singing songs about lost love.

I made my way to the address written on the paper. From the street the hotel looked unprepossessing, even shabby. But when

I opened the door and walked through a cobbled corridor, I suddenly found myself in a lovely tree-shaded courtyard. In the center, the waters of a marble fountain overflowed their basin and trickled into the pool beneath. Old palm and banana trees shaded the perimeter. Above my head, a parrot squawked a greeting.

The desk in the corner under the overhang was deserted. From a room off the courtyard came the sound of radio laughter. A quiz show host was asking a contestant if she could name the current President of the United States. She ventured a guess: Abraham Lincoln. Unnoticed by anyone, I ascended the stairs and made my way to room one-fourteen. It was on the second floor, on a balcony overlooking the courtyard.

The door was louvered. The window that opened onto the balcony was shuttered as well, on the inside. I thought I heard muted voices inside, but when I tapped on the door they fell silent. Then a bolt was thrown back and the door swung open.

I started to scream as the ghosts of Bram and Gray and Paul swam into my vision. One of them clapped his hand over my mouth and pulled me into the room.

Gray shut the door behind me. "Hi, Mom," he said calmly.

I wanted to shout for joy, but I wept instead. I embraced him fiercely and said his name over and over again in a whisper. My son, my sweet boy—could he possibly have grown taller in the few weeks since we had seen each other?

"It's a miracle," I breathed. "I've never had a miracle happen in my life before, and especially not when I needed one. Oh, I'm so glad, so glad . . ."

As soon as I released Gray, Bram wrapped his strong arms around my waist, lifted me high, and kissed me soundly. "Did you really think I'd let Matos get away with this?" he demanded. "Damn it, he sank my boat and made off with the woman I love. He's going to pay for this." He kissed me again, then released me. I wasn't too steady on my feet. Bram seated me on the bed while Gray fetched me a glass of water.

I turned to Paul. He looked more alert, even healthy. "I've missed you so much, Paulie. I don't know what to do with myself when I don't have you around to take care of."

"When you don't have me around to scold and nag, you mean," he smiled. "I've missed you, too, Dessie."

Bram and Gray took turns telling the story. They had drifted in the Gulf for three days and three nights in the *Golden Vanity*'s life raft. Sharks had circled continously but had not attacked. Finally, on the morning of the fourth day, a Mexican freighter had spotted them. They were all suffering from exhaustion and too much sun, but Paul was in the worst shape, barely alive when the sailors pulled him aboard.

The freighter was delivering eight hundred head of beef cattle from Corpus Cristi, Texas, to Puerto Juarez on the Caribbean coast of the Yucatan peninsula. The castaways told the captain that their small sailing vessel had been wrecked by the storm, and he agreed to take them along. They stayed in Puerto Juarez for a couple of weeks until they had fully recovered from the effects of their ordeal. Having lost all their money when the *Golden Vanity* went down, they had to beg food and lodging until Bram received some funds from his company in the States. Then they bought passage on another boat that would take them the eighty miles across the Yucatan Strait to Cuba.

Like a trio of revolutionaries, Bram, Paul and Gray were put ashore at La Bajada on the western tip of Cuba in the middle of the night. They made their way on foot through the Orgone Mountains, arriving secretly in Havana three weeks later. They could not risk word of their presence in that city reaching the ears of Tony Matos.

"You were right about him," Bram said. "Any man who would ram a defenseless little ketch with no warning and endanger the life of his own wife and daughter is capable of anything. If we're going to get you and Grace out of here, we're going to have to be very careful. What kind of security does he have at the house?"

"It's a fortress," I told them. "Guards with machine guns standing on the roof, an alarm system that goes off if anyone so much as looks cross-eyed at the place. The wall around the property is twelve feet high, with three feet of barbed wire on top of that, and men with German Shepherd dogs patrol the perimeter every half hour."

"From what I've heard, Matos needs plenty of protection," Bram said. "At any given moment, the safe in that house could be holding up to three million dollars in cash."

"That much! From what?"

He gave me a surprised look. "Don't you know? Your friend Matos is the world's biggest bag man. Every Monday morning, a limousine pulls up to the gate and a man gets out carrying a suitcase. The man is an underling in the Mob, one of Meyer

Lansky's boys from New York, and he's delivering the government's share of the take from all the casinos and whorehouses in town. Matos takes his cut, distributes some where it will do him the most good, then takes the rest to the National Palace and dumps it on President Batista's desk. He always takes plenty of silver dollars. They say Batista likes to run his fingers through them."

"How do you know all this?"

"It's common knowledge in this town," he shrugged. "Matos is the president's most trusted adviser. After Batista returned to power he rewarded Matos with the fattest plum on the island, mediating between the government and the Mob. Batista doesn't want too much direct contact with the boys from New York—it might look bad on his record in case he ever decides to hold an election. As a result, Tony Matos is one of the island's richest men."

We laid our plans. The house was impregnable, but we could escape from the beach if Bram could overpower the two goons that always accompanied us. Maria and the other two kids were no problem. Bram needed a couple of days to arrange for a plane from Miami; he'd already been in touch with his chief aide back home. We decided to make our move on Thursday, four days hence, or the next good beach day after that. I would not have to contact them again.

On the beach stood a couple of open-sided pavilions roofed with palmetto leaves. Maria and I set up the picnic while the children raced laughing down to the water.

At lunch, Grace noticed that I wasn't eating anything. "Are you sick, Mamí?"

"Yes, darling, the sun has given me a little headache. Don't worry about me. Why don't you run up to the car and tell Paco and Jesús that you would like to share your ice cream with them today? Poor fellows. It's so terribly hot in the sun."

Out of boredom, or because Grace was such a skilled manipulator of men, the two guards came down to the pavilion and accepted their little bowls of ice cream. Neither of them saw the attack when it came. Bram ducked out of the jungle and ran toward us, swiftly and silently. One of the guards, seeing a startled expression of the face of one of the children, started to turn around. Because he still held the bowl of ice cream, he was slow in going for his gun. Bram struck him over the head with the butt of the .38 and he dropped like a felled tree.

His friend was quicker, but when I saw him reach for his weapon, I threw myself against him. His arm flew upward, and the bullet blasted a hole in the palmetto thatch. Bram took no chances. He shot the man in the thigh. The guard reeled and sprawled groaning face down in the sand. Gray materialized out of nowhere and grabbed his gun.

"Get Grace into the car," Bram ordered.

"What about the others?"

Maria was screaming hysterically and crying out in Spanish to the Virgin for help. Juana, the little girl, sobbed quietly. But Grace and little Pedro were staring with utter fascination at the gun in Bram's fist.

"They'll be all right. They have plenty of food and a nice shelter in case of rain. When you turn up missing tonight, Matos will come looking for you. He'll find them instead. Come on, let's move."

We took Tony's Lincoln. It was a perfect escape vehicle: armored, respected by law enforcement officials who recognized the numbers on its license plates, and one of the fastest cars on the island. Bram took the wheel with Gray beside him while Grace and I huddled in the back seat.

"Where's Paul?"

"At Rancho Boyeros airport, bribing a customs man to let us board our plane without the usual exit papers. It arrived this morning, one of the company's Cessnas." He glanced at me in the mirror. "Nice of you to dress for the occasion."

"It's the best I could do." I wore a two-piece bathing suit under a terry cloth robe. "I could hardly pack a suitcase for a trip to the beach. Thank God you found us!"

"We were waiting at Varadero and saw the car go past. We followed on bicycles—no engine noise to tip off the guards. When we saw where the Lincoln was parked, we stashed the bikes in the undergrowth and swung around so we could make our approach from the jungle. They were dumb. They shouldn't have left us so much cover. What if we were legitimate kidnappers?"

The return trip to Havana took even less time than the trip out. The car careened through small villages without slowing its speed, its headlights burning and its horn blaring. Peasants, chickens, and worn-out mongrel dogs scattered with remarkable speed. Kids waved as we shot past.

Grace asked a million questions. I told her she would have to wait and see what would happen next. It was to be a surprise.

Bram drove the Lincoln right onto the tarmac at Rancho Boyeros airport and parked it beside a new Cessna. The guards had waved us past. We hurried to board the plane. "I hope Paul is here," Bram said. "We can't afford any mistakes at this point." He went forward to the cockpit.

Suddenly he retreated backward with his hands held high, the cold, dead, unseeing eye of a pistol pointed at his middle. The hand that held the gun belonged to Tony Matos, splendid in white cambric and crisp linen and a Panama hat with a black band.

"Ah, Mr. Howard, we meet at last, face-to-face." Tony's voice was as smooth as coconut oil. As always, dark glasses concealed his eyes. "I have heard so much about you. It is unfortunate that you and your companions did not go down with your absurd little boat. I must say, you are quite disappointing in the flesh. Nothing like the revered saint my wife has been weeping over since our last encounter."

"Tony, please—" I put Grace down and stepped toward them.

"Get back, Dolores. You have allied yourself with my enemies. You are no longer fit to be my wife, much less the mother of my child. Come, we are wasting time. I trust you will not be so difficult to dispose of on dry land, Mr. Howard."

"Mamí! Papí! What a funny game!" Little Grace laughed and clapped her hands and jumped up and down. Tony scooped her up with his left arm and held her against his shoulder. His gaze never wavered from Bram.

"Move."

Two burley men in ill-fitting black suits and matching guns escorted us across the tarmac to a small hangar. The others were already there, Paul and Bram's pilot and co-pilot. One of Tony's lady wrestlers, Matilda, I think it was, trained a machine gun on them. Tony lined us up against the wall and handed his daughter to Matilda, but Grace burst into tears and succeeded in escaping into my welcoming arms. As my eyes adjusted to the dim light, I noticed something odd. The hangar was empty except for a kerosene lamp, a wooden table, two folding chairs, and a chessboard with ivory and ebony chessmen. I recognized Tony's favorite set from the villa.

Tony spoke. "Now, Mr. Howard, did you really believe your scheme would work? You didn't have a chance. Cubans love to gossip, and if some of them can earn a few pesos for the information they collect, so much the better. The proprietor of the Gran Hotel de Colón is the brother-in-law of the chief of police. Yes, I have known about your presence in this city since the day you arrived."

Paul had been looking pale, and suddenly he crumpled to the floor in a faint. The pilot and co-pilot started to go to his assistance, but at an order from Tony, two pistols and a machine gun coaxed them back into formation. Bram did not move, and Tony took no further notice of Paul.

"But why did you—" I hugged Grace tightly, "why didn't you stop us at the beach if you knew that?" I felt nauseated.

"It wasn't necessary. Maria conveyed the information of your departure—the cooler containing the ice cream also concealed a radio. Maria speaks excellent English, by the way. She was a drama major at Florida State. I had plenty of time to set the scene here at the airport." Tony tucked his gun away, out of sight, then took out a cigar and went through the ritual of piercing, trimming, and lighting it. Paul groaned and rolled slightly, but no one else moved. The fragrant cigar smoke no longer gave me a thrill. My nausea got worse, and I wondered how soon I would be down on the floor with Paul.

"You are in serious trouble, Mr. Howard," Tony continued. "In Cuba, any man attempting to abscond with the wife and child of another is treated as a criminal, prosecuted to the fullest extent of the law as an adulterer and a kidnapper. Added to your other crimes—assault, illegal entry into the country, bribery— this would earn you quite a long sentence on the Isle of Pines, our famous prison off the south coast. But to abscond with the wife and child of Antonio Matos! That is another matter entirely. Your trial is to be a trial of wits, Mr. Howard. As you see, we are set up for a chess game. I have heard that you play chess, also that you like to gamble for high stakes. Are these stakes high enough, Mr. Howard? If you win, you will all go free. I will renounce my claims to Dolores and to my little Gracia. If you lose"— Tony smiled—"you will wish you had drowned off the Yucatan coast."

"Bram, no! He's—"

"Quiet!" Tony barked. The machine gun pointed at the back of Grace's head. "No talking from anyone except Mr. Howard." He turned to Bram. "Well?"

Bram stepped forward. "I'll play, Matos."

Tony and Bram tossed a coin, then seated themselves opposite each other, Bram behind the white pieces. Tony said, "You move first."

"I know."

Despite Tony's warning against speech, Gray whispered in my ear, "Don't worry, Dad's a really good chess player. He beats me all—" Quick as a flash, one of Tony's henchmen lashed out at Gray with his pistol. Gray tried to dodge away from the blow, but the barrel struck him on the left cheek, opening up an ugly wound. He reeled but stayed upright.

I tried to stifle my sobs. Gray's words offered small comfort, anyway. My son was smart, but he hadn't been a Grand Master of chess at the age of thirteen, and neither had Bram.

The game began. After a few minutes, Grace became fretful. I motioned to Matilda that we would like to sit down on the floor. She looked at Tony and then said, "All of you, down, sit side by side. No touching except the mother and the kid."

The bubble of silence inside that hangar was awful. Bram took his time contemplating his moves, yet whenever he shifted a piece, Tony seemed to be lying in wait for him, able to make his own move at once. It was as if he had the whole game mapped out in his head, and he was ready for every move Bram made. Sensing danger, Bram took longer and longer to calculate his moves. The game dragged on for hours—I lost track of the time. Outside, darkness fell. The drone of airplane traffic subsided.

During the whole ordeal, we captives were forbidden to speak to each other. Paul recovered enough to sit up, but he looked like he needed a doctor. He wasn't at all interested in what was happening on the board; from time to time he sucked in his breath or groaned softly, neither of which raised my hopes.

Sprawled across my lap, Grace finally fell asleep. I closed my eyes and leaned my head back against the corrugated metal wall, still warm from the afternoon sun. Bram's pilots were also resting, half-asleep.

Suddenly something happened. The atmosphere changed. Everybody was awake and staring as Bram moved a piece across the table.

"Checkmate," he said.

Tony Matos stood up slowly, his features pinched in fury. "Impossible!" he whispered. He repeated the word, louder this time. "Impossible! I have never lost a match. I was the champion of Cuba at the age of eleven, an international Grand Master at thirteen.''

Bram pushed his chair back. "Okay, everybody, out to the plane."

Tony's gun materialized in his hand. "No, señor, not so fast. Did you really think I would permit you to take my wife and my daughter? I do not believe in keeping promises. The only thing I believe in is this." He hefted the gun.

Bram ducked and came up under the table, which flipped up in Tony's face, knocking him off balance. Tony fell hard and Bram jumped on top of him. They wrestled for control of the gun. At the same time, the pilot and co-pilot attacked the two guards and overpowered them easily, just as Paul dragged himself to his feet and hurled himself at Matilda. She was not expecting an attack from a man she had dismissed as too weak to be a threat. She dropped the machine gun. Paul grabbed it by the stock and brought the butt down hard on her shoulder. With a moan, she sank to her knees. Paul dropped the weapon and kicked it away from him. His energy spent, he sagged against the wall. By this time the pilot and his assistant had disarmed the two thugs and bound their hands behind their backs with their neckties.

Bram scrambled to his feet, Tony's gun in his hand. "All right, out to the plane," he barked. "Move."

The pilots ran out to start the engines and prepare for takeoff. Gray sprinted along behind them. I followed more slowly, leading Grace by the hand. Paul came next. Tony stood a few feet from the overturned table, his hands held high. His glasses had come off in the fight, and his green-gold eyes were burning with fury.

We had just stepped through the door onto the tarmac when Grace broke away from me and ran toward Tony crying, "Papí! Papí, pick me up!" Tony swooped down on her and grabbed her so roughly that she started to cry.

"Grace!" Paul and I ran toward them. "Tony, let her go!"

"Put her down, Matos," Bram said.

Tony shook his head. "She is my shield, my protection, my hostage. You won't shoot while I've got her." He backed away from Bram toward one of the trussed up guards. Stooping, he extracted a small pistol from the guard's sock.

Paul leaped at Tony, who fired low. The shot spun Paul around and sent him crashing to his knees. Tony aimed the gun at his head. His intention was clear: If either Bram or I made a threatening move in his direction, he would kill Paul.

"Get out of here, Dessie," Paul shouted hoarsely. "He won't hurt Grace and I don't care if he kills me. Run!"

I turned to Bram. "I can't leave them. Go now or he'll kill you and Gray, too. Please, Bram!"

Bram hesitated for the merest fraction of a section. Casting me a brief, despairing look, he turned and sprinted away from the hangar to the revved-up Cessna.

Prophetically, clouds had gathered over the city while the chess game was in progress. Now rain started to fall, a steady drizzle that quickly soaked through my cotton robe as I stood on the tarmac in front of the hangar. The plane taxied down the runway, then lifted off. Its lights vanished like sparks into the northern sky.

21

I FIDDLED WITH THE DIAL UNTIL I HEARD THE LAST MARTIAL strains of the Cuban national anthem. I listened while they played two rousing choruses of the "26th of July Hymn." Then, in urgent tones, an announcer of Radio Rebelde reported that the rebels had increased their strength in Oriente, the eastern province. Preparations were advancing for the attack on the town of Las Villas.

He went on to list a string of victories, none of which would be mentioned in Havana's daily newspapers the following morning: Castro's men had blown up a bridge, destroying a convoy of Nationalist trucks that had been heading for the mountains to exterminate the rebel forces. They had also captured a town and been greeted as liberators with cheers, feasting, and dancing in the streets. Radio Rebelde gave an accounting of the casualties incurred by both sides, the only accurate figure the Cubans were likely to get.

I turned the dial to a music station before switching off the radio. I didn't want one of Tony's spying maids to know that I had been listening.

A knock at the door. "Nine o'clock, señora."

"Thank you."

At the hour when most of the locals were settling down for the evening, preparing their smaller children for bed, picking up their knitting and their games, and switching on their televisions, I prepared to go to work. Two weeks after Bram and Gray had escaped from the island, I started doing the only job I knew how to do: singing in the new Havana Room of the Hotel Nacional. Paul and I christened it the Banana Room because the fake gilt the decorators had used was more yellow then gold. Tony turned my opening at the Banana Room into one of Havana's premiere social occasions, a red carpet, by-invitation-only affair. The bankers and diplomats and businessmen came down from their hillside villas, their bejeweled ladies on their arms. At the banquet dinner, the guests were served boned quails stuffed with truffles and caviar. Unlimited quantities of champagne flowed from a fountain made of ice. This monstrosity rested on a refrigerated table, which kept it from melting in the heat from ten thousand candles. Needless to say, the audience was nicely warmed up by the time I made my appearance on the brand new stage, and the applause was enthusiastic.

Just like the old days. The best table near the front of the stage was always reserved for one special customer. Every night at midnight, in time for the second show of the evening, Tony would arrive, order a glass of expensive French wine, light up one of his cigars, and wait for the show to begin. Paul, seated at the keyboard, always greeted him with a respectful nod. When the set was over, Tony and his muscular, well-armed companions departed.

I applied my makeup at home; I couldn't arrive at the hotel looking less than superb. During the last two years, I had become a celebrity in Cuba. I had made a lush recording of "Mi Corazón" with a full orchestra featuring harps and strings. The record was a smash not only in Cuba but in Mexico and Panama and several South American countries as well. Whenever I went out in public, I was mobbed by autograph seekers, most of them teenaged girls. I sang "Mi Corazón" at least four times every night. In the summer of 1958, I had cut another record for the same producer, who had learned his craft in Nashville. He promised American-style that it would blast the top right out of the charts.

My fans did not object to the fact that I was an American. In fact, it added to the luster of my reputation. The Cubans drove American cars, listened to dubbed American television programs, wore American fashions, and read Spanish editions of American newspapers. Many of them spoke fairly good English. The fact that I was an accused criminal and a fugitive from justice delighted them; for once, the Cubans had something the Americans didn't have.

I rang for Digna, my maid. She helped me on with the new sable coat Tony had bought me for my debut at the Hotel Nacional. A fierce *Norte* was blowing outside, and the six-lane Malecon was closed, with traffic being diverted to inland routes.

Before I left the villa, I checked on Grace. She murmured as I leaned over to kiss her. "Mamí." She looked so serene when she was asleep. During the day she was a six-year-old hellion. Tony spoiled her outrageously, and laughed at my protests. "Who can spoil her, if not her own Papí?"

The car was waiting, but Tony intercepted me as I crossed the foyer.

"I will not be coming to the hotel tonight," he said. "I must leave early tomorrow morning for Miami and then Washington. Important business." Perhaps he was trying to persuade the Americans to throw their weight behind Batista, I thought. "I will return in a few days. The staff will look after you."

He kissed me on both cheeks; outwardly we were friends again. In my heart, I loathed him and everything he stood for, but I could not survive with that hatred constantly in my thoughts. For Grace's sake, and my own, we functioned as a family. I forced myself to stop dwelling on revenge and escape, and I tried to give our lives some peace and calm. When Tony came to my room, I took him into my bed. My body responded to him—I could not stop it—but every time he made love to me, I thought of Bram. I wondered what he was doing, and if I would ever see him again, and my soul died a little more.

The Cadillac was parked right outside the door. Even so, the wind from the sea tugged at my head scarf and sprinkled the hairs of my sable with millions of tiny beads of moisture.

The ride downtown was short, only half an hour even in bad weather. Our neighbors' villas slipped past. I had met most of them, English-speaking aristocrats whose children attended American prep schools and colleges. For them, Tony's credentials were impeccable. Besides his connection with Batista, he was a member of the Havana Club, the Yacht Club, and the Country Club. I wondered if my neighbors were really that stupid, or if they were as evil and corrupt as he was. Perhaps they had discovered, as I had to my great regret, that Antonio Matos could be a useful friend.

"For some reason, you sound even better than usual tonight." Paul put his feet up on the chaise lounge in my dressing room and lit a cigar, compliments of the management. "Or maybe it's me. These old fingers feel very limber."

When Paul had found himself living in Cuba, he had switched his allegiance from tequila to rum, and he had taken up smoking cigars. He could not live without some kind of addiction. His cigars weren't up to Tony's standard—even that fragrance made me ill these days—but I never asked Paul not to smoke in my presence. I was so grateful that he was sober enough to play for me.

"Tony won't be joining us this evening, alas." I changed my stocking. I had snagged it on a nail on the corner of the stage on the way out, and sure enough, it had laddered. "He has business in Miami and Washington, *muy importante*. I should warn Mrs. Eisenhower about his line of flattery. She may find him impossible to resist. I did."

We heard a tap on the door, and a waiter entered bearing a salver with a pot of coffee, a plate of little cakes, and a bouquet of roses. I had ordered the coffee and cakes, but not the flowers. An admirer in the audience, I thought. Then I noticed a sheet of buff paper folded in thirds and tucked under the vase.

The waiter lingered while I opened the note. It was in Spanish: "Ernesto G. of Veracruz recalls with great fondness the time he spent with you. Will you meet him tomorrow morning at eleven o'clock?" It gave an address in the poor neighborhood of Jesús del Monte. I glanced at Paul.

"Paul, go smoke that thing in the hall for a minute, will you?"

Seeing that something was afoot, he dragged himself off the chaise. As soon as he had gone, I pulled the waiter into the bathroom and turned on the faucet. "Who are you," I whispered, "one of those underground workers for the 26th of July?" He looked startled and ready to flee, but I gripped his arm tightly. "Don't worry, they can't hear us in here. Who gave you this note?"

"I wrote it myself, señora," he whispered, "on instructions from the leader of my cell. But the message is genuine. It came from Ché himself by radio, in code."

"Then he's not as smart as I thought he was. Imagine trying to arrange a meeting with me in broad daylight! Doesn't he know that I'm the second best-known figure in Havana these days—after Batista? Too many people in Jesús del Monte will recognize me. It's crazy. I can't go."

"Wait, señora, we have a plan. You will go to the Cathedral tomorrow, fifteen minutes before the start of the eleven o'clock mass. Enter through the main doors and turn to the right, walk straight down the side aisle and keep on going toward the baptistry. You will see another door there, behind the statue of the buried Christ. A taxi will be waiting outside. The meeting will be a short one, we can promise you that. The taxi will return you to the church twenty minutes before the mass lets out."

I couldn't help myself. I laughed out loud, then quickly covered my mouth with my hand and flushed the toilet. "That's the stupidest plan I've ever heard!" I hissed. "I'm not even Catholic."

"No, but perhaps you are in need of spiritual comfort. You want to go there to consult a priest. Perhaps you are even considering becoming a convert, Please, señora, will you come? It is very important."

I sighed. "Why is everybody's business so *muy importante* all of a sudden? All right, I suppose I'm a romantic fool. I'll do it. At least my keeper will be out of town."

"Yes, señora." He slipped quietly out of the bathroom. "We know."

My father used to fulminate against Catholics, along with Jews, Negroes, Methodists, Republicans, and other inferior races. I must have felt his influence, for I had never set foot inside a Catholic church in my life. The Cathedral of San Paolo fulfilled all of my most lurid expectations. The place was as cold as a tomb, and so gloomy that I stood blinking for a full minute before my eyes adjusted to the darkness. Some weak light filtered through the dirty stained glass windows, and a little more came from the banks of candles that burned in front of many of the statues. The main altar was a baroque masterpiece, richly carved and heavily gilded, just as the Banana Room should have been. I crept down a side aisle, not wishing to disturb any of the persons I saw kneeling on the hard floor. Except for a few wooden pews near the front, the rest of the marble floor was bare, and worn down in spots by thousands of groveling supplicants.

I caught a movement out of the corner of my eye and choked back a scream. A life-sized Madonna in a black robe beckoned to me. Then I realized that the flicker of candlelight on her white marble hands had made them seem to twitch. She stood inside a glass telephone booth, ludicrous in a black velvet gown embroidered with gold and a black lace mantilla. Through an opening in the bottom on the booth, the faithful had stuffed coins, bills, pictures of their loved ones, and slips of paper bearing their requests. A small plaque read MATER DOLOROSA. Sorrowful Mother.

Next came Jesus Himself, crushed under the weight of a real wooden cross. He had fallen onto one knee, and every single muscle and sinew in his body showed the strain of the burden he carried. His wounds were horribly vivid, great slashes of gleaming crimson on his naked back. His shoulders were bruised and bloody from the cross, and chock full of splinters, too, I imagined. The crown of thorns had gouged deep holes across his forehead, and rivulets of blood ran into his eyes. These were blue and cast up to Heaven. He couldn't have moved another step. On the background of red velvet hung a small fortune in gold and silver jewelry, some of it very nice: lockets, crucifixes, pocketwatches, bracelets, necklaces. I wondered what the donors had been trying to buy with their loot.

A couple of plaster saints came next, tame stuff compared to what had preceeded them. I identified Joseph right away: he carried carpenters' tools and his kindly face was scored by lines of weariness and forbearance. He had put up with a lot from his kid, I suspected. Enough to make anybody a saint.

I bit back another scream. Just in front of me Christ lay entombed in a glass casket. His shroud was stained with blood from the wound on his side. His face was ashen, with the same waxy pallor I had seen on dead people at the funerals for which my father had provided musical solace. The blood had been bathed away from the wounds on His forehead, but the holes left by the thorns were still visible. His hands were folded across His chest; they had been pierced and the ligaments torn. Little crusts of blood had dried around the lips of the wounds.

The top of the casket was slotted, and a scattering of money lay around His mutilated feet.

Two women were kneeling in front of the effigy; both were weeping, one silently, the other emitting loud bursts of choked sobs. For some reason I thought of Gray, whom I might never see again. And Bram. Sorrow overwhelmed me. Hot tears spurted from my eyes. I groped in my purse for my handkerchief.

I felt a touch on my shoulder. "Señora Matos?" I realized that I had collapsed onto a kneeler and had buried my head in my arms. I looked up. A priest was standing over me. "Father Ernesto will see you now. Will you follow me?"

I registered dimly that the plan must have been changed. Ché was here, in this church. I nodded and struggled to my feet. One of the women looked up at me and smiled. She had no teeth.

"Señora Dolores, God will be merciful to you," she cackled. I pressed her hand and whispered my thanks.

Ché Guevara was waiting in a tiny cupboard-lined cubicle behind the main altar. The only furnishings were a small table and two hard chairs. Ché wore a black cassock. The other priest, if he was a priest and not an imposter as well, ushered me into Ché's presence and backed out of the room, closing the door.

Ché said, "Bless you, my child." His Argentine Spanish sounded strange to my ears.

I sat and finished mopping my eyes. "It's a chamber of horrors out there. I've never seen such a display—it was terrible. I couldn't believe it."

He laughed softly. "I forgot, you are not used to Spanish churches. I remember when I was a child, trembling at the horror and majesty of it all. Alas, the incense always aggravated my asthma and triggered an attack. But you were moved to tears, no? Therefore all that symbolism served its purpose. It touched your soul."

His smile was as beautiful as ever. He looked thin but healthy; life in the jungles and mountains agreed with him. "So, Dolores, we meet again. It has been a long time, almost three years. Much has happened in that interval. Our return from Mexico on the boat *Granma*, the journey through the mountains, the fighting. Always the fighting. But the prize is nearly within our grasp. We are close, so close. And you." He reached across the table for my hand. "You are more beautiful than ever."

I stowed my handkerchief away. "I don't suppose you arranged this meeting because you want to make love to me in a church."

"To my great regret, no. We parted as friends. I hope we are still friends. And it is as your friend that I come to you now, to ask your help."

"Do you need a place to hide in Havana? I don't know any—"

"No, I have plenty of contacts with the underground here. And I will be returning to the front this afternoon. My sole purpose in coming to Havana was to see you. I was surprised to hear you were with Matos again. When we met in Veracruz, you were hiding from him."

"No one hides from Tony Matos. He merely decides when he wants to find you."

"Then I am fortunate that he is away from the city at this time."

"Yes. I got the feeling from the waiter at the Nacional that your people knew about his business trip before I did."

Another smile. "If we win this fight, it will be because of loyal soldiers who have been working behind the scenes."

"You mean spies? You don't have spies in our house, do you? I'd never believe that."

"Even the sergeant in the communications room at the Cuban embassy in Washington is one of our men. You see, I am being indiscreet in front of you again. Foolish of me. The police have ways of forcing their victims to talk. But you are under Matos's protection, so you are safe for the time being."

"I don't understand. What do you want from me, Ché?"

"I want eight hundred thousand dollars. It is sitting is Matos's safe in his bedroom at this very minute. We need that money desperately. We managed to divert a British ship on its way to deliver arms to Trujillo in the Dominican Republic and the captain is willing to sell the cargo to us, but at a steep price. Guns, rifles, mortars—everything we need for our final push into Santiago. Once we take Oriente province, the battle is won. Batista will flee, and the country will be ours. But we need those guns. You can help us get them, Dolores."

I felt the color drain out of my face. "Are you out of your mind? I'm no revolutionary. You can't drag me into your fight. No. Absolutely not!"

"This is your fight, too, Dolores." He leaned across the table, and I saw once again the ferocity and single-mindedness that had made him a legendary guerrilla fighter. "You are Matos's slave. You are in thrall to him, powerless to leave Havana because he is holding your child prisoner. Do you think you are any different from the cane cutter who depends on the few pesos the big sugar companies pay him in order to feed his starving babies? The things I have seen in this country—if I had time, I would draw pictures for you, pictures in words. The revolution is for you. We want to free people like you, Dolores. We want to remove Matos's foot from your neck."

"No," I shook my head, "stop. Stop right there. Your propaganda isn't going to work on me. Yes, I know that kids up in those hills are dying of starvation while down here in Havana the bigshots are wondering when they should schedule their next tennis lesson. I'm sorry for them and I'm sorry for myself, but I am powerless to do anything. Powerless. You see these hands?" I raised my fists with the wrists pressed together. "They are bound as surely as if they were shackled by handcuffs. Tony Matos has my daughter. That means he has my life and my loyalty and anything else he wants. I am not going to risk one hair on her head because of some crack-brained scheme to rob him. Why don't you rob Lansky's man before he makes the next delivery?"

"We can't do that. He travels in an armored car, and his guards are armed with submachine guns."

"Well, that's too bad, but armored cars have been robbed before. I feel as though one of those submachine guns was pointed at my head. Good-bye, Ché. It was nice seeing you again. I'm sorry I can't help you."

"Wait, Dolores." His voice stopped me at the door. If I had any sense, I thought, I'd keep on going. But I turned and got a double-barreled blast from those beautiful, imploring brown eyes. "We have a plan, a foolproof plan. You are in no danger, none whatsoever. In fact, you do have an ally in Matos's house. Digna is one of ours. Yes, your personal maid. The police tortured her lover, killed him, and hung up his body as a warning to others. You can ask her. She came to us and offered to help."

"Fine, then let Digna do it."

"She will. But she needs your cooperation in order to sneak our safecracker into the house—"

"Your safecracker!"

"Yes, an excellent man. He learned his trade from his cellmate at Alcatraz. Tomorrow morning, you will telephone your hairdresser and ask him to come to the house. On the way, he will be intercepted and our man—we'll call him Julio—will take his place. Now, Matos's bedroom, in which the safe is located, adjoins your room. Julio could pick the lock on the hall door, of course, but that way he risks being seen by the other servants. The access from your room is safer."

"But that gets me into it up to my neck," I protested.

"Not at all. Digna will do your hair. After she puts in those roller things, you will sit under the dryer in your dressing room. The robbery will take place during the twenty minutes you are in there. Julio enters the room, dismantles the burglar alarm—"

"Alarm!"

"—and cracks the safe. He stuffs the money into his bag of hairdressing paraphernalia, and then he leaves the house. Digna departs soon after—you will send her out to buy a compact or a new lipstick. She never returns. To all appearances, Digna is in league with the thief. But you are in the clear. You made the call to your hairdresser, she overheard you and signaled our men to intercept him. She will be quite safe; we will remove her to the country."

"Good for Digna. But that still leaves me and Grace right there in the lion's den."

"Matos will never be able to implicate you. Never. The money won't be missed—he has plenty, and if he needs more, he will just squeeze it out of his gangster friends. And you can rest easily, knowing that your efforts helped to free the Cuban people. And yourself."

I argued with him, but I couldn't find any weak spots in his plan. Digna had only been in Tony's employ for a year. The goons he had left behind to guard the house were accustomed to the comings and goings of dressmakers and hair—

"Wait. What if the guards check Julio's bag on the way out? They do that sometimes."

"Do they? Digna never mentioned that."

"It's random. My dressmaker told me they made her open her case of fabric samples one day. There's always a chance, and with Julio, a strange face . . ."

Ché was like Tony. He had the ability to see the whole scheme, and to resolve difficulties as soon as they arose. "Then he will give the money to Digna. She will take it with her when she leaves on her errand."

"I don't know." I began to wring and twist my handkerchief. "It's so dangerous. And Tony's so smart. He'll know. He'll know I was involved."

"He won't know unless you give yourself away. I would have thought that you would be accustomed to keeping things from him by now."

I had twisted the handkerchief and wrapped it around my left wrist like a shackle. I squeezed it hard, until my left hand began to redden and swell. When I released the tourniquet, the blood flowed into my fingers, making them tingle.

I said, "I want more than your undying thanks. I want your help. You say you have this vast underground network of loyalists. Very well then, put a few of them to work on my behalf.

Don't let Tony Matos take my daughter out of Havana. I don't care what you have to do to stop him—shoot him or knock him out or throw a grenade in his face. But don't let him take my child! I want to go to the American embassy with Grace and ask for asylum, but I can't do that as long as he has her."

"Everything will be in chaos," Ché said. "The rats will leave Havana in droves, and we want them to leave. The new republic has no use for Batista's friends."

"Take advantage of the chaos. Tony has his own plane, his own pilot. Sabotage the plane. Imprison the pilot. Close the airport. But don't let him go unless he's alone. Give me my daughter back."

I waited breathlessly while Ché considered my terms. Finally he nodded. "Very well, I accept. Your request is not unreasonable."

We rose and he embraced me. "You are a tough case, Dolores," he said. "I had to work hard to win you over."

I drew away from him. "This isn't my country, Ché. It's not my revolution, either. I'm sorry for the people Batista has oppressed, but I've got troubles enough of my own. Politics aren't important to me."

"Politics are important to everyone, but too many people forget that. Most societies get the government they deserve. By the time the people wake up, it's too late. That's why we need revolutions now and then."

The priest was waiting to escort me to the car. The mass had ended. He let my driver see us together. We shook hands. "Come again if you want to talk," he said. "So far Batista's policemen have not been torturing priests. I won't betray you."

"Are you a real priest?"

"Certainly. I am Father Francisco. I like your records very much."

As I climbed into the back seat of the car, I noticed I was still holding the wadded-up handkerchief. No doubt my eyes were smeared with makeup, too. I'm sure I looked like I had just finished a strenuous session of spiritual counseling.

The robbery went without a hitch. "Julio" and Digna played their parts brilliantly. I didn't do too badly myself. Julio was a treat: five-feet-two-inches tall, ninety pounds, with ascending waves of orange hair. He flopped his wrists when he walked and talked with an outrageous lisp. The goons who frisked him as he came in rolled their eyes and fled to the kitchens. Whenever Tony was away, the mice relaxed. Men appeared in shirtsleeves, women in bare feet without stockings or uniforms.

Digna never said a word. While Julio was breaking into Tony's room, she did an expert job of setting my hair. Then she bundled me into the dressing room, clamped the dryer down on my head and thrust a magazine into my hands. Only then did she speak: "Stay out of the way, Señora."

When it was all over, I breathed a sigh of relief, but I didn't congratulate myself. I knew the worst part was yet to come: the interrogation.

It was brutal. Tony returned two days later, an irritated crease on his forehead suggesting that his important business in Washington had not gone well. He discovered the loss right away, and all hell broke loose. The goons dragged me into the imperial presence and the questioning began.

"Why did you telephone the hairdresser?"

"Because my hair was a mess and I had to sing that night. *El Norte* blew it all to pieces and I couldn't do a thing with it."

"Was Digna there when you called him?"

"I don't know. Yes. I think she was making the bed."

"Were the two of them ever alone in your room together?"

"Well, I guess—when I was under the dryer in the dressing room they must have been . . ."

And so on. He didn't bother accusing me of being a Fidelista, or even a sympathizer. He knew me so well: I was completely apolitical, totally uninterested in the struggle going on in the mountains.

The only surprise came when he snarled, "Two million dollars. Those thieves got away with almost two million dollars and no one stopped them. This is the best-protected house in the country, and you let those two rob me blind, right under your nose."

Two million. Ché had expected only eight hundred thousand. Or had he known that the haul would be that generous?

Finally Tony dismissed me. I nearly kissed his hands with gratitude, then I hurried to the nursery. I scooped up Grace and whirled her around. "Soon, soon, soon," I sang in English. Soon the revolution would come, and in the general upheaval, Grace and I would escape from the villa and present ourselves at the embassy, seekers after asylum, fugitives ready to go home, even to jail if necessary. Soon I would see Bram and Gray again. Soon I would put the pieces of my heart back together. Soon.

The political situation worsened—or improved, depending on which side you were on—throughout December. The air was thick with rumors. Even the goons and the servants at the villa couldn't resist speculating on what would happen when Batista fled—as he surely would. Would the Fidelistas be strong enough to take control of the entire country? Or would the Americans intercede at the last minute, with a military force to help prop up the failing presidency? Or would a third force emerge from the wings, moderates who had served the democratically elected president whom Batista's coup had overthrown? The big question seemed to be: Were the Fidelistas Communists? And if they were, what would that mean to the country after they had taken power? Fidel Castro himself, in his broadcasts over Radio Rebelde, declared that he was not affiliated with any movement, party, or foreign power: "We will govern ourselves, without help from Washington or Moscow," he said. But could the Cubans believe him?

I was willing to bet that mine weren't the only ears in town that were glued to the radio every evening at seven and eight, and sometimes at ten if I wasn't working. And I was equally willing to bet that I wasn't the only one hoping that the Second Front would reach Havana soon, and that Batista would pile his suitcases full of money into his private plane and slink off the stage of history.

As Christmas approached, business in the Banana Room and all the clubs and casinos in Havana dropped off sharply. Radio Rebelde was urging people to remember the three C's and to support the general strike: no commerce, no cinema, no cabaret. American tourists hungry for adventure continued to arrive in Havana by cruise ship and airplane, but not in sufficient numbers to gladden the hearts of the hotel managers and their gangster patrons.

Needless to say, the privations of war never touched the residents of our villa. Christmas Eve was a joyous occasion, with Grace and her little playmates receiving the first of their usual avalanche of gifts. Tony always distributed presents to the children on each of the twelve days of Christmas, right up to January 6, feast of the Three Kings. Every time Grace ripped off the wrappings of another box, she would throw her arms around his neck, give him a fat, wet kiss on the lips and say, "Thank you, Papí! You are so wonderful!" This was the kind of love and approbation that he got from no one else. Even so, Tony was not ungenerous to me. I was able to give my black sable a mate, a full length coat of white ermine, and I added a pair of diamond and ruby pendant earrings to my brimming jewel chest. I started sewing some of my jewels into the lining of the sable, in case fortune washed Grace and me up on some unfriendly shore. Diamonds are good currency in any country.

The rumors continued to fly: Batista was leaving; he was staying; a military junta was already forming to replace him; the Americans were coming; they weren't coming; Castro had been killed; he was alive; he was in Havana.

Paul joined me for an early supper at the villa before our New Year's Eve show. Tony had already departed for the traditional celebration at President Batista's country house. Since I didn't have to sing for four hours, I ate heartily, but Paul just picked at the roast pork, black beans, rice, fried plantains, and sugar cakes. In the past few weeks, he had grown thinner and jumpier. His face had lost its color and he was making a lot of wild mistakes at the piano. I was worried about him.

"I heard today that Castro is going to attack Santiago," I said.

Paul picked up his plate and hurled it to the floor. A maid scurried over to clean up the mess. "I am sick to death of the whole thing," he shouted. "Who the hell cares what happens in this stupid country? Do you think it's going to affect our lives one way or the other? We'll end up on the run again, people without a country."

I stood up, shocked, and dabbed at my lips with my napkin. I had seen Paul violently out of control once before, and it terrified me. "I thought we were going back home, to America, aren't we? You're going to turn yourself in, and so am I. Remember?" Tears rushed to my eyes. "Oh, Paul, I want to go home."

"No!" he screamed. "I've changed my mind. I'm not going to spend the rest of my life in a cell. I'll hang myself first." Trembling, he rose from his chair, wavered, and then fell back against the brocade wallcovering. "Goddamn it, somebody call a cab. I've got to get out of here."

"Oh, Paul, are you . . . you're not taking drugs, are you?" I ran to him and grabbed his arms. "Isn't alcohol enough for you? Paul! Paulie! You're not trying to kill yourself with drugs again!"

"Who the fuck cares?"

"Paul, oh, God, Paul! I care! I love you, Paulie!"

He stood motionless, unresisting, while I removed his suit jacket. I had to know. I had to see the needle marks with my own eyes. Then suddenly Paul chopped savagely at my arms with the sides of his hands and pushed me away from him. I careened into the table, overturning the candelabrum and a decanter of brandy. Flames licked at the spilled liquor. The paper doilies on the cake plate started to blaze. I shouted for the maid. By the time we got the fire out and put things to rights in the dining room, Paul had gone.

I thought we would have to cancel our New Year's Eve performance, but Paul was waiting for me at the Banana Room in time for the first show. We didn't speak. I felt like I was performing at a funeral. Paul played more wrong notes than right ones, but nobody seemed to care. The gowns were gaudy, the jewels were bright, but the faces were dead, set in the resigned expressions of those who are still observing rites and following rituals but who have already passed on to the next life in their minds. At midnight, when the waiters served the traditional cups of cider and plates of grapes, the excitement and laughter were counterfeit. I ate my twelve, one after the other, seeds and all, and wished fervently that my luck would improve in the New Year. I sang a few more numbers, keeping them as upbeat as possible. The couples revolved around the room like mechanical wind-up toys. As soon as it was decently possible, they called it a night and hurried back to their homes—and their radios.

Hardly anyone remained in the room as I walked offstage after the last set. Suddenly Paul began to play again. Chopin. "Paradise," the song he had written for me back in the days when I was still performing with King Kingsley. I didn't know what to do. I hadn't sung it in years. I didn't know it in Spanish. But I turned around and walked back on stage and I sang it. In English. Deep and jazzy like in the old days. Half a dozen people, waiters and party-goers, turned to stare, but they weren't much interested. By the time Paul and I finished, the place was empty.

Paul turned to me. Tears were running down his cheeks. My face was awash with tears, too. "You were terrific tonight, Dessie."

I stood there looking at him. I couldn't stand it. "Oh, Paul, you were terrible. I don't want some hop-head playing for me. If you can't balance your work and your recreation, then you'd better give up the work. That stuff you shoot into your veins will take care of the rest." Weeping, I walked out, leaving him slumped over the keyboard.

Back at the villa, I followed my nightly ritual of looking in on Grace before I retired. Her bed was empty. I wasn't alarmed. On special occasions, Tony often permitted her to stay up late. I passed through her room into the nursery.

The large room was stripped bare of toys, furniture, everything except one rocking chair. Tony sat in it, pushing himself slowly to and fro.

"Home at last. Happy New Year, my darling."

"Where is Grace? What have you done with her?"

I raced around the room like a madwoman, opening closet doors, checking the cupboards in the adjoining kitchen, calling out her name.

"You won't find her. She is on her way to safety. The revolution is in progress, you know. This evening El Presidente made the decision to spare his country further suffering. He is on his way to the airport at this very moment. I placed my little Gracia in his care. You could hardly ask for a more illustrious guardian."

"He's nothing!" I screamed. "A deposed dictator is nothing! You're nothing! You damned thug, give me my baby! Where is my baby?"

"You should have thought of the consequences when you agreed to help those ruffians rob me."

"I didn't help anyone," I sobbed. "You know that. You're just looking for someone to blame."

"The police caught Digna, my dear. I made it a point to be present when they tortured her. She was stubborn, able to hold out for a long time, but before she died, she told us everything. I congratulate you, Dolores. Your acting has improved. But you see why you have to pay."

I was on my knees by then, sobbing and pleading, promising him anything . . . anything . . .

"Too many promises," he said severely. "Your word is no good. You will not see your child for one year. That is your punishment. By that time, she may not even remember who you are."

Inside my head, I could hear Grace crying for her Mamí.

"Please," I begged, "please, please give her back to me. Not for my sake, but for hers. She needs me—you know she can't fall asleep if I don't tell her a story and kiss her good night. Oh, God, Tony, don't do this to me."

"You should have thought—"

I reached for his belt and the zipper on his trousers. I could love him into submission, I thought. If I took him into my mouth, made him stupid with sex, he would do anything for me.

Maybe it was all a joke. Grace was still here, in the villa or in Havana—I would make love to him and he would tell me.

He slapped my hands away. "You really are desperate, aren't you?"

"Oh, yes, I'm desperate. Yes, I am . . ."

He stood up. "Get your coat. We are leaving tonight."

I cradled my head in my hands. I barely heard him. "Where?" I asked like a drunkard. "Where are we going?"

"Do you care?"

"No. I just want my baby back. Please. My baby."

"Your belongings are already packed and stowed aboard the *Blue Dolores*. The captain wants to weigh anchor at dawn."

I sat rocking in the middle of the floor. "No, no, this can't be happening. My baby. Please give me my baby."

"Stop that wailing or you will never see your child again!" His voice was like ice. "And you will never see me again. I will leave you to that rascal Guevara and your Fidelistas. You can whore for them."

"Paul," I said into my hands. "I want Paul. He'll help me."

Tony snorted. "He can't even help himself. Go and get him, then. But don't forget, the boat leaves at dawn." He rang for the car and told one of the goons to take me to the Hotel Nacional.

The hotel lobby was deserted except for a group of Americans who were still ready to party. One of the women ran over to me. "Say, ain't you Dessie Heavener? Gosh, you used to sing so pretty, didn't she, Herm?"

"Sure did."

"Can I have your autograph? I want it right here on my skin, on the back of my hand. Ooh, I remember when you sang that banana song. Those were great days, weren't they, Herm? Wartime and all. I danced every night of the week and worked the whole day at that defense plant in L.A. They sure were great days."

Someone handed me a fountain pen, and I scribbled my signature on the back of her hand. Her friends wanted autographs on their hands, too. I was dying inside and here I was signing the flesh of people's hands.

I got away from them and ran up the stairs to the second floor. My escorts stayed down in the lobby, two broad-shouldered men with little black mustaches and deadly little guns tucked into their belts. I pounded on Paul's door.

"Paulie, please, I'm not mad at you. We've got to go now. It's time to leave. Please, wake up. Paulie!"

The pounding was getting me nowhere. The neighbors must have complained because a clerk came up, followed closely by my two watchdogs.

"My friend is in there. I have to see him. Please open the door."

The clerk glanced at the pair of thugs, who nodded and patted their guns. He unlocked the door and I went inside. All the lights were on, but the bed was still made. Paul's tux jacket lay in a heap on the rug. The bathroom door was closed. He must be in the tub. I knocked.

"Paul? It's me, Dess. I've got to talk to you. Paulie?"

I opened the door. He lay curled around the toilet bowl, the needle still in his arm. The clerk crossed himself and murmured "Jesus, Mary, and Joseph" in Spanish before reeling away, his hand pressed over his mouth. I knelt down and gathered my old friend into my arms. He was already cold, and his limbs were beginning to stiffen.

"Oh, Paulie," I sobbed, "don't do this to me, not now. I need you. I need one friend. Don't leave me now."

The three men receded into the bedroom, closing the door behind them. I told Paul that I was sorry for being upset with him that evening, that I would try and behave myself in the future, that I valued his friendship too much to let anything come between us. I had stood by him through murder and flight and drink and drugs and the worst kinds of despair. Now I had lost my second child and I needed him to stand by me.

I don't know how much time passed, just the two of us alone in that bathroom. I looked around at the white tiled walls. So he had ended his life in a cell after all.

I opened the door. "Take him down to the car. He's coming with us. We can bury him at sea. I'm not leaving him to the police or the revolutionaries."

They were reluctant to obey, especially with the clerk watching us with bugged-out eyes. One of them telephoned the villa.

The conversation was brief. He put down the phone and beckoned his partner into the bathroom. I looked for a suitcase but found none. Paul had come here wearing the rags on his back and he had never had any reason to go anywhere until tonight. I spread my coat open on the bed and started to pile Paul's possessions on top of it. They were pitifully few: two tuxedos, a half-dozen ruffled shirts, some underwear, his guitar, the expensive wristwatch I had given him, a few books, mostly poetry and fiction. On a notepad he had scribbled a few bars of music. I didn't recognize the tune.

I ordered the clerk to pick up the bundle and to follow us downstairs. Slinging Paul's arms over their shoulders, the goons lugged him between them as if he were a pal who had had too much New Year's cheer.

The clerk shoved the bundle into the back seat along with Paul and me and we took off with a screech of tires. We went right to the slip at the Havana Yacht Club where the *Blue Dolores* was berthed. Tony watched from the deck as the goons dragged their burden up the gangplank. I brought the bundle.

"I wasn't going to leave him there," I said. "I want him buried at sea. Your captain can read the service, can't he?"

Tony nodded.

I dumped the coat and its contents on the deck. "He was so talented, and so goodhearted. He should have had more than this at the end. Damn." I rubbed my eyes. "Oh, damn. If I had any guts at all, I'd jump into the water and swim until my arms got too tired to hold me up. Then I'd let myself sink down nice and easy. I'd keep Paulie company for a while."

Tony walked away, saying nothing.

I picked up the notebook with the unfinished song. I would keep it as a memento of the boy I had known long ago. I called after Tony, "You gave him the dope, didn't you? He was clean until the robbery. He liked his rum, and his cigars, but nothing stronger. You let me think I'd pulled it off, but all that time you were planning your revenge." My voice swelled to a scream. "You're going to leave me with nothing, aren't you? You've taken my children and my lover and now you've killed my only friend. I still have my voice, but you'll figure out some way of taking that, too, won't you?"

The members of the crew hauled up the gangplank. The engines rumbled. I stood on the deck until the two gateposts of the harbor, Morro Castle and Punta Castle, had dwindled to specks. I was still standing there an hour later when the captain came up and said a few words over the corpse that had been my friend. Tony's goons shoved him over the side. Then one by one I tossed Paul's belongings into the water. The guitar was the last to go. It floated in our wake like an oddly shaped boat for a few moments, then a wave slurped over it, filling the reverberation chamber, and it sank out of sight, its music stilled forever.

22

TONY RESTORED GRACE TO ME ON NEW YEAR'S DAY, 1961, IN his private box at the Teatro Colon in Buenos Aires.

Fifteen minutes before a special holiday performance of *The Nutcracker* ballet was about to begin, Tony slipped away. My heart started to pound. I had been on edge for weeks anticipating my reunion with Grace. But whenever I asked Tony when I would see her, he either dismissed the question without replying or gave me the vaguest sort of answer.

In the audience, fans and programs fluttered in front of bejewelled bosoms and starched shirtfronts. South of the equator, Christmas fell in early summer, and the weather that day had been unusually warm and humid. The air in the auditorium was stifling, and the filmy silk fabric of my floor-length evening gown clung wherever it touched my flesh.

Hearing movement behind me, I turned. Grace stood in front of the red velvet curtain at the entrance to the box. She looked like a miniature princess in a frilly pink dress trimmed with lace and crinoline petticoats that lifted the hem of her skirt nearly to the level of her waist. A pink satin bow rode among her dark curls, and she wore tiny white cotton gloves and carried a tiny white patent leather purse that matched her shoes. I marveled at how much she had grown since I had seen her last, at least two inches. The baby softness had melted away from her cheeks and her limbs. She looked wan and waiflike, too thin for her size and too old for her nine years.

"Gracie!" Moving slowly so as not to startle her, I rose from my red plush armchair and took a step toward her. She retreated a pace, skittish and suspicious, like a fawn in the woods. I knelt down and opened my arms. "Oh, darling, I've missed you so much." Tears spilled down my cheeks.

"You let me go away with strange people." Her voice was accusing, filled with resentment. Her eyes snapped angrily. "You never came to see me."

"I know. I couldn't help it. I'm sorry. They . . . they didn't hurt you, did they?"

"Of course not." Tony stepped through the curtain behind her. "The child has received the best possible care. She wanted for nothing."

"I couldn't help it," I repeated weakly. Defeated by her sullen stubbornness, I dropped my arms. "Don't be angry with me, Grace. I couldn't stand it if you decided to hate me after all this time. I've thought about you every day, every minute. I've been so lonely without you—it was awful, like being sick but knowing there was no cure. Until now. Oh, my darling, I love you more than anything else in the world, and I always will."

One long minute passed during which neither of us moved or spoke. Then all of a sudden Grace launched herself at me and threw her arms around my neck. I hugged her tightly and buried my face in the cloud of tulle and lace that swirled around her. Together we wept for the year we had lost.

I gazed at Tony over the top of my daughter's head. "I will never forgive you for this," I whispered. "Never. As long as I live."

He shrugged. "It was your own doing. You have only yourself to blame."

Grace sat on my lap through the entire performance, her arms wound around my neck and her head pressed against my shoulder. Our pleasure in being together again was so great that we hardly noticed what was happening on the stage, although Tchaikovsky's beautiful music certainly provided a fitting accompaniment to our joy. More than anything, I wanted to be alone with my little girl, either at the elegant apartment Tony maintained on Avenida Callao or at his ranch house about forty miles away from the city. But Tony refused to leave the theater until the last curtain call had been taken.

After the ballet, we had a late supper in the tearoom at the Plaza Hotel. I was too excited to eat, and Grace hardly touched her ice cream. I grieved at the changes I saw in her. The carefree child I had known in Veracruz and Havana had vanished. Her laughter was no longer spontaneous and joyous. When it came at all, it was timid and strained. She had grown watchful and wary, suspicious of strangers. She had never been like that before. As an eight-year-old, she had been proud and independent. One year later, she seemed to have returned to infancy, clinging to her Mamí like a limpet, fearing to let me out of her sight for one moment.

Back at the apartment, she insisted that we sleep together in my bed and that we leave all the lights in the room burning brightly. She dozed off in my arms as I crooned a lullaby, the first time I had sung in a year.

At three in the morning, Tony shook me roughly.

"I want you. Now." He didn't bother to whisper. Grace whimpered and stirred in her sleep, but she did not awaken.

I hated to leave my child, but I was terrified of displeasing my husband. I had survived a solid year of hell, but I doubted that I could endure even one more day without Grace. Reluctantly, I accompanied Tony to his room. His lovemaking that night was passionate and prolonged. I was exhausted, emotionally and physically wrung out by the tension of the past few weeks, but I had to force myself to counterfeit pleasure I did not feel because lack of response always angered him. Tony finally fell asleep at dawn, and I was able to slip back to Grace. I didn't want her waking up alone in a strange room.

As I curled my body around hers, the rising sun gleamed through the slats of the louvered shutters outside the windows. A pattern of gold bars appeared on the brocaded walls around my bed. Those bars might as well have been made of steel. My prison was as solid as a granite fortress. Grace and I, lying in a genuine Louis XVI bed with satin sheets and a silk coverlet, were chained as firmly as if we had manacles on our wrists and shackles around our ankles.

The wind came roaring off the flanks of Cerro Lopez, raising a cloud of snow that obscured Lake Nahuel Huapi, which shone hard and blue in the sunlight like a Limoges platter. Then a miracle happened. The sun turned the tiny prisms of snowflakes into a dancing fairy wearing parti-colored gauze, a genie released from a bottle. Grace and I stared, fascinated. But in the wink of an eye, on another breath of the wind, the genie vanished. Like all our hopes and fancies.

Behind us, a door opened. "Dolores. Grace. It is time to go." Tony stepped onto the veranda of the Swiss-style chalet in which we had been staying for the past week.

Bariloche was Argentina's most scenic and popular mountain

resort, located high up in the Andes on the Chilean border. Architecturally, its hotels, ski lodges, and private chalets were faithful to their Alpine prototypes. But from anything I had heard, the crystal lakes, soaring volcanic peaks, and dizzying rock formations around Bariloche surpassed anything in Europe. Certainly Europe could not offer skiing on the fourth of July.

Swathed in black cashmere, with black-lensed glasses shielding his eyes from the glare of sun on snow, Tony looked like an ebony carving, an icon to evil. How, I wondered, had I ever thought him handsome? How had I ever fancied myself in love with him? For longer than I had loved him, I had loathed him with all my heart.

Grace clung to my hand. "Mamí, I don't want to go alone. Don't make me go by myself this time."

Kneeling, I embraced my daughter. Whenever we traveled through the countryside, Tony insisted that Grace be driven in a separate vehicle for her own safety, so that any attempt on his life would not imperil hers. My pleas to him to change his mind, or at least permit me to accompany Grace, went unheard.

Tony strode over to us, wrenched Grace out of my arms and passed her over to one of his drivers. She screamed and called out to me, "Mamí! Mamí!" as she was borne through the house and out to a waiting car. I clapped my hands over my ears to shut out her cries. Tony grabbed my wrists and jerked them down.

"That is just the reaction she was hoping to achieve by her behavior," he snapped. "You are the one who has taught her how to overdramatize a situation for maximum effect. I find you both intolerable."

"Then, let us go," I pleaded tearfully. "We'll get out of your life and never bother you again. I don't want anything from you, Tony. Just our freedom."

He released me, straightened the black Homburg on his head, and turned on his heel.

We left Bariloche in three cars. The Cadillac in the lead carried our luggage, a couple of Tony's bodyguards, and three of the household servants. Tony and I followed in a Rolls Royce, with an armed chauffeur and a bodyguard seated in front of us. A Daimler that had once belonged to an ambassador from Great Britain brought up the rear, with Grace and my maid, and another armed driver.

Although Tony had instructed the three drivers to stay together, we lost sight of the Cadillac on the twisting road down through the mountains. Fierce winds had swept the slopes bare of snow. The terrain was barren and so strewn with rocks that it resembled a moonscape rather than a landscape.

We had been on the road only thirty minutes when we heard a muffled roar. The explosion reverberated through the valleys and caused the roadbed under our wheels to tremble. The car halted abruptly, pitching Tony and me to the floor. I heard a popping noise somewhere in the distance. Firecrackers, I thought. Fourth of July. Independence Day. I started to rise, but Tony shoved me down again and told me to stay there. He barked a command to our driver. More popping at closer range. No. The Fourth of July was meaningless here. Not firecrackers. Guns.

"Grace! They're trying to kidnap Grace!"

I straightened up and looked around. Men wearing camouflage suits and black hoods were emerging from behind the pillars of rock that flanked the road. Tony's bodyguard leaned through his open window and started firing. A bullet pierced his throat. He fell back, clutching his neck and gurgling horribly. Blood spurted all over the interior of the car. I wrestled with the door handle and tumbled out of the Rolls just in time to see the Daimler pulling up behind us and more hooded gunmen converging on it. Tony screamed at our driver to get us out of there. Our car didn't move; bullets had ripped through the engine and shredded all four tires.

I shook off the lap robe that had become entangled around my legs and stumbled toward the Daimler. Suddenly strong arms were flung around my neck and the cold nose of a pistol nudged my ear.

"Walk slowly, Dolores," Tony gasped. "It is not Grace they want, but me. If they wanted to shoot you, they would already have done so."

He was right. The commandos held their fire, although they continued to point their weapons at us. I heard Grace calling to me. I tried to break away from Tony, but he held me fast.

"I swear, I will kill you myself if you don't behave," he hissed.

The Daimler's driver was standing on a boulder about ten feet above the road. He shook his fist at Tony. *"Viva Ché!"* he shouted jubilantly. *"Viva la revolución!"*

One of the commandos was hunkered down, holding Grace

around the waist. He wore no hood, and the sun picked out brown-gold highlights in his hair. I screamed at him in Spanish to take his rotten hands off my daughter. He straightened up to look at us, and for a moment I stopped breathing. Bram Howard. Bram, an automatic weapon slung across his back, a pistol shoved into his belt. Bram, looking perfectly at ease in this company of terrorists.

"Let her go, Matos." He stepped in front of Grace to shield her with his body. "Throw down your gun." Two of his men moved toward us.

"Stay back, all of you!" Tony drove the muzzle of the pistol into the side of my neck. I bit off a cry of pain. "If you take one step in this direction, I will kill the woman, I swear it. Hand over the child. I'm taking her, too."

"No!" I shrieked. "You can't have her! Save her, Bram, for God's sake!"

"You're not in any position to make deals, Matos," Bram said. "As I see it, you have exactly the time it takes to fire one shot. Pull that trigger and you're a dead man. And you know it. Let Dessie go, put down the gun, and then we'll talk."

"Talk," Tony sneered. "You mean your guns will talk. I have no desire to listen. We have reached a stalemate, my friend. You want the woman. I want to go free. So long as I have her, I am safe from your guns."

Tony and I came abreast of the Daimler's passenger door. It was open. Tony gave me a shove. "Inside. Behind the wheel. Hurry!" I obeyed numbly. At any moment, he might turn his gun on Bram.

Tony climbed in beside me and pulled the door closed. The pistol jabbed my temple. "Drive!" he ordered.

Although I had ridden in Tony's cars often enough, I had never driven any of them. This one was a British import with the controls on the right. I had to start the engine with my left hand, a somewhat awkward process. The car clearly resented being handled by a rank amateur. It stalled twice, and even after I got it going, it bucked and heaved as we pulled away. I soon realized why: I was trembling so violently from head to toe that my foot was jerking spasmodically on the gas pedal. Tony snapped at me to concentrate on my driving. I glanced at the black gloved forefinger curled around the trigger of his pistol and decided to obey. Concentrate. Hold steady. Get him away from Grace and

Bram. Save them. My lover. My baby. Save them from him. The rhythm of the engine smoothed out.

I swung wide to avoid the body of the fallen guard beside the Rolls. A few yards away, our chauffeur lay at the side of the road, his face a mask of blood.

A powerful landmine had exploded in the center of the road in front of the Cadillac. The driver had swerved to avoid it and had plowed into a tree. The car's hood was crumpled and its engine belched smoke and steam. The occupants of the Cadillac stood in a small circle under the watchful eye of a quartet of commandoes. One of them held a radio to his ear. Someone on the other end must have issued an order, for although two weapons swung around in our direction, the gunmen held their fire.

I eased the Daimler around the crater left by the mine. The road ahead of us was clear of obstructions. Tony brandished his pistol and ordered me to go faster.

"Oh, go ahead and kill me," I said through gritted teeth. "Do you really think I care at this point? Why don't you drive the damned car yourself?"

"Shut up!" he snarled. "Don't you think I would If I could?"

Stunned and terrified as I was, I almost giggled. Antonio Matos, bastard child of the barrio, had ascended so swiftly to the ranks of the privileged that he had never mastered the skills of the middle class. He had owned dozens of cars in his lifetime, but he didn't know how to drive.

I took the Daimler around a tight curve without slowing down. The big car heeled over sharply, the wheels on the left side breaking contact with the ground for a fraction of an instant before the machine righted itself with a jolt.

"Be careful or you'll kill both of us!" Tony yelped.

"You told me to go faster."

Bram. Dear Bram. He had found us, clear down at the bottom of the world. Once again he had tried to save us, and this time he had half succeeded. At this very moment, Grace was with him, resting in his arms, safe and secure for all time. Tony couldn't touch her anymore. I expelled a long, relieved sigh.

Only Tony and I were left, and as the driver of his car, I was in control. I had to find some way to destroy him. I had to do it, in order to save Grace.

Soon we would be leaving the mountains. On the flat treeless plain, my chances of wrecking the car would be slimmer. Crashing into a building or another vehicle was out of the question. I didn't want to hurt anyone else. Just Tony.

I couldn't wait much longer. As soon as we reached a town of any size, Tony would stop and telephone his ranch near Buenos Aires for reinforcements. I knew him so well. Without a phalanx of guards and guns surrounding him, he felt exposed and vulnerable. Men would come, dozens of them, flying down in airplanes and helicopters, and in just a few hours I would be right back where I had been for the past ten years, a prisoner of love that had never really been love at all, but a sort of madness.

I tried to recall the final leg of our three-day journey from Buenos Aires. Hadn't there been a sharp bend in the road, just beyond a village—what was its name? San Martin de los Andes, that was it. The progress of our caravan had slowed considerably. Tony had been nervous about the delay and had asked the driver to hurry. The chauffeur had explained that this part of the road was tricky and dangerous, particularly after a snowfall. Through the window on the right, I had seen a low wooden railing marking the top of a steep canyon, or *quebrada*, which was littered with boulders as big as bulldozers. On the opposite bank, a cluster of crosses commemorated the victims that the spot had claimed over the years. I remembered one cross in particular; fastened to the horizontal piece was a laminated photograph of a smiling young man sitting astride a motorcycle.

Two more crosses would add lustre to the turn's reputation as a dead man's curve. But how far ahead was it? How many miles? Two? Three? No matter. I had to be ready.

At my side, Tony lowered the pistol to his lap. "We will stop soon." He sounded tired. "At San Martin."

As I suspected, he was ready to summon reinforcements. I guided the Daimler around another twist in the road, praying for the cluster of crosses to appear ahead of me. But the roadsides were clear. This stretch was damnably safe.

I leaned forward and gripped the wheel more tightly. Tony noticed the movement. "What is it? What's the matter?"

"Just trying to get comfortable. This seat is too far back for me."

"You'll manage. We're nearly there."

Another kink in the road, this one to the right, with a distant Lake Lacar shimmering in the gap between rocky slopes. Then an ascent so steep that it put a noticeable strain on the engine. Yes, I remembered now. Right after the deady curve, we had plunged downhill for a long time before resuming our climb to the mountains.

There it was at last, a disorderly crew of white crosses, some wrought iron, some wood, some prim and straight, some leaning drunkenly, a few bearing photographs of the dead. Faded plastic flowers added a hint of color to the blighted landscape. And ahead of me, like a low easy hurdle beckoning the horses in my engine to jump it, the guard rail.

I braked slightly going into the curve, then at the point where I would normally have given the car a little more gas to carry it through the rest of the way, I tramped the pedal all the way to the floor and jerked the wheel hard to the right. The Daimler flattened the railing as if it had been made of toothpicks and took a nose-dive off the cliff.

The din was horrible, deafening, a cacophony of shattering glass and crumpling metal. And beside me, Tony Matos screamed.

I smiled. Good for you, you bastard. Good for you.

23

I HAD NOT EXPECTED HEAVEN TO BE SO INHOSPITABLE, NOR death to be so agonizing. Perhaps I wasn't in heaven at all. Perhaps this was really hell.

I tried to speak, to ask someone—the guardian demon or gatekeeper or whoever was in charge, but I couldn't move my jaw or any part of my mouth. The groan I emitted sounded distorted and faraway, as though it had come from someone else. I checked the other areas of my body: toes, fingertips, eyelids. Nothing moved, or even twitched. I had no vision either. Just weight and pressure all around me. And pain. A coffin of pain.

"Dessie, can you hear me? You're in the University Hospital in Buenos Aires, and you're going to live." The voice spoke in English, slow and soothing. "You're a little banged up, and you'll be out of commission for a while, but the doctors and surgeons have done everything that can be done for the time being. Now we just have to wait and see what happens. I'm holding your hand. I guess you can't feel it. Your hands are in plaster, too. But they'll heal. I'll be right here, darling. I won't leave your side for a minute. I'm right here."

The pain clamped down on me like a vice. I screamed.

"Mamí, can you see me?"

Shadows moved behind a white screen.

"You had bandages all over your eyes, but they're gone now. Can't you see me?"

I strained to focus. Gradually the bobbing shadow gained depth and detail. Dark curling hair, eyes like polished onyx beads, a pink smiling mouth. A little face, as beautiful as an angel's.

"Unnh," I said.

"You do! Look, Gray! Look, everybody! Mamí can see!"

Another form appeared, longer and taller with fair hair and sad eyes. A pale face loomed close to mine.

"Mother, it's Gray. Do you know me? You . . . you look . . . oh, Dad, why did this have to happen?" The pale face disappeared. Someone was crying. The noise irritated me. Why didn't these people go away and leave me alone?

". . . more surgery to reset the bones in her leg—fused some of the vertebrae in her spine—infection cleared up—still in a great deal of pain—something less dangerous than morphine, not nearly so effective."

A man was standing beside my bed, reciting this litany of horrors into a telephone receiver.

"Are . . . you . . . doctor?"

Well, well, I could finally move my jaw. I tested the mechanism. Up and down. Side to side. It made a cracking noise, but at least it held together. I wondered if the hinges were showing. I lifted my hand—

"Dessie, you're awake."

Something intercepted my hand on its way to my face. The doctor leaned over me and gazed into my eyes.

"I'm Bram Howard, Dessie. Don't you remember? Bram. I love you."

"Am I . . . good patient?" Speech was awkward, if a little painful. Not really worth the effort.

He laughed. "Yes, you are. A very good patient. It's been three months since the accident. Do you remember anything that happened?"

Accident? I couldn't recall any accident. I studied the white wall and tried to concentrate. The mist shifted slightly. No accident. I wanted to kill someone. Turn him into a mass of bloody pulp and splintered bone just like myself. But who was he? Who? I struggled to sit up.

The doctor pressed my shoulders down. "Matos is dead, Dessie. He died in the crash. It's all right. He can't hurt you anymore. You're free."

Free. He said the word as if it meant something. I didn't feel free. I felt heavy and tired and profoundly uninterested in what was happening to me. So there had been an accident, a crash. A man had died. By some fluke, I had lived. Why? I didn't know. Life, like freedom, meant nothing to me. I was breathing,

I was speaking, but deep inside my head and my heart, I was dead.

"One foot in front of the other." The nurse-therapist was homely and hearty and tiresomely British. "Grip the bars, that's right, dearie. Don't worry about falling down, I'm right here to catch you. Now take the walker and go toward Mr. Howard. See him waiting for you down there? You're doing beautifully, yes, you are. Pick up the walker and move it along. Don't be afraid to let your legs take the weight of your body. They may be stiff, but at least they're in one piece!" She laughed. I didn't understand the joke. "Everyone says it's a miracle that you're walking at all. Right foot, left foot. Move the walker. Right foot, left—"

He stood about six feet away from me in front of the window, a tall man wearing a tan suit and a blue shirt. A graying forelock drooped above his eyes, which were also blue. A memory tugged at the edges of my mind—no, I couldn't place him. Howard who?

He didn't move. He didn't smile. Those cool blue eyes watched me toiling along, stiff-legged and stiff-armed as a robot. They were such compelling eyes. Once they caught my gaze, they did not let it go. I wanted to look away, but I found I couldn't. Those eyes reeled me in on invisible cables, forcing me to push on, step after painful step.

His face was the oasis on the horizon, the cathedral rising from the plane, the shoreline glimpsed from the vastness of the sea. I was the parched traveler, the weary pilgrim, the castaway. As I drew nearer, it grew in size until it filled the whole field of my vision. My sense of familiarity increased. I grasped at the memory of a landscape long forgotten, recognizing contours of chin, cheekbones, nose, and forehead.

We stood toe to toe. I gripped the walker with my aching hands.

"I know you," I said slowly. "You're Blair's brother. Abraham. Charles Abraham Howard. They call you Bram, don't they? What are you doing here?"

"Oh, Dessie, I've been here for four months," he said. "I'm in love with you, Dessie. Don't you remember?"

I struggled to grasp the wisps of memory that drifted through my brain. Then he reached out and touched my cheek. That sparked an image: a room in a cold cellar, like a prison cell. A flickering lantern. Two bodies melting into one.

"Yes, I think I remember. Am I in love with you, too?"

He put his arms around my waist and pulled me into a tight, lengthy embrace. He was hurting me, but I didn't say anything because I felt him shuddering and I knew he was crying and I didn't want to make him feel any worse than he already did. Behind me, I heard the nurse sniffling.

I leaned against him. "I'm so tired, Bram. You'll have to tell them I can't sing tonight. What's the matter with me?"

Behind me, the nurse said, "Don't worry, sir. The confusion can last for several months, sometimes longer. She'll get over it."

Now that my mind was clearing, Bram was able to explain how he had found us. "Eight months after the revolution, your old friend Guevara arranged a secret meeting with me in Mexico City. He said he owed you a favor."

Ché had handed Bram a slip of paper on which was scrawled a Buenos Aires telephone number. "These men have instructions to help you. They are friends from the old days. I wish you much luck, señor. But take care. This Matos is a dangerous and slippery character, as we have both learned to our sorrow."

When Bram arrived in Argentina, he discovered that Ché's friends were keeping close watch on Tony's movements. One of their men managed to infiltrate his household, but he was unable to discover where Tony was keeping Grace. Bram knew that they could not make a move to liberate Grace and me until we were reunited, and even then it would be difficult. Tony's ranch was isolated and well-guarded, the compound around the main house even more heavily fortified than his villa in Havana had been. Grace and I were virtual prisoners, under observation at all times.

Then in June, Tony announced that we would go to the mountains for winter sports. Ché's man sabotaged his jet by adding sugar to the fuel supply, forcing us to take the cars. Bram planned the ambush for the day of our departure from Bariloche. He admitted that his men should have prevented Matos from grabbing me and using me as a shield.

"When I saw the two of you driving away in that Daimler, I wanted to kill somebody," Bram said. "Of all the damned incompetence . . ."

I squeezed his hand. "When I saw you there with Grace, I knew my prayers had been answered. After that, I didn't care if I died. At least she'd have someone to love her."

"Sweetheart, you're not going to die. Honestly, you'll probably outlive your grandchildren." Bram leaned over and kissed me. "You're on the mend now, ready to go places. Guess what? We're flying to Paris next week."

"Paris? I don't have to sing, do I? I'm so tired. I don't think I can sing."

"No." Bram's smile looked tight and unnatural. "You need to see a few more doctors before you can sing. They want to do some plastic surgery."

"Plastic?"

He took my hands and held them firmly. "Dessie, that accident left you in pretty bad shape. Almost every bone in your body was broken, and your face has some scars. They couldn't start reconstructive surgery until they were sure you were out of danger from your other injuries, but now they can go ahead. Dr. Roland is the best man in the world for this sort of thing. He learned his business on the battlefield in World War I. He's a pioneer in reconstructive techniques. He's examined you, he's seen your X-rays and your records and he's confident that he can repair the damage so that no one will ever notice."

An orderly looked in and told Señor Howard that he had a message at the nurses' station. When he had gone, I lifted my hands to my face. For the first time, I felt the crooked place on my jaw, the hump in my nose, the depression where my left cheekbone used to be. And the scars. They were smooth and silky and deep. One of them ran all the way down the right side of my face from my hairline to my neck.

"No!"

The room had no mirrors. Even the mirror over the sink in the corner had been taken down and a colorful art print, a Renoir mother and child, hung in its place. A chrome-plated tray rested on my bedside table. I shifted the pitcher and glasses and held it up in front of my face.

A leering grotesque looked back at me, grinning crookedly out of a mouth that was pulled down at one corner by the scar. The new tufts of hair that sprouted out of her shaved scalp were white, her skin was sallow and shrunken, except for the livid scar tissue which was the color of ripe plums. This creature was not Dessie Heavener.

I replaced the objects on the tray. When Bram returned, he found me lying peacefully with my eyes closed. He leaned over the bed and kissed my forehead. I shivered. How could he bring himself to touch the monster I had become?

Dr. Roland was small, white-haired, bearded, with hands no larger than a child's. After he had examined me in his Paris clinic, he told me that when he was finished, I would look half my age.

Why was he lying to me?

We moved into a house near the forest of Fontainebleau. Dr. Roland could not operate until I regained some of my physical strength. He ordered three hearty meals a day, plus a concentrated program of physical therapy to rebuild my shrunken muscles and improve my circulation.

But at Fontainebleau, I sank into a deep depression. When the therapist, a strapping grim-faced German named Dieter Kleinschmidt, came into my room, I clung to the arms of my chair and refused to cooperate. Herr Kleinschmidt had no sympathy for anyone who didn't want to get well.

"Rehabilitation is in the mind, Frau Matos," he would say, "and your mind is still asleep. Wake up. Wake up!"

On other occasions Herr Kleinschmidt would tell me how much Bram was paying him to work with me twice a day, seven days a week. "But money isn't everything, believe me. What kind of satisfaction can I get out of doing this when you fight me every step of the way? I could be helping people who want to be helped."

He forced me to stand without wavering. He insisted that I walk long distances between parallel bars. He berated and scolded me and made my lift my legs and bend my knees and flex my elbows and wrists by hoisting half-pound barbells with my aching hands until I begged him to leave me alone.

One day after our afternoon session Herr Kleinschmidt made an announcement. "After today I quit. I told Herr Howard that I have done all I can. He can hire someone else to work with you if he wants, but he will be wasting his money and that person's time."

I thought that the ungenial German's departure would mean a reprieve for me. I was wrong. Bram did not hire anyone else. He took over the job himself, and he was even tougher than Herr Kleinschmidt.

"I'm not asking you to walk to the windows, Dessie, I'm telling you. On your feet."

"I won't," I protested. "I want to stay here."

He lifted me under the arms and kicked the chair away. "Walk," he said. "I'm right behind you to catch you if you fall. Don't be afraid."

"I'm not afraid. I just don't want to do it."

As soon as he released his hold around my rib cage, I slumped in a heap on the floor. He dropped to his knees beside me. "All right, if you won't walk, then we can do floor exercises right here. You know how much you hate those."

"I know how much I hate you," I muttered.

He pulled me around so that our faces were almost touching. "How much?" he demanded. "How much do you hate me? Do you hate me for taking Gray away from you? Do you hate me for abandoning you before he was born? How about for letting Matos sink my boat? Come on, Dessie, tell me. How much do you hate me? Why do you hate me?"

He wanted to make me angry; he was trying to elicit some response besides apathy. I said dully, "I hate you for loving me."

Gray left me alone. Once or twice I turned my head on my pillow and caught him staring at me from the doorway, but he never came in. The sight of my shattered body upset him, but no more than my defeated attitude. He wanted me to fight for life now as fiercely as I had once fought to gain custody of him. But I couldn't do it. I wanted to die, and he knew it, and he couldn't bear to watch.

Grace, however, pestered me constantly. She would come into my room and climb right into bed with me.

"Don't you want to get well, Mamí?"

I shrugged my shoulders.

"But you have to get well. I want you to sing songs to me, and help me play with my dolls, and take me to the park. Gray takes me every day, but I want you to come, too."

"I can't darling," I sighed. "I'm too tired."

"Sing to me," Grace begged. "Sing 'Mi Corazón.' Please? You feel better when you sing. You always said you did."

I moved my head weakly on the pillow. "No, Gracie, not now. Maybe later. Maybe . . . tomorrow."

"Do you want me to sing it for you? I know all the words, and I can dance, too."

"Some other time, darling. I'm too tired to listen to any songs right now."

Disappointed, Grace went away. I turned my gaze to the window. The gardeners were busy planting bulbs in the crescent-shaped bed on the grassy terrace below the house. Tulips and daffodils for spring. I hoped I wouldn't be around to see them.

That evening, after the private duty nurse had put me to bed, Bram came to my room. He carried a record player and a pile of albums. He plugged the thing in and dropped a record onto the turntable. I heard myself singing "Snakebelly Blues":

> I feel lower than a snake's belly, my-oh-my,
> So low that I just want to cry and cry and cry.
> If my man don't come back soon,
> I'm just going to die, yes, I am, I will surely die.

I had recorded the album in Havana with a group of old jazz men and a few young ones. It had sold very well in Europe, where I had a following, and also in the States, where *Billboard* magazine called it the best example of a white woman singing the blues since Mildred Bailey. Bram played it through, then flipped it over.

The arrangements were good, very good. That recording session had been fun, earnest young conservatory-trained musicians playing right alongside white-haired black men whose hands were so swollen and gnarled that it seemed impossible that they could ever make music. But make music they did, on the cornet, the drums, the trombone. They had been touring, and had stopped at the Hotel Nacional because Hotshot Grayson had told them I might be glad to see some boys from back home. My Cuban A and R man had listened to our impromptu blues session, and the record was born.

> Blue in the morning, blue at noon,
> Blue when the sun goes down,
> And singing the blues at the moon.
> I'm the color of night, baby,
> Like shadows and old wine—

The record ended with applause from the patrons at the Havana Room, where we had recorded live. When I closed my eyes I could see the faces of the people I had sung for all my life, in churches and dance halls, on battlefields and Hollywood sound stages, in little clubs and in the public square in Veracruz. They had listened so attentively, and when I finished, they had always applauded, adding a coda of their own to the music I had given them.

The music started again. "Mi Corazón." Paul at the piano.

"Stop it," I said. "I don't want to listen anymore."

"Why not? It's a beautiful song. It did pretty well back home, too, did you know that? They sang it on the Hit Parade ten weeks in a row. Dinah Shore had good luck with the cover she made of it."

"Dinah Shore? Dinah Shore recorded my song?"

"Well, you weren't around to promote your own record. Don't worry, anyone who knew anything thought yours was better. I especially like that flamenco wail you do at the end."

He couldn't have devised a worse torture. Every record he put on evoked floods of memories, and reminded me that singing had been the greatest joy of my life, the sole constant, the one thing I could do with some degree of pleasure when everything else had gone sour. The sound of my own voice mocked me. Something inside my head said, "You'll never do that again. Never." Tears rolled down my cheeks.

Bram sat on the side of the bed. "I know what you're thinking. But you're wrong, Dessie. You'll be singing again before you know it. I have absolute faith in Dr. Roland, and I have faith in myself: I promise you, I will do everything in my power to get you up on stage again, if I have to spend every cent of my money and use every bit of my energy to do it. Why can't you believe in me? And in yourself? You've accomplished so much in your life, despite incredible odds. This fight is just going to be a little harder, that's all. Inside that broken body, your spirit is still the same. Believe you can do it, Dessie. Believe."

"There is no Dessie Heavener," I said. "She was just somebody I made up because I wanted people to notice me. But she's gone now."

"Where's Grace? Why hasn't she been to see me?"

Bram stood at the foot of the bed. "Grace is in school, Dessie. I decided it was time she had the company of kids her own age. Gray is taking some courses at the Alliance Française, and she wanted to go to school, too. It's her third day already and she loves it."

I stared at him. "School? Grace in school? That's ridiculous. Grace is terrified of leaving me. She doesn't want to be apart from me for even a few minutes."

He shrugged. "She may be a child, but she's old enough to realize that she can't do anything for you as long as you're content to lie in bed and vegetate. That's no fun for a kid to watch."

Feebly, I kicked the covers off my legs. "No, it's wrong, all wrong. Her place is with me, not with strangers. She's terrified of strangers. You had no right—she needs me. Me! I'm her Mamí. We're never going to be apart. Never!"

"That's not very realistic, is it?" Bram said. "She isn't going to be a baby forever. She's got to start letting go, and so do you."

"I'm going to find her, bring her back."

I dragged myself out of bed and stumbled to the wardrobe. A week without exercise had frozen my joints and allowed my muscles to atrophy again. Behind me, Bram said, "You want to keep her in some kind of prison, just like Matos, to serve at your whim—"

"You don't know!" I tried to pull off my nightgown. Failing to get it over my head, I ripped the front neckline to hem and cast it aside like a rag. "You don't know what she's been through. That man kept her locked up for an entire year. I never saw her, not once, but I could hear her crying. Night after night, I heard her. 'Mamí! Mamí!' It ripped through my heart like a knife. I couldn't stand it. 'Mamí!' " I fancied I could still hear her voice. "We haven't been apart since, not for five minutes—"

"You've been apart for six months," Bram corrected me gently. "Half that time you were comatose or else you didn't recognize her or want anything to do with her. Half a year is a long time for a kid. She needed to make some adjustments, learn to trust herself again. She's going to be just fine, you'll see."

"You're lying to me! Something's happened, hasn't it? She's been kidnapped and you're afraid to tell me." Haphazardly, I dragged garments from hangers. "Tony—one of Tony's friends has her. A Cuban, a gangster just like him." I whirled on Bram. "Tell me the truth, damn you! Where is my baby?"

"I told you the truth, Dessie. She's at school. She'll be home in just a few hours."

"I don't believe you. I've got . . . I've got to find her." My fingers fumbled with the hooks on my brassiere. Bram must have seen my predicament, but he made no move to help me.

"She's just beginning to learn about the real world," he said. "Go on, chase after her, drag her back. But what are you going to do when she starts to cry because she misses her new teachers and her new friends? She spent too many years living under Matos's thumb. She won't tolerate that kind of tyranny from you, Dessie. If you love her, you'll start letting go. Now."

"Are you crazy? I can't let her go. I won't let her go. Never." I abandoned the recalcitrant brassiere. Digging further into the wardrobe, I found a loose smock with no fasteners and no belt and I struggled into it. My muscles screamed in protest. "She's my baby, my little Gracie. I can't let them take her away from me—vultures and hyenas—waiting to pounce—"

At that moment I caught a glimpse of myself in the mirror over the dressing table and I stopped cold. The woman who stared back at me would have scared the devil himself, much less a classroom full of ten-year-olds. She was weak and frantic and incoherent. Her clothes hung on her wasted frame. Her face alone, awash with tears and streaked with purple scars, was enough to put any hungry lumberjack off his lunch.

"Why aren't you helping me?" I demanded weakly. "Why?" Sobbing, I slid to the floor.

Bram knelt beside me and put his arms around me. "You don't want any help," he reminded me. "You told me to leave you alone. Remember?"

"You did this! You took Grace away from me, just like you took Gray when he was her age. You still hate me for what happened to Blair. Still punishing me—"

"You can get well or you can stay right where you are," he said. "It's your choice, Dessie. I'm not punishing you. I can't force you to do anything you don't want to do."

"I want my baby back! I want my Gracie!" I hid my face in the curve where his neck met his shoulder. "Hold me, Bram. Hold me. My babies are gone, both of them. They're growing up and they don't need me anymore. What can I do? I don't have anything left."

Bram smoothed the pitiful wisps of hair away from my face. "You have more than you know, Dessie. It's time you realized that being an invalid isn't going to bring you anything worthwhile. You've never been the kind of woman who was content to sit in her armchair and let life pass her by."

My mother had been one of those, a spectator rather than a

participant, a refugee from reality who sought sanctuary in the bottle.

Bram hugged me and rocked with me until I was calmer. Then he found another nightgown for me, helped me into it, and put me to bed.

"Don't leave me." I clutched his hands. "I don't want to be alone anymore. Everybody's leaving me . . ."

"I won't leave." Bram kissed me tenderly. "I'll be right here, as long as you want me or until forever, whichever comes first."

Two months later, Dr. Roland declared himself satisfied with my physical and mental condition. I was ready for reconstructive surgery. I checked into his clinic on a Friday and came out the following Thursday, my face and neck swathed in bandages. A week later he came to the house to remove them. I sat in a chair near a window and listened to the snipping of his bandage scissors and his murmured comments: "Yes, that looks quite good, amazingly good. Hardly a trace of a scar."

When he finished I said, "I want to see."

"You are still badly bruised from the surgery," he warned, "but the bruises will disappear in a few weeks and in time the puffiness will also vanish. Still, this will give you some idea of what you will look like." He held a mirror up in front of me. "I am a great fan of yours, madame. I have all your records. I used the photographs on the jackets as my guides during the surgery. I felt happy, knowing I was restoring a work of art."

Yes, I was certainly bruised and puffy, but the horrible scars were gone, the crushed cheekbone reconstructed, the nose and mouth straight. I laughed out loud. "Why, I look fine, just fine. All I need now is more hair."

"It will grow out and hide the scars on your scalp," Dr. Roland promised. "No one will ever know that you have had surgery unless you tell them."

That night when Bram climbed into bed beside me, I put my arms around him and kissed him. "Thank you."

"I didn't do anything. Dr. Roland is the magician."

"Well, I wish I was in bed with Dr. Roland, then. I would like to express my appreciation to him. If we turn the light out, I can pretend you're Dr. Roland and you can pretend I look like my old self."

"We'll leave the light on," he said. "I'm pretty happy with things the way they are. No pretending for me."

358

* * *

Every day I walked a little farther, stood a little straighter, felt a little stronger. I started to sing again, the old familiar tunes I had always sung around the house. I couldn't open my throat to full volume, but at least I knew my voice was still there.

I continued to report to my doctors for regular checkups. I returned from one such visit to find Bram in his study conducting business by telephone.

"Are you richer than you were an hour ago?" I asked when he had finished.

He leaned back in his chair and locked his hands behind his head. "I just sold some company franchises for six million dollars. Can I buy you a piece of the moon, or will a major galaxy do?"

"It doesn't matter." I sighed despondently. "The doctor says I have to go back to bed and stay there for the next eight months."

"What?" Bram sat up straight. "I don't understand. You were doing so well."

A slow grin spread over my face. "I have to be extra careful if I don't want to lose my baby."

He looked thunderstruck. "Your—what?"

"My baby. Our baby. You're going to be a father, Bram. I was careful not to have another baby with Tony, but after the accident I just forgot all about it. And now Grace is growing up and I'm going to have another baby to take her place. I love you and I love children and I'm thrilled to be having one with you. Aren't you excited?"

"Well, of course I am. I just never expected you to be able . . . really, I'm delighted."

Bram forced himself to smile, but I could tell he was deeply worried. I leaned over the top of the desk and kissed him. "Don't be afraid," I said. "This baby is a special gift, a sign that everything will be all right."

Thus began the long period of my confinement. The doctors who came in periodically to check my condition shook their heads and tut-tutted and issued all sorts of stern warnings. I wasn't to let myself get upset or worried, I wasn't to exert, I wasn't to lift anything heavier than a pencil. I merely smiled at them. They were far more worried than I was. The months of therapy and exercise after the accident had barely lifted me out of a deep depression, but now my spirits soared. I was carrying a baby inside my body, Bram's baby, and I felt ecstatic.

Our son Charles was delivered by Caesarian section in March, 1963. He was healthy, perfectly formed, and endowed with a terrific pair of lungs. I had to spend several weeks in the hospital, and apparently I gave Bram and my children some bad moments, but by April I was home again and in reasonably good shape.

"You need to recover," Bram said. "Why don't we go to Greece, where it's warm?"

I shook my head. "No, not Greece. Take me home, Bram. I want to go home."

24

"LET ME CARRY HIM."

"No, I want to hold him. I feel better holding him." I hoisted the baby up on my shoulder.

"Ready?" Bram made sure he had a firm grip on Grace's hand, then he put a protective arm around my waist.

"I suppose so." We passed through the doors from the customs area onto the main concourse, into a blaze of lights from TV cameras and flashbulbs. I shielded Charlie's eyes from the glare. He whimpered a little but did not awaken. His first flight over the Atlantic had been a bad one, and he was exhausted. Even without the turbulence that had given us a bumpy and uncomfortable ride, we would have been on edge, wondering how the scene at New York's Idlewild airport would play itself out.

"Hey, Dessie!" Voices called to me from all directions. I kept my gaze fixed straight ahead and tried not to squint into the lights from the TV cameras. "Wow, Dessie, you look terrific!"

"Dessie, over here!"

"How does it feel to be back in this country after eleven years?"

"Are you going to be singing anytime soon?"

"Is it true that Tony Matos kept you locked up in a dungeon, and Grace, too?"

Grace looked up at me, suddenly curious. "Mamí, what's a dungeon?"

My head was reeling. Why hadn't I listened to Bram? Alerting the press to our arrival had been stupid.

"Miss Heavener?" An authoritative new voice cut through the din of the yelping reporters. A badge appeared under my nose. "Jim Forrest, U.S. Marshal. I have a warrant for your arrest. I will now advise you of your rights." He proceeded to do just that while two other government agents escorted Bram and me and the children to the nearest exit.

I heard a shout. Turning, I saw Gray and another man running toward us. Gray embraced me, swooped his little sister up in his arms, kissed the baby, and shook Bram's hand. "Sorry we're late," he panted. "Traffic on the expressway was terrible." He swung his head around and faced the marshal. "This is Phillip Blackman, Miss Heavener's attorney."

Mr. Blackman spoke up. "May I see a copy of that warrant?" The cameras purred, taking it all in. Charlie woke up and started to scream.

We were taken to a Manhattan courtroom, where I was charged with having been an accessory to the murder of Samuel F. Martin and Francis X. McGuinn on the night of March 6, 1952. The judge set bail at one hundred thousand dollars. Bram paid promptly, and I was released into his custody.

As the cab pulled away from the federal courthouse he said, "I think we should have stayed in Europe for a few more months."

"I couldn't wait any longer." I adjusted the corner of the baby blanket under Charlie's chin. Grace had been so wound up and excited that I knew it would take her hours to settle down. At my suggestion, Gray had taken her to F.A.O. Schwarz to buy her a welcome home gift, her choice of any toy in the store—a scheme I had cause to regret later when they returned with a stuffed toy giraffe, half lifesize. "I want to get it over with. After I pay my debt to society, then I can sing again. Maybe I'll start a choral group in prison: Dessie and the Desperadoes. What do you think?"

"You are not going to prison." Bram's tone was strained. "No judge will—"

"I don't mind if you play my records for Charlie, but please don't show him any of my movies until he's older. I'd hate for him to have bad dreams about me."

"Goddamn it, you are not going to jail!" Bram's shout brought a loud wail from the baby. The cab driver swung his head around to look at us. He was a middle-aged black man whose tired brown eyes had seen it all.

"Look, man," he said, "if the chick wants to go to jail, let her go to jail. What's the big deal?"

We finished the ride to the Waldorf Astoria in silence. A mob of reporters was waiting for us in the lobby.

"Miss Heavener, do you have a statement to make about what happened in court today?"

Bram said, "Miss Heavener has nothing to say—"

"That's not true. I would like to say one thing." I paused in front of the bank of elevators. "I will abide by any decision the judge makes in my case. I will not dispute it. I will not appeal it. I want to put my past behind me so that I can go on with my life."

"Have you lost your mind?" Bram exploded when we were alone in our suite. "If you get any kind of prison sentence, even one day, we'll appeal it. You can be damned sure we'll appeal it! A judicial decision can always be overturned if you fight long enough and go high enough."

"I'm not going to fight," I told him. "I am guilty of helping Paul escape. If I had let the police handle it, he might be alive today. He didn't mean to hurt anyone. That shooting wasn't premeditated. They wouldn't have executed him. He'd be out of jail now and he'd be making music. I shouldn't have interfered. But I did, because I loved him. And you love me, which is why you're trying to save me. Don't, Bram. Please. Stop trying to arrange my life. That's my job. If I mess it up, then I'm the one who has to take the consequences."

"What about your children? What about Grace? What about the baby?"

"Oh, Grace will be all right, now that she has you and Gray. And Charlie will be fine, too. I trust you to take good care of both of them until I get out."

"I think you've lost your mind," Bram raged. "That accident must have damaged your brain cells. You are not competent to take charge of your own life."

"I'm as competent as you are, Abraham Howard," I said sharply. "I know what's best for me. If it doesn't fit in with your plans, that's just too bad."

I bore the baby off to the bedroom for his fourth feeding of the day. We were off schedule, and my breasts were beginning to leak.

I was still nursing him when Bram came into the room. He stood over us. "I think we should get married right away."

I didn't look at him. "Do you think you'll be able to control me better if I'm your wife?"

"Damn it, I love you! I want us to be a family, you and me and the three kids."

"I love you, too," I said, "but I won't marry you. I've been married twice and that's enough. I will gladly spend the rest of my life with you, Bram. I will raise our baby and look after you when you're sick and old and I trust you to do the same for me. You've already done more for me than any ten men. I'm sorry, my darling, but we've had this discussion a hundred times already. Don't ask me to marry you. Please."

He stood silent for a moment, trying to contain his anger, then he said in a low voice, "You're still angry with me about Gray. After all this time."

"Oh, Bram, don't be silly. Anyway, I can't make plans until after the hearing." Charlie's belly was taut and he was breathing deeply. I burped him, then laid him down in the crib the hotel had provided for him. "Imagine what your mother would say, her son marrying a saloon singer—and a felon to boot. The Howards of Woodlands don't marry girls like me, remember? The consequences are just too terrible. They might sleep with us, though." I straightened up and gave him a crooked smile. "Are you still interested?"

"You are the most exasperating woman I have ever met. All you have to do is crook your little finger and you know I'll come running."

"Consider it crooked." I put my arms around his waist. "We might not get too many chances. Except on visiting day."

"Why?" He held me away from him. "Why are you being so damned negative about all this? You sound like you really want to go to jail. Why can't you believe you'll go free?"

I shook my head. "Every piece of good luck I've ever had has been balanced with bad. It never fails. If something terrible can happen to me, it happens. Anybody else might be able to beat this rap. Not me. If it's possible for me to go to jail, I'll go. I want to get used to the idea in advance. I think it's about time I got smart and stopped expecting my luck to change."

I gave dozens of interviews to the press and on television in which I described my life in Mexico, Cuba, and Argentina. This barrage of publicity certainly won me the public's sympathy. Now that they knew how powerful Tony's hold over me had been, they were all rooting for me.

The hearing was held at the end of August, on the hottest day of the year, in the courtroom of Federal Judge Albert T. Albright. I pleaded not guilty to a charge of murder and guilty to everything else: possession of firearms, aiding and abetting a fugitive, and evading arrest. The judge asked Phillip Blackman, my attorney, and the federal prosecutor to approach the bench. Blackman came back looking pleased.

"We've had a piece of luck," he told Bram, Gray, and me. "They're going to drop the murder charge. The judge has received an affadavit from Clayton Striker's attorneys. It seems Striker got religion when he was in jail, and he's changed his testimony about your involvement in the shooting. He denies absolutely that you had anything to do with what happened in that room. The judge is willing to accept your other guilty pleas. He'll pass sentence in six weeks."

"Why so long? Why can't he do it now?"

"He needs to review all the evidence. He'll take into account your conduct since the incident, and your present situation; that is, the fact that you're recovering from a near-fatal accident and that you have an infant to care for. We want him to take all the time he needs."

"Can I talk to him?"

"Who?"

"The judge. I want to talk to him for a minute. Can't I do that?"

Mr. Blackman looked doubtful. "I don't know. I mean, that's what you have me for, to represent you . . ."

"I don't need representation, honey. I'm right here. Why can't I talk to him?"

Gray and Bram exchanged looks and rolled their eyes. Blackman shrugged. Then he stood up. "Your Honor, my client wishes to approach the bench."

"You may do so, Miss Heavener."

Blackman and Gray started to follow. I turned to them. "Thank you, boys, but I don't need you up there with me. What I have to say is strictly between Judge Albright and myself." I waited until they had returned to their seats, then I looked up at the austere, black-robed man who held my future in his hands.

"Your Honor," I said, "I'm not trying to excuse what I did. The whole thing was ugly and wrong and if I'd had any sense at all I would have walked out of that nightclub at the first sign of trouble. But I'm not strong on sense. I left school in the tenth grade and I've never been back. Everything I've learned, I've learned the hard way, by making mistakes. But I suppose I should say that if the same thing happened today, if I saw my oldest friend in trouble, I'd probably act just as I did then and hang the consequences. Paul Miller was very dear to me. I had to help him."

The judge looked unimpressed. "According to the evidence, your friend shot two men. You were a witness."

"But his friend was in trouble. Clayton Striker, I mean. I never liked him myself, but he was a fine musician and Paul worshipped him. I think you should know that Paul paid for his crime. He didn't have a peaceful moment until the day he died. His father was a judge like yourself. It killed Paul to know what a disappointment he had been to his daddy. I think even if he had gone to jail, he wouldn't have been satisfied that he had paid enough. I believe he still would have died with a needle in his arm and his head in the toilet."

The judge looked startled.

"We exiled ourselves from this country, Your Honor, and not a day passed that we weren't sorry. We both wanted to come home. Paul never made it. But I did and here I am. I would be grateful if you would sentence me as quickly as possible. I want to start serving whatever time you give me right away, before my baby gets any older."

"Do you have a husband, Miss Heavener?"

"No, sir. Mr. Howard is the father of our child, but I have declined to marry him. I don't want him tarred with my brush."

"We no longer administer tar and feathers in this courtroom," the judge said wryly. "Very well, I will expedite this matter. Sentence will be passed in one week's time. Court is adjourned." He rapped his gavel and stood up. Before he stepped away from the bench, he leaned over and said in a low voice, "You sang for my platoon in Naples about twenty years ago. I've never forgotten it." Then with a swirl of black robes, he vanished into his chambers.

Back at our table, I hugged Bram and Gray. "I have a feeling that something is finally going to go right for me. I don't know if I should trust it—I'm almost scared to—but the feeling is very, very strong."

"I hope you're right, Dessie," Bram murmured. "I hope you're right."

The judge sentenced me to two years in prison, but he suspended the sentence in view of the time that had elapsed and the hardships I had endured.

Minutes after my sentence was passed, I told Bram to hire a theater. "It's time I got off my duff and did some singing. I don't want to keep taking your money. I need to earn some of my own."

He looked amazed. "What are you talking about? You're a rich woman."

"I'm not rich. I haven't made any money in years."

"You're Tony Matos's widow, right? Everything he had belongs to you now. The money in his Swiss accounts is still intact. You have over eight million dollars, Dessie. If you wanted to, you could buy this hotel."

"That's not my money. Tony stole it. Send it back."

"To Cuba? We can't do that. The government of the United States has suspended relations—"

"Why not? Why can't I just write a check and mail it to Fidel? You can arrange it. Listen, I was a revolutionary, too, for a short time. I helped throw Batista out, didn't I? Those people need it more than I do. Return the money. I don't want it."

Bram grinned. "You can't fool me. You just want an excuse to work for a living."

We scheduled the concert for November, three months away. I would need every minute of that time to get my voice and my body back in shape—if I could do it at all. I found a pianist who had known Paul in the old days, and I worked with him six days a week. Bram rented a house in Connecticut. I had the living room stripped of drapes and rugs and a grand piano brought in. I didn't want any soft surfaces to muffle my mistakes; I needed to hear them.

The rest of the summer passed quickly. Gray, in his third year at Harvard Law School, visited frequently. Grace adored him, and he didn't seem to mind being pestered by his little sister. They went riding and sailing together, and in the evenings she would entertain him with songs from her own vast repertoire, sung in English, Spanish, French, and most astonishingly, Welsh. Apparently one of the women who had looked after her in Buenos Aires had been descended from Welsh settlers, and still spoke the language fluently.

Bram booked Carnegie Hall for one night. Tickets went on sale in early October and sold out in a day. My new agents started talking about a Broadway engagement, a one-woman show.

I was amazed. "I'm not sure this woman can get through even one show. Can't we wait and see?"

I tried not to think about what it would be like, facing an audience again after so many years. I concentrated on my music and let Bram and the talent agency take care of the details. I had to select the songs, decide whether I wanted twenty musicians on the stage with me or three or one. Then I needed to hire the instrumentalists and arrangers and a conductor.

One day I started making a list of all the songs I knew, starting with the very first blues songs Clara Mae had taught me. Spirituals, hymns, big band songs and jazz songs, show tunes and standards, Mexican and Cuban folk songs, a few Italian songs and tangos I had learned in Argentina. My list grew to two thousand, seven hundred, and eighty-four. How could I choose? How could I best share my gift with my listeners, most of whom had not heard me sing in over a decade?

I sang more than I talked. Walking around the house and the grounds, driving in the car, shopping, holding the baby, sitting with Bram and the children in the evening, I sang, and whenever a song struck me as particularly meaningful, I made a note of it. Some songs had associations which gave them special power. "Go 'Way from My Window" had seduced Bram, even as "Fast Walkin' Blues" had attracted his brother. I remembered the songs I had sung to my babies, the lullabies and the nonsense tunes, songs for play and songs for quieter times. Songs of sorrow. Songs of triumph. I had a right to sing them all, because I had lived them.

I was lying in bed with Bram when the solution to my dilemma presented itself. I sat bolt upright and said, "I'll tell them the story of my life, only I'll do it in song. If they don't like me then they won't like the program, it's as simple as that."

I decided to open the concert with a scorching version of "Frankie and Johnny," which Clara Mae had sung to me when I was just a toddler, before she was saved. The story it told had fascinated me, so much so that when anyone asked my name in those days, I said, "Frankie Ann Johnny." Oh, yes, poor Frankie loved her Johnny, but he was cheatin' on her, so she got herself a gun, a powerful .44, and she killed him dead, the rascal. My listeners would surely appreciate the irony of my singing that song so soon after I had won a reprieve from jail on a shooting charge.

After that, the rest was easy. I chose the songs that mattered to me. Some had been hit records. Some I had never recorded. Some I had sung only for the people I loved, and some for myself, when I needed to express something but couldn't find the words. "Hava Banana" would be on the program, because I wouldn't have had a career without it. And "Mi Corazón," which had made me a star in Veracruz.

My old friend Pepper Wellington came to see me. He was editing the new jazz magazine *Riff*.

"How does it feel to be making a comeback?" he asked

"It's not a comeback," I told him. "It's a continuation. I don't have anything to come back from. Only life, and everybody has that."

He laughed and adjusted the volume controls on his tape recorder. We talked about the changes I had gone through musically in the past few years, and about what I thought of contemporary jazz and the stuff kids were dancing to now, rock and roll. As a matter of fact, I didn't mind it at all. I had always liked a good strong beat behind me when I was singing, and the new rock bands certainly provided that.

At the end of the interview, Pepper asked a strange question: "Why do you sing, Dessie?"

I thought about it for a long time. "Everything I have ever felt inside, someone has written a song about. I'm not smart and articulate like you, Pepper. I can't talk brilliantly and I can't write two sentences without making a mistake. But music never fails me. When I can't think of the right words to say, I can always find a song that says them for me, and a tune that expresses my mood. The music helps me know what I'm feeling, and then I can tell the world. When I think of all the composers and songwriters who have helped me communicate over the years—they've not only given me the words to say, they've also given me the best way to say them."

"You sound like you're getting more from the music than you're giving," Pepper said.

"Oh, yes," I nodded, "of course I am."

He switched off his tape recorder. "You'll forgive me, Dessie, but I can't agree with you. When you're up on stage, you give more than any singer I've ever seen. And come November, the whole world is going to know it. No one else in the business comes close. I have a feeling that this concert is going to be the start of a long lucky streak for you."

* * *

In the weeks that preceded the concert, I could feel nervousness and fear coiling up inside me like tightening springs. These were feelings that my songs did not express, and so I kept them to myself. Pepper's words had pleased me, and I hoped he was right, but I was terrified that my black star would ascend again. I worried that my voice would fail me, or that my health would fail. What if I blacked out, forgot the words, made a fool of myself? I didn't want to disappoint Bram and embarrass my children. The concert might be so terrible that nobody, anywhere, would ever want to hear me sing again.

For the concert, I selected two gowns, one for each half of the program, the first a flowing white chiffon with gold bands on the sleeves and cape, the second a narrow sequined sheath of midnight blue, my trademark color.

Bram remarked on the symbolic progress of my life from innocence to experience.

I laughed. "In that case, the first half of the show should last no more than five minutes. I didn't stay innocent very long."

My spasms of nervous terror grew more intense. The week before the show, I turned down all interviews because I was afraid I might lose control and start sobbing in front of an unsuspecting journalist. I became obsessed with my physical health. Whenever I went out of doors, I wrapped my throat in a cashmere muffler. I drank plenty of carrot juice and popped vitamins as if they were candy. I forced myself to eat three balanced meals every day. I knew I would need all my strength in order to sustain my energy over two and a half hours.

I met regularly with my arranger and conductor. Three days before the concert, I had my first rehearsal with the full orchestra. Five minutes before we were scheduled to begin, while my twenty-one musicians were setting up their stands and unpacking their instruments and looking over their music, Clayton Striker came striding into the rehearsal hall carrying his saxophone case. He walked straight up to me.

"I hear you got a gig comin' up. I'd like to sit in on it."

I stared at him, unable to make a sound. These days he was a respected figure on the musical evangelism circuit, a sort of Old Testament prophet of bebop and cool jazz. He gave concerts and testimonials all over the world, on college campuses and at jazz festivals. He had also been active politically, leading voting rights marches in the south, speaking out on civil rights, having his picture taken with Attorney General Robert Kennedy and

Martin Luther King, Jr. Oh, yes, Clayton Striker was a reformed man. But I still hated his guts.

He tipped his head to one side and grinned at me. "You look like you seein' a dead man. Hey, I'm a cat, Mama, remember? A hep cat. A cool cat. A cat with as many lives as I need to get done what I got to do. That's why I just keep comin' back."

When I found my voice, the anger that was boiling up inside of me brought forth an hysterical shout. "You've got a hell of a nerve coming here, you son of a—"

"I know it." He assumed an expression of abject humility. But not for long. His eyes twinkled. "I hear you told that judge that you never liked me but that I was a fine musician. Now why'd you tell him that?"

"Because it was true, damn you." I lowered my volume to an infuriated hiss. "Paul was so crazy about you that he wanted to emulate everything you did, including that damned heroin. If that gun had belonged to anyone else, he never would have used it. But because it was your gun, and you were in trouble, that made it all right."

Clayton sighed. "I miss the little fellow, Mama," he said. "I been clean for eleven years and maybe I even got saved 'cause of him. I figured no sense both of us dyin' hooked into the needle. Hey, you remember that night when I taught you how to sing?"

"I remember."

He chortled. "I taught you real good, didn't I? You still singin' the way I taught you?"

I said, "Look, I'm only paying union wages. I didn't plan to take on any Bible-beating superstars."

Still laughing, Clayton joined the other players in the brass section. "I'm just an old jazz man lookin' for a place to play his horn, Mama. Union wage is plenty good enough for me."

When the rehearsal was over, he came up to me. "Good thing you still singin' right, Mama, 'cause I ain't givin' no more free lessons."

I didn't like Clayton any better, but with him sitting behind me in the band, I suddenly felt safe. Not because he was a superb musician; any one of the professionals on that stage could produce a quick obligato or a riff to cover me if I slipped up. But he was a link with my past. I had the strangest feeling that maybe Paul had sent him to look after me.

* * *

"I can't do it. I can't go out there."

The heating system backstage at Carnegie Hall was working overtime and the temperature was eight-five degrees, but I was shivering. The musicians had already taken their places on the big, bare stage. When the curtain opened, I was supposed to walk out there, stand in front of them, and start singing. Like fun.

Bram said, "Are you feeling sick?"

"Sick? I'm going to die. I feel worse than I did after the accident. My heart's going to stop."

"Well, you'd better kick-start it again. The maestro wants to start the overture."

I was aware that my conductor was searching frantically for my signal to begin. "I'm sorry, I can't start yet. Something's wrong. It's the program—that first song, it's wrong somehow. It doesn't say what I want to say. Imagine a kid in a white dress singing 'Frankie and Johnny.' It's not how I want to open the show. That song can't be first."

"This is a hell of a time to decide—"

I turned to the stage manager. "Tell them to turn up the house lights. I want to see the audience. I want to feel like I'm connecting with them. I want to see their faces."

Bram protested, "You can't bring the lights up now. The audience will get confused. Please, Dessie, you've already kept them waiting twenty minutes . . ."

"All right, leave them down, but bring them up as soon as I start to sing, okay? I want to see their faces. And no overture. That's out." I dispatched a stagehand with a verbal message to the conductor, then I sent Bram to his seat out front. I wanted his honest appraisal of my performance, and he couldn't give it from backstage.

"All right," I told the stage manager, "let's go." The curtain rose on a silent stage. I took a deep breath and stepped out from the wings.

The burst of applause rattled me. I hadn't sung in a big hall since my Hollywood years, and I had forgotten just how loud and unnerving applause from three thousand people could be. Not sure how to respond to their ovation, I stood stock-still in the center of the stage and bowed my head. I let the din wash over me as I waited for it to crest and start ebbing. Behind me, the musicians sat perfectly still, as I had requested.

When the house had gone quiet, I stepped down to the footlights, away from the microphone. I wasn't worried about being heard. In the days before artificial amplification, plenty of good singers had filled this hall with their voices. Lungs were invented before microphones.

I cleared my throat. "This is for Paul." I hummed softly to myself to find my note, then without any accompaniment, I sang:

> Amazing grace, how sweet the sound
> That saved a wretch like me.
> I once was lost, but now I'm found.
> Was blind, but now I see.

Clayton picked up on the tune on the second verse and together we carried it like strands of colored ribbon, passing the melody back and forth, weaving something new and special in sound, a song of our own invention that had never been written down or recorded. I brought the song forth not just from my throat and my diaphragm, but from every cell in my body, from my blood and from my bones, from between my legs and out of my ears and my eyes and my nose. My face contorted, my body twisted, but I didn't care. Back in Hollywood, I had been instructed always to look beautiful when I sang. In those days, I had been a mannequin whose only moving parts were supposed to be a mouth and fluttering eyelashes. Not now. The music was boiling around in me, and I was letting it out the best I knew how. My song wasn't gospel, it wasn't jazz. It was me. I wasn't singing. I was giving birth, and being born at the same time.

As I sang, the lights in the auditorium came up very slowly. I could see my own people in the front row. Bram had taken his seat in the center, with Grace on his left side and Gray on his right. Beside Gray, Clara Mae was mopping her eyes with a handkerchief the size of a pup tent. Dizzy Dillon was there, and Judge Albright with his wife, and Pepper Wellington. In a burst of warm feeling, I had sent my father two tickets. His seats were empty.

Hotshot Grayson sat on the aisle. He was going blind from glaucoma, but music still filled his spirit. His hands twitched in front of his chest as he fingered an invisible trumpet, jamming with Clayton and me as he had jammed with Paul back in Grace, Mississippi, the night my daughter was born.

I lifted my head, sending the notes of the song out beyond the walls of the hall, into the streets and into the sky.

> Through many dangers, toils, and snares,
> I have already come;
> 'Tis grace hath brought me safe thus far,
> And grace will lead me home.

I knew Paul was listening.

27 million Americans can't read a bedtime story to a child.

It's because 27 million adults in this country simply can't read.

Functional illiteracy has reached one out of five Americans. It robs them of even the simplest of human pleasures, like reading a fairy tale to a child.

You can change all this by joining the fight against illiteracy.

Call the Coalition for Literacy at toll-free **1-800-228-8813** and volunteer.

Volunteer Against Illiteracy. The only degree you need is a degree of caring.

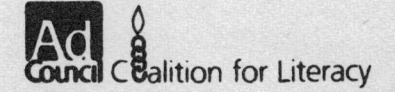

Ad Council Coalition for Literacy

LV-3

THIS AD PRODUCED BY MARTIN LITHOGRAPHERS
A MARTIN COMMUNICATIONS COMPANY